A PATCHWORK QUILT

By the same author:

All in the Telling
The Art of Illusion
Escaping Freedom
Too Close to Home
Facing the Music
The Confessions of Dudley Sims
Where Past Truths Lie
Old Boys

Short Stories: *The Man Who Loved Books*
                 Mixed Fortunes

A PATCHWORK QUILT

BRIAN SMITH

Smith, Brian
A Patchwork Quilt
ISBN: 978-0-646-97922-9
pp384

In the Beginning

Jane was four houses from home when a tall boy of about her age sauntered around the corner. Squinting into the late afternoon sun, she could see he was wearing a school suit and tie but no cap and his auburn hair tumbled over his forehead and ears. His face was in shadow but she was confident he was not one of the local boys.

He scrutinised each of the houses he passed like a tourist taking in the streetscape of a foreign city. Jane had never seen anyone in her neighbourhood behave like this before. The boy seemed to be quite unaware of her approach, an unusual experience for her. Sometimes boys observed her in a shy, surreptitious manner, while the more confident ones would smile or even greet her. If in a group, one often muttered something she couldn't hear and the rest would laugh self-consciously. Surely this boy would have to notice her soon.

But he did not. Instead, he paused to examine the house which shared a common wall and was the mirror image of her own: a two-storey terrace with a cream stucco façade. The black wrought-iron gate creaked as he pushed it open, stepped onto the black and white tiled porch and disappeared into what Jane thought of as the Swanson's place.

She hurried in and called to her mother, 'Hey, Mum, the new people have arrived next-door.'

'Don't shout, dear.' The reply came from the front room.

'I've just seen a boy go in there,' Jane said as she entered.

1

Edith Glover closed her copy of *The Women's Weekly*. 'The McBrides have two sons. Their van arrived with a surprisingly small amount of furniture this morning. The wife is a bit mousy but quite friendly. The husband runs a newsagency in Victoria Street, somewhere at the Richmond end.' She made it sound like a far country rather than just across Punt Road. 'I imagine they must be renting.'

'You don't miss much, Mum.'

'I took in a cake. Made one for us, as well. Would you like a slice before you start your homework?'

'Danny, is that you?' Mary McBride called from the kitchen.

'Hi Mum.'

Mary stopped unpacking crockery and came to stand in the kitchen doorway. 'Where have you been? Sean's been home for ages. I was beginning to worry.'

Danny dropped his bag in the hall. 'Thought I couldn't break the habit and went to the old place, did you?' He leaned down to kiss her cheek. 'I had to stay back so Brother Peter could give me a pep talk.'

'You're not in trouble, are you?'

Danny shook his head. 'Not really. He says I'm doing OK but thinks I can do better and wants me to put in more work.'

'He's right, too. You're a bright lad and who knows what you might become if you knuckled down and studied hard.'

'No, Mum. I know what I'm going to be and you should be happy about that.' Danny looked over his mother's shoulder into the kitchen.

'Would you like some? The lady next door, Mrs Glover, brought it in for us. Wasn't that kind?'

'We can try it at last.' Danny's brother, Sean, bounced down the last few stairs. 'Mum wouldn't let us have any until you were home.'

'Go up and get your father. I'll make some tea.' Mary went to fill the kettle.

'Hey, Dad, Mum's cutting the cake,' Sean shouted up the stairs.

When they were seated around the table, each with a cup of tea and a slice of cake, Bernard drew a satisfied breath and said, 'Better than that pokey kitchen at the shop, wouldn't you say, old girl?'

'It's lovely,' Mary said. Danny noticed the dutiful note in his mother's voice and saw his father glance quickly at her. 'I do like the extra space we have here. Now the boys have separate rooms, they'll be able to study more easily and ...'

'I've already put your machine and materials in the room for your quilting,' Bernard said.

'After all these years, it'll be strange going to sleep on my own,' Sean said.

'Don't worry, brother. Just prattle on and pretend I'm lying there saying nothing like I always do. That way you won't notice any difference.'

'How do you like the cake?' Mary asked.

Bernard licked the last crumbs of cake from his lips. 'Not bad. Didn't take to Mrs Next-door, though. She's a bit too la-di-da and nosy for my liking.'

'Did you cop the girl next-door?' Sean asked Danny.

'No. When?'

Sean sighed and shook his head. 'Just now, you dozy dill. I saw her from the window upstairs. She was right in front of you when you got to our place — a blonde.'

Mary grinned at them. 'That will be the Glover's daughter, Jane. Her mother told me she goes to Merton Hall.'

'Pity there isn't a good Catholic family next-door, but I s'pose you can't have everything.' Bernard squared his shoulders. 'Time to get cracking, you boys. There are boxes waiting to be unpacked in your rooms.'

'And, Danny, don't leave your bag cluttering up the hall,' Mary called after them as they dawdled from the kitchen towards the stairs.

Bernard waited until the boys were out of earshot before he said, 'You're not as happy as I thought you'd be.'

3

'I *am* happy. The house is great, the extra space is wonderful.' Mary sipped her tea and glanced over at the boxes awaiting her attention. 'I'm just worried we've overcommitted ourselves.'

Bernard ran his hand through his thinning ginger hair. 'Mary, love, I've told you. Mick gave me the tip this place wasn't selling and the owners were up against it. We got a bargain.'

'I know Michael's a good friend but he's also an estate agent. Every house they have for sale is a bargain — at least that's what they tell buyers.'

'You heard Mick. Most people after a house round here want something grander and are put off by that add-on at the back. He told the owners they should pull it down but they wouldn't have a bar of it and we shouldn't, either.'

Mary pushed back her chair and started clearing the table.

'Crikey, love, Kevin Crawford is a mate, but do you think he hands out mortgages from his bank without being sure he's got the debt well and truly covered? And he knows better than anyone how we're placed.' When Mary turned away from him without replying, he quickly said, 'Anyone but you, of course.'

As she began to wash the cups and plates, Bernard slowly hauled himself up from the table and hobbled over to take a tea-towel. 'After all, you were the one who insisted we needed to free up space at the shop to build the business and I was the one who needed convincing.'

'I'm really happy about that,' Mary said. 'It's just I had a more modest place in mind.'

'Cheer up, love. We can trust Mick and Kevin to look after us. They're my mates. I keep telling you the time I spend with them at the Oak Tree after work on a Friday is time well spent.'

The boy who walked towards Jane this time was about the same age as the previous one but bore little resemblance to him. He was short with neatly arranged dark hair and, instead of carefully finding his way down the street, tripped along with a cheerful smile. When still about twenty paces away he greeted her with, 'Hello. I'm Sean, one of your new neighbours.'

'Pleased to meet you,' Jane said primly. 'I'm Jane — Jane Glover.'

'Have you lived here long?'

'All my life.'

'It's awfully quiet,' he said in a tone which surprised Jane who had been brought up to see it as one of the advantages of living in this corner of East Melbourne.

'It's lovely having the park across the road,' she said, pointing at the generous green square dotted with tall gums, oaks and elms where a woman was throwing a ball for her fox terrier.

'I s'pose.' He turned to scan up and down the street. 'At our old place we had people walking past all the time and there were plenty of cars and trucks on the road — trams as well. You felt as though you lived in the centre of things.'

'I'm sure you'll enjoy it once you settle in.'

'Have you met my brother yet?'

'I saw him the day you moved in but we didn't speak.'

'Typical. Danny's a man of few words. Not like me, eh? But if you can get him going, he makes a lot of sense. Again, not like me. You don't have any brothers or sisters?'

'No, just me, I'm afraid.'

'No good being afraid. That's what I say. What do you do with all those spare rooms?'

Sean switched topics with such speed that Jane was having trouble keeping up. 'What do you mean?'

'Your house must be the same as ours. When you count the ones at the back, I reckon we have enough rooms to sleep a dozen people.'

Here was Jane's chance to give her new neighbour some of his house's history. 'We don't have that set of back rooms. Long ago — I think it was in the twenties — the owner extended your place and had it as a guest house. They say he went bust in the Depression.'

'Really? No wonder the house has a bit of a haunted air to it.' Jane would have liked to ask him what he meant by that but he gave her no chance. 'You should meet Danny. You'd like him once you got to know him.'

'You're quite a fan of his. Not many boys I know are fans of their brothers.'

Sean waved away some bothersome flies. 'Probably because they don't have a brother like mine. He's only a bit over a year older than me. Do you play any sports?'

'I've been learning tennis at the courts down the street. Do you play?'

'No.' Sean shook his head. 'I'm no good at ball games.' His face brightened. 'Danny is, though. Cricket. Football. He's in the school teams. I reckon he could play for a league team one day. Who do you barrack for?'

Jane hesitated, before remembering her father was a member of the Melbourne Cricket Club. 'We barrack for Melbourne,' she said.

'Like to get with the toffs, eh? But there's really only one team: the mighty Tigers. He paused to fill his lungs and then, as though commanding an imaginary tiger in the park across the road, shouted 'Eat 'em alive!' When Jane started at the force of his voice, he grinned and went back to a previous topic. 'I don't think Danny's played tennis, but I'm sure he'd pick it up pretty quickly. You should give him a game sometime.'

Jane was still grinning when she entered her house. 'Who was that you were speaking with?' her mother asked.

'One of the boys next door. The younger one, Sean. He's quite a character.'

'Jane, dear, it's not ladylike to indulge in conversations with strangers in the street. You know that.'

'Mum! He's our neighbour. He showed no signs of trying to molest me, so you can relax. In fact, I had more fun chatting with him for a few minutes than I ever have with those stiff Melbourne Grammar boys at dancing class.'

Danny was at his desk when Sean bustled into his room. 'I met Jane, the girl next door. I reckon you could do well there. She's got a bit of class — a step up from those girls at the church. Have you ever played tennis?'

Danny put down his pen and turned to face his brother. 'Tennis? Why would I play tennis? Cricket and footy are enough for me.'

'Play your cards right and I reckon she might invite you for a game. I doubt she's much good, so you ought to be able to get by.'

Danny leaned back in his chair and tilted his head at Sean. 'Have you forgotten she's a Proddy? Still, if you're so keen, why don't you take up tennis? Concentrate on your own love life and leave mine alone.'

Next Saturday Jane stepped onto the street with her tennis racquet in hand as Danny emerged from his house. He wore a school blazer and held a cricket bat and was gazing about vaguely as if still emerging from sleep. When their eyes met, she smiled but he didn't respond. Perhaps he was shy. Not like his brother. 'Hello,' she said, 'I'm Jane, Jane Glover, your next-door neighbour.'

'I'm Danny McBride,' he replied flatly.

Jane had expected him to make some attempt at conversation but, when he said nothing, she had to improvise. 'I'm glad the rain's cleared, although it's been good for the gardens and the grass over there in the park is already fresher.' She thought of Sean's discomfort with open space. 'Do you like living here? I don't think your brother does.'

'He'll adjust.'

'I'm off to a tennis lesson. It's handy having the courts just around the corner.' If he was interested in sport, he might see this as an advantage.

He turned to walk along the street and Jane fell in beside him. 'Where are you going to play cricket?'

'Saint Kevin's.'

'Sean says you're very good.'

'Sean exaggerates.'

'Nice to have a brother who talks you up you, though.'

Danny continued to stare straight ahead but Jane caught a wry grin. 'He doesn't do that all the time.'

He told me you don't play tennis but thought you'd be good at it.'

'Are you?'

At last he had asked her something. 'I'm not as good as some of the girls at school. I'd love to play really well.'

'Why?'

Jane found Danny's question puzzling. 'Because I like to do well at the things I take up. Don't you?'

'I can see why it would be fun for you.'

The breeze was blowing Jane's hair onto her face, adding to her irritation. 'You mean it's not a real game, but good for girls?'

'No, not that,' Danny said quickly. 'It's not a team game. That's what I like about cricket and footy. At least with tennis you're able to go when you feel like it and have a fair chance of getting a game. You can't do that with team games.'

'I still need at least one to have a hit up with. If you want to try it sometime, I'd be happy to give you a game.'

'Nah, I think I'll give it a miss.'

Jane had enjoyed talking with Sean, but how different was his brother. Not only a droob but a condescending one as well. 'I suppose you wouldn't want to be shown up by a girl.'

'Are you challenging me to a game?' The wry grin returned. 'Seeing I've never played, it shouldn't be too hard for you to give me a hiding.'

Jane wasn't going to take any of that. 'There aren't too many people about after school, so you wouldn't be too embarrassed.'

'You're the one who'll be embarrassed by bringing along a clueless idiot. Not sure what I'm doing next week. I'll let you know.'

They had reached the gate to the courts where a fair-headed man in shorts and T-shirt stood with three other girls. 'Come on Jane,' he called to her. 'We're waiting for you.'

'This is where I leave you,' Jane said. 'Don't forget to tell me when you're ready for our match.'

Jane tensed her body and rang the bell. When there was no response, she let out a relieved breath and turned away. She would have to come back, though. She couldn't let him get away with brushing her off like that. As she reached the gate, the door opened and Jane turned to find a short woman whose expression made Jane wonder whether she had awoken her from a nap. She thought her mother's description of Mrs McBride as 'mousy' was unjust. True, she was not as fashionably dressed as her mother, but the autumn shades in her simple skirt, blouse and cardigan blended well with her colouring. She might have been quite pretty when she was young.

'I'm sorry to keep you waiting so long,' Mrs McBride said. 'I was so wrapped up in my quilt I was slow to react.'

'Your quilt?' It was a warm November day and no normal person would need to wrap themselves in a quilt, even for a nap. What could be wrong with her? Was she going a bit gaga like some old people did? She couldn't be much older than her mother.

Now Mrs McBride's eyes cleared and she smiled. 'I'm working on my latest patchwork quilt and was reluctant to break from it to come to the door.'

Jane frowned. 'I've heard of patchwork quilts but I don't really know what they are.'

'Let me show you.' She turned and led Jane up the stairs. They entered the room that in Jane's house was her father's office. The floor was strewn with cotton and silk fabrics of different textures and colours. In one corner, a sewing machine sat on a narrow wooden table. On the other side of the room, an ironing board had been erected and, in

9

the centre of it all, a partly completed quilt was draped across another wooden table. The quilt comprised strips of plain silk in burgundy, royal blue and olive-green nestling against multi-edged patterned and embroidered cottons in a host of colours complementary to those of the silks. The longer she gazed at the quilt, the more Jane was struck by the rhythm and harmony of the total effect.

'You can see why this is called a Crazy Quilt,' Mrs McBride said.

'I've never seen anything like it. How do you do it?'

'Some people have carefully laid out designs and pre-plan the fabrics they will need but mostly I allow myself to go where the mood and the fabrics take me.'

This was interesting but did not answer Jane's question. 'How do you make the different shapes and how do you get them to line up so neatly?'

'Cutting and sewing. For some I use paper templates, but it's not difficult once you get the hang of it. Some people think it's tedious and takes too much time to achieve a result, but I enjoy immersing myself in it.' Her apologetic smile appeared again. 'I'm sorry. I kept you waiting on the doormat, rushed you up here and still haven't asked why you called.'

'Oh yes.' Jane was brought back to earth. 'I'm Jane Glover from next-door. Is Danny at home?' That sounded silly now when it was pretty clear Mrs McBride was alone in the house.

'No, he's not. I'm sorry.' She sounded as though she meant it. 'After Mass the boys went to the shop with their father. Now we no longer live above the shop, we're increasing our display space by putting anything we don't need to have on show up there. I'm so looking forward to increasing our range of products.'

'You work in the newsagency?'

'Oh yes, I help out in the shop when needed. I also do the accounts and handle most of the routine paperwork. Before we were married, I was a bookkeeper — I'd be called an accountant these days. It's very much a family business.' The dreaminess in Mrs McBride's manner had completely disappeared. 'Always has been and I guess always will.'

She smiled at Jane. 'I don't often get the chance to devote myself to quilting so that's one reason, I suppose, that I get so involved when I do find some time.'

It had never occurred to Jane that her mother might take a job. Perhaps she could help out her father at the office.

'You're very kind to listen to me prattling on about my quilt-making,' Mrs McBride said, 'but I'm delaying you. Is there a message I can pass on to Danny?'

'Yesterday he and I arranged to play tennis after school one day next week.' Jane knew it was more of a vague suggestion but wasn't going to let Danny off the hook that easily. 'This morning it occurred to me he might not have a racquet. Please tell him he can use my father's if he would like. Dad hasn't played for years, but I checked and the racquet is still OK.'

'What a good idea. Your mother was so kind to bring us a cake when we arrived and now you're making Danny welcome. I'll pass on your message as soon as I see him.'

'There is one other thing … I know how busy you are.'

'What is it, dear?'

'One day, if you could spare the time, I'd like to learn more about patchwork quilts.'

'Really? You've hardly seen anything. Come.' Mrs McBride took Jane to a room at the rear of the house where a single bed carried a quilt similar to the first Jane had seen. Here the pattern of different shapes was even more random and the colours brighter.

'Danny's brother, Sean, said he wanted his quilt to liven up the room when he shared with Danny. You can see how he likes bright colours.'

'Yes, you can,' Jane said as she took in the glossy posters of footballers and action heroes covering the walls, the red painted cupboard and the lacquered wooden desk with its carefully arranged papers, books, pens and pencils. She thought of Sean who jiggled from one foot to another as he jumped from topic to topic, yet maintained a very tidy room. 'I don't think I'd want a quilt this crazy, though.'

Jane hoped she hadn't offended Mrs McBride by her comment and was relieved when she laughed before saying, 'No, neither would I. When I make a quilt for a particular person, I try to imagine what would suit them best. That one I'm working on now is for an old friend who has suffered a lot in the past year. I want the quilt to be cheerful but nowhere near as bright as this one for Sean. Let me show you something very different.'

Mrs McBride took Jane to the front bedroom where a double brass bedstead bore a quilt in shades of blue and green. It was more subtle than the ones she had already seen and the sinuously intertwined strips gave the room an air of tranquillity.

'That is beautiful,' Jane said 'It's much quieter than the crazy quilts and suits the room so well.'

'I cut up a couple of my old dresses to make this one. I'd say you have an eye for colour and form. That's a great advantage in quilt-making.'

Jane could appreciate from her clothes and her quilts that Mrs McBride certainly had colour sense. 'I like to draw and paint, but I'm not nearly as good as some of the girls.'

'And you sew?'

'Mum taught me. I make some of my own clothes. Nothing very grand: tops, skirts, that sort of thing.'

'Your mother will be wondering where you've got to. Let me show you one more and then you must go.' She crossed to the room on the other side of the house and came to a sudden halt in the doorway. 'Oh dear, that wretched boy. I'll have to get onto him.' Over Mrs McBride's shoulder Jane could see what had upset her. A small desk at the window was covered in stacks of papers, leaving scant room for a blotting paper pad and a few nondescript pens and pencils. Books were piled on the floor and some cast-off clothes lay in one corner. The bedclothes on the single bed lay twisted as though someone had only just got up. 'That Danny, he can never keep things tidy.' Mrs McBride straightened the bedcover and Jane was able to see how different it was from the others she had been shown. Precisely aligned triangles alternated between black and a variety of browns, fawns and beiges. 'Danny doesn't go in for bright colours,' Mrs

McBride said. 'I thought a quilt in the style of one of the old Waggas might encourage him to take more care with the rest of his room. It didn't work when the boys shared and it hasn't worked here.'

Jane felt she ought to say something to cheer Mrs McBride but nothing would come to mind. Instead she asked, 'A Wagga? What's a Wagga?'

'They're part of our history,' Mrs McBride said. 'When bushmen stitched together crude blankets from chaff bags, the tops of wool bales, flour sacks and the like, they called them Murrumbidgee blankets or Wagga rugs. When times were hard and farming families could no longer afford wool, the women created their own Waggas with a skill that made them fit to be seen in any home.' She paused and pursed her lips. 'Listen to me boring you to death with all this. Trouble is, when I get going it's hard to stop.'

'No, I asked you.' Jane considered the quilt again. 'The materials here are different from the others you showed me.'

'I was able to get a batch of suiting off-cuts from the tailor along the street from our shop and used a paper template to ensure the triangles matched perfectly.' She paused to survey the room. 'My boys are so different.'

Jane was about to say, 'In so many ways,' but held back. 'You certainly know and care a lot about quilts and they come in such varied forms.'

'Much more varied than my efforts. If you like I could show you how I go about making a quilt and you could borrow some of my books.'

Jane was delighted by the prospect. What would her mother say?

'I probably won't be able to do that until into the New Year,' Mrs McBride said. 'It's such a busy time for us in the shop and we haven't fully settled in here yet. But now you must go. I'll make sure to give Danny your message.'

'Here we are, love,' Bernard called from the doorway. 'Is lunch ready?'

'Won't be long,' Mary said as she came from the kitchen into the hall.

Bernard laughed. 'No chance of an early lunch when you've been at your quilting.'

Mary returned his smile and said, 'I've had an interesting morning. I have a message for you, Danny, from Jane, next-door. She says, if you'd like, you can use her father's racquet when you have your game of tennis after school next week.'

'What? A game of tennis with Jane?' Sean smirked 'You kept quiet about that.'

Danny felt the colour rise in his cheeks and bowed his head. 'There was nothing definite. I don't know if I can fit it in with cricket practice and homework.'

'Don't be such a wimp' Sean told him. 'The lady has gone to the trouble of finding a racquet for you. You can't insult her by begging off.'

'If you want to take up tennis, you know there's a group at the church who play,' Bernard said.

'I don't want to take up tennis, Dad.'

'Sean's right,' Mary said. 'When the people next door have been so nice, it'd be rude to turn her down. Go straight in there now, before we have lunch, thank the Glovers for the offer of the racquet and work out with Jane which day would suit her best.'

Danny hung his head and did not move.

'Go!'

⟍𝓁

Jane was quick to appraise Danny when he arrived for their game of tennis. Although the shorts and T-shirt were grey rather than white, they were acceptable at this time on a weekday and the sand shoes were fine. She handed him her father's racquet.

'Don't be too late. Remember your homework,' her mother called from the living room.

Jane pulled a face which got a small grin from Danny. As they walked up the street, she suggested it might be best they had a hit up rather than embark straight away on a match.

'Whatever you like,' he said curtly.

'I just thought you might get the hang of it more quickly if you didn't have to worry about winning points. Do you know the rules and the scoring?'

Danny swished the racquet like a cat flicking its tail. 'I haven't played but I follow quite a few sports, including tennis. Stayed up to listen when Rod Laver won Wimbledon earlier this year.'

When they reached the courts, Jane was surprised to find the coach was working with five children who were so young they could barely see over the net. Beside the court sat a number of mothers. 'Sorry, I forgot about the class that Tony runs for primary school kids on a Wednesday.'

'Perhaps I should join them,' he said.

'Let's go over to the far court out of their way. I have some balls.'

Jane had been modest in rating her ability to Danny and wanted to make this clear to him. She strove for fluency in her strokes and moved quickly to position herself for returning his shots even when many of them were miss-hits. He chose to adopt a two-handed grip for his backhand — playing modified cricket shots with some success — but was insufficiently side-on when playing his forehand and his grip was far from ideal. It was obvious he had a good eye and, despite the deficiencies in his technique, was doing far better than she thought he might. After her mistake in questioning his knowledge of the game, she decided against offering any advice.

When the class for the young children finished, Tony stood watching Jane and Danny before wandering over to join them. 'Who have we got here, Jane?' he asked with that cheesy grin she so disliked. 'You haven't brought him before.'

'Tony, this is my neighbour, Danny McBride. He hasn't played tennis before, so I brought him to try the game.'

'Good idea.' Tony went to stand beside Danny. 'What do you play, Danny? Cricket? Footy?'

'Yeah, they're my sports.'

'And you're pretty good at both, I'd say. You've got the eye and the balance of a natural ball player. Your tennis technique could do with an overhaul, though. Let me show you.'

Tony conducted a ten-minute clinic on the fundamentals of ground strokes which resulted in a marked improvement in the consistency of Danny's shots. 'Now, you need plenty of practice. Do that and you'll be ready for the next step.' He turned and walked back to what he called 'The Clubhouse', an old brick building with a tiled roof. A faded cream portico added to its ancient air.

Danny watched him go before calling to Jane, 'Should we be packing it in. There's your homework.'

Jane shook her head and scowled. 'We've hardly started. If we're going to have a proper game sometime, you'll have to be able to serve and we haven't tried that yet.' She hit several balls to him. 'Here, have a go.'

As Danny struggled to achieve the flight and direction needed for a valid service, Jane, emboldened by the way he had responded to Tony's coaching, offered him some tips which enabled him to do better. 'Not bad for a start,' was Jane's verdict. 'Shouldn't overdo it the first time, though. I'm thirsty. Would you like a drink? Coke? Fanta?'

'Water will do me, thank you.'

'Come and sit outside while I get the drinks.'

After she returned with his water and a Coke for herself, they sat silently sipping their drinks until Jane said, 'The other day you surprised me by asking why I wanted to be able to play tennis really well, but when I asked you whether you liked to do well at the things you take up, you didn't answer.'

'It depends. Sometimes you can have fun just being average at something and trying to be really good takes the fun away.'

'You think so?'

'Take school work. One of my teachers, Brother Peter, is giving me a hard time because he reckons I should try harder and do better. What's the point of that?'

'He sounds like he thinks you could be a brain and do really well. Then who knows what you might become?'

Once more that wry grin. 'You sound like my mum. But I know what I'm going to be and that's fine with me?'

'Really? You know for sure? What are you going to be?'

'I'm going into the newsagency with my dad and, when he's had enough, I'll take over from him. That's what he did.'

'I can see it's easy for you to follow your father, but is it something you really want to do? I think each of us should have a goal, something that's important for us to achieve in our lives.'

'You reckon?' For a moment Jane thought Danny was putting her down, but the way he continued to gaze at her made her feel she had roused his interest. 'Being a newsagent isn't something I feel I have to achieve. I know that backing up my dad, like he did for his father, is a good thing to do and I'm happy to do it, but it's not an achievement like winning the best and fairest or coming top of the class. On Sunday Father Maloney at our church said God has a plan for each of us. That doesn't mean He plans for every one of us to be the best there is in something or other. Maybe His plan might be something quite ordinary, but Father Maloney said true happiness comes when we fulfil that plan, so we have to watch out and recognise it when the chance comes along. I reckon I'll find that chance when I get into the newsagency.'

'You're religious?'

He frowned, giving her question serious consideration. 'Not like a few of my mates who are going to be priests. The Church has always been part of my life and I've tried to follow its teachings.'

While some of the girls at school were active members of the Anglican Church, Jane had not met anyone of her age who spoke like Danny and was intrigued. 'And you think by becoming a newsagent you're carrying out God's plan for you?'

'You after something grander? What are you going to be? A doctor? A lawyer? A scientist?'

Jane laughed, surprising Danny. 'I don't have Brother Peter telling me I could be a brain. At my school they divide us into brains and others.

17

They don't call us that, but that's what we are and I'm one of the others. We others aren't going to make it to university. We're expected to become something like a typist or kindergarten teacher or shop assistant while we wait for Mr Right to come along, but I know what I want to be.'

'What's that?'

'I want to be a nurse. If I was one of the brains, I'd be a doctor, so nursing is the next best thing — something worthwhile I can do really well.'

'What do your parents think of your plans?'

She'd never had a boy ask her questions like these before. 'Dad would like me to be a solicitor like him but he knows that isn't going to happen and is easy about it. He's easy about most things. Mum wants me to squeeze into university somehow; not so I can be a doctor, but so I can meet a superior set of possible husbands.'

Danny drank more of his water. 'I reckon you'll make a good nurse. It needn't stop you getting married, though. Would you like to get married?'

'I'm flattered by your offer but it's too soon. I hardly know you.'

Danny frowned and shook his head. 'Seriously. I think everyone should get married and have a family.'

'You are a serious boy, Danny McBride.'

Danny glanced around as if reconnecting with the here and now of the tennis courts. 'Hey it's getting late. We'd better go before your mum thinks I've spirited you off.'

Jane recalled her mother's disapproval of her speaking with Sean in the street. What would she think of her discussing marriage with Danny? 'You're right, we should be going. I'd like to do this again, though.' She saw Danny studying her and wondered whether, like her, he found the conversation more rewarding than the tennis. 'We could play a match next time.'

'Hey, that smells good,' Danny said as he stepped into the kitchen.

Mary turned from stirring a pot bubbling on the stove. 'Just the usual spaghetti, but I'm trying a different sauce. Now I've had the chance to get used to the new stove and oven, I think it's time I gave you something more interesting than the old faithfuls I've been serving since we came here. How was the tennis?'

'Yeah, not bad. I didn't make as much of a fool of myself as I expected.' He hesitated before adding, 'Actually there's a guy at the courts, Tony, who does coaching. He thought I showed promise.'

'Will you take it up?'

'Nah. Cricket and footy are more fun.'

'I thought, when I saw you bring in the racquet, you must be going to use it again.'

Danny peered at his hand as though surprised to find the racquet there. 'Oh yeah. I was carrying it and didn't think to give it to Jane when we got back here. I'll take it in now.'

'No, wait until later. Dad will be home soon and he'll want to eat straight away.' She took a breath and smiled at him. 'And how did you find Jane?'

'OK I s'pose. But she's different from other girls I've met.'

'Different? How?'

'Hard to say. She doesn't mind telling you what she thinks.' Danny didn't tell his mother about Jane's drive to excel at whatever she took up. Nor did he mention her questioning him about his beliefs. He had never spoken with any girl about such things before. Nor had he done so with many boys. Kevin and Paddo, the two friends at school who were planning to go into the priesthood, were probably the only ones.

Mary had not told her husband or sons of Jane's interest in patchwork quilting, either.

Final Year

McBride's Newsagency was housed in a slate-roofed, red-brick building, flanked by a greengrocer and a branch of the State Bank. Wire-encased posters, emblazoned with the headlines from the *Sun, Herald, Age, Truth* and *Financial Review*, lined the bottom quarter of the wide front windows. Four smaller windows in the upper storey looked down onto the street. When Bernard, who stood in the doorway gazing out, said, 'Quiet today,' Mary came to stand beside him.

'I thought you might enjoy a few days of quiet after the Christmas rush.'

'Didn't we do well with all the new stuff? The toys and the extended range of cards went like a treat. The extra space made all the difference. Just as well I got the boys to help out. Sean's not that much use yet but Danny was great.' Mary's smile at his approval of her innovations froze when he spoke of the boys working in the shop. She noticed how his dependence on the gnarled stick which had belonged to his father was growing each year and she saw how much effort he needed to lift the bundles of newspapers he once tossed around with ease. Bernard still refused to acknowledge any deterioration in what he called his 'gammy leg'. For how many years would he be able to continue and what alternative was there to involving the boys in the business?

She swept her eyes around the shop before replying. 'I think we need to display our new lines so they catch the eye of anyone coming in. We can put the papers and magazines, the tobacco and cigarettes more towards the back.'

'But that's our bread and butter,' Bernard said

'Exactly. Anyone coming in for them needs no persuasion. We have to catch their eye with the things they haven't come to buy but might when they see what's on offer.'

Bernard put his arm around her shoulder and gave it a squeeze. 'You've been happy with the shop the way it was all these years. What's brought on this drive to change everything now?'

She didn't remind him that, when the boys were young, she had little contact with the shop. She didn't mention that, until she had persuaded him to move from above the shop to East Melbourne, there was little room for expanding the business. Now the way was clear. 'I guess I'm just slow to get new ideas.'

'Rubbish. When it comes to new ideas, I'm the tortoise.'

There *is* one other thing. I was thinking we might do well to add a range of paperbacks. More and more people are reading them.'

'What? Take over from the bookshop down the street?'

'Bernie, be serious. I know we've done well last year but we can do so much better if we lift our sights.'

He drew himself up, as though he was about to deliver an address to the faithful. 'Yeah, we should be ambitious, but as I keep telling you, we can't get ahead of ourselves and forget our bread and butter.'

'You know the real bread and butter of this place is your reputation for integrity and your concern for your customers. Best of all, they like you and always enjoy a chat with you when they come in.'

Bernard waved her compliments away. 'That's about all I'm good for these days. When Danny joins me, he'll bring the energy to kick us along.'

She had held off earlier; she couldn't do so again. 'Talking of Danny, you know this is his last year at school.'

Bernard nodded enthusiastically. 'That's what I was just saying. Next year I'll have him with me full-time. It'll be good to have someone to do the heavy work.' So, he was admitting it at last. 'And when I'm sure he can cope on his own ...'

'Brother Peter is keen for him to go to university. He says God has given him the talent and he shouldn't miss the chance to develop it to the full.'

Bernard laughed but it was forced and lacked his usual good humour. 'Come on Mary, love. Those teaching brothers have spent so much of their lives in schools and universities they can't imagine the satisfaction which comes from actually earning a living and building a business. Danny can, though. I know he's keen to get started. If it wasn't for you, I'd have him with me now. You don't need to worry about Danny — not on that score anyway.' Bernard paused and pursed his lips. 'He's seeing a lot of that girl next door.'

'Bernie, he hasn't turned seventeen. There's no harm in a few games of tennis with Jane. She's a nice lass. I like her.'

'There are plenty of nice lasses at the church.'

Jane was dressed for tennis and had her racquet, but stood uncertainly in the doorway of her house. 'I think it's too hot for tennis today.'

'Bothered I beat you last time?'

'For the first time,' Jane said. 'I thought you needed some encouragement.'

'Baloney. You were going flat out.'

'What say we get an ice-cream from the milk bar and sit under those trees?' Jane gestured at the park across the road.

They brought their ice-creams back to the park and sat on the grass in the shade of one of the oak trees.

'How was your holiday at Point Lonsdale?' Danny asked.

'OK I s'pose. The weather wasn't great.'

It had not been the weather that disappointed her. This year, on what she considered the family's annual pilgrimage to Point Lonsdale, she had been allowed to invite her best friend, Sally Courville, to accompany them. Jane had looked forward to Sally enlivening what had become a predictable two weeks at the beach. As it turned out, Sally focussed on enlivening the interest of the boys at the surf club and Jane been a willing accomplice.

'Play any tennis?' Danny said.

Jane remembered her distaste for the boys' raucous behaviour, nowhere more irritating than when trying to have a decent game of tennis. It made her realise just how much she enjoyed her matches with Danny, despite his quirks. 'Played a bit of doubles with my friend Sally and a couple of the boys from the surf club.' She was disappointed when Danny's only response was to lick the dribbles of ice-cream which were running down the side of the cone.

'Has your mother had time to work on her quilt?'

'We were all flat out in the shop up to Christmas and in the past few weeks she's been working on Dad to change the set-up in the shop. He's being a bit hard to persuade, although her ideas have been really successful so far. Why do you ask?'

'No particular reason,' she said before attending to her ice-cream. 'Did she mention she offered to show me how to make a patchwork quilt?'

'No. When did she do that?'

Jane shrugged, attempting to suggest the matter was of no importance to her. 'Oh, ages ago, before Christmas. She was too busy then, but I thought if she had some time it would be good to get started before we go back to school. Only a bit over a week to go, worse luck.'

Danny nodded but his thoughts were elsewhere. 'Have you seen *West Side Story*?'

'The movie?'

'Yeah. Sean and I often go to the pictures on a Saturday night. He wants us to go to *West Side Story* but I'm not keen. It's a musical. I don't like musicals, but Sean says this one is different from the rest.'

'We don't go to the pictures much. Mum and Dad aren't keen. Mum's a bit of a prude and thinks many of them are unsuitable for the young lady she'd like me to be. I'd love to see *West Side Story*. Some of my friends saw it and thought it was great.'

Danny flicked away a fly that had taken an interest in his

ice-cream. 'Yeah, that's what I'm worried about. I think it might be a girl's movie.'

'What? It's a musical version of Shakespeare's *Romeo and Juliet.* Is that a girl's play?'

'I hope you're right. Sean's very keen and, if I don't go, he'll be snaky with me.' Danny glanced across at her. 'Would you like to come? It'd be good to have someone else with me so I don't have to put up with Sean on my own.'

'You really know how to charm a girl.'

'What?'

'Yes, I'll come. I enjoy Sean's company. He's a lot more fun than some I know.'

'Are you sure you have the time. I don't want to trouble you.'

'I'm only sorry I took so long to get around to it. I hadn't forgotten, although it wouldn't surprise me if you thought I had.'

When Mrs McBride led Jane into her quilting-room, Jane noticed the addition of a chest of drawers and another chair.

'As you can see, I've made very little progress with this quilt since you first saw it. Come and sit next to me while I take you through the basic steps.'

They began with what Mrs McBride described as 'piecing': the production of segments from the oddments of different cloths. 'Since this one is a crazy quilt, I don't need paper templates but I do need to mark out each segment.' She placed a floral fabric on the table and using a ruler and tailor's chalk, marked out a triangular shape. 'You need a good pair of sharp scissors,' she said as she took up a black-handled pair and cut out the triangle. Mrs McBride then explained the necessity of frequent ironing to ensure the material remained strictly flat during stitching. When they came to stitching, she showed Jane how to bring the faces of the pieces together and how to sew a straight seam with a small margin for safety. At first Jane did it by hand but later graduated to using the sewing machine and was pleased when Mrs McBride admired her competence.

'That's very kind of you, Mrs McBride, but you've made it easy for me to follow you.'

'Oh, call me Mary, please, Jane. Quilters don't stand on ceremony.'

It seemed they had been going for only a short time when Mary checked her watch. 'My goodness, look at the time. Would you like a drink?'

'No, I'm fine thank you Mrs ... Mary.'

Jane was keen to continue but Mary disappointed her. 'That's probably enough to get you started. If you would like to make a quilt, I suggest you try a crazy quilt. They're more forgiving. And if you run into any difficulties or would like me to show you some more advanced techniques, then don't hesitate to come in again.' She stood up and was about to usher Jane out when she clicked her tongue. 'I said I'd get out some of my books for you. Here they are over here.' She took two substantial volumes from the top of the chest of drawers and flicked through the leaves of one so Jane could see many pages of close type-script and photographs of a wide variety of quilts. 'Take them home and, when you get a chance, dip into them. There's much more to making a quilt than selecting and carefully sewing patches of material together.'

'I can see that,' Jane said, wishing they could return to doing just that. 'I suppose it's a bit like painting a picture.'

Mary took a breath, considering what Jane had said. 'That's true when you pre-plan the design before you start. With crazy quilts, you could say they're more like abstract paintings. Instead of sloshing and dripping paint onto the canvas like Jackson Pollock, you piece together the disparate scraps. But I think of it as more like a novelist writing a story. The author of a novel doesn't tell you everything the characters do or say or feel. Instead the writer chooses what to relate — bits and pieces, if you like, which when sewn together tell the story. Some of the pieces may be humorous, some poignant, others full of tension and so on.' She paused and, as if embarrassed by her speech, said, 'Well that's how I think of it, anyway.' Recovering her composure, she added, 'The other thing is, as I've already explained to you, quilting has a long history and I'm so pleased to be able to share in that tradition. I hope you will feel the same.'

The pleasure Jane had gained from her time with Mary led her to say, 'What a pity you never had a daughter.'

Mary stiffened and her cheeks reddened. It was as if Jane had struck her.

Sean sat in the park, his back against one of the gum trees, his knees spread and his head down. He looked up as Jane came to join him. 'Hi, Sean,' she said. 'Are you starting to enjoy the open space of East Melbourne?'

He did not return her smile. 'No, I'm escaping a sectarian argument.'

'What's that?'

'You really don't know?' He climbed to his feet and, after casting an anxious glance over his shoulder, said, 'Let's not hang around here. Let's go for a walk.' Without waiting for her he took off across the grass.

'Hey, slow down a bit. We're not running for the bus,' Jane called. After catching up to him, they walked in silence. This was much more like a walk with Danny. 'You haven't answered my question.'

'Oh yeah. You do know the Christian religion is divided into the Catholics and the Proddys?'

'I remember being told at school there were more than that.' Jane had not been much interested and had to search her memory. 'There's a church called Eastern Orthodox, I think, and ... I can't remember the rest.'

'Yeah. Yeah,' Sean said. 'But let's just concentrate on the Catholics and the Proddys. We're Catholics.'

'Yes, I remember one Sunday your mother telling me the whole family had been to Mass.' Jane thought it best not to mention her discussion with Danny about the Church. They had reached the far side of the park and she turned to continue along the perimeter of the grass but Sean strode on. She had to change course quickly to stay with him. It was as if he wanted to escape the neighbourhood.

'The priest at our church, Father Maloney, bangs on about "The One True Church". In other words, we're the ones who've got it right and the rest of you are wrong. The priests and their die-hard followers reckon we should not get too close to anyone who isn't a Catholic. They reckon this'll damage our faith. Can't be much of a faith, I'd say, if that's all it takes.' He was breathing heavily now and she didn't think that was because of the fast pace he had set. 'In places like Ireland the Catholics and the Proddys even try to kill each other. Both sides call it "Sectarian Conflict" as though that makes it OK. Over here we haven't come to that, yet.'

'So, what sectarian argument were you escaping from?'

Sean's smile was scornful. 'You're a Proddy aren't you?'

'We go to the St. Paul's Cathedral at Easter and Christmas.'

'Do I have to spell it out?' When Jane did not reply, he sighed. 'Dad's the real problem. He's one of the die-hards and isn't happy about Danny seeing so much of you. Apparently, he's been sounding off to Mum about it and she got fed up. She hadn't told him she was teaching you how to make quilts and, when she did, he hit the roof.'

'What's the harm in a bit of tennis and going to the pictures with you boys?'

'Exactly what Mum said.' His face lightened and he added, 'She's quite a fan of yours. I guess it's the quilting.'

'Is she still a fan?'

'She was half an hour ago. Why do you ask?'

Jane hesitated. She had been planning to ask Danny, but Sean might be more forthcoming. 'When she was talking with me about quilting the other day, I said it was a pity she didn't have a daughter and I could see how much I upset her. She broke off the lesson straight after.'

'That'd be cos of Bernadette.'

'Bernadette?'

Sean paused to allow a cyclist to ride past them. 'She was born two years after me. Nobody ever speaks about it, but the birth must have gone badly. Bernadette only lived for a day or so and Mum nearly died.'

'Oh, how terrible. What can I do? I should go and apologise but, after what you've just told me, I probably should stay away.'

'Don't worry. It's only the old man sounding off. Mum'll calm him down. She always does.'

⸙

Jane liked the sound of gravel crunching under the tyres of her father's car. It matched the sense of opulence she felt as they approached the portico of the Palladian style mansion. The white building gleamed in hidden lighting like a diamond set in the ring of the surrounding garden.

Her father pulled into the ample area where about a dozen cars were already parked and others were disgorging stylishly dressed men and women.

'Not just young people,' he said.

'I told you, Dad. This is a celebration to show off their new house. Mr and Mrs Courville have invited their friends. Sally has been allowed to invite some of hers and her brother, Byron, has invited some of his.' After telling him when he should come to pick her up, Jane left the car, feeling very pleased with herself. The powder blue dress she wore had been chosen in consultation with her mother who, knowing something of the wealth and position of Sally's parents, was happy to spend a good deal more than Jane would have ever thought allowable. Appraising herself in the mirror before she left home, she thought she had never looked better. She walked up the marble steps and through the wide doorway to the chandeliered hallway where Sally's family stood welcoming the guests.

'Jane, what a lovely dress.' Jane brushed a kiss on Sally's cheek, careful not to disturb the make-up or lipstick on either of their faces. 'The dance floor for us is through that archway over there. Byron's brought a bunch of his pals from Scotch so you should be able to do well for yourself with them. Don't go for Andy Forsyth, though. He's mine.'

Jane did do well. She was never short of a dance partner and was taken to the lavish supper by Richard St John, a handsome boy with impeccable manners. When the band continued after supper, Richard was reluctant to give her up to others and they were dancing cheek-to-cheek in a slow waltz when Jane was dismayed to be informed her father had arrived. Surely, he had the time wrong. But no, it was just after midnight. She should have asked him to come much later. Richard insisted on accompanying her to the car, pausing en route to ask for her phone number.

Jane had just stepped off the bus in Punt Road when Mary came up behind her. 'How nice to see you. It's been quite a while.' Mary showed no sign of animosity or even any hint of coolness towards her. 'How are you going at school this year?'

'Pretty well,' Jane said.

They walked side-by-side along the street and Jane no longer had a clear view of Mary's face. Was she just being polite?

'What about your quilting? When you didn't come in to piece your materials, I thought that maybe you were too busy at school to go on with it.'

'No, Mum got me what I needed from a friend of hers who used to be quilter. I've found it hard to find the time since school started, so I haven't done much but I will finish it.'

'You must show me when you do. Or, if you run into any problems along the way, I'd be happy to help.'

They continued in silence while Jane searched for the right words. Eventually she blurted out, 'I want to say how sorry I am. I want to apologise.'

'What?'

'Saying it was a pity you didn't have a daughter. Bad enough if you hadn't had one, but much worse when you did.'

Mary put her arm around Jane. 'No need to apologise. You're not the first to say something like that and always I'm torn. Yes, I did have a daughter, but only for a short time. Her name was Bernadette. There were lots of problems when she was born and she only lived for two days. I nearly died, too. I knew you meant well and you'd be embarrassed if I told you the truth. On the other hand, I felt bad about not mentioning Bernadette. I felt as though I'd denied her. Now it's obvious I should have told you straight away and I'm the one who is sorry to have made you feel bad.'

As they approached home Mary said, 'You haven't had much time for tennis lately.'

Jane could hear the question in Mary's voice. 'No. What with school ... and I've been going out a fair bit, too.' She wondered whether Danny would mind or be relieved.

'I understand you have a new friend.'

'Who told you that?'

'Your mother mentioned it when I bumped into her recently. No doubt in my mind he has won her heart.'

Jane could feel her cheeks burning and was not sure whether this was because of her feelings for Richard or annoyance with her mother.

Danny knocked on the door of Father Maloney's study and waited anxiously to be invited in. It was Sean's fault, nothing to do with him, but his dad insisted he come with Sean.

'Come in lads,' sounded through the door in the lilting Irish accent of Father Maloney, the long-time parish priest at St John the Evangelist. Danny recalled his father saying the only remaining signs of Father Maloney's upbringing in County Cork were his accent and his dislike of anything English.

Danny led Sean into the study and was greeted with, 'Ah, boys. Good to see you both.' The look Father Maloney gave Danny confirmed the priest was particularly pleased he had come. This was not the first time Sean had been in hot water with Father Maloney who clearly thought of Sean as a smart-arse kid given to annoying him by questioning the teachings of the Church. On the other hand, Danny knew the priest viewed him as a devout follower of his dad's faith. Was he supposed to put a brake on Sean if he started to get out of hand?

'Please take a seat here in front of me.' Father Maloney did not get up from behind his mahogany desk but waved at the two hard-backed chairs opposite him. When they were settled, he said, 'Your father tells me there was a family discussion after Mass last Sunday when I mentioned the situation developing in Vietnam. He thought it would be good if I could expand a little on my remarks with you tonight.'

Sean was quick to reply. 'Thank you, Father. Before we get to that, though, it would help me if we could go back to one of your sermons from a few weeks ago.'

'Really? Which one do you have in mind?' Danny could see the priest's surprise. Like Danny, he must be wondering what Sean was up to.

'You spoke about Christ's teaching that the Old Testament practice of taking an eye for an eye should be replaced by turning the other cheek. You said this didn't mean passive acceptance of the wrong done to us. Rather, we should encourage the wrongdoer to reform by engaging with them. I liked that.'

The priest nodded his acknowledgement of Sean's compliment but his face remained wary. 'And you found difficulty in harmonising those teachings with the need to oppose Communism wherever we find it?'

'Not exactly, Father. I can see the need to question the propaganda of the Communists and challenge their attempts to gain power. It's just that I was puzzled by the Prime Minister's announcement the Government is sending an army training team to Vietnam and a squadron of Sabre fighters to Thailand to assist South Vietnam in their fight with the North. Then on Sunday you advocated Australia lift its military commitment even higher. Since what is going on in Vietnam is a civil war between its citizens with no sign of invasion from Communist China or anyone else, I wondered what Jesus would think of this.'

Danny saw Father Maloney's eyes flare. Sean's casual mention of

Jesus had done it. Would it all be downhill from here? 'How blind you are,' the priest thundered. 'A creeping tide of Communism is flowing through Asia, destroying Christianity wherever it finds it. Its tentacles are already reaching into many countries including our own. It is entrenched in North Vietnam and, without desperately needed support from the outside world, South Vietnam will be overrun. You may be unaware but there are many devout Catholics in South Vietnam. We cannot fail them. Unless Communism is stopped now, we'll have it ruling our country and we'll have abandoned Jesus. Already followers of the Anti-Christ are infiltrating our trade unions. We cannot allow its soldiers to advance closer and must mount the strongest resistance we can muster.'

Sean was unflustered by the priest's tirade. 'So, when it comes to the Communists, we should destroy them before they destroy us, not seek a peaceful solution to the conflict, even though there's no immediate threat to our country?'

Father Maloney lifted his head and took a deep breath. Danny could see his anger remained, although that was now mixed with puzzlement. 'I cannot fathom how any son of Bernard McBride can believe we should not do what we can to keep invaders from our door.'

'What's Dad got to do with it?' Danny asked. He had intended to remain silent while Sean and Father Maloney slugged it out but could not understand why the priest would portray his father as some kind of defender of the nation. He was pleased to see his question had quenched some of the priest's heat.

'I was referring to your father's distinguished war record as an example of a committed Christian who went to great lengths to defend his country from an aggressor intent on destroying our way of life.'

'He doesn't talk about it but, as I understand it, he joined up, went to New Guinea, was injured and sent home,' Danny said.

'He hasn't described to you how he and his fellow-members of the gallant 39th Battalion kept the Japanese at bay and saved Australia from invasion?'

'I overheard someone mention it once,' Sean said, 'but Dad cut them off.'

Father Maloney stared at them, giving Danny the impression he was having trouble deciding what to say next. Eventually he said, 'I know Bernard is a modest man who does not like to speak about himself, but to deprive his sons ...' He seemed to be speaking to himself not them. 'I expect you know in the early years of the war your father provided strong support for his father in the newsagency.'

'He and Mum never talk about those times,' Sean said.

'Ah, I see.' Father Maloney smiled at Sean, something Danny had not expected to see tonight. 'Let me tell you.' He sat up and squared his shoulders, just as he did before embarking on one of his homilies. 'Although Bernard was keen to play a role in protecting the world from the evil doctrines of Nazism, his responsibilities to his father kept him at home. When Japan began its merciless sweep towards Australia, both the McBride men knew the time had come for Bernard to play his role in resisting the aggressor. He enlisted in that heroic band of men known as the 39th Battalion while your grandfather's contribution to the war effort was to get by without his son.'

Father Maloney then embarked on a detailed account of the raising of the 39th battalion in late 1941, largely from young men with no military training who, with scant preparation, were sent to garrison Port Moresby but almost immediately called from that role to oppose the unexpected advance of the Japanese over the Owen-Stanley Ranges. He described the difficulties and privations of the Kokoda Trail, the resistance put up to the better equipped Japanese by the greatly outnumbered 39th. Gradually they were forced back down the trail, suffering huge casualties and inflicting great losses on the Japanese who poured more and more of their soldiers into the fight. Encouraged by the questions from the boys, he went into detail on some of the battles, so they could better appreciate their father's contribution. He told how them how the climate, the terrain and disease also took a great toll, yet the 39th, an ever-dwindling force, refused to give in. After

33

some five weeks of unrelenting battle the 39th had stalled the Japanese and allowed reinforcements to be brought up. The surviving members of the 39th, many carrying injuries, malnourished and disease-ridden, returned to Port Moresby while the reinforcements pushed the Japanese into retreat. Of the over fifteen hundred men who served in the 39th, less than fifty remained fit for service.

Danny was entranced by the priest's account and he could see Sean was, too. He flinched when Sean said, 'How do you know all this, Father?' but Father Maloney did not take offence. Instead he gave a modest smile and said, 'One of my interests away from the Church is military history and I have read widely on the battles fought by Australia's courageous soldiers in the Second World War. Your father was one who played a distinguished role, was badly wounded and carries the effects of that wound to this day. He is a brave man who fought to save his country and yet modestly shuns any mention of it even to his own sons.' Father Maloney leant forward and spread his arms, appealing to them. 'I believe I have done right in revealing the truth to you, but ask that you respect his wish not to speak of his achievements. You must keep what I have told you to yourselves.'

Danny said nothing, still absorbing what he had been told.

'I need say no more tonight, but ask you boys to think carefully about the example your father has given you.'

He wasn't going to escape that easily, though. Sean, emerging from the restraint the priest's words had put on him, said, 'You're saying we should not be aggressors, but when our family or community or country is threatened by others, we have the right to resist as strongly as we can. That still leaves open what kind of a threat the war in Vietnam is for us. I'm glad you told us about my Dad, though. He's kept that very quiet.'

Anxious to avoid setting the priest off again, Danny said, 'Father, I'd like to ask you about a different matter that's bothering me.'

'Of course. Of course. What's the problem?'

'I can see why Catholics should marry only Catholics. That makes sense.'

'Yes,' the priest said in a wary voice

'What I can't understand is why Catholics can't be friends with Protestants.'

Father Maloney beamed benignly on Danny, 'But they can. We both know there are places in the world where there's hostility between the two, but here in Australia we peacefully co-exist. There are some matters on which we don't quite see eye to eye and that can be a barrier to close friendships but need not prevent us getting along together. The Church encourages us to be neighbourly.'

'Neighbourly! That's right.' Sean said. 'You know we moved to a new place last year. The family next-door has a daughter, Jane. She's good to chat with. Mum has been showing her how to make a patchwork quilt, Danny's played a bit of tennis with her and she has come to the pictures with Danny and me a few times. She's a Protestant, though, and Dad seems to think all this is sinful.'

'No, not sinful, but possibly leading to problems.'

'Problems?' Danny said. 'Sean and I know full well we're going to marry Catholic girls and, even if we were stuck on this Jane, which we're not, she's not interested in us, except as friends — she's in love with a bloke from Scotch.'

The priest rested his elbows on the desk, interlaced his hands and leaned towards them with a benign smile. 'I like to see our young men and women enjoying one another's company under the auspices of the Church. I'm sure this is the best possible way to bring our young people together and foster those relationships which ultimately form the basis for building strong families like your own. Wouldn't you agree?'

'Coming back to the point, Father,' Sean said. 'I wish Dad could see he has nothing to worry about and it's fine for Mum, Danny and me to be friendly with Jane.'

'I understand your point of view but, remember, your father has seen a lot more of the world than you and people's attitudes towards one another can and do change. In your friendship with your neighbour, heed his concerns.'

When he was in bed, Danny reflected on Father Maloney's suggested path to marriage. He would have been surprised and probably horrified that Danny had spoken with Jane about marriage. Danny had never mentioned it to any other girl and certainly did not agree with Father Maloney's idea that the Church should be some sort of marriage broker. Yes, he chatted with the girls at the church and went to the annual dance the school organised with the Catholic Ladies College, but not to search for a life partner. Yes, he flirted with the more attractive girls, but only because some of them were so encouraging he didn't like to disappoint them. Danny understood his knowledge of sexual matters was limited, though it did include some experience with lust.

It had started as a confused reaction to some of the prettier girls at the church: a pleasure in looking at them and a fear of actually engaging with them. Some of the more streetwise members of his class furthered his education by circulating their copies of Carter Brown and Mickey Spillane paperbacks where he read of leggy dolls and the macho men who enjoyed them. He experienced lusty fantasies and learnt how to raise and release the excitement of such fantasies. Later in his teens he came to the view that such thoughts had no place in real relationships and believed that you had to love a girl before you could properly kiss her. He also believed that one day, probably not for some time yet, he would meet the one destined to be his soul-mate and would immediately recognise her. Where did these beliefs come from? He didn't know. Like a number of his beliefs, he just knew them to be true.

Jane gazed out at the rain and wind from the latest storm lashing the trees in the park. It had been a long and rotten winter but her gloom had nothing to do with the weather.

It had started so well. Richard called her within a few days of their first meeting and invited her to go with him to the Capitol on

36

the following Saturday where they saw *Breakfast at Tiffany's*. Audrey Hepburn was delightful but not as delightful as Richard taking her hand and gently squeezing it. After the film, he insisted on taking her to a dimly lit bistro he knew. They sipped coffee, sitting on carved chairs with velvet covered cushions. She had not done anything like this before and felt so grown up. He put his arm around her as they walked from the tram and, reaching her door, where the porch light blazed like a beacon, he said 'Jane, thank you for a wonderful evening,' before lightly gripping her shoulders and kissing her on the lips.

So began a series of outings to the pictures, parties and dances. On their return from the pictures Richard was careful to steer her into a laneway where they could enjoy a lengthier farewell prior to reaching her door. She was surprised the first time he put his tongue into her mouth but came to expect and enjoy it.

She was delighted when Richard got his licence and they could enjoy the privacy of his mother's car. They found a place on the opposite side of the park where the overhanging trees prevented any light from the streetlamps betraying their presence to prying eyes. Their times there became increasingly lengthy and involved. The first time he fondled her breasts she had a moment of disquiet but it was such a good feeling she had no inclination to discourage him.

Some weeks later they were parked in their favourite spot when his hand wandered lower and she gently pushed it away. It wasn't that she didn't want him there. Indeed, she was excited by the idea, but some instinct told her she should slow him down, make him wait. He didn't take it well. 'Come on Jane. No harm in it,' he said in a wheedling tone.

'Maybe not, but I'm not ready just yet.'

'Keeping yourself pure?' he asked. 'A bit late for that.'

'I'd like to go home, please.'

'You mean home safe and sound,' he said and started the car.

He didn't even try to kiss her goodnight before she stepped out. He didn't call her either. She thought of calling him but pride prevented that.

Eventually she did receive a call. It wasn't from Richard but from

Barry George, one of Richard's friends who Jane thought of as 'the shy one' — shyness was not common among Richard's group. He sounded even more awkward on the phone, hesitantly asking how she was and mentioning that he hadn't seen her for a while. He had been at the party which preceded her falling out with Richard and that was only a little over a fortnight ago. There was a silence before he blurted out, 'Have you seen *To Kill a Mocking Bird*. They say it's very good.'

'No, I haven't. Richard and I were going but something else came up and we put it off.'

'Would you like to go with me?'

'How did you get my number, Barry?'

'I ... I ... Richard gave it to me. He said it would be all right.'

'For him perhaps. Not for me. You can tell him that. And you can tell any of your friends who are inclined to ring me I am not available.'

Sally was never one to hold back but, over several days, it became clear she was bothered by something she was unwilling to share with Jane. Eventually Jane said, 'Sally, for heaven's sake, what's biting you?'

'I don't know whether I should tell you.'

'You'll have to now.'

'OK. OK. Last Saturday I was at a party and Richard was there, too.'

Jane had an inkling of what was coming and attempted nonchalance. 'So what?'

'He was there with a girl from St Catherine's. Her name was Marilyn — a bit of a tart if you ask me.'

'Why should I be bothered by that? I've given him the flick.'

Sally's face lit up. 'You have? Good for you. Sussed him out, did you?' When Jane did not reply, she said, 'It was just that I was talking to one of the other St Catherine's girls and she said he's known for playing the field and dumping any girl who won't let him go as far as he wanted.'

The rain had cleared and the sunshine confirmed spring was approaching, but Jane was in no better frame of mind. The School Dance was only three weeks away. She had assumed she would be taking Richard. Perhaps she had been hasty warning off Barry and that crew. Still, she could never have asked any of them. There was that bunch of Grammar boys she got to know at dancing class last year. Jonathon Gardiner had taken her to their dance. What a grind that had been. Besides, she hadn't as much as spoken to any one of them for about a year. Could she stand the embarrassment of taking her cousin, Peter? No, she couldn't. Just about as bad would be to have Sally fix her up with a blind date — Sally was certainly capable of that and would be willing. No, she had to find a partner for herself. Worst of all would be not to go. There was Danny but ...

A cold breeze gusted through the park beside the tennis courts as Jane sat huddled on a bench. She had already seen Sean pass along the street on his way home from school and was relieved he had not noticed her. Where was Danny? At last, ambling along in his usual fashion. She rose and walked down the path at a rate she calculated would allow her to meet him at the corner. He hadn't noticed her yet, wrapped up in his own thoughts. Seeing his creased suit and loosened tie, she almost changed her mind but there really was no alternative.

'Hello Danny,' she said, feigning surprise. 'I'm glad I bumped into you.'

'Hi Jane.' He gave her his wry grin before saying, 'What makes you glad to bump into me? You're not wanting a game of tennis?'

Jane turned to walk along with him. 'I was wondering,' she said. 'I was wondering ...' She turned her head to examine his face and could see his puzzlement. 'Do you like to dance?'

'Dance?'

'I remember you saying once you went to a dance at your school. Did you enjoy it?'

'It was all right.'

'You don't just stand around like I've seen some boys do at Ormond Hall. You can dance?'

Danny sniffed, reminding Jane of the annoyance he'd shown with her on the first day they met. 'I can dance. I told you we have a dance the school organises with the Catholic Ladies College. If you can dance with some of those girls you can dance with anyone.'

Was he suggesting she might be a poor dancer? 'It's the same at Merton Hall but we bring a partner. As it happens, it's on the Saturday after next.' She paused to regard him again. 'Would you like to come with me?'

'To the dance? What about ... Are you sure you want to go with me?'

'Why else would I ask you?'

Her hands tightened into fists as he paused, apparently giving her proposal thought. Was he working out what had happened? Should she say she was no longer going out with Richard — maybe say she'd had enough of him?

'OK. Saturday week, you say. Sean will have to go to the pictures on his own.'

Danny sat with a straight back and knees pressed together on a couch in the Glover sitting room. Mrs Glover had made it obvious she was appraising him carefully after Mr Glover showed him into the room. She had little to say, Mr Glover doing his best by starting with the weather — the forecast rain had not yet arrived — and moving on to ask how Danny was faring with his tennis. As he hadn't played since the early autumn, there was not a lot he could say, but mentioning his preparation for the start of the cricket season gave Mr Glover the opportunity to ask Danny's views on the upcoming Ashes series. That occupied them for a while before they lapsed into an awkward silence.

'Where is that girl?' Mr Glover said. 'Very rude to keep us waiting like this.'

At last Jane entered the room, her hair stylishly arranged and her cheeks softly glowing. She wore a sleeveless dress of pale pink satin with a sculpted neck and full skirt. A dark pink cummerbund around her waist set off the remainder of the dress superbly.

Danny, who had never seen her dressed for a dance or a party, was staggered. From early on he had seen she was pretty but tonight she was stunning. He rose to his feet and mumbled, 'Hello Jane. I've brought this for you.' Tentatively he held out a gardenia corsage his mother had bought for him.

'Oh Danny, how thoughtful of you.' She raised the gardenia to take in its scent and eyed him over the top of her hand.

He wished he had been able to do better than his school suit but his mum had pressed it and produced a natty tie for him to wear.

When Jane was refreshing her make-up in the ladies' room, Sally stood beside her. 'Hey, that Danny is really something different,' she said as she beamed at the mirror.

Jane had been relieved at the improvement in his appearance. His hair was its usual undisciplined self, but he had taken quite a bit of trouble and the corsage was a lovely thought. Nevertheless, she couldn't dismiss the fear he wouldn't measure up with her friends. 'What do you mean?'

'Well, for a start, he's a terrific dancer. You two are great together.'

Jane was delighted with the compliment. She had been nervous when they first took the floor and didn't begin well. Danny had quietly told her to relax and encouraged her to follow him as he took the lead. At the end of that first dance, when she expressed her appreciation, he said it was like tennis: you just had to go with the flow of the music like you did with the bounce of the ball. 'You really think it's that simple?' she asked.

'Wouldn't have said it if I didn't.'

Sally continued to enthuse. 'I'm not much chop on the dance floor but he even made me feel at home. And he's so different from the other blokes. Doesn't have much to say but, a bit like his dancing, he leads you into talking and listens carefully to what you say. The further Sally went the better pleased Jane became until: 'Where did you pick him up?'

'He lives next-door.'

'The one you played tennis with? You said he was a bit daggy.' While Jane had said that, she was in no mood to admit it now. 'He could do with a good barber and a good tailor,' Sally said, 'but get him those and you've got a winner. I'll take him in hand when you get tired of him.'

Mr Glover pulled up in front of their terrace. 'Danny, it will be easier for you to get into your house if I drop you here before I take the car around to park it in our garage at the back.'

'Thanks, Mr Glover.' Danny wasn't sure what he should say to Jane. No one had spoken much on the drive home. He had enjoyed himself much more than he had expected and was surprised by how pleasant Jane's friends were.

'I'll get out here, too, Dad. I've got my key.'

They stood together watching Mr Glover drive around the corner before Jane said, 'I hope you enjoyed yourself.' Before he could reply, she hurried on. 'And thank you for being so nice to me and to my friends.' She stood on tiptoe to kiss him on the cheek and hurried away. He had kissed and been kissed before but that had always been for a lark or bravado. And this one was only on the cheek. But it was different.

Jane lowered her rolled-up quilt onto the doormat and, maintaining her grip of the two bulky books Mary had loaned her earlier in the year, rang on the bell. After a short time, Mary opened the door and beamed at her. 'Hello, dear.'

'First I must give you these books.' She held them out to Mary. 'I'm sorry, I shouldn't have hung onto them for so long.'

'That's all right. I was happy for you to have them. I don't suppose you've made much progress with your quilt. Do you intend to go on with it?'

'Here look,' Jane said proudly, bending down to unfurl it.

'Come, into the living room. Lay it down so I can see it properly.'

Mary took her time inspecting the quilt before giving her verdict. 'You've done well. It's very good for a first attempt.'

Jane, conscious of the flaws in the stitching, heard the reservation in Mary's voice. 'Could do better,' she said in the tone of voice she imagined her teachers used when compiling her school report.

'You can always do better,' Mary said. 'I always want to improve. It's part of the fascination.'

'Not like your son.'

'What do you mean?'

'Ages ago,' Jane said, 'Danny told me he thought you could have fun being average at something and trying to be really good often took the fun away. We argued about it.'

'Good for you. I hope you won the argument.'

'Hard to win an argument with Danny. He slips away from you.'

'You are getting to know him well. Speaking of Danny, how did you enjoy your school dance with him?'

'That was back in September.'

Mary gave a rueful smile. 'Too true. All I got from Danny was something along the lines that it was fine. You weren't around for me to ask — your mother tells me you've been totally taken up with school work. That's why I thought you might not have gone further with your quilt.'

'I had to finish the quilt so I can take it with me when I go to the Alfred in the New Year.'

Mary's face clouded. 'Are you OK?'

Jane laughed. 'I'm not going into hospital. Not in that way. I've been accepted to do nursing. It's what I've always wanted to do. Didn't Danny mention it?'

'I've just been complaining to you that Danny doesn't tell me things. I'm delighted for you. Congratulations. But back to the dance. How was it?'

'I had a good time and I think Danny did, too. He's such a good dancer.'

As she neared home on her way from school, Jane saw Danny walking towards her. Just like the first time, the sun prevented her from seeing his face clearly. It occurred to her that it must be close to the first anniversary of that puzzling occasion. This time he did notice her and stood waiting for her to reach him.

'Hello, Danny.'

He did not greet her but stood eyeing her uncertainly. 'When we were at your school dance, your friend, Sally, told me you like to go dancing at ... is it, Ormond Hall?'

Sally hadn't mentioned this to her. What she had said was that Jane should invite Danny to go with them to Ormond Hall or Powerhouse but Jane had rejected the idea. It had been demeaning for her to have to ask him to take her to the school dance. Her pride demanded that next time, if there was to be one, he would have to invite her. 'I've been a few times,' she said.

'Sally said it was good fun. Would you like to go with me one night?'

'When did you have in mind?' She wasn't going to rush in. Let him think she needed to consult her appointments book to see if she was free.

'I've promised to go with Sean to the pictures next Saturday. How about Saturday week?'

She looked across at the park, forcing him to wait. 'Yes, that should be fine.'

Leaving Home

Jane wrinkled her nose as she emptied Mrs Crawford's bed-pan. She must have emptied hundreds of them by now and yet she still felt her gorge rise every time she did it. Was it the smell? Some of the body odour she had to contend with when washing patients was obnoxious but she was able to cope much better with that. When she first came into the wards, she was unable to escape the pervasive hospital smell of ill health and antiseptic. Now, like people who live beside a busy highway but never notice the traffic, she was unaware of it. When would she become inured to bed-pans? She'd been in the ward for only four months but what a difference those months had made to her understanding of the role of a nurse. How naive she had been.

She had marked the day she first entered her room at the Nurses' Home on Punt Road as the day she began a new life. School was behind her and she was an independent woman, no longer accountable to her parents. Her room was smaller than she had hoped but hers alone. After she had unfurled her quilt and set it on the bed, she was delighted by the way it gave the room a distinction it had lacked. She took special care dressing in her new uniform and set off to meet her new colleagues. Those already waiting in the downstairs lounge of the home eyed one another with anxious expectation. The recruits were not only starting their careers but facing the opportunity and the challenge of making new friends.

Once gathered, they did not enter the hospital but were led by a nursing sister past those disappointingly aged buildings to the Preliminary

Training School in St Kilda Road. Seated on the tightly aligned rows of straight-backed wooden chairs they were once more in school. Her teacher had become a lecturer in the full regalia of a nursing sister and Jane had swapped her Merton Hall uniform for that of a trainee nurse: white-and-blue checked blouse, white pinafore, blue cape and banded cap.

Over the next eight weeks, they were instructed in basic anatomy, medical dosage, bandaging, injecting, preparing beds and washing patients. On the rare occasions they set foot in the hospital it was to observe a particular procedure or the demonstration of a certain technique. There was no patient contact, no real nursing. Compared with the image Jane carried of her career, this was unexciting and unrewarding. Still, she reasoned, it was preliminary training, something to be endured before the real work began.

Her initial experience was hardly more uplifting. Her first duty after arriving on shift was to provide tea and toast. Her main duties were to wash backs, empty bedpans, clean sputum mugs, make beds, give enemas and keep everything neat and tidy. She worked under the eye of Sister Johnson, the dragon in charge of the ward, who was seldom satisfied with Jane's performance: she was a minute late, she had not aligned the wheels of a bed with precise accuracy, the corners of a newly made bed were not sufficiently sharp, she was spending too much time chatting with one patient when others demanded her attention. When the doctors came on their rounds, Sister Johnson met them with extreme deference until after they had departed when she sighed and muttered at their arrogance. Jane was determined that, when she completed her training, she would be as efficient as Sister Johnson, happier in her work and more pleasant to the trainees.

It wasn't easy. As time wore on, she came to view her training as a test of stamina, like struggling up a long hill to a distant finishing line while surmounting various obstacles put in her way. There were good days, when a patient expressed thanks for her work or managed a tolerant smile as she put them through some indignity. On other days, she found herself asking, 'Why am I doing this?' Some of her classmates did give up but not her.

The parties held in the homes of her fellow trainees provided a welcome respite from the hospital. After the first few, she wondered whether she should invite Danny but decided against it. There was very little dancing of any quality at these parties — the cramped space and crush of people would not allow it — and the hubbub of frivolous conversation was not really Danny's scene. Besides, she enjoyed the attention of men who found her attractive, although none appealed sufficiently for her to do more than flirt.

Jane saw Sister Johnson bearing down on her and wondered where she had slipped up this time. 'Glover, a word. I've just been speaking with Sister Tomlinson at the Training School. She wants to trial what she calls "a total care experience". There's a patient coming in later who's scheduled for an op. tomorrow. Tomlinson wants one of our nurses to settle the patient on arrival, get to know her, take her to the holding room for the pre-op., observe the procedure, take her to recovery and look after her prior to returning here. The nurse involved is to write a report on the assignment. You can do it. You like to chat.'

The patient, Mrs Teasdale, a tiny lady in her late seventies, arrived near the scheduled end of Jane's shift. She had a soft voice and troubled blue eyes. Jane did her best to cheer and encourage her as she prepared her for bed and carried out routine tests.

'Apart from the birth of our children, this is the first time I've been in hospital,' she said.

'How many children do you have?' Jane asked, hoping to divert her.

'They're all grown up now, of course. Judy lives in Brunswick with her family and both my boys are interstate — Scott in Rockhampton and Marty in Adelaide.' She hesitated before saying, 'I didn't want to worry them or have them come to Melbourne, so I've told them I'm in for a minor operation.'

Suddenly a commanding figure strode into the ward like a schooner under full sail. He was tall, heavily built with a mane of thinning fair hair. In a charcoal grey suit and with gold cuff-links gleaming from his sharply ironed French cuffs, he marched along the line of beds until opposite Mrs Teasdale when he peeled off. 'Ah, here is the lady herself.' His eyes moved quickly to explore Jane. 'And with a charming attendant.' Mr David Davenport was renowned for his surgical skill, his self-confidence and his wandering eye.

Sister Johnson hastened towards them. 'Just checking my patient has arrived safe and well,' Davenport told her. Again, his eyes passed over Jane before coming to rest on Mrs Teasdale. 'As I've told you, the growth is to be quite extensive but you've nothing to worry about. I'll take my time and go carefully so we can make sure we have all of it and you'll be right as rain from now on. Get a good night's sleep and remember: nothing to eat or drink after eight pm. I'm sure the nurse has that well in hand.' He smiled at Jane who felt compelled to smile back. 'I expect all was fine when you checked.' He picked up the log Jane had filled in and placed at the foot of the bed, scanning it briefly before saying, 'Yes, as I thought.' He bade them farewell and sailed out of the ward much as he had entered it.

Mrs Teasdale gripped Jane's hand. 'That man frightens me. He makes me feel so insignificant. I have no idea what to expect and don't dare ask. Will you be there?'

Jane told her she would and thought, were it not for the trial, she would have been unable to give this assurance. Best of all, she was playing a role which mattered to the patient. This was what nursing was all about.

When Jane entered the ward ahead of her usual time, she found a pale-faced man in a surgical gown beside Mrs Teasdale's bed. As she approached, he turned to appraise her over the top of his glasses.

'I'm here to bring Mrs Teasdale to the holding room and ...'

'The orderly will come when we're ready for her. You can get on with your other duties. I presume you have something useful to do.'

'I'm supposed to accompany Mrs Teasdale and observe the whole process. It's a trial ...' Jane struggled to recall the words Sister Johnson had used. '... giving trainees experience of total care.'

'What?' The man laughed scornfully. 'We don't need you gawping. The operation will be fraught enough as it is. Now Mrs Teasdale, this angina of yours, has it been giving any particular problems over the past few days? At least you can be sure Mr Davenport will do a good job. It'll be up to me to get you through the procedure and, fortunately for you, I do a good job as well.'

After he walked away, Jane asked, 'Was that the anaesthetist?'

'I don't think he said. He did introduce himself. Dr Crossley? Would that be right? Is he the one to put me to sleep?'

'He does that and he cares for you while the operation is proceeding.' Jane needed to say something to reassure Mrs Teasdale and was hard put to find anything appealing about the crabby anaesthetist. 'A pity Dr Crosspatch is so grouchy first thing in the morning, but I'm sure you'll be safe with him.'

Mrs Teasdale's face brightened at Jane's name for the anaesthetist but quickly clouded again. 'You will be there with me?'

'Of course,' Jane said, hoping that would be true. She wouldn't put it past old Crosspatch to have her excluded.

When the orderly arrived, Mrs Teasdale insisted Jane walk beside the gurney where she could see her. In the holding room a nurse Jane administered a preliminary sedation to Mrs Teasdale and gave Jane a questioning glance. Jane followed them into the operating theatre where she found Mr Davenport, Dr Crossley, another man and three nurses all masked and in surgical scrubs. Immediately the anaesthetist reacted as Jane had feared he would, but with words that increased her concern. 'David, I've told you we shouldn't put a woman this age with her heart problems through the trauma of this operation. I'll have my work cut out keeping her alive. The last thing I want is to have the theatre cluttered with spectators.'

The surgeon's eyes twinkled above his mask. 'Gerald, like all the top performers, an audience brings out the best in me, as I'm sure it does for you. Besides, it'll be good for this young lady to see masters of their craft at work. No, let her stay.' It was clear he was the one to decide. 'Better get kitted up though.'

The tumour was even larger than had been thought, so its removal required stamina, intricate surgery and a lengthy time during which Jane went through a range of emotions. At first, she was shocked by the bloody brutality of the surgery and feared for the safety of Mrs Teasdale. Then, as the doctors settled to their work, she was amazed by the way they chatted to one another, like a couple of women doing their knitting. Triggered by Crossley's earlier objection to the operation proceeding, they embarked on a debate about the justification for surgical intervention when the patients were aged. 'We are obliged to extend life wherever we can,' Davenport said. 'That's what we do.'

'What's the point of a few more months of painful existence?' Crossley said.

'I'll ask you when you reach that age.'

What impressed Jane the most, though, was the quiet, almost imperceptible, efficiency of the nursing staff, often predicting and always responding swiftly to the calls made upon them by the doctors. They were an essential part of the surgical team and must gain great satisfaction from their work. She was determined, one day, to join them.

After the operation the recovery room nurse was happy to allow Jane to monitor Mrs Teasdale. Eventually her eyes flickered and, seeing Jane, she gave a weak smile and murmured, 'Jane. How nice,' before slipping off again. The next time she awoke she was more coherent. Her smile was still weak but her voice stronger. 'I'm still here. I must have survived.'

By mid-afternoon Mrs Teasdale had recovered sufficiently to return to the ward. Jane went to sit beside her but Sister Johnson would not allow that. 'Mrs Teasdale is fine now and, apart from writing up your report which you can do in your own time, your little junket is over. There's plenty for you to do at the other end of the ward, so go down there and get cracking.'

Mrs Teasdale reached out her arm and took Jane's hand in a gentle grip. 'Thank you, Jane. I'm so glad I had you to care for me.'

Jane was busy for the remainder of her shift with the needs of other patients but kept glancing to where Mrs Teasdale was quietly resting. Just before the relieving shift was due to arrive, Jane risked the ire of Sister Johnson by going to farewell Mrs Teasdale. At first Jane thought she was asleep but, on examining her more closely, saw there was no sign of intake or outflow of breath. Jane took her cool hand and before she registered the absence of a pulse knew that Mrs Teasdale was dead. Her cry brought Sister Johnson and several other nurses hurrying to her. The sister pulled the curtains to screen the bed from the rest of the ward before confirming the death. She gave Jane a smile which chilled her. 'Your trial has an unexpected postscript. Before you go off you can prepare her for transfer and clean up.'

'I haven't done that before,' Jane said. She didn't say this was the first time she'd seen a dead body.

'I'll get you started and Sister Markham will be here in a few minutes to take over from me.' She waved a dismissive hand at the others who had remained staring. 'The rest of you get on with preparing for handover.'

Instructed by the senior nurse, Jane found preparing the body of Mrs Teasdale even more gruesome than she had feared. As she recalled from one of her lectures, the onset of death is often accompanied by defecation and Mrs Teasdale was a mess. When initially helping her prepare for bed, Jane had noticed the frailty of Mrs Teasdale's body, but in death it was even more wasted. Nevertheless, Jane had trouble moving her lifeless limbs and, despite receiving assistance, found difficulty in turning her body to ensure she had cleansed every part. Jane could not rid herself of the grisly sense that this was not Mrs Teasdale she was laying out but the carcass of some alien creature. After the orderlies had removed the body Jane thought her work was done, but the sister now in charge disabused her of that hope and specified how she must deal with the bedding and disinfect the bed. Finally, when that was done to the satisfaction of the sister, she was released to return to her room.

Bernard had decided only one of them need wait for the *Sporting Globe* on this wintry Saturday night and gone home, leaving Danny to wonder whether his father was keen to warm himself in front of the fire or knew Danny was taking Jane dancing.

Since she moved to the Alfred, they had settled into a monthly routine of going to Ormond Hall. It had a good band and was within easy walking distance of the Nurses' Home, so they had enough time to enjoy themselves before her curfew of 10.30. Danny had also started going to the dances organised by the Young Christian Workers but he missed Jane with whom he was now able to dance at a level he had not achieved before. Although he let her know how much he enjoyed her company, he held back from confessing that, when dancing with her, he found great pleasure in striving to get better and better.

That night something went wrong during the printing of the *Sporting Globe* and delivery to the newsagency was delayed. By the time the papers had arrived and been sold to the impatient crowd — both Richmond and Collingwood had won that afternoon so there were plenty of locals anxious to read about their side's victory — Danny knew Jane would be wondering what had happened to him. As he was locking up, he checked his watch again. It was so late he was likely to have a long wait for the bus to take him to the Nurses' Home. He thought of the van sitting in the small yard at the back of the shop.

When his father bought the dark green Morris Minor panel van, 'a bargain' from Harry, the proprietor of the used car lot in Chapel Street, his mother had seen it as an unnecessary expense. Bernard insisted they needed a van in which he could undertake deliveries when one or more of the paper-boys had let him down, pick up urgently required stock for the shop and ease the burden of transporting papers to the kiosk they had established on the North Richmond station.

When Danny came into the newsagency full-time, Bernard said he should be able to drive the van and immediately took on the job of teaching him. As a result, he had been able to gain his licence soon after he turned eighteen. Danny knew his father insisted that the van was only to be used for business purposes, but who was to know?

After the trauma of the morning, Jane was in no mood to go dancing and the longer she waited for Danny the more unhappy she became. Danny didn't worry much about being on time but he'd never been this late before. Was he ill or had he had an accident? She daren't ring his home in case Mr McBride answered the phone. When she was told he had at last arrived downstairs, she was relieved but knew there was no way she could face going to Ormond Hall.

She found him standing glumly in the room where callers were required to wait. 'I'm so sorry,' he said. 'What happened was ...'

'Don't worry about it. I'm not up for dancing tonight anyway.'

She saw how closely he was examining her and realised how terrible she must look. 'Are you sick?'

'No, not sick. I'm sorry you made a wasted trip but ...'

'That's OK,' he said consolingly and took her by the elbow. 'Come with me.'

'But I've just said I don't want to go.' She was glad it was so late none of the other girls were around to see her.

'We're not going to Ormond Hall.'

Keeping a firm grip on her elbow he steered her to the front door and, as they were about to step outside, she pulled back. 'I haven't got my coat.'

'You won't need it.'

'But it's cold.' The earlier rain and wind had abated but the pavement was still wet and the air damp.

'The van has a heater."

'What van?

Without responding he drew her across the road and she saw the small van with the sign, McBride's Newsagency, highlighted by an overhead street lamp. She didn't even know he could drive. He opened the passenger door and ushered her into the narrow bucket seat. By the time he came to sit beside her she had recovered a little of her spirit. 'This is a surprise.'

'I know a place at Elwood,' he said, started the engine and checked the rear vision mirror before pulling away from the kerb.

She couldn't understand what Elwood had to do with anything but decided not to distract him; he must have just got his licence. While they travelled down the length of Punt Road, she recalled her times in Richard's mother's car. This certainly was different.

Just after the road circled around the hill at Point Ormond, Danny turned off to the right and came to a halt in a car park overlooking Elwood beach. There was no moon and no horizon, the merged sea and sky unremitting black. The only light came from a few navigation buoys and the muted glow of Williamstown across the bay. Two or three other cars were parked beside them.

'How do you know about this place?' she asked in an arch tone. The bucket seats would present a problem for him.

'On hot days we sometimes come here for a swim. This is as far as you can go on the Punt Road bus.' He turned to face her. 'Now, tell me what's troubling you. What's the problem?'

She stared out into the darkness. 'I shouldn't have let it get to me. I should be able to cope. What's the point of being a nurse if ...'

'Tell me.'

She turned to him and took a deep breath. 'OK, I'll tell you.' Haltingly at first and then more fluently as she saw the close attention Danny was paying her, she described what had upset her. Towards the end of her story, her voice became choked with her tears. When she stopped speaking and sat dabbing her eyes with a small handkerchief, he took his much larger one and handed it to her. 'Blow.'

Jane, surprised by his tone, glanced at him quickly before obeying his order. She wiped her nose and went to return the handkerchief but he took her hands in his. Jane waited for him to say something but he did not speak.

'I face my first real test as a nurse and I fail miserably.'

'That's not the way I heard it.'

'If I'd stayed with her, I might have been able to save her. Mrs Teasdale died all alone without her family even knowing how ill she was. And I hadn't said goodbye to her. She's the one who suffered and all I can do is blub about how awful it was for me.'

She felt Danny tighten his grip of her hands. 'Mrs Teasdale died quietly in her sleep freed from what would have been a painful aftermath to an operation which may have done little to improve her life or even prolong it. Did you cry when you were at the hospital?'

'What? No, I wouldn't do that.'

'So, you did what nurses are supposed to do, except that you've let your sadness about what happened blind you to the really good part.'

'What good part?'

'In her last hours Mrs Teasdale gained a new friend who supported and encouraged her in what was for her a frightening experience. She didn't die alone. She died knowing her friend was close at hand.'

'You are kind to me, Danny.'

'Soon after we first met, you told me you thought everyone should have a goal in life that we wanted to achieve and your goal was to be a good nurse. You've found achieving your goal is harder than you thought it'd be, but what's just happened shows you have what it takes and you've honed your vague ...' Jane went to protest but Danny continued. '... your vague idea of what you wanted to achieve as a nurse into a clear ambition to be a theatre nurse. You're very lucky.'

Jane leant across but her efforts to kiss him were thwarted by the bucket seats until he let go of her hand and grasped her by both shoulders, hugging her to him. She was disappointed when he let go of her and said, 'I'd better get you back. It's getting close to ten thirty.'

Sean was at his desk when Danny, returning from the shop, came into his room. 'Hard at work?'

Sean looked up from writing on a pad beside an open textbook. 'Yeah. Only a few weeks now till the exams.'

'Are you on for the pictures tomorrow night?'

'Why don't you ask Jane?'

Danny was surprised Sean would see going with Jane as an alternative and not an add-on. 'I think she's working this weekend. Besides, you know she has very little free time these days and when she does, we prefer to go dancing. Have to stay with the books, do you?'

'No.' Sean hesitated as if unsure what he should say. 'It's just that Conor and I are going to the film at the Savoy. It's French.'

Danny sat on the bed and asked, 'Conor? Who's Conor?'

Sean shook his head impatiently. 'We're doing the same subjects this year. We study together and hang out.'

'I don't remember you saying anything about him.' Danny pursed his lips. 'I thought I knew all your pals but I've never heard of Conor'

'Well, get used to it. We're both planning to go to Melbourne Uni next year.'

Danny's eyes widened in surprise. 'Have you told Mum and Dad?'

'Mum will be keen on the idea. Dad will probably carry on for a bit but he'll come around.'

'You reckon? I'd say he's just as keen for you to come into the business as he was for me.'

'Bollocks. He says he loves to have us with him but when I do get involved at Christmas, he gets pissed off with the way I go about things. Besides, there's really only room for one of us and it suits you. Honestly, I'd go mad working there every day.'

'You'd get used to it.'

When Sean shook his head, Danny expected some kind of retort and was surprised when he said, 'You're right about Jane having very little spare time. I've hardly seen her since she went into nursing. How is she?'

'It took her a while to settle in but she's thriving now.'

'Next month it'll be two years since you had that first game of tennis with her.'

Danny could hear the question in Sean's voice but chose to ignore it. 'Yeah. She's become a good friend.'

'Isn't that a line for movie stars. "We're just good friends".'

Danny shrugged. 'We enjoy dancing together and are getting quite good at it. I like talking with her. I think she feels the same about me.'

'So, no romance?'

'What about you? Have you got some girl you haven't been telling me about?' Danny grinned at Sean. 'It's not really Conor you've been hanging out with.'

Sean eyed Danny quickly before shaking his head. 'There's no girl. None of them take me seriously. Conor does, though.'

Bernard was much later home from the meeting of the Newsagents Association than Mary had expected. He bent over to kiss her but, as she was sitting low in the spongy lounge chair, he overbalanced and ended up planting his lips on her nose.

'Steady on, Romeo.' While Bernard occasionally arrived home from the Oak Tree in an ebullient state, this was a new development. He attended meetings of the Association to stay in touch but seldom found much to enthuse about. Had he been drinking? She couldn't smell any liquor.

Bernard sank into the chair opposite her. 'Just been having an interesting chat with Luke Taggerty.'

Mary was well acquainted with Luke, the owner of a newsagency in Smith Street, Fitzroy. Over the years they had consulted one another over a variety of regulatory, administrative and financial issues affecting their businesses and had developed a strong mutual respect. When he sought her out a fortnight ago, she had been delighted by what he had to say but insisted that any approach had to be made to Bernie.

'Ever since you asked me if I'd ever thought of opening a second shop,' Bernard said, 'I've been checking around and I reckon Luke's place would be ideal. Now we live here, we're about midway between the two. I've made a point of chatting with him from time to time and know how he's placed. Trouble is he doesn't have sons like I do. He does have a wife — a bit of a nagger I'd say — who wants him to give up the newsagency and go somewhere up north where it's warmer.'

'So, what happened tonight?' Mary was keen to find out how far the two men had progressed and was impatient with being told things she already knew.

'He's not ready to sell just yet but asked me if I'd be interested.'

Mary tried not to show too much of her interest. 'What did you say to that?'

'Told him the timing could suit us very well.'

'I s'pose you're right. If we continue to do as well as we have, we should be able to finance the purchase in a few years.'

Bernard beamed at her. 'We could do it now. Kevin could chalk up another great investment for the bank. I wasn't thinking about the money side.'

Mary did not reply — she knew what was coming.

'Now Danny's settled into the shop, I need to find a place for Sean.'

'Sean? Why should you worry about finding a place for him? He'll be very happy doing other things.'

'It's always been a family business and he's a member of the family. I have an obligation.'

'But, Bernie, none of your brothers came into the shop.'

'Ah,' he said, nodding his head, 'We were too small to be able to offer them a place. That's why they cleared out. My dad always felt bad about that.' He gave Mary a triumphant smile. 'When we get Luke's business,

Danny will be right to take over there while I train up Sean. Then we can enjoy a relaxed life watching over both of them.'

He grinned expectantly at her but she made no immediate response. She had her own plans and had been waiting for the right opportunity to raise them with Bernie. But how should she put it to him? 'It would be good if we can make it work.' Bernie nodded approvingly and was about to respond but she continued. 'You've overlooked one thing. You won't just be creating a bigger newsagency; you'll be creating a much larger and more complex business. We've got by with me as book-keeper, but you'll need a business manager.'

'Maybe. Shouldn't be too difficult to find someone.'

'I know just the man: Sean.'

'I'll need him in the shop,' Bernard said.

'You'll need extra staff but Danny can take charge of both. Sean has a good brain and, with the right training, will make a good business manager.'

'The right training?'

'He can go to university next year and by the time we're ready to move he'll be qualified to deal with the financial and legal aspects of our expanded business.'

Jane hurried down wind-chilled Flinders Lane searching for Chez Renoir, a restaurant she had not heard of until Sally called to suggest lunch. She had not seen Sally since she went overseas just after Jane began nursing — over eighteen months ago. During that time Sally had made no contact other than sending six postcards which Jane had kept: a view of the Eiffel Tower, a bistro in Montmartre, the ski fields at St Moritz, a bull-fight in Ronda, the palace at Windsor and a fjord in Norway. Scrawled on the back of these cards were different words but the same message: 'I'm having a great time and you would love it here.' Sally did not say what she was doing and gave no details of the people she met or the places she visited.

Entering the restaurant, Jane was immediately charmed by its intimate warmth. Overhead lamps in diaphanous orange shades cast a soft glow over the white table cloths, silver cutlery and elegantly curved wooden chairs. Sally rose from a small table against the wall and hurried towards her with arms wide apart. She wore a rust red woollen suit under a matching cape, around her waist a casually tied black leather belt and on her head a wide-brimmed hat of the same material as her suit. 'Jane! How great to see you.'

Following their embrace Sally stepped back. 'Nursing suits you. You must tell me all about it.'

'But what about you? Where did you get that gorgeous suit? And that hat? Only grandmothers wear hats to lunch in Melbourne — nothing as chic as that number, though.'

'I stocked up before I left Paris. This is what they're wearing over there. But sit down. I've already started on the champagne and you must join me.'

After they had clinked glasses and drunk one another's health, Jane said, 'Will you be happy to stay here? After your experiences, Melbourne must be very dull.'

'That rather depends on what I do about Antoine.'

Jane could see the mischief in her friend's eyes and was tempted to pretend no interest as she might have done when they were at school. 'Antoine? Who is Antoine?'

'Antoine Chalon is the youngest son of the family which for many generations has resided at Chateau Chalon in Burgundy where they continue to produce some of the best wine in France. Sally picked up a leather covered folder and handed it to Jane. 'We should decide what we're going to eat.' The menu was set out in French with English sub-titles appended discreetly in smaller print. 'I'm told they do fish very well and the lamb is usually good, but you may like an entree first.'

Jane was keen to get back to Antoine. 'You choose. I'll have what you're having.'

It took only a slight lift of Sally's head to bring the glossy-haired young man in black to their table. 'Mademoiselle?'

Sally ordered in French gaining an appreciative smile from the waiter and a commendation which Jane could not translate. She had forgotten most of the French she'd striven to master at school but could appreciate the marked improvement in Sally's accent and fluency.

After the waiter had gone, Jane frowned sternly at Sally. 'Stop beating about the bush. What do you need to do about Antoine?'

'I need to decide whether to accept his proposal.'

'To marry him?'

She grinned at Jane. 'He made a number of earlier proposals but, when he saw I wasn't interested in those, he got around to proposing marriage. He isn't the first to want to marry me but he is the first worth considering.'

Jane reflected that the changes in her friend were of a magnitude she had not come close to imagining. It was as if Sally had spent her time since they last met moving quickly into full womanhood with its experiences, opportunities and choices, while Jane remained stuck in her teens. 'So, what are you going to do?'

'It's tempting. I've enjoyed enough of the life he leads to know how well off I would be. He has a beautiful apartment in Paris. He's handsome, entertaining and has many friends.' Again, she grinned and her voice, which had been thoughtful, became impish. 'He's a passionate man and is wooing me with ardour, charm and persistence.'

'But?'

'I've never felt as free as I have been since I went away. I fear that becoming a member of the Chalon family — dynasty you might call it — will bring obligations and restrictions I'm not ready to take on. But is this the best chance I'm going to get? Antoine is a man used to getting what he wants. If I try to keep him dangling for long, he won't hang around.' She sighed, all the earlier mischief completely gone. 'What would you do if you were me?'

'But I'm not you.' Jane was sure the life Sally was contemplating would have no appeal for her. Having a great time could never become a satisfying career and surely must soon lose whatever gloss it might initially have, resulting in boredom and dissatisfaction. She knew none of these views would be welcome.

Sally took a long draught from her glass. 'So, what about you? How's your love life?'

Jane laughed, relieved to change the subject and amused by the contrast between them. 'What love life?'

'No handsome doctor anxious to sweep you away?'

'One or two have cast their eyes in my direction but, unlike you, no proposals of any kind. The nurses in my group are good at organising parties, though. We need some light relief. I've had a few dalliances there but nothing worth continuing.'

'And what about nursing? Has it lived up to your expectations?'

Jane had been looking forward to telling her friend how her career had developed. The first six months were tough and I soon learnt that my expectations had been far too rosy.' She started to elaborate on her experiences during those early days but, sensing that Sally was becoming bored, she moved on to describe what she now thought of as the key event in her career so far: the episode with Mrs Teasdale. It was only when she mentioned Danny that Sally showed any interest.

'Danny? The boy next-door? Don't tell me he's still around?'

Jane was surprised by how much she was offended by Sally's tone. Yes, he had his deficiencies, but he didn't deserve to be considered of such little account. 'We still go dancing and have become very good at it. Some people suggested we should go in for competitions but neither of us is interested in that.' Conscious of Sally's continuing sceptical gaze, she added, 'I'd say since you went away Danny has become my best friend.' This was a new thought for her and she wondered where it had come from. Maybe her irritation with Sally had brought it on.

'Really?' Sally's scepticism had become outright disbelief.

Jane was tempted to say Danny had given her far more comfort and encouragement than she would ever have gained from Sally. 'That was the turning point for me. The more experience I get, the easier it is for me to deal with problems or difficulties and the more rewarding I find the job. I know I've found the right career. Another year to go and I'll be qualified.' Jane could see Sally had no understanding of how fulfilling nursing had become for her. A gap had opened between them which most likely would continue to widen.

'I don't get it. When I ask you about your love life, you say you don't have any. Then Danny pops into the story as your best friend. What's going on?'

Jane was saved from the need for an immediate reply when the waiter returned with their meals. A whole grilled trout eyed her from the plate. She liked fish but had never had to contend with the whole creature before. Sally began dismembering her trout with confident aplomb and Jane followed her lead. She did not recognise the sauce which bathed the fish but it was delicious as were the accompanying mounds of finely sliced vegetables.

'I thought you'd like it. A bit different from the old fish and chips.'

Jane jabbed her knife into the fish, bringing away some of the bones with the flesh. A bone caught between her teeth and she turned her head away to pull it out with her fingers. Sally raised the champagne to her lips. Was she hiding a smirk? Jane thought of Danny's lop-sided grin and wished she was eating fish and chips with him. He wouldn't have smirked; he would have laughed, but in a way that made her join in. Was she falling in love with him? He'd never fitted the image she had of a lover. Best friend had sounded like an apt description until Sally had shown it to be inadequate. What could she say? She stopped eating and looked at Sally directly.

'It's hard to explain. We get on very well together both on and off the dance floor. I enjoy my conversations with him better than I have with any other guy. I think he feels the same.' She paused to consider what she had just said. She'd thought Danny was holding back in recent times and wondered whether he was tiring of her. 'But there's nothing romantic between us. Yes, I give him a kiss when we meet and part, he hugs me sometimes, particularly when he needs to cheer me up. But that's as far as it ever goes.'

'Jane, you're a nurse not a nun. Sort yourself out.'

Uncertainties

'Would you give me a hand at the shop?' Danny said as he and Sean left the church after Mass. 'There are some things I need to sort out. It won't take long.'

'In that case can't you do it on your own? My last exam's on Monday and I need a final go over some sections of the course.'

'I said it won't take long. We can have a chat. With you at uni night and day we haven't had a good chat for ages.'

Sean laughed at him. 'Don't tell me you're missing me. That would be a first.' When Danny made no reply but continued to gaze at him in unspoken appeal, Sean relented. 'OK but we'll need to make it quick. Come on, the lights are about to change.' Immediately he took off across Punt Road and Danny had to dash to avoid the oncoming cars. As they walked along Victoria Street, Sean said, 'I haven't been along here since the start of the year. It's like coming back to a former life.'

As if to welcome him back, one of the old green and yellow trams trundled along the street before stopping under the railway bridge to allow a single passenger to alight. With the shops shut and their customers absent, there was no other sign of welcome. When they were almost to the newsagency, Sean said, 'I thought you wanted to talk but you haven't said a word. You want me to do all the chatting like in the old days?'

Danny pulled some keys from his pocket and used one of them to open the door of the shop. 'We need to bring the Christmas toys down from upstairs where they've been stored. It's time to put them on sale. He walked to the back of the shop and led the way up the stairs.

Sean surveyed the small room they entered. 'Brings back memories. How long is it now? Getting on for three years since we used to kip in here.'

'Grab this box. It's bulky but not too heavy.'

Sean wrapped his arms around the cardboard box and walked to the stairs, saying over his shoulder. 'I can understand why you're so keen to do this when Dad isn't around? On the way to church this morning I could see how heavily he's leaning on that stick of his.'

'Hurry up. I'm right behind you. There are four more when we get these two down. Put yours over by the far wall.'

After they had the six boxes on the floor of the shop, Danny opened one and began handing Sean a number of dolls. He nodded at a row of empty shelves and said, 'Put them anywhere over there. Mum'll want to come in tomorrow and arrange them to her liking.'

After they had emptied the first box, Danny glanced across at his brother. 'I bumped into your old pal Corky at the cricket yesterday.'

'Corky? He was never keen on sport. I tried to get him to come with me to see the Tigers but he never did. Had even less interest in cricket.'

Danny opened the second box which contained toy cars and trucks, each in its own carton. He handed some to Sean and said, 'Unlike you, since leaving school he's become an active member of the Old Boys. He came to support us.'

'It upsets me the way you waste your time with the Old Boys. Worst of all was going back to the footy team when you should have stayed with the Tigers — given it a proper go when they invited you and not wimped out with the Old Boys. You couldn't expect to make the firsts at the Tigers straight off, but after a year or so you'd have been a star. They wanted you.'

Danny turned away to carry another batch of toys to the shelves. 'Yes, they wanted all of me. Everything was footy. You carried on like this when I first went back to the Old Boys. I told you then I had no interest in having footy dominate my life like it does if you play for a league team. You didn't cut any ice with me then and dredging it up now won't divert me.' He glared at Sean. 'After Corky told me he was doing commerce, I surprised him by saying he must be seeing a fair bit of you. He knew for sure you weren't doing commerce but couldn't be certain exactly what course you're in since he hardly ever sees you — too busy with Conor. What are you up to?'

Sean straightened himself from depositing toys on the bottom shelf and turned to face Danny. 'I'm doing an arts degree.'

'An arts degree? How's that going to help you when you come into the business?'

'I'm not going into the business. I never have been.'

'That's not what Mum and Dad think.' Danny stared fiercely at his brother. 'Have you told them?'

'Mum wanted to make sure I didn't waste my talent like you did. You could have been an engineer or a scientist. Instead you buried yourself in this nothing job.'

'Don't try to put me off. When are you going to come clean with them?'

'After my results come out.'

'Dad'll be furious.'

'Nah. He'll be miffed he didn't know earlier but he'll get used to the idea pretty quickly. The only reason he wants me in the business is his obsession with keeping all the family involved. Once he accepts that's not going to happen, he'll be relieved. Besides I'm moving out. Next year I'll be able to support myself without any help from him. Conor and I are going to rent a place with Ted and Julian, two guys we've got to know.'

'Where's the money coming from?'

'From a teaching studentship. I'm going to be a teacher with the Education Department. Just so long as my results this year are as good as I expect, it's in the bag.'

Danny tilted his head and grinned at Sean. 'What a pity you didn't latch onto teaching when you were at school. You could have gone into the Church and become a teaching brother. Dad would have been rapt.'

Sean chuckled. 'Yeah, that would have been something. But I did decide I wanted to be a teacher when I was still at school. Never a priest though. No thank you. Maybe that's why I didn't mention it. I didn't want the hassle. I told Conor. He has the same ambition.'

Danny gave eyed Sean sceptically. 'Just about anything you say these days has Conor in it somewhere, yet we've never met him. What's going on?'

'Nothing's going on.' Danny noticed how quickly and perhaps even defiantly his brother replied. 'The better I come to know Conor the more I've come to like and admire him.'

'You make him sound like he's your hero.'

Sean took one of the toy cars from the shelf and inspected it as though considering buying it. 'When we lived here you were my hero — the big brother who could do no wrong. Good at maths and science when I struggled with those subjects. Terrific cricketer and footballer when I was hopeless at sport. Calm and collected no matter what. I wished I could be just like you. But look at you now. You let your life drift along taking you where it will. It's true of your job. It's true of Jane. You know there's no future with her and yet you keep on with her. I don't know why she doesn't have the sense to give you the flick. She's not a drifter like you. She's got a worthwhile career.'

Danny tried to keep his face blank but felt as though Sean was raining blows upon him. 'Don't be so snooty about the newsagency. It's been good enough for Dad and will be good enough for me.' His declaration gave no clue he had been wondering why God was taking so long to reveal the challenge he had expected to find through working in the newsagency. Was he supposed to be satisfied with the humdrum routine? His gathering doubts had now been given voice by his brother.

'Dad is very different from you. He likes nothing better than chatting with whoever comes into the shop and drinking with his mates afterwards. He never had other options and has made the best of it. You, on the other hand ...'

'Another batch of books came in on Friday. We should unpack them.' Danny went behind the counter, picked up a cardboard box which he carried to a display rack containing a range of paperbacks and began to add the new arrivals.

Sean came to stand beside him. 'God!' he exclaimed. 'Georgette Heyer, Agatha Christie, Ian Fleming, Wilbur Smith. Can't you offer some decent literature? Penguin has a great range of classics available.'

'You're able to lay down the law on literary merit as well.'

'I've always had a better appreciation of literature than you. English is one of my majors.'

Danny could hear them sniping at one another like when they were little kids and hated it. 'What are your other majors?'

'Only one: politics.'

'You aren't thinking of going into politics?'

'I've told you I'm going to be a teacher. That's an honourable profession. Politicians make me sick. You heard Menzies last week. He doesn't have the guts to tell the Australian people how badly that useless war in Vietnam is going. The Yanks had no need to get involved in the first place but mistakenly thought this would shore up their conflict with China despite them not being involved in Vietnam. Even the Communists there are suspicious of China, but the Yanks are pushing them into China's arms. When things start to go badly for the South, the Yanks engineer a military coup which achieves nothing but further chaos. So, they call on their lap-dog, Menzies, for help and bit by bit he gives them what they want. Now he's announced the reintroduction of conscription with conscripts being sent to Vietnam. Before you know it, your marble will drop and you'll find yourself dying in the jungle in support of America's futile gamble.'

'Is this what you talk about in your politics classes?'

'I get more from people in the peace movement.'

'The peace movement?'

'We've been holding some teach-ins on the Vietnam war. They've

69

been well attended, too,' he said proudly before giving a small grin. 'Not as well attended as our open-air concerts of protest where we've combined speakers on the war with live music. We're learning how to stir interest, though. Did you see the newspaper and TV coverage of our rally outside the US Consulate on Hiroshima Day, protesting against the bombing raids after the Tonkin Gulf fiasco?'

'You were in that?'

Danny had rarely seen Sean so pleased with himself. 'Yeah. There were about two hundred of us. Next year will be even bigger. They're about to start the Youth Campaign Against Conscription at Sydney Uni and we won't be far behind.'

'Do you have time for this and your studies?'

'Don't worry about me, brother. I'm passionate about the need for the world to strive for peace not war. But that's a cause. On the other hand, teaching will be my career. It's selfish, I know, but getting through my degree and becoming a teacher rates more highly with me than alerting people to the dangers we face, even though the consequences of ignoring them will likely be disastrous.'

Danny didn't know how to reply. Foremost in his mind was the thought that both Jane and Sean had found a mission to which they were committed. Envy was an emotion he had not met before. Jane had been right the very first time they played tennis when she said that everyone should have a goal, something they saw as important to achieve in their lives. Working in the newsagency could not compete with caring for the sick and injured or teaching kids. At least conscription might allow Danny to escape for a while.

Danny and Jane dodged a tram as they crossed Victoria Street into Fitzroy. The rays from the setting sun and the glow of the Christmas lights in a number of the shop windows combined to give Smith Street a festive air which was at odds with Danny's memory of a rather drab street enlivened only by the press of shoppers.

'Carol told me it was somewhere along here on the left before you get to Gertrude Street,' Jane said, beginning to doubt whether the directions her friend at the Alfred had given her were correct.

'We'll find it. At least we don't have to worry about the rain or the cold. It's taken until the week before Christmas for us to have any decent summer weather.'

'Let's hope Café Georgette lives up to Carol's recommendation,' Jane said. 'If we ever find it.'

'There it is.'

They paused outside the narrow shopfront window and peered in at the assortment of timber tables and benches. The restaurant was lit by candles stuck into the necks of wine bottles. Danny pushed open the heavy door and, as they stepped into the room, a squat woman in her fifties waddled from a rear corridor, wiping her hands on her striped apron. She brought with her the appetising aroma of the kitchen. 'Bon jour. Welcome,' she said with a heavy accent. 'Deux? You are two?'

Jane nodded.

'Over here.' The woman led them to a table against the wall and gestured for them to sit. She took a lighter from her pocket and lit their candle. 'I come back soon.'

In front of them on the table were two dog-eared sheets, each containing a hand-written menu. 'I s'pose this is how they do it in France,' Danny said.

Jane thought of Chez Renoir and wondered what Sally would have said if she had returned the favour of their lunch by bringing her here. 'Of course, choose what you like, but Carol told me the speciality of the house is Bouillabaisse — fish stew with a spicy sauce.'

'That'll do me. What about something to drink?'

'I suppose we should have wine. How about the house red?' She sniffed. 'Or do you want to stick with beer.'

'Not if that isn't the French thing to do.'

Their hostess returned to deliver food to the foursome at a table across the room. Jane wondered whether she was the proprietor and

71

was intrigued to know if her name was Georgette. Two more groups of four came through the door and Georgette, as Jane had decided to think of her, hurried to settle them at tables and light their candles. Finally, she came over to them.

'We would both like the Bouillabaisse,' Jane said. Perhaps it would have been polite to allow Danny to order for them but it had taken quite a bit of work for Carol to tutor Jane in the correct pronunciation and she didn't want to embarrass him. Besides, she had invited him.

'To drink?'

'Two glasses of the house red, please.'

Georgette shook her head and smiled, showing the gaps between her front teeth. 'Better white. The house wine, Sauvignon Blanc, very good for the Bouillabaisse.' Her pronunciation of Bouillabaisse made Jane reflect that Carol wasn't as good a tutor as she had thought. After the woman had departed, Jane sighed and said, 'Glad that's out of the way.'

'Are we celebrating something special?' Danny asked. When Jane did not answer immediately, he said, 'It just we haven't done this before — a change from dancing or the pictures.'

Here was further evidence he was tiring of her and dancing had become a bore. She had told herself it wouldn't be the end of the world if that were the case but she wanted to know where she stood. That's why she'd suggested the meal. 'It's a while since we had a good chat.'

Georgette arrived with two large glasses of white wine.

'Good luck,' Danny said and raised his glass.

'Cheers,' Jane replied and reached out to clink glasses before taking a sip. She preferred her drinks to be sweeter but the aftertaste was pleasant.

'What's happened?' he asked.

Of course. He was so used to having her tell him about her problems and concerns. No wonder he'd become bored. She took another sip of wine. 'I'm worried about you.'

'Me?'

'You've never been one to say a lot about yourself, but in recent times I've noticed you going further into your shell. Are you unhappy?'

Danny hesitated over his reply. 'I'm sorry if you think that There are a few things that have been bothering me lately and maybe I haven't been paying you the attention I should when we're together.'

Jane laughed. 'Danny, you make being with me sound like an obligation.' Was that how he felt?

'I'm concerned about Sean.' He began to recount the recent conversation with his brother. When he paused to take some more wine, she leaned over to touch the hand he had resting on the table.

'Almost the first time we spoke, you told me how important your family was to you, and I can understand why you're so upset. I'm sure the breaches can be healed, though. Your mum is such a caring person and I know Sean thinks the world of you. He'll listen carefully to any advice you give him.'

'Maybe once. Not any longer. You should have heard the scornful way he told me how I disappointed him. These days he has a new hero, Conor, who has Sean under his spell.'

Georgette returned carrying two large bowls of what appeared to be very thick soup which she placed before them. Jane took in the spicy aroma from the bowl containing pieces of fish, mussels, prawns, tomato and other vegetables she could not identify. 'Bon appetite.'

Neither spoke as they gave their full attention to the Bouillabaisse, both finding difficulty in dealing with the mussels and prawns. Jane enjoyed the blend of flavours and needed frequent mouthfuls of wine, as did Danny. About half way through their meal she decided she could return to their conversation.

'I don't think you need to worry about Sean. I found moving out of home helped me get on better with my mum.'

Danny hesitated before saying, 'It's his pal Conor I'm worried about.'
'Why?'

Danny picked up his glass and, finding it empty, placed it back on the table. Georgette, who had just served the table next to them, caught his eye. 'Another?'

'Thank you.'

After she had moved away, Jane persisted. 'Why are you worried about Conor?'

'I don't know. There's something about the way Sean speaks of him. I think Sean has got into something he'll regret.'

'Danny, you're talking in riddles. Spit it out.'

'I'm worried Conor has got Sean into a relationship that isn't healthy.'

At last Jane understood. 'You think Conor has corrupted Sean. Or do you think Sean might be gay?' She liked the term she had heard one of nurse friends use. It was softer, more accepting.

'Gay?' Danny took a second to grasp her meaning. 'I don't know. He's never shown a lot of interest in girls.'

Georgette returned with another glass of wine for both of them. Jane hesitated before accepting it. Already she felt a little light-headed but it would risk the rapport she was striving to establish with Danny if she left him to drink alone. She emptied the first glass and licked her upper lip before smiling at Danny. 'He's always been very friendly to me.'

'Yeah but that's different.'

Jane stiffened and the colour rose in her cheeks before she gave a braying laugh. 'Poor little me. Different from other girls. Not bad if all you want is a chat but she never stirs romantic thoughts in guys like other girls do.'

Danny frowned at her. 'You know that's not true.'

Jane wondered how he could be so sure. Was he recalling that unhappy episode with Richard St John? He wouldn't know about her unexciting flirtations at the nurses' parties.

'I've seen the way the guys at Ormond Hall gawk at you.' Did he mind that? If so, it was a side of Danny he'd kept well hidden. 'All I meant was that the two of you are good friends — a bit like brother and sister might be.'

'Like us?'

When Danny took some more wine rather than answer her question, Jane decided this was the time to speak up. She leaned forward over the table and asked, 'Are you becoming bored with me? Have you found another girl you prefer?'

'Bored? Me bored with you?' Danny produced one of his wry grins. She hadn't seen one of those for a while. 'One of the home truths Sean gave me when he was dressing me down was about you. He accused me of keeping on seeing you when I knew there could be no future with you and he didn't know why you hadn't given me the chop. I could understand if you did but I would mind. I'd mind a lot. I do care for you. There's certainly no other girl.'

'No future with me? What's this future? Are you talking about marriage? Why should that be a problem now? We're both far too young to think about marriage.'

Georgette had returned to their table in time to overhear what Jane had just said. As she leant over to take their bowls, she turned to face Jane, winked and nodded her head in approval, causing Jane to giggle. Straightening up, the woman asked, 'For the dessert?'

Jane took up the menu from the side of the table.

'Tarte Tatin is very good,' Georgette said. Seeing Jane's dubious expression, she added, 'Apple pie upside down,' and gave her gap-toothed smile. 'Or the Créme Brûlée?'

'The tart please.'

'I'm fine,' Danny said in a grumpy voice.

'Come on Danny, you can't leave me to eat on my own.'

Georgette nodded her acceptance of the double order before Danny could respond. As she turned away, she said, 'And deux café.' It occurred to Jane that maybe she wasn't the only one concerned about the extent of her wine consumption.

After she had gone, Jane giggled again and said, 'She thinks I've just rejected your marriage proposal and reckons I've done the right thing. Remember when I pretended to do the same the first time we played tennis. She considered Danny's unsmiling face. You weren't amused then, either.'

'Years ago, when Dad was giving me a hard time over my playing tennis and going to the pictures with you, I went to talk to our parish priest. He assured me there was nothing wrong in becoming friendly with a Protestant but warned me that sometimes people's feelings change and that can cause a problem.'

'What feelings of yours are changing?'

'To tell the truth, when we first started playing tennis and talking together, I was intrigued to find a girl who wanted to talk about serious topics and even give me a hard time when you didn't agree with me. I hadn't met a girl like that before and I enjoyed my struggles with you on and off the court. I guess it was when we started to go dancing that things started to change. Like you said, even then I didn't have any romantic thoughts about you.' He broke off to look around the café.

Jane had the impression he was trying to decide whether he should continue with what was becoming more and more like a confession. 'Go on.'

'You'll probably laugh at me like you do, but for a long time I've believed that one day, certainly not yet, I'd meet the girl I would marry and I'd immediately recognise her.'

'Really?'

'See, I said you'd laugh.'

Georgette returned bearing two plates of Tarte Tatin. Jane spooned some of the tart into her mouth and mumbled, 'Delicious.'

Danny nodded his agreement and took a second spoonful.

'I wasn't laughing at you,' Jane said. 'I was surprised, but I shouldn't have been. I can see how you'd think that. I remember you once said you believed God has a plan for each of us and we have to watch out for it until it comes along. It's not an idea I like at all, but I've never forgotten it. You mightn't have met many serious girls. I haven't met many sincere boys. But, forgive me, what I see as your fantasy about marriage fits with your belief in God's plan.'

'And deep down I guess I still believe that, although I'm not as sure as I once was.'

Jane saw Georgette coming towards them with two large cups, so waited for her to deliver the thick, dark coffee before she asked, 'You're not confessing to having a few romantic thoughts about me?'

'I've already told you I care for you. I'd be sorry but could understand if you gave me the chop. Are these the romantic thoughts you were talking about? They aren't the ones I expected but they may be and, if so, that's not fair on you.'

She him gave an encouraging smile. 'I appreciate you being so honest with me. Now it's my turn.' She sipped her coffee. 'I've gone down a different path from you but I'd say I'm heading in the same direction. My first impressions of you were of a dull, sloppily dressed guy.'

'Really? That bad?' Danny grinned sheepishly.

'I didn't like the way you condescended to me but I did enjoy the talks we began to have — a new experience for me. Maybe that would have fizzled out after a while but then you came with me to the school dance. That night you managed to make yourself fairly presentable and dance better than anyone I have ever met.' She paused to take another sip of coffee. 'Dancing with you has got better and better and you're so kind and attentive to me that I described you to Sally as my best friend.' Danny shook his head as if denying he could be her best friend. She had never seen him so coy before but did not let that stop her. 'I care for you and, just like you, this is not what I expected.' She grinned at him. 'So we're both stuck. Maybe we're in love. Maybe we aren't. I guess if we keep hanging out together, we might find out which it is.'

'I suppose you're right.' He sounded far from convinced.

'Cheer up. I don't think things are as bleak as you feel they are. Take Sean. I'm sure you won't agree but I think it's great he's keen to pursue a teaching career. You know I believe it's important to have a mission. I have my nursing and you have the family newsagency. I can't see you and Sean sharing that happily even if it is what your father would prefer.'

Danny gave a humourless laugh. 'I don't think I've envied anyone before but, listening to the way you speak about nursing and Sean about teaching, makes me feel I'm missing out.' He lifted his chin and gave a small sniff. 'If I'm called up next year, a spell of conscription might give me the chance to work out what I should do.'

Jane sat back as if avoiding a blow. 'You're not wanting to being called up. That'd be terrible. I haven't been game to mention it. What if they send you to Vietnam?'

'I guess you and Sean might say I'm just drifting along again but, if I am called up, I'll just have to be on the lookout to see if that has anything to do with God's plan for me.'

'Is your God a gambler? I can't see Him going in for conscription lotteries.' When Danny made no response, Jane said, 'I think you may be worrying unnecessarily over Sean. When I was at school it was common for girls to get crushes on other girls. It seldom lasted long. I don't know how it is with boys but maybe he just had a schoolboy crush on this Conor.'

'They're not at school now.'

'OK, if you insist, let's say he is gay. What's so wrong with that?

'It's a mortal sin.'

'A mortal sin? What's that?'

Danny finished his coffee and wiped his lips with his paper serviette. 'It's what the Church calls it when your sin is so severe your soul is deprived of divine grace.'

'You're quoting from some creed, aren't you? Do you have any idea what those words actually mean?'

'They mean what they say,' Danny said doggedly.

'But if two people love one another, that's a joyful event, even if they are both men or both women. Among the nurses at the Alfred there are several couples and they get along fine.'

Returning along Smith Street, they did not speak, each preoccupied with their own thoughts. For Jane it had been a very successful evening. She had cleared the air with Danny and, while she had not been completely open with him, felt much clearer on the way ahead. If her feelings for him were to become love, he would need to change. She had already told him of her dismay at his sloppy dress and remembered his untidy room. No, the main issue was the one she hadn't mentioned. She was incredulous he found it hard to doubt he would know the instant he met the woman he was destined to marry. She, on the other hand, had always imagined the blossoming of love would be accompanied by courtship and looked forward to being wooed by her lover. True, she'd been sadly misled when Richard had been so keen in his pursuit of her. She wished Danny would show at least a little of Richard's enthusiasm and, to put it crudely, become more physical.

They crossed Victoria Street and approached the moonlit tennis courts, but Jane was taking more notice of the lane which led off the street before they came to their corner. It was here that she and Richard would pause before reaching her porch. 'Here, let me show you something,' she said and led Danny into the darkness of the lane. 'I know we're still deciding whether we're in love but I want to kiss you properly.' She reached for him and was delighted when he took her in his arms.

*

'Hello, stranger. I've hardly seen you since you moved out in January.' Having just entered the front door, Danny beamed at Sean who stood in the doorway of the living room with a serious face.

'Dad not with you?'

'No, he left earlier. He's doing that more and more. If he's not here, then he's at the Oak Tree. It's good to see you. How do you like living away from home? Or is that it: you've come home for some of Mum's cooking?'

'I'll just be here for a few days. Come with me.' Sean turned and led Danny through the house to one of the rooms in the add-on at the rear. The family had still to find any use for these rooms and the contents of this one were a broken display case that Bernard thought might be repairable, two battered suitcases and the smell of disturbed dust.

Danny became aware of Sean's sombre manner. 'What's wrong? What's happened?'

'I need to find a new place. It shouldn't take long.'

'Hasn't living with your pals worked out?'

'I thought it would be better to have some space between us.'

'Is Conor moving out with you?'

Sean scanned his face. 'Do Mum and Dad know about him?'

'What is there to know?' When Sean did not reply but studied the floor, Danny added, 'Come on, mate. You didn't bring me out here to exchange pleasantries.'

'What do you know about Conor and me?'

Now it was Danny who was reluctant to speak candidly. It was as if Sean had called his bluff. 'Seeing we've hardly spoken in recent months, not much. But I do have concerns. Perhaps you can tell me whether I should be worried.'

Sean pushed at one of the suitcases with his toe. 'Depends what you're worried about.'

Danny groaned. 'OK. You won't bite the bullet so I will. Is Conor your boyfriend? Are you gay?'

Sean surprised Danny by smiling. 'I see you're up with the latest terminology.'

'Jane taught me. You haven't answered my questions.'

'Jane? You are having interesting conversations these days.'

'Sean!'

'The answers are no and I'm not sure.'

'Meaning?' Danny was only just managing to control his frustration with Sean's reticence.

Sean gave a sigh. 'We have been very close. I felt great affection for Conor and thought he cared for me. Yes, we fooled around a bit but nothing too heavy. He's now moved on to Julian and, from what I can tell, that is heavy. That's why I need to move out and coming home was the only immediate option. Finding a room in the middle of term is difficult.'

Danny waited for Sean to go on. Eventually Sean shrugged and said, 'What I said is true. I'm not sure and that's what's bugging me. Girls have never turned me on. There's a start. I used to have a crush on you until you began to disappoint me but that was really me searching for a hero, not a boyfriend. It started the same way with Conor but became something else. Was that his doing or mine? I think he made it easy for me but I wanted it. There are plenty of gay men at the uni but I haven't found any that appeal to me. Not yet, anyway.' He frowned at Danny. 'Before you ask, I have been looking, but in the way I imagine you casually check out a bunch of chicks.'

'So, where do you go from here?'

'You're not disgusted with me? You're not angry? You don't mind?' Sean spoke as if reciting a list of surprises but Danny heard them as a catalogue of his fears.

'I'd be lying if I said I didn't regret finding you are the way you are. But I'm not angry with you. I'm sorry for the problems it creates for you. It must be very hard, particularly in a family like ours.'

Sean scoffed at him. 'The good Catholic family having to confront mortal sin.'

'I can see how troubled and confused you are. Yet you trusted me enough to tell me. I want to help.'

'I asked you if Mum and Dad know about Conor.'

'They know the two of you are close friends. I can't be sure but I'd guess Mum has her suspicions — not much gets past her. On the other hand, I don't think Dad would have a clue. If I were you, I wouldn't say anything to either of them right now. If you like, I could try to suss out what Mum thinks and how she feels. Is there someone you could consult? I feel inadequate and obviously you wouldn't want to go to Father Maloney.'

Sean gave a twisted grin. 'No, I've never found him much help.' He straightened up and squared his shoulders. 'We'd better get back. Mum was upstairs making sure my room had all I needed. She'll be wondering where we are.'

When they walked into the kitchen Mary was there to greet them. 'There you are. I didn't know where you'd got to.'

'We were just checking those derelict rooms at the back. We really should do something useful with them.' Danny knew his hastily invented lie would not have fooled his mother and noted how she kept her eyes on Sean.

'You could have warned me, dear, that you were coming tonight.' She turned towards the stove where a large pot was sending forth a savoury aroma. 'Fortunately, we're having stew and I've been able to add some extra, so we won't starve.'

'Smells very good, too,' Bernard said from the doorway where he had arrived unnoticed. He ignored Sean and grinned at Danny. 'You found a derelict on the street and brought him in for a meal did you, son?' Now he turned to examine Sean. 'I reckon he could do with a decent feed.'

'Good to see you, too, Dad.'

'Sean is spending a few days with us,' Mary said. 'Won't that be nice?'

The awkwardness among them was not dispelled when they sat around the table to eat. Sean had withdrawn into himself, not even complimenting his mother on her cooking, while Bernard had nothing he was keen to share with them. Eventually he smiled at them and said, 'Mick had a good story for us tonight. It's about the bloke who went to apply for a job. He'd filled out his application and then had to front his hoped-for new employer. He waited anxiously while the man read his application. Eventually he said, "We have an opening for people like you."

"Oh, great," he replied, "What is it?"

"It's called the door!"'

'You trying to tell me something, Dad?' Sean snapped at him. 'I'll be gone by the end of next week at the latest. You can be sure of that.'

'Oh dear,' Mary said. 'You men are so difficult to deal with these days.'

'I have some reading I have to do before tomorrow's lecture,' Sean said. 'I'll be up in my room.'

When he had gone Bernard appealed to Mary. 'I was just trying to lighten the mood. What's got into him?

When Danny poked his head into Sean's room, his brother was not reading but lying on his bed with an open book beside him, staring at the ceiling. 'You'd didn't need to be so hostile with Dad. Surely you haven't forgotten how he is when he's trying to climb down from some past falling out. Tonight he was more ham-fisted than usual but you've seen all that before.'

Sean wriggled into a sitting position and looked up at Danny. 'Yeah, I'm sorry. You said it yourself: I am troubled and confused. Hopefully I'll get over it soon.'

Danny hesitated before saying, 'I've been thinking. If you're stuck for someone to talk with, you could do a lot worse than have a chat with Jane.'

'Jane? You've got to be kidding.'

'Hear me out. Unlike other girls, you've never had any trouble talking with her. She's not Catholic and she has a very sympathetic view of people who are gay.' He paused to smile at Sean. 'When we were talking about it, she told me there were some gay nurse couples at the Alfred and gave me a lecture on how she believed that if two people loved one another it didn't matter whether they were men or women or one of each.'

'What brought all this on?'

Danny was pleased he had sparked Sean's interest and decided to risk a further step. 'I've been worried about you since before last Christmas and I told Jane. We talked about it. That's how I know you could talk with her.'

Sean made no response, perhaps absorbing the surprise his secret had not been as well hidden as he had imagined, perhaps considering whether he should take up Danny's suggestion. Eventually he said, 'There's something else I wanted to mention. You realise next week you'll find out whether your number came up.'

'Next week? Having registered back in January, I'd sort of forgotten about it.'

'Well some of us haven't. We turned up to protest at the National

Service Office in Swanston Street on the day the ballot was drawn. There were about twenty of us there and people going to work accused us of being traitors, Communists and cowards. Some of them even spat on us. It makes you proud to know you're trying to save people like that from the horror of war. We're arranging to offer support to those who'll find out early next week they've been called up. If you have, I'll be here to help you decide what you should do.'

When Danny and Bernard came into the kitchen after work, they found Mary sitting at the table staring absently at a brown envelope which lay in front of her. She raised her head and said, 'There's a letter for you, Danny. An official one.' She made no effort to hand it to him. He walked to the table, saw his name and address typed under an OHMS logo and picked up the envelope. She continued to gaze down at the table as he tore open the letter, took out the single, sharply folded sheet and read the opening lines. 'I made it. This is my call-up.'

'Congratulations, Danny,' his father said, grasping his hand. 'I know you'll give a good account of yourself.'

Mary picked up her untouched tea and walked across to the sink.

'What's going on?' Sean asked as he came into the room.

'I've won the lottery.' Danny held out the letter. 'See.'

'Bugger,' Sean said, taking the letter.

Bernard, who was taking a bottle of celebratory beer from the fridge, turned to frown at Sean and tilt his head in Mary's direction. Sean scanned the letter and said, 'You're off to Puckapunyal.'

'Am I? Where does it say that?'

Sean began to read in an official tone, 'You are required to present yourself at Flinders Street Railway Station on the twelfth day of April, 1965 to the National Service Reception Officer for onward transport to Puckapunyal.' His tone changed as he said, 'That's if you can't get an exemption.'

'Why would I want to do that?'

Mary turned from the sink. 'How will we get by in the shop without you?'

'I'll miss Danny, of course, but I'll get by,' Bernard said. 'My contribution.'

'There's a thought,' Sean said. 'It's too late for you to go for conscientious objection. You had to apply for that when you registered. But you could seek deferral on exceptional hardship grounds.'

'What hardship do I have?'

'Not you. Dad. Let's face it, Dad, you may have been able to get by without Danny a couple of years ago but now you depend on him for all the lifting and quite a bit else as well. You won't be able to get by on your own.'

Bernard gave a wide smile and raised his hands in a gesture of gratitude. Danny saw his mother wince and guessed what was coming next. 'Thank you, Sean,' Bernard said. 'I hadn't realised you were so concerned about me. But now I needn't worry. I can see you'll be happy to defer your studies and take Danny's place. That'll be your contribution.' For once Sean was lost for words. 'I thought so. When I went into the army my dad was a lot worse than I am now but he got by somehow. So will I.'

Sean transferred his attention to Danny. 'You should talk with Guy Norton. He's a lawyer we're working with to help those who've been called up gain exemption or deferral. He's very good.'

'Are you one of those wretched uni students trying to undermine our security?' Bernard said.

'The only thing undermining our security is our government's persistence in joining this American invasion of Vietnam, putting our soldiers and our country at risk.'

Bernard puffed out his cheeks. 'Pah. You students have no experience of the world and think you know it all. I've heard how the Communists are seducing you lot with their anti-American propaganda. I'd hoped you had more sense.'

'Dad, stop listening to the demented preachings of that obsessive fool, Father Maloney, and consider the facts. Nothing good will come from our involvement in Vietnam.'

'I mightn't be going there,' Danny said.

'Get out of my house,' Bernard bellowed.

'He just needs a few more days,' Mary said.

'I'll shelter no Communist fellow-traveller under my roof,' Bernard said. 'Go, Sean, and go now.'

In the Army Now

When the train reached Dysart siding, the recruits could see a line of khaki trucks awaiting them. Emerging onto the timber platform, they were met by a small group of non-commissioned officers who herded them onto the trucks before they set off along a pot-holed dirt road, the convoy creating a choking plume of dust.

As they approached Puckapunyal, Danny felt the same mixture of excitement and apprehension he remembered feeling on the day he commenced primary school. His view of the camp was of a flat, sparsely treed expanse with row upon orderly row of rectangular huts, putting him in mind of the temporary classrooms which were so common around the suburbs of Melbourne. When he climbed down from the truck he was met by the smell of bare earth and diesel fumes.

Immediately a sergeant ordered him to join a long line of recruits awaiting the issue of their kit. After standing for an age in a chilly breeze, he staggered off to his allocated hut with a load that included toilet gear, greatcoat, two uniforms, beret, slouch hat, drill trousers, khaki shirts, boots, shoes, underwear, socks, pyjamas and towels. Now, equipped for service, his problem was how to store his gear in the confined space he shared with the ten others who were facing the same challenge.

The reactions of those around him to their first minutes of military service were mixed. The short, wiry one with spiky black hair who said his name was Skeeta Philips quietly went about organising his space.

Billy Jones, also short but gingery and overweight, grumbled that none of his clothing fitted and no one he complained to was bothered about it. Arnold Cordell told Billy he should get used to it — the army was like that. Arnold did not say where he had gained this knowledge. 'Well, I s'pose the only thing we can do is make the best of it,' was Skeeta's response.

A loud shout ordered them to don their uniforms and parade outside 'quick smart'. Standing between the adjacent huts in small disconnected groups, they were confronted by a man in slouch hat, sharply pressed uniform and gleaming boots who bore three stripes on his shoulder. 'Quiet,' he bellowed, immediately stilling their desultory conversations. 'Line up. Three ranks, ten in each. Quick about it. We haven't got all day.' After some jostling, they arranged themselves in something approaching the formation he had ordered while he continued to glare at them.

'You'll get better at it with practice,' he said. 'The quicker you do, the less time we'll have to spend practicing.' He smiled at them in a way Danny found more threatening than his glare. 'Welcome to Puckapunyal, your home for the next ten weeks. I am Sergeant Braddock. You will call me Sergeant ... as in, "Yes, Sergeant ... No, Sergeant ... Three bags full, Sergeant." Should you have a question, or in the unlikely event you have something worthwhile to say, you will raise your right hand in the air and wait to be given permission to speak. Then, and only then, will you utter a sound. Are we clear?'

Mutters of assent set him off again. 'The correct answer to that question is, "Yes, Sergeant," given in a firm, clear voice. Understood?'

'Yes, Sergeant.'

His face suggested another rebuke was coming, but he moved on. 'My job and that of my colleagues is to ensure that by the end of these ten weeks you are fit to take up your designated post as a soldier. If we succeed, you will still have a lot to learn but at least you will not be a liability to your unit. It's clear I'll have my work cut out but I don't give in easily. Neither will you.' After this homily he pointed out the locations of the mess hall, the exterior of which was more like a factory than a restaurant, and the various toilet, ablutions, laundry and drying blocks. Then he lectured them on the importance of maintaining their gear and their quarters in 'top-notch' condition. 'Now, return to your quarters and I will come through for a preliminary inspection.'

Awaiting the arrival of Sergeant Braddock, they could hear his displeasure echoing from further down the building. On reaching their end, he directed his attention to Danny and exploded. 'Straighten yourself up, man. Put your shoulders back and stand tall like a proper soldier even if you aren't one. And, for God's sake, do up your buttons. You've got two of your pockets gaping. We'll deal with your hair later. And that bed! These are military quarters not a doss-house.' He turned to assess the job Skeeta had done on his bed. 'There, this bloke can give you a clue. Not the best I've ever seen but not bad for a first try.' He checked on the others. 'Both of you need to improve, too, but at least I've got only one out-and-out hopeless case here.'

After he had gone Skeeta said 'I've always found that the louder bullies shout, the less you have to fear from them. I don't think Boofy Braddock will cause us much trouble once we settle in.'

Dinner that night was served cafeteria style on metal trays which Danny, Skeeta, Billy and Arnold carried to one of the long tables in the mess. Danny thought, the main course, a form of beef stew with plenty of thick mashed potato and boiled carrots was OK and nodded his agreement when Skeeta said, 'Not as good as what Mum cooks.' Billy complained the servings were too small and Arnold surprised them by admitting the food was not much different from what he had in his college at the university.

'Hey, Skeeta,' Billy said, 'How did you get that name?

'Dunno,' was the laconic reply. 'I've always been Skeeta.' It was as if the question had never occurred to him.

'Where do you come from, then?' Billy asked.

'We have a property at Mundarlo between Junee and Gundagai: fine wool. The family's been there for years.'

Billy shook his head in regret and Danny wondered what could be wrong with Skeeta's answer this time. 'You could have put in for a deferment. Hardship. They specially mention blokes needed on the family farm.'

'Yeah, I s'pose I could have,' Skeeta said and Danny could see the ghost of a smile. 'Probably wouldn't have gone too well, seeing I've got three older brothers and me dad is still fit as a bull.' Skeeta appraised the layer of stomach protruding over Billy's belt and clapped him on the shoulder in a friendly gesture. 'I'm surprised you didn't manage to fail the physical. That would have got you off, no problem.' This was the first time Danny noticed Skeeta never met hostility or provocation head-on but bided his time and coated his rejoinder with good humour. Perhaps he had developed the technique when surviving the attention of three elder brothers.

'I'm surprised it needs four of you to run the place,' Billy said. 'Must be quite a size.'

'We do other things as well. Mick works as a shearer. Pat uses his truck for carting and Tom helps out on other properties when they're short.'

'What about you?' Billy asked.

'I'm good at fixing things.'

'Fixing things? What things?' Billy would not give up.

'Pretty much anything: pumps, ovens, tractors, broken tiles.'

Even after their short acquaintance, there was something about Skeeta which appealed to Danny greatly.

After they had returned from their meal and were preparing for bed, Billy challenged Skeeta again. 'The sergeant says you're the one who knows how to make a bed army-style. You'd better give us a lesson.'

'Yeah, if you like. Not a lot to it. You just have to be careful about keeping everything square.'

Jane had once mentioned her boss's obsession with bed-making. 'Keeping it square' had been one of her demands. He wondered how

Jane was feeling now they were apart for twelve weeks. Since that night at Café Georgette, he had enjoyed the pleasure of fondling and kissing her. His affection continued to grow but he had no idea how or even if he could make everything square between them.

'And who taught you this? Got a soldier in the family?' Billy always made his questions sound like challenges.

'Me dad was in the war but it was me mum who makes us do it the way she likes. Don't know where she got it.'

'Was she a nurse?' Danny asked.

'Yeah, she was before she married me dad.'

'There you are,' Danny said.

Billy turned to Danny. 'From your efforts, I'd be surprised if you had a soldier or a nurse in your family.'

'Would you, Billy?' Danny thought of the way Skeeta was handling Billy. 'Well my old man was at the war, too, and I know a nurse.'

Skeeta grinned at him. 'Lucky you.'

Settled in their newly-made beds at lights out, they laughed when a call came from the other end of the building. 'Only sixty-nine days to go.'

'Poor sap,' Arnold said. 'Doesn't he realise the full count is seven hundred and twenty-nine.'

When she returned to the Nurses' Home from her shift, Jane was told Sean McBride had rung and asked her to call him on a number she did not recognise. Danny had told her about his conversation with Sean and warned her he might call her. Had it taken this long for Sean to overcome his reluctance and seek her out?

Her call was answered by a man who announced himself with the words, 'Guy Norton speaking'. When she gave her name and asked to speak with Sean, she was told she certainly could and heard him being called to the phone. Guy Norton sounded somewhat older than Sean and had the mellifluous tones of an ABC newsreader.

'Jane! Thanks for calling back. How are you?'

'Fine, thank you, Sean. How about you?'

'Couldn't be better.' He certainly sounded like the old, ebullient Sean who would not need her help or advice. 'Haven't seen you for ages and would like to catch up. How about coming up to Carlton and having a coffee at Genevieve's. The coffee in the caf at uni's rubbish.'

Having followed Sean's directions to take the Number 1 tram up Swanston Street and get off at the University, Jane walked down Faraday Street past the Carlton Movie House and came to Genevieve's on the next corner, just as he had described. Entering the door, she was struck by the clamour of conversation and the smell of roasted coffee beans. There was a good deal of high-pitched laughter and posturing, reminding Jane of some of the parties she had attended with Richard. Was this how university students spent their time? She thought of her lunch with Sally when she felt Sally had grown up while she remained a teenager. Now Jane felt she was the one who had matured while many of these students had yet to have done so.

She turned to find Sean entering the cafe. 'Sorry I'm late.' Her first impulse was to give him a peck on the cheek but she thought better of it. He probably would not like to be kissed by any girl, no matter how chastely. 'Let's grab that table over in the corner.' Once they were seated Sean asked, 'How do you like your coffee? Cappuccino? Latte? Flat white? They have a wide range.'

'A cappuccino, thanks Sean.'

He rose and hurried to the counter. In jeans and black T-shirt under a navy bomber jacket, he looked as chipper as he had sounded on the phone.

Returning with their coffee he grinned at her and said, 'What about my warfaring brother? I guess you've heard from him.'

'He's not the most dedicated letter-writer, but I get the impression he's quite enjoying himself. He has a new friend by the name of Skeeta who comes from a sheep property in New South Wales. I don't think Danny knows many people from the bush and is intrigued by Skeeta.'

'You're right. Our family has relatives in Queensland and Western Australia who are on the land but we never see them.' Again, he grinned at her. 'Missing you, of course.'

'Not that he's said.' Jane sipped her coffee. 'Though I wouldn't expect Danny to put anything like that in a letter to me.'

Sean nodded his amused agreement. 'And you? Are you missing him?'

'Yeah, I do miss him.' Jane had expected she might be counselling Sean, not talking about herself. 'Him being away has made me appreciate just how much I like having him around.'

'Do you love him?'

Sean's blunt question was one she continued to ask herself. 'I think so. Yes, I'm becoming more certain.'

'You're wrong there.' Sean spoke with the confidence of someone newly converted. 'If you love someone, you know. If you're not sure, you don't.'

Jane felt the heat grow in her face. How presumptuous of him to pontificate on something as complex and many faceted as love? Did the university give its students the misplaced idea they knew better than anyone else? 'You're speaking from your vast experience of the subject, of course.'

'Hardly vast.' He surprised her with his coy expression. 'I know very little about love but I'm completely sure I am in love.'

Jane thought of Conor, but Danny said he had moved on. 'That was quick.' Immediately she regretted what she had said. She was thinking aloud but it had come out as a cheap shot. So much for Danny's confidence Sean would benefit from speaking with her. 'Danny used to believe he'd know straight away when he met the girl he'd marry. Is that what you're saying?'

Sean leaned towards her with his arms outstretched and crooned:

'Some enchanted evening, you may see a stranger.

You may see a stranger across a crowded room
And somehow you know, you know even then,
That somehow you'll see her again and again.'

'Sean, I didn't know you could sing.'

He sat back, ignoring her compliment, and said in a scornful voice, 'That only happens in the movies. I've known Guy for over a year now and ...'

'Guy? Guy Norton? The man who answered the phone when I called you?'

'Yeah. He's a human rights lawyer who's been a great help to those of us in the peace movement. For sure he'll go into politics one day and you'll hear a lot about him then. When I needed somewhere to stay, he suggested I move in with him. It didn't happen overnight but. I know. It's why I wanted to talk with you.'

'I don't understand.'

'I miss the family, Danny in particular, but Mum as well and, to my surprise, even my cantankerous old man. Would you let Danny know he doesn't need to worry about me and please tell him about Guy?'

Jane had a better idea. 'He finishes at Puckapunyal next week and will be home for a few days before going up to Sydney where he's been posted. Why don't you speak with him directly?'

'I don't want to create any more hassles at home by turning up there. Tell him about me and give him my number. He might like to call me.'

Two young men and a woman who were making their way out of the cafe turned to approach their table. 'Hey, Sean,' one of the men said, 'we missed you at the meeting last night. Where'd you get to?'

'Had better things to do.'

'Like chatting up young ladies?' the girl said with a sneer.

Sean turned to face Jane. 'Sorry about these pests. Just ignore them.'

'Bye Sean,' the other man said with a laugh and the threesome continued on towards the door.

'What was that all about?' Jane asked.

'Those three are some of the drippier members of the Labor Club at the uni. I'd joined, too, but since the Federal Executive of the party has got behind the myth that the war in Vietnam is needed to stop the Communists from threatening us, I'm putting my efforts elsewhere. You could hear what bird-brains they are.' Sean shrugged. 'Where were we?'

'You mentioned how you missed your family. I'm sure your mum is worried about you.'

'Yeah, I s'pose so.' Sean took up his cup and drained what remained of his coffee. 'Would you have a word to her as well?'

'Wouldn't you prefer Danny to do it?'

'I think you'd do it better. From our last conversation I don't think Danny's properly come to terms with my ... with my situation. He said you'd be more sympathetic to me.'

'Are you saying you want me to tell Mary about ... about Guy Norton?'

'Yeah, that'd be good.' He made it sound as though Jane had come up with the suggestion.

'Sean, if you're going to tell your mother, it must come from you directly and face to face.'

'You think?'

'I'm certain.' Jane could hear an echo of Sean in her confident asser- tion. A man at the next table stood up to call out to three others who had just entered. The din around him meant he had to wave his arms and continue shouting before they saw him.

Sean leaned forward so their heads were closer. 'Perhaps I should do it after you've spoken to her. I'm sure she'll be fine with it, but she might like a bit of time to get used to the idea before I speak with her.'

'I know she loves you and will continue to love you but I don't think she'll be happy.'

Sean frowned at her. 'Mum's not a homophobe like Dad is.'

'I'd be surprised if she was, but in this country homosexuality is still a crime and in your church it's a mortal sin.'

'It's not my church.'

'I'm just trying to suggest why your mother will find your revelation very painful. I'm sure she won't condemn you, but she will be very sad that things are as they are. If I were you, I'd concentrate on re-establishing a connection with your parents. Sure, tell them where you are staying and mention Guy Norton but don't go beyond that. Certainly not at present. I'd also make sure to speak with Danny when he's down.'

A weak sun did nothing to warm the group of national servicemen standing on Seymour station waiting for the train to take them home. Despite the chill, Danny was buoyed by the thought of spending a few days of comfort prior to taking up his allocated posting. As the train to Albury came into view, Skeeta, who was on the platform opposite him, raised his arm in a mock salute. 'Give my love to Miss Bluebell,' Skeeta called across to him before disappearing behind the locomotive and carriages of the train. After the train had gone Danny felt a sense of loss. The train to Melbourne was not due for another half hour and Danny had no inclination to chat with any of the others, preferring to contemplate how this friendship between sheep-farmer and newsagent had been forged over the past ten weeks.

The weekly arrival of a blue envelope lightly scented with Yardley's Lavender soon caught the interest of his mates. On the third occasion Billy was quick to say, 'That'll be from your nurse.' As far as Danny could tell he was the only one to have a girlfriend. 'What's her name?'

'That's Miss Bluebell,' Skeeta said before Danny could reply. 'You'd better treat her with respect, mate. You never know when you might end up in hospital.'

Danny had been surprised. Was Skeeta protecting him from one of Billy's grillings? Was this how their friendship began?

The weeks that followed, the drills and inspections, the sessions on the firing range with rifles, machine guns and rocket launchers, the route marches and combat training in the bush around the camp, all contributed to Danny's growing appreciation of Skeeta's qualities and, Danny felt, a reciprocal growth in Skeeta's good will to him.

The weather had been dry for the first half of autumn but, after they had been in camp for a few weeks, the rain arrived and turned the earth to mud. The exercises conducted in the surrounding bush, designed to introduce them to patrolling, entailed a good deal of crawling through the mud. Skeeta was the least concerned about getting down and dirty. Throughout the training — despite bad weather, degrading tasks and bullying by the N.C.O.s — Skeeta never complained. He seemed to accept whatever he had to bear as part of the natural order or, as he would have put it, part of the natural disorder. Danny guessed he had gained this acceptance through the misfortunes that were always part of farming. He remembered the poem they had studied at school about a sunburnt country with flood and fire and famine paying us back threefold. From Skeeta's tales of life on their farm — the only times he spoke at any length — Danny had the impression the Philips family seldom received such a rate of return. Most of Skeeta's stories were sardonic accounts of major and minor calamities. Bad luck was always an excuse for laughter, not for railing against a malicious fate or God. Indeed, as far as Danny could tell, God played no role in Skeeta's view of the world.

On the other hand, Skeeta was surprised by Danny's tolerance, even enjoyment, of what he considered boring and repetitive drills. Danny, too, was surprised by the pleasure it gave him to participate in a sequence of marching drills where he strove to stay strictly in step and maintain a tightly aligned formation with his platoon.

'What do you get out of brain-dead drill?' Skeeta had asked.

'Do you play footy?' Danny said.

'Footy. What's that got to do with it?'

'Do you play?'

'Played at school a bit. A few games with the Mundarlo team, but the way I'm built, spent most of the time with me face in the mud.'

'The thing I like best about footy is when the team plays well and you're part of it,' Danny said. 'I get the same sort of thing out of drills.'

'Everybody has their own form of insanity,' Skeeta said.

The first visit of Danny's platoon to the firing range was on a still, rain-free day. Each of them loaded their rifles and lay on groundsheets covering a mound that ran across the range. About 100 yards away Danny could see circular targets, about six feet across, opposite each firing position. After he had fired his first shot, the instructor said, 'Not bad but relax the shoulders a little more and the lightest touch when you squeeze the trigger.

After Sergeant Braddock had marched the platoon back to their hut, he took a sheet from his pocket and announced their results. Skeeta and Arnold received 'satisfactory' ratings while Billy was deemed 'not satisfactory'. Danny was amazed to find he alone achieved an 'excellent' grading.

'You belong to a club?' the sergeant asked.

'No, never fired a shot before.'

'Strewth! Keep this up and you could get a post as a sniper.'

Danny did not like that idea. From what he had seen at the movies, a sniper led a solitary existence, hidden away waiting for a target to dispatch.

Skeeta offered a more attractive option. 'Any time you want to come up to our place we can find plenty of foxes, rabbits or the occasional plague of roos for you to clean up.'

While Skeeta's prowess with the rifle could not match Danny's, he was by far the best at maintaining firearms. Unlike Danny, he took great care keeping his rifle in first rate condition and demonstrated an unmatched skill in the speedy and efficient disassembling and reassembling of any machinegun. 'We'd make a good team,' he told Danny, perhaps recalling their discussion of drill. 'You do the shooting and I keep the guns working.' Skeeta had said he was good at fixing things.

Danny was not the only one to get along well with Skeeta. Many people were happy to chat with him, enabling him to be remarkably well-informed and to 'wangle things', as he put it. One of his wangles was to arrange for the four of them to spend one Saturday on leave in nearby Seymour. When closing time was called at six o'clock, Skeeta was able to persuade the publican at the Royal they qualified as out-of-town travellers and could remain drinking there.

The final weeks at Puckapunyal brought discussion of the postings each of them might seek. Skeeta said, 'I've heard there's a new battalion, 5RAR, being set up at Holsworthy Barracks in Sydney. I reckon I'll try my luck there?' He turned to Danny. 'Why not come with me? It'd mean going interstate just like coming here was for me. With your reputation as a hotshot we should be able to wangle it, though.'

Danny was immediately flattered by Skeeta's invitation. 'Yeah, OK.'

'Great. I've also heard 5RAR is likely to be sent to Vietnam, although the government is saying nothing yet. Stands to reason, though. Why else set up a new battalion? We should have some fun in Vietnam.'

Danny frowned and did not reply. He hadn't been able to decide whether he wanted to go to Vietnam or not. If Skeeta's prediction was correct, he would be going while still undecided. More than likely he would also remain undecided about Jane.

Whether it was his reputation as a marksman or Skeeta's skill at wangling or sheer luck they would never know, but both of them were told during their last week that they had been posted to 5RAR.

Danny had expected to enjoy a warm welcome on his return from Puckapunyal but was surprised when his father greeted him like a hero returning from war. 'Here he is, our boy taking a well-earned break from serving his country. We owe a lot to the men who've had the courage to stand up against those who'd threaten our way-of-life. Beats me how those layabouts who try to stand in their way have the cheek to show themselves.' Danny could see how his dad's slighting reference to Sean dimmed his mum's happiness at having him home.

Bernard insisted Danny sit down and give him a detailed account of his experiences. Almost every incident he described caused his father to break in with one of his own reminiscences of joining the 39th Battalion at Darley Camp which he said was near Bacchus Marsh. Danny was surprised his father had retained such a detailed memory of events from twenty-five years ago. More amazing was that this man, who refused to speak about his heroic service in New Guinea, should get such pleasure from recalling the unremarkable experiences of his early training.

When Danny tried to distract him by asking how he was getting on without him in the shop, Bernard assured him that he was getting by, having recruited Jack McGowan, the son of one of his fellow-drinkers from the Oak Tree. 'Not a patch on you and he knows he'll have to go when you return.'

Later, Bernard insisted on taking him for a drink at the Oak Tree, something he had never done when Danny was working in the shop.

'I've brought along my son, Danny,' Bernard announced to his friends. 'You'll have met him when you came into the shop, but he's in the army now.'

Danny was embarrassed by the way his father made it sound like he had risen to an exalted state and wondered why he would want to show him off like a prize bull.

—✗

For the third time in the past twenty minutes Jane checked her appearance in the bathroom mirror. It was still a few minutes before Danny was due, but he couldn't be late tonight, surely. Carol had been highly amused when Jane insisted she leave an hour ago and forbade her from returning until late tonight.

The sound of the bell brought her straight to the door where she hesitated. She shouldn't appear too eager. After a moment's delay she threw open the door and rushed to embrace him. After a while, she said, 'Danny! Your hair! What have they done to you?' She tried to pretend distress but couldn't keep the smile from her face or her voice.

'No cracks about Sampson. I've had enough of those from Dad already.'

'You know I've always thought you could improve the styling of your hair but ...'

'Standard army cut. Can I come in?'

Jane took him by the hand and led him to the couch in the living room. 'Would you like something to drink?'

'Thanks. A beer would be good.'

'You haven't been captured by the demon drink at Puckapunyal?'

'No chance of that. A night in Seymour Skeeta wangled for us was the only time we were let off the leash.'

'I'll get our drinks and then you must tell me more about Skeeta.' She frowned at him. 'From the little you wrote I gather you and he have become good friends.'

'There wasn't much time for writing. Besides, I'm no good at putting words on paper. Let's have that drink and I'll tell you all about him.'

Settled on the couch with their drinks, Danny was in the midst of describing how Skeeta's approach to life had intrigued him when Jane said, 'Miss Bluebell? He called me that? A bit soppy I s'pose, but he must be quite a romantic soul, unlike some of his friends.'

Danny did not rise to her bait but continued with his account of Puckapunyal which, to her relief, he brought to an end by saying, 'I know a fair bit about you from your letters, but what haven't you told me?'

Jane wondered whether he was hinting at her suppressing details of her social life which — she had no inclination to tell him — had been pretty dull during his absence. Perhaps he was suggesting she had held back on any bad news. He was used to her telling him of any problems or disappointments she encountered, but these had been rare during the past ten weeks. The closer she got to qualifying, the more interesting and more challenging she found her work. She had written to him about her time in surgery, confirming her intention to seek a place there when she qualified as a staff nurse.

'I haven't had a chance to tell you Sean invited me for a coffee last week.'

'I've been wondering about him. So, he eventually got around to taking up my suggestion he speak with you. How did it go?'

'First, I must tell you Sean has found a good place to stay and is very happy. It was clear he had no problems he wanted to discuss with me and his main purpose was to have me pass on to you the message that all was well with him.'

'Where's he staying?'

'With a man called Guy Norton. Guy is a human rights lawyer. Sean's known him for about a year.' Jane picked up her Pimms and eyed him over the top of her glass as she took a mouthful.

'Go on,' Danny said.

'I can tell you Guy Norton has a beautiful speaking voice. If you want to know more, I suggest you call Sean and speak with him yourself. He's given me his number.'

'Come on, Jane. I've only got a couple of days and doubt I'll be able to spend any time with Sean, particularly seeing that Dad threw him out of the house before I went away.'

She gave him an appealing smile. 'He would really like to speak with you. He's missing the family.'

Danny was unmoved. 'What else did he tell you?'

'He gave me a lecture on love.'

'What?'

Pleased to see she had stirred his interest this time, Jane said, 'He's totally convinced that if you love someone, you're certain of it and, if you're unsure, then you don't.'

Danny hesitated before saying, 'Did he mean us?'

'He has no time for your belief that one day you'll meet a girl and immediately know she's the one for you.'

Danny shook his head. 'I've come to see it's more complicated than that. You know I have.'

'And has your time away given you any more confidence in us?' This time it was Danny who chose to drink rather than answer, causing Jane to say, 'If we are still a work in progress, you'd better put down your drink and come closer, so we can see whether our separation has stirred any new romantic thoughts.'

~

When Danny called, Sean took much the same line he had taken with Jane, proclaiming the certainty of his love for Guy Norton. His manner and tone suggested he was explaining a situation to a child who lacked the experience needed to have any real understanding of what they were being told.

'It'd be good if Jane spoke with Mum,' Sean said. 'Will you make sure she does?'

'Jane said you should wait until you're back in the family. She's talking good sense.'

'You don't get it,' Sean said and soon afterwards ended the call.

Commitment

Danny had watched to see if Skeeta boarded the train at Junee but saw no sign of him. It was a different story when he reported in at Holsworthy Barracks. 'Private McBride, Daniel. Yeah, your mate, Skeeta Philips, has been wondering where you were. You're in Hut 3 in the Gallipoli Lines.'

His first impressions of Holsworthy were more favourable that those of Puckapunyal. For a start, the weather was mild and sunny. When he walked between the cannons mounted on either side of the entrance, he felt he was entering a military establishment of some importance. His positive view of the barracks continued as he walked along a formed foot-path among a number of shade trees but ended abruptly when he entered his hut in the Gallipoli Lines. These huts had been constructed to house the national service intakes of the early nineteen-fifties. Their reuse for 5RAR meant that Danny was in a hut housing nine men with what was called a 'jack room' for the section commander. 'Down here, Mac.' Skeeta was waving from the far end of the hut. 'Your bed's next to mine.'

'McBride?' A thick-set man with a deeply tanned face had come up behind him. 'Where the hell have you been?' He had the twin stripes of a corporal on the sleeves of his uniform.

'I've just come up from Melbourne.'

'You were s'posed to be here yesterday.'

'My travel warrant was for yesterday but the train didn't get in until this morning.'

'You travelled on the Spirit?' His inquisitor sneered at him. 'Wanted the luxury of a sleeper?'

'No, I sat up.'

'Yeah, I can see that. You need to smarten yourself up, man. You're in the real army now. Why didn't you travel on the Daylight? That would have got you here last night with the others.' When Danny did not reply the corporal said to no-one in particular, 'We've got a real one here.' He turned his attention back to Danny and told him, 'Dump your gear next to your mate, Skeeta. We're on parade in a few minutes.'

Danny and Skeeta had time for only a brief greeting before the call came for their platoon to assemble and Skeeta shepherded Danny into the line headed by the corporal he had just met. They were addressed by a lieutenant by the name of Dennis Markham who looked no older than Danny and told them he was proud to lead the platoon. 'As most of you know, 5RAR is one of the first to be composed of a mixture of regulars and national servicemen. I want to give a special welcome to those nashos who have just arrived. You'll have a major role in enhancing the reputation of 5RAR. You newcomers need to know our battalion colours are black and gold and our mascot is a tiger. We're the Tiger Battalion.'

Danny wondered what Sean would say when he learned Danny was once more with the Tigers.

After the sergeant dismissed the parade, the corporal called his section to gather around him. Danny was reminded of standing to listen to the coach's three-quarter-time harangue. All that was missing were the oranges. The corporal began with, 'All we're likely to get in our section are now here, so I reckon it's time we got to know one another. I'm Smacka Fitzroy and I'm in charge.' He pointed to a tall man with blue eyes and a glint of red in his hair. 'My 2 IC is Taffy Williams. Taffy and I served together in Malaya. The bugger saved my life at one stage so I like to keep him close. Next to him are the other two regulars, Butch Gordon on the left and Tich Page on the right.'

Butch was squat and muscular with fair hair and an unsmiling face. Tich was a huge man who grinned shyly when introduced.

'Then there are you nashos.' The corporal's tone did not match the platoon commander's welcoming one. 'I know you're Skeeta Philips,' he said to Skeeta, 'so that's alright.' Danny had a sense his pal had passed some form of test. 'And your late mate,' he said, turning to Danny. 'What do they call you, McBride?'

'Most people call me Danny.'

The corporal was not pleased. 'That won't do. We'll have to think of something.'

The slightly built nasho next to Danny was accepted as 'Simmo Simmonds'. The only other one left without a nickname was a dark-haired, handsome man. 'I am Carlo Da Silva,' he said as though announcing himself to a theatre audience.

Smacka eyed him up and down before saying, 'Da Silva, you're Goldie now.'

He turned back to Danny with a broad grin. 'I know, "Baby Something's Wrong". Heard it last night. Really good Chicano soul.'

'What?'

'Not a fan of Danny and the Dreamers? You should be. Apart from the good music, the name suits you. From now on you're Dreamer.' Smacka swivelled his head to make eye contact with each of his men in turn before saying, 'One final thing. You nashos have spent a few weeks starting to learn what it is to be a grunt. You still have a lot to learn and the most important thing is teamwork. When we're on patrol there are no individuals, just the team. Teamwork's what makes sure of our survival and success. That's why we sleep, eat, drill, train, shit, shower, shave, drink, even bloody fight together.'

Perhaps Smacka had been a football coach. He certainly sounded like one.

The early months at Holsworthy were taken up with routine training. They were taught the formations they would use on patrol. They practised patrolling, setting up defensive positions, ambush formations and assault tactics. They marched across rough terrain and drilled on the parade square. When Danny again demonstrated his marksmanship on the firing range, he earned grudging praise from Smacka. 'Very sharp, Dreamer,' he said.

They knew that 1RAR had arrived at Bien Hoa air base in May and been supplemented with additional artillery, engineers, army aviation and logistics in September. There were rumours of a planned build-up to two battalions in Vietnam and a belief within 5RAR they would be one of those battalions. Skeeta had it 'on good authority' that the announcement was imminent but months passed with nothing. The inauguration parade in early November lifted morale for a time but, as Christmas approached, the absence of confirmation was wearing on most of them.

'What's the point of doing all this training if we're just going to hang around here for the rest of our time in the army?' Skeeta said.

'I reckon that could be better than going off to Vietnam,' Simmo said.

'Where's your sense of adventure, mate? 'What d'you say, Dreamer?'

'Better than hanging around here, I reckon.' Danny realised how his attitude had changed He had joined the battalion with no great desire to serve in Vietnam but was happy to go if sent. After this long period of uncertainty, though, he was becoming like a house hunter who is ambivalent about a particular property until told it has been sold before auction, whereupon he becomes bitterly disappointed at missing his chance.

'Hello dear,' Mary said with a welcoming smile. 'Do come in.' She led Jane into the living room but did not invite her to sit. Instead she grasped her by the shoulders and planted a kiss on her cheek. 'Congratulations. Now a qualified staff nurse.'

'Thank you. But how did you know?'

'Your mother told me. She is so proud of you, as she has every right to be.'

'Mum told you?' Jane knew her father was proud of her. He had said so. But she still had the impression her mother was disappointed she had not followed a more prestigious career or, better still, found an eligible husband among the doctors at the Alfred.

'Do sit down and tell me about your plans. What will you be doing next year?'

'I'm very pleased I've got a position in surgery. Quite a bit of it will be in the wards but I'll have the opportunity for theatre work and that's what I'm really keen to take up.'

'That sounds great. And how are you apart from that? Missing Danny, I suppose, like we all are.'

Jane did not want to tell Mary just how much she was missing Danny. Carol had insisted she go with her to a number of parties but none of the men could dance like Danny, she found their conversations boring and was tired of fending off unwelcome advances. Stuck in the flat alone, she thought she might take up quilting again. She didn't want to do another crazy quilt. She should get Mary's advice on what to choose — the reason she had called today. 'Yes, I am missing him. But it does give me some extra free time and I'm keen to do more quilting. There's been very little chance until now.'

'He's not good at keeping in touch and we haven't had anything from him for ages,' Mary said.

He hadn't written to Jane in weeks and, rather than tell Mary that, she said, 'Danny only writes when he has something to tell and I think he's finding the army a bit dull at the moment.'

'Yes, that could be it.' Mary did not sound convinced. 'I'm sorry, what was that you were saying about quilting?'

After Jane repeated her words and added that she hoped Mary might be able to show her a few of the more advanced techniques sometime, Mary's mood lifted. 'You couldn't have chosen a better time. Come and I'll show you what I'm working on.'

Just as she had the first time, Mary sped up the stairs and into her room. There was a partially completed quilt, patterned with an array of interlocking hexagons in a variety of fabrics. 'Remember me telling you how you could use paper templates for piecing the fabrics. It was invented in England centuries ago and is still called the English paper piecing method. It comes into its own when you're quilting with interlocking shapes. You can see this one consists of hexagons but it also applies to squares, triangles and diamonds. I used this method for Danny's quilt with the matching triangles. Some people even use curved shapes but I've never ...'

'I remember reading about that in one of your books. I think they called them apple core and clam shell.'

'My, I'm impressed you remember that. Let me show you how I go about it.' Mary took up a hexagon cut from stiff paper and placed it over the back of a small sample of blue and white checked cotton. She pinned the paper in place and cut around the template leaving a quarter of an inch margin which she folded over and sewed onto the template. After removing the pin, she took up another hexagon, formed from a similarly checked cotton in green and white, and sewed this to the one she had just formed. 'That's it,' she said to Jane. 'Now you have a go.'

The lesson continued until Jane had assembled a small group of inter-locking hexagons and was confident she had grasped the technique. She was examining her creation with satisfaction when Bernard entered the room 'Here you are. I thought ...' He saw it was Jane sitting at the table.

'Bernie. You must congratulate Jane. She's finished her training and is now a qualified staff nurse.'

Jane felt the colour rush into her face as Mr McBride took his time to appraise her. 'A fine occupation, nursing,' he said. 'My sister was a nurse. Married a Yank after the war and has lived in Baltimore ever since. Hardly ever hear from her these days.' He gave a small grin as if finding that amusing and said, 'A bit like our Danny. He been in touch with you?'

'Not much,' Jane said. 'I'd better be going.'

'Don't let me send you off. I know you quilters. And congrats you'll be a good nurse, I reckon.'

In early January there had still been no formal announcement, but everyone in the battalion knew they had three months to be ready for operational commitment in Vietnam. Training was now undertaken with a sense of urgency. Practice at the range began in the early hours and went on into the night. The nights were also used for lectures on Vietnamese history, culture, customs and language. When Danny learnt that Vietnamese courtesy demanded he not beckon with one finger, speak in a loud voice, touch upon the back or point at anyone, he wondered how Smacka would be able to operate.

In February they went to the Jungle Training Centre at Canungra in the dense rain forest of Southern Queensland. They practiced creeping through the jungle without getting lost in the maze of apparently identical valleys. All of them were impressed by Skeeta's ability to recognise differences in the terrain that were invisible to them. 'Be handy having you up front with me,' Smacka told him. Danny's fitness and agility showed through when, drenched by drumming rain or his own sweat, he was required to push over rope courses, swing across rivers on flying foxes and stumble through dense foliage on assault exercises. Most memorable, though, was the hell he experienced when completing what had been named 'the confidence course' by an officer with a dark sense of humour.

They took off from the top of a hill kitted for patrol — webbing, water bottles, ammunition pouches and rifles slung over their shoulders. Danny left with the shout of an instructor ringing in his ears. 'Don't muck around, you dickhead. If you take too long, you do it again. Don't wait for your mates.'

He hurtled down the hill, slipping and sliding with the weight of his kit forcing him on. The smoke of grenades and the staccato beat of machine guns surrounded him. The first obstacle consisted of three long parallel poles, caked in mud and green slime, which spanned a wide and swiftly flowing creek. Simmo bent down with the intention of crawling across until an instructor shouted, 'Get up you bloody idiot. You'll be a sitting duck. Run across. Go.'

Danny saw him make it to the midpoint before losing balance and plunging into the creek. Spluttering in the freezing water he began to wade to the far bank. Skeeta, who had stayed upright by taking careful steps despite the shouts for him to get cracking, was soaked by the splash from Simmo's fall and started to totter before dropping forward onto his pal who had begun to clamber up the bank. Danny sensed that momentum would be his friend and took his pole at speed. His feet slipped a couple of times but he was able to right himself on the next step and arrived on the other bank in time to reach down and help the others up. 'You heard it. Don't wait for your mates. Now you're all dead,' came across the creek to them.

He stumbled through choking smoke and came to three long pipes. Following the instructions they had been given before the start, Danny entered the pipes backwards, only just fitting, and inched his way through before falling into a foul-smelling pond. He struggled from the pond and ran down a narrow track with machineguns firing over his head. Next they had to swing by a rope across a moat. Danny went first, thinking to show Simmo how to do it. Following his example, Simmo was successful but suffered rope burns on his hands.

Off and running again. 'Shit, the wall.' Skeeta croaked. Logs had been mounted one on top of the other to form a wall about ten feet high. Danny shinned to the top and reached back to pull Simmo over. Skeeta slipped and banged into one of the logs, blood streaming from his face. Danny was taking shallow breaths which burnt his throat. The weight of his wet webbing felt as if it had doubled.

At the next obstacle he dropped to the ground and led them under a tangle of barbed wire strands while deafened by machinegun fire and smoke grenade explosions just above their heads. Danny's webbing caught on the wire and he could not reach to free it. He called to Simmo the who crawled back to rip the wire away, cutting his hand as he did it.

Up a ladder to a platform from which two wires were strung across a creek. The lower wire was so slack he wobbled and twisted. This time the shout from the bank was, 'You're hanging in the breeze like washing on the line. A shooting gallery for the VC.' Crawling under a cargo net through a scungy pool, Danny heard, 'You're running out of time you bloody snails.'

They came to another wall, shorter than the first and he took heart from the relative ease with which he scaled it, only to drop into a pit full of putrid mud. He crawled, slid and pushed to escape the muck and came to a vertical cargo net that climbed into the sky. Once over that he crossed a tarred road and struggled through a series of car tyres to be confronted by a tower erected above a river. At the top an instructor asked Danny 'Swimmer or non-swimmer?'

'Yeah I can swim,' he puffed and his answer was relayed to two divers waiting below.

'Arms away from your body, off you go.'

Just before jumping Danny cheered himself with the thought that at least the water would wash off some of the crap that had stuck to him. On hitting the water, he sank like a stone but was grabbed by the divers before he was captured by the mud at the bottom. He collapsed on the riverbank, soaked to the skin and was soon joined by Skeeta who was shivering with the cold of the water. 'Where's Simmo?' He looked back to the tower and saw him still hesitating to jump. This time the instructor did not shout at him, just gave him a hefty push and Simmo hit the water with an enormous splash. The divers brought him to the bank where he lay like a beached whale. 'You did it, mate.' Skeeta said. 'We all made it.'

Buoyed by the realisation their ordeal was over, Simmo managed a small grin. 'Nothing in Vietnam will be as bad as this.'

Danny wondered whether that would be true.

Later that night, as the section sat salving their cuts, bruises and exhaustion with stubbies of beer, Smacka went from man to man having a brief conversation with each of them. When he came to Danny he said, 'Simmo says he doesn't reckon he would have made it without your help.'

'Don't know about that. He was the one to cut his hand getting me unhooked from the barbed wire.'

'Didn't you hear the instructors yelling at you not to wait for your mates?'

'We weren't waiting for one another. We were working as a team like you said.'

Smacka eyed him carefully. 'Belonged to many teams, have ya?'

'Yeah, I play cricket and footy.'

'We might be playing here but we sure won't be playing in Vietnam.' He appraised Danny again. 'I can see you're a fit bugger, Dreamer. What position d'you play?'

'Centre-half forward mostly.'

'Centre-half-forward?' Smacka's disgust was plain. 'You Mexicans with your Aussie rules. Up here, footy means rugby league. I reckon you might make a decent winger or full-back. You should give it a go.'

In January Sir Robert Menzies retired and Harold Holt became Prime Minister. In March Holt announced the formation of the First Australian Task Force (1ATF), comprising the two battalions 5RAR and 6RAR together with artillery and other support units, which was to serve in Vietnam and be located in Phuoc Tuy Province. This would be the first commitment of national servicemen overseas.

The officer who came to brief the troops of 5RAR began by stating that the origins of the current conflict in South Vietnam arose from an attempt by the Communist government of North Vietnam to conquer the South through a campaign of terrorism and guerrilla warfare. War was waged through a combination of regular army formations from the north and a locally based organisation created by the North Vietnamese government and known as the National Liberation Front or, more commonly, the Viet Cong. The South Vietnamese army, known by the initials ARVN, was struggling to deal with the threat and would likely have been overrun were it not for the support of the United States and, more recently, Australia. If the North were to prevail, not only would the long-term inhabitants of the South be cruelly treated but those who had migrated from the North, many of whom were Christians, would suffer greatly. Furthermore, the Australian Government believed it would not stop there, but the Communists would continue their aggression deep into South-East Asia.

Danny was familiar with most of what the officer said. He had heard it first from Father Maloney and then his own father. He had also heard the rebuttal mounted by Sean. Unlike those three, the officer spoke with a calm authority which impressed Danny. The officer also quoted considerable evidence to back up his assertions.

The briefing now turned to the role of the Task Force which was to secure the peace of the province of Phuoc Tuy. Phuoc Tuy, south-east of Saigon and to the north of the major port of Vung Tau, had a rich farm area dotted with villages and hamlets, a long coastline, a complex delta area of mangrove swamps and channels, isolated ranges of rugged mountains and a large area of uninhabited jungle. The main occupation of the people was growing rice, but there was a rubber plantation, formerly owned by the French, to the north of Nui Dat, the site chosen as the base for the Task Force. There were also several fishing villages on the coast. At this stage the South Vietnamese Government's authority over Phuoc Tuy was restricted to the vicinity of the provincial capital, Bia Ria.

The first mission of the Task Force was to establish its base at Nui Dat, a site on a low hill in the centre of the province. A start had been made by 1RAR in conjunction with the US 173 Airborne but the bulk of the work would fall to 5RAR and 6RAR. Once the base had been secured the Task Force would move on to its principal objective, the pacification of the province and the restitution of the authority of the South Vietnamese authorities.

The officer made it clear the task they were to undertake would be difficult and potentially dangerous, but convinced Danny of how important it was they should succeed. At last he felt he had found a challenging and important role, one he would undertake as part of a team.

On the holiday Monday of the Moomba Festival, Bernard and Mary were seated in front of the TV watching the news. Bernard was in a benign mood, having enjoyed the indulgence of two days in a row free from the newsagency. After the fanfare died away, the newsreader announced in a stern tone that the Moomba parade had suffered disruption by anti-war and anti-conscription protesters who had staged a sit-down on the route of the parade. A group of protestors were shown brandishing a variety of placards which condemned the war, told the Prime Minister and his Government to go to Vietnam themselves and called on the public to 'Make Love not War'. Scuffles broke out as the police arrived to remove the protestors.

'Disgusting,' Bernard said as he leant forward to scan the melee. 'There's Sean,' he shouted. 'See in the centre. He's just been grabbed.'

'That's not Sean,' Mary said.

'I'm sure it is. His own brother about to take up the fight and all he can do is get in the way of people enjoying the Moomba procession. I'm ashamed.'

'I tell you that was not Sean. He's not going to those protest demonstrations anymore.'

The certainty in Mary's voice surprised Bernard. 'How would you know that?'

Mary braced herself with the thought she had already waited too long to put Bernie in the picture. 'Because he told me when we spoke last week.'

Bernard got up, walked over to the TV set and turned it off. 'You spoke with Sean?'

'When Danny was home before going up to Sydney, he told me Sean had found a good place to stay and gave me his phone number. I've kept in touch with him since then but didn't want to upset you by saying anything.'

Bernard continued to stand in front of the TV. 'What upsets me is you'd do this and not tell me.' The frown left his face. 'Has he seen the light? Given up on all this anti-war rubbish? Getting away from that Conor must have given him a chance to come to his senses.'

'Bernie, dear, I don't know what's caused Sean to stop going to demonstrations but I'd be surprised if it's as you hope.' She appealed to him with her smile. 'We have to accept that both our boys are now men. They have their own opinions and beliefs, not all of them the same as ours, but held just as sincerely. I told you I don't know what's changed for Sean but I'm pretty sure he's just as strongly convinced that participating in the war in Vietnam is not the right thing to do. He holds those views as strongly and sincerely as you hold yours but, for some reason, he no longer wants to convince others by public protest.' Bernard began to reply but Mary continued over him. 'I'll tell you one thing which will surprise you. He's missing us. All of us, you included.'

Bernard came back to his chair and sat down. 'He makes me very angry, the way he carries on sometimes,' Bernard said. 'But I miss both of them. It's not the same without Danny and Sean being around.'

'I've been thinking,' Mary said. 'In a few weeks Danny will be down before he goes to Vietnam. Why don't we give him a farewell party and invite Sean?'

'Yeah, I'm really keen to talk with Danny. You don't think Sean will want to spoil things by carrying on the way he did last time?'

'I told you something's changed. I don't know what it is, but he's less heated. Not depressed. In fact, he sounds very happy with life in general. He just doesn't want to go in the protests. I'll see if I can find out before he comes.'

'It'd be great to have the whole family together to farewell Danny.' Bernard drew in a breath and sighed. 'I suppose we should include that girl, Jane.'

Mary beamed at him. 'Bernie, that would be lovely. I'm sure they'd both be delighted.' She thought it quite likely Jane would be uncomfortable confronting the whole family and Danny might well be embarrassed, but she wasn't going to say anything that might cause Bernard to change his mind.

'She's a pretty thing and obviously gets on well with all the family except me. And she has what it takes to be a nurse. That's no mean feat. If only she was a Catholic.'

⚹

'Come on Danny, let me take you for a drink at the Oak Tree. There won't be many pubs in Vietnam. Your mother's been with you all day and now it's my turn.'

'But, Dad, it's seven o'clock; the Oak Tree will be closed.'

'Not any longer. While you've been scooting around the jungle, the Government's abolished six o'clock closing. The usual crew won't be there and we can have a good chat.'

⚹

Bernard carefully scrutinised the room as he led Danny into the Oak Tree and made for a table in the far corner away from the four other patrons who were close to the bar. He brought their glasses of beer to the table and raised his in a toast. 'Good luck, Danny. I'm so proud of you.'

'Good luck, Dad and thanks for making do without me so willingly.'

Bernard waved Danny's thanks away. 'I see you're no stranger to a glass of beer. The army teach you that or had you kept it quiet until now?'

'After what we went through in the heat and wet of Canungra, we needed a drink.'

'Nothing wrong with that either. The trick is not to drink too quickly.' He took a mouthful from his glass as if demonstrating how to do it. 'I've could never understand why the Government was so slow to realise the six o'clock swill caused far more drunkenness than extending the hours ever would.' He wiped his lips. 'But that's not why I brought you here. I want to tell you a story.'

'Yeah?'

'I want to tell you why your going to Vietnam is so important to me.' Danny glanced in surprise at his father as Bernard supped his beer. 'I've told you how I joined the 39th when it became clear we

117

were under threat of invasion from the Japanese and how we trained at Darley before we got the order to prepare ourselves for shipment to New Guinea. They didn't send us up to the jungle in Queensland, though. No, our one training exercise was held in the flat country of the Western District.

'What could you do there which would be any good?'

'Absolutely useless. We left on Boxing Day in '41 by train to Sydney and sailed from there to Port Morseby. Despite our poor preparation and our shortage of equipment, we were keen to take up the fight with the Japs. Instead, we get sent to defend the Seven Mile Aerodrome just out of Morseby. We had no tents, no blankets, no mosquito repellent and no medicines in an area riddled with malaria. On top of that we were put to work like a bunch of navvies building defence works and unloading stores.'

Danny saw his father was now staring down at the table as if it carried pictures his unit working in New Guinea. 'All of us were totally pissed off, but I was the only one careless enough to trip over the side of a trench we were digging and fall onto a pick someone had left there. That's how I busted my hip. The doctors did what they could but, like us, were short on equipment and experience. My malaria and my hip got so bad they decided to ship me home. When I got back, I laid as low as I could, partly because I felt so sick but mainly because I was hugely embarrassed that I'd put myself out of the fight before I could fire a shot.' Bernard continued to stare down at the table and was breathing heavily.

'Another beer before you go on, Dad.'

He looked up at him as though surprised to find Danny there. 'What? Yeah, why not.'

When Danny returned, Bernard took a mouthful, wiped his lips and said, 'Then the reports started to come in about the Kokoda Track. I could read between the lines that my mates in the 39th were doing it tough. I didn't know then just how tough. I don't know who started the rumour. Maybe it was my dad. But the story got around I'd been badly injured fighting the Japs.'

Bernard gazed at Danny with an expression he had not seen before. Was it shame? Humiliation? Danny raised his glass to his lips and glanced over at the bar.

'I should have come straight out and told everyone the rumour was a load of codswallop but I didn't. It'd been a huge load for Dad to run the newsagency on his own, so I could join up. It's no excuse, but I could see how he was bathing in my reflected glory. I felt I owed him and shouldn't take that away from him. I don't think I did it for myself, but who knows.' He gave a crooked grin. 'We're pretty good at kidding ourselves when it suits. What I do know is that I was bloody ashamed of living a lie when the gallantry of the 39th and the losses they suffered became known. By then it was too late to put the record straight. I'd have humiliated the family if I'd admitted the truth to everyone.'

Bernard paused and Danny stared at him, searching for something to say.

'There it is,' Bernard said. 'Your father is and has been a fraud and will forever remain one. Now you can see why I won't talk about my part in the war and try to close down anyone who does. But can you also see why it's so important to me you take up the fight against the Communists in Vietnam? You can bring some honour to the family. You won't make up for my dishonour, but at least I'll have something positive to hold onto.'

Danny recalled the version of his father's war service he had been given by the priest. 'Did you never confess and receive absolution from Father Maloney?'

'He wasn't here back then. Anyway, I was in a state where I couldn't confess to anyone, even myself. Before telling you tonight, I haven't spoken of the war for decades.'

'I should tell you, Dad, that when I joined up, I didn't know who was right, you or Sean. Now I'm sure it's you. For me, though, there's more to it than that. For a while now I've been searching for something I can really commit to. I reckon the opportunity to play a part in the success of the war in Vietnam is just what I need.'

Jane continued to enjoy and value the opportunities she had to participate in theatre. Even though her role was to assist and provide support,
she saw her work as an essential part of the process. She was fascinated
with what could be achieved and in awe of the skills shown by the
surgeons. In the main they were an outgoing, confident lot. The anaesthetists were more circumspect and of less interest to her, though Jane
did find one of them, Dr Townsend, rather intriguing.

In the long open-heart procedure they had just completed, the heart-
lung machine malfunctioned and the patient might have died on the
table. Although only recently qualified, Dr Townsend was unflustered. Without lifting his voice, he superintended the installation of
a replacement machine and ensured the patient suffered no failure in
blood supply. Then the surgeons encountered unexpected difficulties
in replacing two heart valves, requiring the operation to continue far
longer than scheduled. All of the doctors and nurses were under pressure, yet he appeared the least stressed of them all. Eventually, as they
headed towards a successful conclusion, the doctors were able to relax
and chat with one another as they usually did, but he remained silent.
There was something machine-like about him.

Jane had dumped her scrubs and was washing her hands and face
when she was surprised by a movement behind her and Dr Townsend
entered. He still wore his gown but no longer had his cap or mask.
'Sorry to startle you. I thought I was the only one left.'

'It took me a while to tidy up,' she said.

'I've been down in intensive care. I wanted to make sure our patient
was as comfortable as he could be and the staff were fully aware of his
condition.' This was her first opportunity to study him out of theatre.
He was of medium build, a little taller than her, with straight fair hair
cut quite short. He had thin cheeks and dark brown eyes. 'You seem all
in.' His voice lacked the sympathy or concern that usually accompanied
such words and sounded more like a medical diagnosis.

'I'm not used to such a long and demanding operation. Do you think he'll survive?' She had never asked a doctor this before. It had not taken her long to realise theatre staff did not appreciate such questions.

'Hopefully, yes. Realistically, the first night in intensive care will be crucial. That's why I went there. The staff are very good but they'll need all the help we can give them.' Again, he spoke in a matter-of-fact voice and she noted he used the term 'we'. He passed his hand over the top of his head as though patting down his hair, although Jane thought it was already tidily in place— nothing like the mop Danny had before joining the army. 'How do you like Indian food?' he asked.

'Pardon.'

'After a theatre session like we've just had, I go to a little Indian restaurant in High Street. A humble place, but when Mrs Gupta does her magic I'm restored. I'd say you could do with a dose of Mrs Gupta. Do you want to give it a try?'

Jane had by now been asked out by a number of boys and men. Never before had she been invited to dinner as though receiving a recommendation for medical treatment. Nor had it ever been so easy to refuse. When he asked her if she wanted to give it a try, it was as if he were making a casual suggestion to a male pal of his. 'No big deal mate, but come if you like.' She could refuse without being concerned she might hurt his feelings or cause him disappointment.

'Thank you. I wasn't looking forward to getting myself something when I got back to the flat. My flat-mate will have eaten.' She was rather pleased with herself. She thought she had managed to match his style.

There were not many cars left in the car-park but Jane was surprised when Dr Townsend led her to a sleek green sports-car with an oiled canvas hood. 'It's a TC built in 1948. This was the best model MG ever produced. I was so lucky to get it.' His face had come alive and his eyes sparkled.

Now that she considered it more closely, she could see the car was in remarkably good condition for its age. The pristine body-work gleamed in the lights of the car-park as did the silver radiator grille and wheel spokes. He opened the passenger door and held it while she clambered into the low leather-covered seat, the first time he had treated her as a woman. He climbed in behind the wheel and said, 'This car is one of my obsessions. What's yours?'

Jane had never thought of herself as being obsessive over anything. She thought of her ambition to be as good a nurse as she could, but that was not in keeping with an MG car. 'I enjoy quilting,' she said, desperate to fill the silence.

'Quilting?' he repeated as he started the engine which set up a growling pulse.

'Yes, patchwork quilting. It has a very long history and tradition. I've only recently started out but I'd love to be good at it. Those made by experts are so beautiful and convey such a variety of emotions.'

He turned the car into Commercial Road and nodded. 'It's good to have a worthwhile ambition, isn't it?' Despite what he'd said, she couldn't see owning an old MG, no matter how stylish, as a worthwhile ambition. 'Tell me about patchwork quilting. I know nothing about it,' he said.

Jane began what she hoped would be a sufficiently brief account, but the questions he kept interjecting showed not only a keen interest in what she was saying but a swift understanding of some of the complexities of quilting and a curiosity to know more of its history. Most of what she told him came from the pages of Mary's books rather than her direct experience and Jane was glad her enthusiasm for quilting had led her to pay the books close attention. She was still speaking when he pulled the car into a spot a few doors down from a brick shopfront which carried the sign BOMBAY HOUSE.

He held the door open for her and Jane entered the spicy atmosphere of the simply presented room: white painted walls from which hung photographs of Indian street life, green linoleum on the floor and Formica table tops. It was as he had said: a humble place. Coming towards her was an Indian woman wearing a royal blue sari and a beaming smile. 'Doctor! Welcome. Welcome. You have come for the restoration.'

'Indeed, I have Mrs Gupta and I've brought a colleague who is more in need of your magic even than me.'

Finally, Jane received some of the smile. 'Welcome. I will do my best for you.' Jane wondered whether Mrs Gupta thought she was a doctor. She could not remember a doctor referring to a nurse as a colleague before.

Freed from the need for examining a menu, the couple sat for a moment in silence, each glancing around at the other diners, almost all of whom were Indian.

'Now we are away from the hospital, I think we can dispense with the formal titles. I'm Gordon. Forgive me, I don't know your first name.'

'I'm Jane Glover,' she replied. The doctors seldom got beyond 'Nurse' or 'Sister' so Jane thought it wise to give her full name.

'Yes, I knew the Glover. I asked after you had been in theatre with me a few times.' He had been interested in her, after all. Had he staged this whole episode? 'I was impressed by your work. For someone only just through, you do very well.'

Jane blushed, partly from the pleasure of his compliment and partly at her misplaced suspicion. 'Thank you. The theatre is where I want to spend my time.'

He shook his head and pretended a scowl of annoyance. 'I've just said we are away from the hospital and here we are back at it.' It was amazing how that placid face could become so animated when he wasn't working. She had not met anyone who drew such a sharp line. 'I hope you're not rostered on tomorrow. You've earned a week-end off.'

She sighed. 'Tomorrow is a family party farewelling my boyfriend who is one of the nashos going to Vietnam.' When she was on a date or at a party she avoided talking about Danny. She never denied him and most people knew of him anyway, but she thought it rude to bring him into the conversation when socialising with another man. Tonight, it seemed the right thing to do.

'I can see why you aren't happy about that. Despite some of the conflicting views, though, I'm convinced he's on a valuable mission. I'm thinking of going myself.'

'To Vietnam? Are you going to join up?'

He smiled at her amazement. 'Not militarily. You've heard of the medical teams the Alfred is sending to Bien Hoa now that so many of the local civilian doctors have been taken into the army?'

'I heard something about them but didn't pay a lot of attention after I was told they want older nurses with more experience.'

'The first team is up there now. The second one is gearing up to relieve them shortly. I'm hoping to go in August.'

The longer the time Jane spent with Dr Townsend — it was hard to think of him as Gordon — the more intrigued she became with this unusual man. 'When we were in the car you said it was good to have a worthwhile ambition. What's yours?'

'I want to be the best anaesthetist in the business and introduce new methods and techniques which will make all operations safer and more effective. There's much I have to learn and explore.' He paused as if he were reconsidering what he had just said. 'I know it will never be down to me alone. At the heart of all operations is teamwork and I have to develop ways of enhancing that as well.' His dark eyes had been glowing as he spoke and he now looked away as if embarrassed by his passion. It occurred to Jane that Danny would like Dr Townsend.

Mrs Gupta broke the silence when she arrived at the table bearing three richly smelling bowls. 'Here you are. I have the Lamb Achari, Dhingri Matar and Kubuli Pulao.' She placed her dishes on the table and clicked her tongue. 'You haven't touched the Nan. You must eat.'

When Bernard McBride opened the door, Jane took a breath and greeted him with a smile. 'Thank you for including me in the party tonight. It's very kind of you.' She knew it would have been Danny and Mary she had to thank for the invitation but was determined to be on the front foot with Mr McBride.

'Not at all, my dear. We're pleased you were able to come,' he said in an unexpectedly cordial voice. He led her into the living room where she kissed Mary on the cheek and Danny on the lips, determined not to be intimidated by her first dinner with the family.

Mary was smartly dressed in a woollen jersey dress with a paisley design in pastel colours that suited her admirably. The men were well turned out, as well. She had never seen Mr McBride in a business shirt and tie before. It was a chilly night but the house was warm and he had abandoned the ageing green jumper he usually sported in cold weather. Danny, who had chosen a well-pressed pair of grey trousers and a navy roll-neck, was far more neatly turned out than she was used to. He stood tall with his shoulders back and Jane wondered whether this could be the influence of the army. She was relieved she had chosen to dress up for the occasion. When she had bought the dark blue dress of fine wool, her mother had described it as being too old for her and that was just what she wanted this evening. Her red high heels were intended to confirm she was no longer the girl next-door but an independent woman with a career.

After Bernard went off to get drinks, Mary chatted to Jane who, with her eyes on Danny, had trouble concentrating on what Mary was saying.

Bernard returned with their drinks on a tray. 'Here we are: Pimms for the ladies and beer for the men.' He handed round the drinks, raised his glass and said, 'Cheers.' He smiled at Jane. 'Welcome again.' Glancing around, Jane could see she wasn't the only one to be taken aback by Mr McBride's affability and he had only just started. 'You must tell us about your work at the Alfred.' When Jane began to describe her time in theatre, he said, 'Tough work. I admire anyone who can cope with that.'

'Sometimes it can be hard but it's wonderful to be part of the team when you have a good outcome.'

'So now you know what I was trying to tell you ages ago,' Danny said.

'Yes, I do and you were right.'

'What's that all about?' Bernard said.

'I think that might be between Jane and Danny,' Mary said.

'What's going on between them now?' Sean stood grinning in the doorway with a bottle of red wine in each hand.

Mary jumped to her feet and went to embrace him. 'It's so good to see you. You startled me coming in like that.'

Sean glanced across at his father. 'Glad to see you haven't changed the locks and my key still worked.'

'Welcome home, son,' Bernard said and advanced to shake Sean's hand, forcing him to put the bottles on the floor.

'I didn't know you'd be here, Jane,' Sean said. He went to her and kissed her on the cheek before turning to Danny. 'And it's great to see you too, mate.'

'Would you like a beer?' Bernard asked.

Sean picked up the bottles and held them out to his father. 'Thanks Dad. I've brought some wine but we can have that with the delicious dinner I can smell.'

The meal did not begin immediately they were seated at the table with plates of roast lamb, potatoes, parsnips, tomatoes and peas before them. Sean was adamant each of them must 'at least try' the wine he had brought. A search for wine glasses produced four that could justify that title and two others that would do. Sean went from place to place pouring the wine and when he was finished Bernard raised his glass and said, 'We're here to wish Danny well, serving his country in Vietnam. Good health, son.'

'Yeah, here's to you, mate,' Sean said and raised his glass, as well.

'May God bring you back safe to us,' Mary said almost inaudibly.

Bernard sipped his wine, the others following him. 'Not a wine man,' he said, 'but this isn't a bad drop.'

'I thought you'd like it,' Sean replied. 'Guy knows a lot about wine and this is one of his favourites.'

'Guy? Who's Guy?' Bernard asked.

'Come on, start eating,' Mary said quickly. 'Don't let the meal get cold.'

'Hasn't Mum told you about Guy?' Sean said. 'He's a human rights lawyer I met about a year ago. It's his house I live in these days. Very comfortable it is, too.' He grinned at Jane and said, 'See, I've taken your advice.'

Jane did not smile back. She knew he was referring to her concern he not tell Mary about his love affair with Guy Norton and she felt sure the others would want to know what he meant. She was relieved when Bernard said, 'I didn't know you were in touch with Jane. Am I the only one you haven't been talking to?'

'Well here we are back together, so we can talk all you like,' Sean said cheerily.

Jane saw the need to change the topic and had a ready-made alternative. 'I'd like to propose another toast. Danny, on one of the days you were stomping around the jungle in Queensland, it was your birthday and you formally became an adult. I'd forgotten to ask if you got my card, but happy twenty-first.'

'Oh, Danny, yes, forgive me,' Mary said. 'We sent a card as well but I should have said something before this.' She raised her glass and took a sip.

'Not to worry.' Danny laughed. 'I forgot all about it myself and only remembered when we got back to Holsworthy. Of course, all we nashos turn twenty-one sometime in these six months.'

'What about you, Jane?' Bernard said. 'When's your big birthday?'

'Mine's not until next year. Like you, I suppose, Sean.'

Bernard stopped eating and sat with his knife and fork pointing upwards. 'You'll have to register in a few months, son.'

'Yeah, in July,' Sean said.

Bernard eyed him carefully before saying, 'I wondered how you'd feel about that. Your mum tells me you aren't going in the protests these days.'

Sean swallowed the mouthful he had been chewing and took more of his wine while an anxious silence hung over the table.

'It's complicated, Dad,' he said. 'I still believe as firmly as I always have that our involvement in Vietnam is wrong, but the fact that next

127

year I might be fighting there myself changes things. That and a few other issues.'

'You'll go if you're called up?' Bernard asked with a hopeful expression.

'Yeah. Guy has represented a number of conscientious objectors and wants me to put in for exemption, too. He's pretty pissed off that I won't do it. I don't want to be in that war but I'm not going to lie to get out of it. My objection is not to war under any circumstances; just to this one. That's not grounds for exemption and Guy knows that better than I do.' Jane could hear a tone of resentment in Sean's voice and thought of the euphoric way he had described his love affair with Guy when they talked at Genevieve's. Perhaps all was not as rosy as it had been.

'I hate to think you may have to go as well, but how does that change things?' Mary said with a worried frown.

'I've found that those who go in the protests have different aims. Some of them, like me, want to get people thinking about what is at stake and not just swallow the line the Government peddles.' Bernard stirred at this but Sean continued. 'Some want to oppose whatever the Government puts up, regardless of what's right or wrong.' He turned to smile at Jane. 'You met a few of them the day we had coffee together. Some come along hoping for a fight. They're the ones who annoy me most. They aren't interested in the cause and they do it great damage.' He sighed before saying, 'And finally there are those who are scared of going to Vietnam and want to get out of it any way they can. I'd hate to be taken for one of those guys, but there's every chance that's how my protest would be viewed. Now, Dad, I hope you can see why I said it was complicated.'

'Yeah, son, I can. Both Danny and I think you're wrong about Vietnam but I'm pleased you're acting according to your principles, even if some of them are different from mine.'

Sean laughed, releasing the tension that had been mounting. 'I'm not Groucho Marx. I can't tell you I have principles and, if you don't like them, I have others. You'll just have to hope I do get called up. If I'm not, I'll be free to be the pain in the arse I used to be.'

'That was great, thanks Mum,' Danny said, triggering murmurs of agreement from the others.

'I thought we should have your favourite dinner,' Mary said. 'So now there's Lemon Meringue Pie.'

'I'll come and help you serve it,' Jane said.

'This wine is not too bad at all,' Bernard repeated. 'Any more left?'

Sitting back in the living room with a cup of tea each, the atmosphere was far more relaxed than it had been around the dining table. Jane wondered whether this was because the contentious topics had been either dealt with or avoided. Perhaps it was the wine She was able to sit quietly while the McBride family recounted favourite stories of past escapades and embarrassments. Sean had the best store of them except for those from the newsagency where Mr McBride came into his own and showed himself to be quite a raconteur.

Eventually she said, 'I've enjoyed myself very much but I'm afraid I have to get home.'

'Well that's not far,' Bernard said with a laugh.

'Yes, I know your parents enjoy having you home,' Mary said.

'No, I'm at the flat. Mum and Dad are away this weekend at Point Lonsdale staying with friends. They're thinking of buying a place for themselves down there.'

'They're going to move?' Mary said with a concern that surprised Jane.

'No just a weekender.'

'Danny,' Bernard said. 'We can't let this young lady struggle home alone on the bus. Go with her and take the car.'

'You mean the van?' Danny asked in a surprised voice.

'Of course not. I mean the EJ.' Danny was plainly even more incredulous.

'Thank you, that would be very kind,' Jane said. She'd hoped he would accompany her to the flat but thought they would have to go by bus.

Having bade her hosts goodnight, they were about to leave when Bernard said, 'There is one other thing. I nearly forgot. I was speaking to Father Maloney the other day. He's going to give a special prayer for Danny at Mass tomorrow morning. All the family will be going, of course. He said he'd be happy if you came too, Jane. Would you like to?'

Caught by surprise, she made no immediate response but could see Mary was embarrassed, Sean highly amused and Danny ... Was he really that angry?

'I'm afraid I'm on duty tomorrow. That's why I have to rush off now. But thank you. Perhaps I could come another time. I've never been to a Catholic Mass and would like to.'

Danny grabbed her by the arm and propelled her along the passage to the back door and into the garage. Tight lipped, he opened the passenger door for her, climbed in himself, started the car and drove into the street.

'Why are you so angry?' she asked.

'We need to talk but I don't want to do it now. I've never driven this car before and I need to concentrate. If I put the slightest dent or scratch on it, I won't be going to Vietnam; Dad will have killed me. Wait till we're at your flat.'

Once again Jane had prevailed on Carol to be at least out of sight if not away from the flat when she returned. She led Danny to the couch, sat beside him and said, 'Now, what's this all about?'

Danny's face was flushed and his voice loud. 'My bloody father. How could he do that to you?'

'Shush,' she said. 'Come with me and don't wake up Carol.' She took his hand, led him into her bedroom, shut the door and perched herself on the side of the bed, patting the space beside her. 'Sit here and calmly tell me why your father has so upset you.'

Danny was sucking in breaths as though he had been running in a race. 'Surely it's obvious. He's seen how close we are and has given up trying to steer me away from you. Instead he's going to have you become a Catholic.'

'Is that such a bad thing?'

'What? You can't be serious.'

'I've been thinking about it and didn't know how to raise it with you. Your dad kindly did it for me.'

Danny glared at her. 'But why would you want to be a Catholic?'

Jane returned his glare. 'To marry you, of course, you big egg.' Danny went to object, but Jane spoke over the top of him. 'I went to a Church of England school and my family turns up at the Cathedral at Christmas and on Good Friday. That's all it's taken to make me a Protestant. I don't subscribe to the beliefs or creeds of the Anglican Church in any serious way. I may as well become a Catholic and solve our problem.'

'You mean, solve his problem and create one for us.' Danny shook his head sorrowfully. 'This is worse than I thought. I expected you to be angry Dad would want to convert you. You know I take my religion seriously. That doesn't mean I take everything the Church says as holy writ, but it does mean I can't accept you glibly signing up to join the Church without any commitment, just so we can marry.'

'Just so we can marry? Just?' Her voice rose, matching Danny's earlier level. What did she care if she was overheard? 'That's my commitment to you. Where's yours to me?'

'What do you mean?'

'Do you love me or don't you? Is this Catholic versus Protestant business just an excuse?'

'I don't want the cost of marrying you to be forcing you into a sham conversion to my faith.' Jane made no response but continued to glower at him. 'I'm going to Vietnam in a few days. There's no time to decide what we're going to do about getting married. But please, while I'm away, don't do anything you may later regret. I promise you, if I have to choose between my parents and you, it'll always be you.' He smiled at her. 'We should be happy with what happened tonight. Since we've known one another, Dad has been opposed even to us being friends.

131

Now you have him for an admirer and he wants us to marry. The way he wants us to do it is wrong, but he'll come around. Mum will see to that. She always does.'

'I'm still not sure you want to marry me.'

'Of course I do. But only in a way we can both be happy about.'

'There's always a but.'

'We've always been honest with one another,' Danny said. 'It's one of the things I love about you.'

Jane wriggled herself closer to him so they were pressed together from shoulder to thigh. 'Here it is, our last night together before you go away for a year and we end up arguing. This is not how I planned it.'

Danny lifted his arm to encircle her shoulders and pulled her even closer. 'You planned it? How did you plan it?'

'I thought this is the last chance I get for ages to seduce the man I love. I need to lure him into my bedroom and let nature take its course. I've made preparations.'

'What?'

'There's a packet of condoms in the drawer.'

Danny jerked himself away from her. 'You must know how I would feel about that.'

'To tell the truth, I wasn't giving your feelings a lot of thought. It was my feelings I was focused on.'

Danny laughed. 'The devil sure has got into you tonight. You tell me, the good Catholic boy, that you intend to become a Catholic and at the same time you plan to defy the Church's teaching, not just on sex before marriage but birth control as well.' He laughed again and Jane was unsure whether he was laughing at her, at himself or at their predicament.

'OK then, let's see how far you are willing to go before the fear of mortal sin holds you back.'

Vietnam

'We're going on the Sydney?' Danny looked up from cleaning his rifle. 'Are you sure?'

'That's the drum,' Skeeta said.

'A two-week cruise through the tropics isn't a bad way to start our tour,' Simmo said.

Goldie spoke from where he was stretched out on his bed. 'My parents came from South America to Australia by boat. They swore never to go to sea again.'

'But they didn't travel by aircraft-carrier,' Simmo said.

'Not any more she isn't.' Smacka had come to join them. 'Sad really. In her young days she was the flagship of the Navy and now they've pulled her out of retirement to ferry grunts like us and our equipment.'

After they boarded at Garden Island and made stately progress down Sydney Harbour in the early morning sun, Danny began to feel Simmo might be right. The sea was flat and the shoreline resplendent. It was only when they were on the open sea somewhere off Avoca Beach that the wind rose and the ship began to roll in a heavy swell. 'I don't feel so good,' Tich said.

'That's a shame,' Smacka said, a note of sympathy not often heard in his voice. 'But don't worry. I've been on a troopship before. You'll be fine after the first fortnight.'

Tich was the first to throw up but more of them soon joined him.

Their next challenge was to set up and hang a hammock. Skeeta had not had a sailor in his family but still showed the way it could be done in the cramped space with little more than a foot between the hammocks. Much of the flight deck was taken up by vehicles and stores so they were forced to spend a good deal of their spare time below decks in what they came to view as a hot and humid stink-hole.

Danny was the one who made the best of it. He coped well with the circuit training carried out each day around the expanse of the deck. He distinguished himself in the target practice, arranged by wafting balloons off the stern, and he took more interest than his colleagues in the continuing classes on Vietnamese language and culture. The only bright spot for some of them was the single can of Fosters they were allocated each night.

The Sydney anchored off Cape St. Jacques early in the morning and the men, lined up on the deck, heard the chatter of an approaching helicopter. Danny watched as it swooped in and touched down on the deck. The assembled ranks were called to attention as a group of officers clambered from the helicopter. Among them were two heavy-weights Danny recognised from their photographs: General William Westmoreland, Chief of the Armed Forces in Vietnam, and Brigadier Oliver Jackson, their own leader. In a gravelly voice, Westmoreland addressed the parade. 'Gentlemen of the Fifth Battalion, I salute you.' He snapped a salute to the several hundred men lined up on the deck and not long after departed as quickly as he had arrived.

'Nice of him to drop by and welcome us,' Danny said with a grin.

Skeeta shook his head. 'He said "Gentlemen". He couldn't have meant us.'

Next to arrive were a flotilla of landing craft. After they were along-side, cargo nets were thrown down to assist the men scramble down the side of the ship. They wore their slouch hats with the sides up, carried canvas packs on their backs, clutched a rifle in one hand and a kit bag in the other. Once on the landing craft, the officer-in-charge ordered them to fix bayonets. 'What the hell is this?' Smacka grumbled. 'Have the VC taken over Vung Tau?'

There was a bang as the ramp of their landing craft dropped forward, water poured in and they waded onto the beach where a group of Yanks were standing, laughing at them. One of the Yanks called out, 'Put those pig-stickers away before you hurt yourselves.'

Danny wrinkled his nose. This pantomime was a caricature of the Gallipoli tradition, not the arrival he had envisaged when committing himself to the fight in Vietnam.

On the esplanade a line of trucks awaited them. Across the road a group of children smiled and waved One of them called out, 'Eh, Uc Da Loi.'

'What did he say?' Skeeta asked.

Danny's attention to the language classes enabled him to answer. 'People from the South — that's what they call us. There you are, Skeeta. Better than Westmoreland. The kids are pleased to see us.'

They clambered into the trucks and were taken to a staging camp which had been hastily constructed on an uneven stretch of dunes known as Back Beach. Closely packed tents laid out in company areas would become their home for the next two weeks spent acclimatising in the sand dunes and the jungle near Vung Tau, anxious to begin yet nervous at what they were about to face.

Danny sweated in the steamy heat of the early morning as he stood, fully kitted up, waiting for the American helicopters which were to take them to Nui Dat, the site for the Australian base. On arrival, the choppers blasted sand into Danny's face as he struggled forward to climb aboard. He felt the crush of bodies as more and more men crammed into the tight space until the door gunner shouted the load was too heavy and used his boot to shove a would-be passenger back onto the ground. The chopper struggled into the air, bucking and weaving as it climbed to take its place in the closely packed line bobbing across the sky. In the crush, Danny had only a limited view of the ground covered in their flight. They followed a road through flat country with a line of densely wooded hills along one side. In the mist not yet burnt off by the sun, the country appeared to be only just awakening — no sign of war.

As the chopper came down on a broad cleared area in front of a rubber plantation, Danny felt the sweat trickle from his armpits. Now he was at war for real. He assembled in his platoon, watched by a group of Americans. One of them drew on a cigarette before saying his group had seen some hard fighting, but the place was pretty well cleaned up now. His grin and wink chilled Danny. The thump of mortars and artillery further undermined the American's claim.

The initial task given 5 RAR was to clear the area north and east of Nui Dat, so that enemy mortar fire could not reach the base. When that was achieved, they were to patrol the area to ensure the security of Nui Dat while the base was established. Danny was pleased his battalion had been chosen for this role and felt sorry for the others who would be little more than builder's labourers, like his father had been in New Guinea.

The company divided into its three platoons and moved to the area it had been allocated, west of the landing zone. Once in position, Smacca led the section away in an arrowhead with Skeeta as forward scout and Butch, the gunner, behind him. Heavy cloud now obliterated the sun and the gentle hills Danny had seen from the chopper had become a low mountain range rearing up behind them. Ahead lay a huge rubber plantation surmounted by a low hill. 'Wonder what that hill over there is called,' Simmo said.

'Shut up you guys and keep your eyes skinned,' Smacca said.

They came to a bitumen road they knew from their briefing as Route 2, the highway which split Phuoc Tuy in two. There was no sign of traffic, the wreckage of the bridge ahead of them adding menace to the silence. A short distance further on was a hamlet that Smacca's map identified as Ap An Phu. All that remained of it now was a pile of smouldering timber. Not far beyond they came upon an old couple standing by the track. Their faces showed neither welcome nor hostility, their posture and expression conveying only exhaustion and resignation. From their briefings Danny knew it would be necessary to clear the villages around Nui Dat and relocate the inhabitants, so that the Viet Cong could not use the sites to direct mortar fire on the base. It was clear the old couple understood nothing of this. Had they missed the call to move away or had they chosen not to go? Danny knew the Viet Cong would be violently opposed to the arrival of the Australians but had thought the bulk of the South Vietnamese would welcome being liberated.

Cautiously they continued their patrol, eventually entering the rubber plantation with its knee-high ferns and thorny undergrowth. No air stirred in the gloom of the plantation and soon their jungle green shirts were black with sweat. A commotion up ahead brought the section flat onto their stomachs in the fire position. They inched forward until a crackle of gunfire halted them again. They had trained for just this situation and Danny had been confident he would perform well, but the fear which gripped his stomach was totally unexpected. He was under fire and had no idea what was going on. Who were his attackers? How many were there? Most importantly, where were they? He had known fear before. There was the time he had been set on by a couple of hoods in a lane off Little Bourke Street. He had taken a couple of blows but his fear then gave him the adrenalin to push them off and outrun them. Once, a weirdo had come into the newsagency waving a knife and calling for retribution against all Catholics. His fear that time was of being trapped without an escape.

A nudge from Taffy brought him back to the present where Smacca was signalling to move into a defensive perimeter. The light began to fade as they lay in the corridors of precisely aligned rubber trees. Suddenly all light was sucked from the plantation. A blinding flash, a booming explosion, a rush of wind. Danny was soaked by pelting rain. More lightning, more deafening thunder, the rain drumming down on him. He pulled out his Hootchie and wrapped himself in the plastic sheet. The rain streamed across the sheet to funnel inside his shirt and pants.

As suddenly as it had arrived the rain was gone, replaced by the steady drip from the rubber trees. He strained to hear threatening sounds, but nothing stirred. From the midst of the darkness came another flash and bang. Was it thunder? The rattle of automatic gunfire from across the plantation said it was not. Again, he emerged from his sheet and rolled into the fire position. Red tracer bullets flew through the darkness. Smacka said the company HQ might have been rocketed but he wasn't sure.

Simmo, next in line to Danny, whispered, 'I didn't reckon it would be this bad.'

'Maybe this is as bad as it gets,' Danny said, striving to be optimistic. A faint hope on their first day.

Danny lay enveloped in darkness as though in a sealed room. He was able to confirm he still had sight from the glimmer of his luminous watch. All he could hear was the sound of his own breathing and the faint whisper when a nearby member of the section tried to ease the cramp in his arms or legs. At last Smacka passed on some good news: the company HQ had not been hit. It had been merely a parting shot from the monsoon. The comfort of that news was short lived when word spread that Errol Noack, a national serviceman, had been killed. He was in another company but had been with them during initial training. The loss was both personal and symbolic — the first nasho to die.

'I was wrong,' Danny said. 'It can get worse.'

Danny spent an uncomfortable night trying to sleep when offered the chance and trying to stay awake when on watch. In the morning the platoon moved on through country which varied between low scrub, overgrown banana plantation and chaotic jungle. Progress was slow as they had to be on continuous watch for an enemy ambush. Once their section came upon several huts hidden in the bush. Each hut contained a bed and, under the bed, a bunker. On the roof of one hut Smacka found grenades triggered to detonate. He ordered them to set fire to the huts and stand well back as the grenades exploded. Danny recalled the burnt-out hamlet they had seen the previous day. It would be good if they could be more constructive, but that would probably have to wait until they had cleared out the VC.

The rest of the morning was spent searching for more signs of Viet Cong. Danny, continually primed for dealing with an attack, was frustrated by the slow rate of progress with so little to show for their efforts. In the late afternoon they were ordered to be part of an ambush which was set up on a track beside the bank of a river. Two machine-guns were sighted along the track. Their section spread in pairs through the bush between the guns while another section and machine-gun protected their rear. Danny was paired with Simmo and they took it in turns for one to be on alert while the other tried to relax and grab some sleep. The gurgle of the river provided a welcome contrast to the silence of the previous night. The monsoon provided fewer fireworks this time, but Danny was doused just as heavily.

Suddenly one of the machine-guns erupted, sending red tracer bullets across the track. The second joined in and there was a shriek as some of the bullets found their mark. Danny, jerked from his numb reverie, saw shadowy movement on the track. Those VC who had not been hit by the initial burst but were cut-off by the intersecting stream of bullets dropped to the ground and began to return fire. The fear that had frozen Danny last night was just as severe, but this time there was something he could do to combat it. Again, he was under threat of death but this time he knew where that threat lay and could channel his fear into returning fire. He fired at any sign of movement, real or imagined, emboldened by the confidence he had in his own marksmanship. He was sure he could shoot straighter than any of his assailants.

After the early flurry of attack and counter-attack, the darkness returned to silence, as if it, too, was holding its breath and waiting for the next explosion.

Unable to sleep, Danny reflected that, marksmanship counts for very little when neither side presents a clear target. You were probably more likely to be hit by a stray bullet, even a ricochet, than a direct shot. It had been drummed into him during training that the only likely result of firing indiscriminately would be to reveal his position to the enemy. Danny remembered Smacka saying to him when they were at Canungra that training was one thing but being under enemy fire was something quite different. Now he knew what Smacka meant.

Morning light revealed no sign of life on the track. The VC had retreated, leaving nothing behind but a trail of blood and footprints.

'They don't abandon their wounded or their dead. I'll say that for them,' Smacca said grudgingly.

Skeeta pointed to a line of flattened brush, some of the leaves tinged with dried blood, and followed it to where, ten metres from the track, he found a crumpled body. 'Over here,' he hissed and then in a louder voice, 'My God, it's a woman.'

Danny wondered if he was the one who had killed her. He was relieved when Smacca looked up from examining the body and said, 'Judging by the mess, I'd say it was one of the M60s that did for her.'

'So, they're happy to abandon their women,' Goldie said.

'Probably couldn't find her in the dark and the chaos,' Smacca said.

Goldie was unimpressed. 'Took her rifle, though.'

Smacca sighed. 'Which she would have dropped on the track when she was first hit.' He tossed her bullet-riddled back-pack to Goldie. 'Go through it and see if there's anything useful we can get from it.'

'I didn't know the VC used women,' Danny said.

'You were told that back in training at Holsworthy,' Smacca said. 'Weren't you listening, you dreamy bastard? They're just as dedicated to the cause as the blokes. You can bury her. Get on with it while the rest of us see if there's anything more to be found.'

~

After several weeks of patrolling, always wet in the stifling humidity and with continually blistered feet, Danny began to search for relief from a range of unlikely sources. The helicopters that brought food and water every few days were welcome, not so much for the food — he had only a small appetite when in the jungle and the menu of biscuits and cheese, pork and beans or cold turkey loaf was not all that tempting — but for the link they symbolised with dry, clean clothes and a comfortable bed. When the monsoon returned each mid-afternoon to drench him, he enjoyed watching it whip the foliage of the jungle into a throbbing dance. With the rain came refreshment, shining the leaves and washing him clean of accumulated mud and sweat. The jungle which so often sought to bar his path, enfold him or trip him up also brought him fascinating sights: insects of many shapes and sizes, butterflies with large black and turquoise wings, friendly brown lizards. When unable to sleep and suspicious of the night sounds, he could gaze up from the floor of the jungle to marvel at the beauty of the stars.

Smacka returned from a briefing by the platoon commander, far happier than he usually was after such meetings. 'I've been ordered to tell you that within a week we'll be moving into an area around Nui Dat where we're going to set up a permanent camp.'

'You bloody, beauty,' Goldie said. 'That means a place with toilets, mess halls, a tent, a cot. Shit, even a hot shower.'

'You sure about this, Smacka?' Danny was having trouble believing their month of patrolling might be coming to an end.

'Would the army allow an officer to mislead us?' Smacka asked, feigning offence.

'We might even get some real food instead of combat rations,' Goldie said.

Skeeta turned to Danny. 'There'll probably be some mail — a letter from Miss Bluebell.'

Danny had often escaped into thoughts of Jane in the past weeks. In particular he had replayed that last night on her bed many times. Given another chance he might not hold back like he had. Her letter was unlikely to be as stimulating as that thought.

'The skip also asked me to tell you not to expect a bloody holiday. The war isn't over. We'll have plenty of wiring, digging weapons pits and still be patrolling and ambushing.'

After the images wishful thinking had planted in Danny's mind, Nui Dat was a bitter disappointment. They approached through a 500-yard stretch of land which had been stripped of vegetation to provide fields of fire and a clear view of any VC approaching the perimeter fence. The area allocated to 5 RAR was in what had been a rubber plantation to the north of the air strip. A dirt road provided entry to what was planned to be their quarters but which the continuing wet season ensured was currently no more than a sea of mud.

Soon they were at work enhancing their defences. The base perimeter was ringed by a barbed-wire fence, which had to be extended and strengthened with the laying of Claymore antipersonnel mines. Each platoon had to dig bunkers and mortar pits, the job made more difficult by the pits immediately filling with water. Each section manned their machinegun through the night preventing any of them from enjoying an uninterrupted night's sleep.

Then they had to build their camp. At first there were no tents and, when these arrived, some were found to be without poles. When they were erected, the men had to build sandbagged walls around them to protect against mortar attack. They also laid sandbags on small logs to prevent pathways from turning into slush. The longed-for showers did not arrive for weeks.

Now Danny had first-hand experience of the frustration suffered by his father. It occurred to him his dad had been better off since he didn't have the threat of bombardment or mortar attack, ever present at Nui Dat. Danny wouldn't have believed it when he arrived at Nui Dat but found he welcomed going back on patrol as a respite from duty on the base.

Eventually Danny and Skeeta shared a tent with Smacka and Taffy. 'So I can keep an eye on Dreamer,' Smacka said, 'and I know Skeeta won't let Dreamer go anywhere without him.'

The tent provided a roof over their heads and was air-conditioned by permanently raising the sides to allow any breeze to pass through. The floor was formed from duckboards and each of the men was issued with a canvas stretcher for a bed, a mosquito net and a metal trunk. Any furniture was knocked together from old mortar boxes and shell cases, a skill at which Skeeta was particularly adept, even creating a wardrobe of sorts from a few planks of wood.

The mess hall, which had been created in a marquee-like tent, was not what Goldie had been envisioning. Neither was the food. Cool rooms and refrigeration had yet to be installed so that fresh food soon became inedible. Frankfurters and sweet corn were the staple diet for some weeks.

It was late before Jane could clean up and leave. What had started as a day of routine surgery had become more fraught the longer it lasted. The scheduled anaesthetist had gone down with the flu and was replaced at the last moment by the inexperienced Dr Roberts. Jane had not worked with him before but quickly formed the view he had little of Dr Townsend's calm competency. He was incessantly talkative throughout each of the scheduled operations and was much more focussed on his own concerns than on monitoring the wellbeing of the patients. When Jane drew his attention to a deterioration in the condition of one patient, he said, 'Yes, yes, no need to panic,' in an irritated tone. As it turned out he was correct but Jane remained aggrieved by the manner of his response.

They were in the process of finishing the last operation for the day when told that a patient with a burst appendix had been admitted and would be brought for urgent surgery. 'What?' Dr Roberts said. 'I have a game of billiards at the club before dinner tonight. I can't miss that. We'll need to be quick.'

The patient, a man in his mid-fifties, had hardly reached the surgery table before Roberts had him anaesthetised and was urging the surgeons to get a move on. He was in the midst of a detailed account of one of his recent games of billiards when Jane noticed a slight movement in the patient's limbs and feared the anaesthetic was not as effective as it needed to be. After the earlier rebuke from Dr Roberts, she hesitated to alert him but eventually had to risk another dose of his irritation. 'What?' he said. 'Let me see. Damn. You should have told me earlier.'

Jane wanted to tell him to make up his mind but held back. This time it was Roberts who was beginning to panic. Hastily he adjusted the flow of gas and repositioned the tube in the patient's breathing passage. For a while it was touch and go but the patient's condition stabilised and the removal of the appendix was completed successfully.

What she needed was some of Mrs Gupta's magic.

When she entered the restaurant, Mrs Gupta greeted her with a warm smile. 'How nice to see you again.' The smile became a frown of concern. 'But I see you have need for my magic.' After she had led Jane to a table she asked, 'Dr Townsend? Will he be joining you?'

'No, not tonight.' Jane did not know whether he had been in one of the other theatres that day. Working with him after their visit to Mrs Gupta's, he was back to being the serious, formal anaesthetist she had first known. She had to admit she would have liked to have found him here tonight. In addition to Mrs Gupta's dishes, part of the magic of her first visit had been the transformation in Dr Townsend. Since Danny joined the army, Gordon had been the only man she met who was of the slightest interest. It was as if he were made up of two differ-ent people. At the hospital he commanded respect and was always in control, but conducted himself like an emotionless automaton. Away from the hospital he was transformed to an engaging man with youthful interests and enthusiasms. How could the division be so stark?

Today had been one of those days when she really missed Danny. It would have been so good to be able to tell him about her troubles and be consoled by him. From the two letters she had received since he left, she thought he might need some consoling of his own. It was more what he didn't say. He had set off keen to fulfil his mission to rid South Vietnam of the Communists but only wrote about an unexciting sea voyage and a long period wandering around the jungle before eventually reaching camp. She didn't know whether he'd been involved in any fighting. He did say the jungle could be beautiful, but she got the impression that was only on rare occasions.

Again, Mrs Gupta had not asked for direction and now brought her selected dishes to the table. After she had described them to Jane, she did not turn away to attend any of the other diners but stood with her hands clasped in front of her. 'You are sure Dr Townsend will not be joining you?'

The gleam in Mrs Gupta's eyes caused Jane to say, 'As sure as I can be. I've seen very little of him at the hospital lately.'

'Mrs Gupta pursed her lips and shook her head. 'A pity. I worry about him coming here alone. He needs the company of a gracious lady like yourself.'

Early in the morning the entire battalion marched out of Nui Dat in a column that stretched to the north along Route 2 before turning into the trees of the rubber plantation, crossing the Song Cau river and heading west past the area, which Danny recognised as having been their landing zone on arrival eight weeks ago.

Danny reflected that the slog of those weeks had failed to satisfy his aspiration to rid the province of the Communists. The constant patrolling his section carried out — 'search and destroy' as the army liked to call it — entailed a lot of searching and setting of ambushes but very little destroying unless he counted the demolition of empty VC huts and bunkers. After that first fire-fight they had seen only the occasional enemy soldier and seldom been involved in direct confrontation. However, the threat of conflict was constant as they struggled through the jungle or lay in ambush. One benefit of exhaustion was that it dulled fear. The company commander made a point of assuring them their efforts were denying country to the VC where they had previously been unchallenged, but it was hard to see this as winning the war he had come to fight.

At least today's operation was one of those described as 'cordon and search'. Danny had been involved in a couple of those and found them more satisfying. In the night a cordon was thrown around a village, which the VC were known to use and control, denying escape to any who were found the following morning when the village was entered and searched. In this way they had taken a number of prisoners and, while the villagers remained circumspect, it was possible to see the relief many of them felt at being freed from the control and the taxes the VC imposed.

Today's operation was directed at Binh Ba, a large village of some two thousand people. Here was the headquarters for the French-owned and French-managed Gallia rubber plantation which continued to operate despite the VC being in control of the village. Danny was cheered by the belief that clearing Binh Ba of the VC would be a major step toward the goal of re-establishing Government control of the province.

They continued for the remainder of the day over open country, through clumps of bamboo and across muddy swamps before reaching the company harbour area in jungle dotted with small clearings. 'Good to sit down,' Danny said as he threw off his pack and delved into it for the tin of cold meat which was his first meal since breakfast.

'No dramas yet,' Smacka said. An essential requirement for all cordon and search operations was that the cordon must be firmly in place before its presence could be detected by the villagers. If not, all the

146

company was likely to find was an ambush or a village empty of Viet Cong. The size and scope of this operation made secrecy even more difficult. They were forced to gather in the jungle two miles from the village and not enter the surrounding rubber plantation until after the tappers had finished work for the day.

The light was already failing when they left the jungle and filtered into the plantation where they halted. Near midnight, before the moon had risen, the order came to move forward to their final position. To maintain cohesion in the pitch dark each man was ordered to fix a short rope between his pack and that of the man in front of him. Smacka had been an outspoken sceptic of this idea since he first learned of it. 'Bloody ridiculous,' he told them. 'Besides, when I get hitched, I don't want it to be with any of you bastards.' When the procession moved off, some of those at the back were too slow to react and found the packs they had yet to put on disappearing into the inky blackness.

'Hey, stop! Where the hell are you?'

'Stuff it,' Smacka said. 'Untie those bloody ropes and keep your hand on the shoulder of the bloke in front.'

They stumbled through the rubber trees and across the small banks and channels which ran through the plantation until the late-rising moon gave them some light and they were able set the cordon undetected an hour or so before dawn. At sunrise a plane fitted with loudspeakers flew over the village instructing the villagers on what they needed to do and reassuring them that they would not be harmed. While the men in the cordon maintained watch, some detachments entered Binh Ba to search the village and begin arranging for the company intelligence officer to interview the inhabitants. The males of military age were taken by trucks under armed escort to the village of Ba Ria where provincial staff had set up to interrogate them.

These enquiries by the provincial authorities were scheduled to take place over three days before the men would be brought back to Binh Ba. Meanwhile, the task of the battalion was to maintain guard against the possibility of the VC attempting to infiltrate back into the village.

They were also told to move around meeting the people and establishing a positive image. Danny's section was one of those involved in what Smacka called 'the hearts and minds stuff'.

At first the villagers kept their distance. 'Wouldn't you?' Simmo said. 'You've been under Charlie's thumb for ages before this foreign bunch sweep in and take control. How long are they going to stay? We might piss off again in a few days and the VC will be back taking it out of you for cosying up to the enemy.'

'You're right,' Smacka said, 'but I'm told we're going to keep a company here until local troops move in, so we won't be leaving them on their own again. The boss wants us to spread the word if we get a chance. He didn't say how we'd do that.'

Walking through the streets of Binh Ba, Danny found much to enjoy. The influence of the French was widespread and benign. Green lawns surrounded a collection of villas with gardens abounding in exotic flowers. The smaller cottages for the plantation workers had brick and cream plastered walls, red tiles on the roofs and were surrounded by gardens of vegetables and ornamental shrubbery. The houses and the rectangular pattern of intersecting streets gave the village a suburban air. It was unlike anything Danny had yet seen in Vietnam. Eventually the reticence of the villagers was overcome through the curiosity of the children and the rations the soldiers offered to share with them.

The children were entranced by Goldie's skill as a conjurer when he swallowed coins and recovered them from behind their ears or made some of their small possessions vanish and pop out of another child's hair or clothes.

Taffy also found Goldie's ability revealing. 'Now I can see why you win so many of our poker games.'

Danny's attempts to converse with the locals in their native tongue were met with uncomprehending but delighted laughter.

Their efforts to ingratiate themselves were interrupted when a Roman Catholic priest in black robes and beret cycled towards them at such a slow pace it was miraculous he could stay upright.

'Bon jour,' he called as he passed them.

'Bon jour mon pere,' Danny called back.

Skeeta was impressed. 'I didn't know you spoke French.'

'Learnt a bit at school. Hardly any left now.'

'What hidden talents these nasho boys have,' Smacka said to Taffy. 'You'd never think it to look at them.'

'But the priest? Where did he come from?' Danny said.

Goldie turned from taking a piece of chocolate from the ear of one child and flicking it to another. 'I guess he's the local man. By local standards this is a pretty big place and I remember hearing in one of our briefings back in Holsworthy there are quite a few Catholics scattered among the Buddhists in the south.'

'Haven't seen a church,' Danny said.

'Well lift your eyes, Dreamer.' Smacka pointed to a hill rising behind the village. 'I'd say there's a bit of a steeple over there.' Now Danny could see a cross on the top of a square, white steeple poking above the roofs of the furthermost villas.

On their return to Nui Dat, the company commander told them the operation had led to the capture of a considerable number of Viet Cong cadre and guerrillas based in the village as well as sympathisers who had been giving the VC material aid in considerable amounts. The cordon had taken them completely by surprise and nearly seventy VC had been captured without the loss of a single man in the battalion. He went on to say two thousand people had been brought back under Government control and the road to the north of the province cleared, allowing the possibility of regaining control over another ten thousand people.

Danny felt much happier than he had been at the start of the mission. He was proud to have played a part in a complex exercise involving not just the battalion but elements of the local forces and the provincial administration. Apart from the fiasco of the roping together, it had gone exactly to plan and even that hiccup had been overcome quickly.

The realisation there must be a significant number of Catholics in the village was the icing on the cake.

For the first time since landing at Vung Tau he could be satisfied he was part of a team undertaking a challenging and important role in the restitution of South Vietnam. He would have loved to have spoken with the priest who had cycled past them. It would have been great to learn about the state of the Church in Binh Ba. Probably, the priest would have been able to give him a good picture of the situation across the whole province. It was surprising he had been allowed to continue ministering to the Catholics of Binh Ba when the village was under VC control. Even more surprising, the French-owned rubber plantation had been allowed to continue with French management staying in place. How had the hated French been able to come to an accommodation with the VC? And how did he explain the considerable number of VC sympathisers among the villagers?

—⟩

Jane was pleased to find Gordon Townsend on duty and unsurprised when the scheduled operations were conducted smoothly and in good time. Cleaning up afterwards, she grinned at the thought a more ardu-ous day might have provided the benefit of another invitation to Mrs Gupta's. A few moments later she became aware of him hesitating in the doorway. 'Sister Glover, thank you for your assistance today. You were your usual efficient self.'

'As were you, Doctor.' If he insisted on continuing the formality, she had better do the same, although it grated. 'As it turned out everything went very smoothly and we were not challenged.'

'Yes,' he said and it was clear to Jane he had something else on his mind. 'Can I buy you a coffee?'

Jane wanted to say, 'How about dinner at Mrs Gupta's,' but settled for, 'Of course. Thank you.'

Only after they had collected their coffee and were seated at a table in the hospital cafe did it occur to Jane how the gossip would spread if she were seen here with Dr. Townsend. Fortunately, none of her friends or acquaintances were around.

'Your boyfriend in Vietnam?' he said, 'How is he getting on?'

'Danny doesn't say a lot in his letters. I think it's quite a hard slog for him.'

'Yes, I imagine so.' He paused as if stuck for something to say and took a sip of his coffee.

Jane filled in with, 'Are you still going? It's August now.'

He beamed at her as if she had said exactly what he wanted to hear. 'You remembered that. We'll be off next week. Actually, that's why I wanted to speak with you. One of the nurses, Sister Johansen, has had to pull out at short notice. I wondered whether you would consider joining us.'

'Really? I thought you were taking more experienced nursing staff.'

'That is the preference, but time is short and I have to admit we are scrambling a bit.' Some of the pleasure Jane felt at being invited dissipated with his untactful admission. 'But you know I admire your competence and have persuaded my colleagues you will do very well.' That was better. 'I'm sorry to press you but we need your answer as quickly as possible.'

'How long will I be away?'

'We're scheduled to return in January.'

'So, I'll be away for Christmas.' Jane saw the disappointment cloud his face and found herself saying, 'OK. Thank you. I'll come.' Had she been rash? She knew very little of what was involved. A trip overseas sounded exciting, though, and working closely with him over an extended period might give her a chance to understand how and why he managed to have two different personas.

He beamed and for a moment she thought he might hug her. 'That's great. I'm so pleased. It takes a great load off my mind. I didn't know what we would do if you hadn't been willing.'

He certainly knew how to flatter her one moment and deflate her the next. Danny could be like that. Both of them shared the same transparent honesty.

Although returning from patrol continued to mean picking up a hammer or shovel, Danny was pleased to see things at Nui Dat were improving. A picture theatre boasting a large screen and two 16-millimetre projectors was nearing completion while entertainers including Col Joye and Little Patty had given concerts at the base. All the tents were in place, cool rooms had been erected and refrigeration installed. Even better, Smacka arrived with the news, 'We're off to Vungas for three days R and C.'

'What's R and C?' Simmo asked.

'Rest and Convalescence,' Smacka said. 'Three days of sun, sand and sex.'

'You forgot the booze,' Taffy said.

'I never forget the booze. It's understood in everything I say and do.'

The plane dived steeply from the clouds above Saigon and began to lurch and judder in the severe turbulence, raising Jane's fear they were about to plummet into the jungle below. Instead, they recovered to land safely at an airport crowded with military aircraft. In her ignorance, she had expected Saigon to be well away from the war zone and was shocked to see the plethora of fighters, bombers, military helicopters and freighters.

A man from the embassy was there to meet them. He focussed his attention on Mr Charles Brookner, the distinguished surgeon who was the leader of the group. The rest of them were left to tag along as he led Mr Brookner to a small bus. Jane had not been in theatre with Brookner but had seen him in the ward and, knowing his reputation, was impressed he had given priority to a stint in Vietnam. At the pre-departure briefing, when Brookner had gone out of his way to thank her for volunteering at such short notice, she wondered how this special recognition had gone down with the other three nurses, each of whom was more senior than her.

The bus took them through streets crowded with trucks, cars, bicycles and pedicabs to a hotel which was surmounted by a pagoda-like tower. As they stood waiting to check in, Gwen Forster, the elder of the nurses, said, 'Shall we go for a stroll after we freshen up? I think we should be cautious at first and there's safety in numbers.'

Jane thought the doctors and nurses would make an unwieldy group on the crowded footpaths but realised belatedly that Gwen was speaking only to the nurses. The usual demarcation between doctors and nurses, which had shown some signs of softening during their flight up, remained firmly in place, at least in Gwen's mind.

They walked through throngs of bustling Vietnamese, a number of the women wearing attractive conical lampshade hats, clinging white jackets and long trousers. There were also quite a few American soldiers, some of whom greeted them and were keen to chat, but the nurses walked on. They passed a variety of shops, street stalls, bars and even a cinema, which was showing *Spartacus*. After a while Ellie Wilson said, 'Hey, how about we have a beer in that bar over there. It seems reasonably clean.'

Jane had not met Ellie during her time at the Alfred but was already envious of her superb auburn hair and liked her suggestion, not so much for the beer as for the opportunity to get some relief from the humid and pungent air choking the street.

'Great idea Ellie.' It was clear Mia Champion, the fourth of the nurses, was a good friend of Ellie.

'Do you think they'd do a pot of tea?' Gwen said.

Once they were settled around a table with Gwen's tea and three glasses of beer — Jane had decided against asking for a Coke — Ellie said, 'Well here we are for the next four or more months. From what I've seen of those doctors we've brought with us, we'll have to make our own fun.'

'Yeah,' Mia said but then brightened. 'There's the US air base at Bien Hoa. From what I've heard there are some charmers over there.'

'We're lucky to have such a senior man as Mr Brookner leading us,' Gwen said.

Ellie grinned at her. 'You don't think he's come just to put the icing on his CV for that knighthood they say can't be far off?'

Gwen ignored her. 'He's a smooth operator. Without actually saying so he made it clear there was to be no carrying on between doctors and nurses.'

Jane was surprised to hear her regretful tone. Gwen would have to be about the same age as her mother.

'When did he say that?' Mia asked.

'Remember the bit about how we would be working and living together under the same roof and it was important we got on well together throughout our time in Vietnam?'

'What's wrong with that?' Ellie said.

'It was what came next. He said to achieve this we needed to avoid building relationships which excluded others. In other words: no carrying on.'

'I missed that,' Mia said. 'I tend to switch off when I hear a surgeon going on about working together — it's usually just a call for the nurses to lift their games.'

'I don't reckon Graham Fisher heard him either,' Ellie said. 'He's already given me the eye a couple of times.'

Mia put down her glass. 'At least he's got a bit of spirit. Most of them are past it. Gordon Townsend is young enough, but there's more life in a block of wood.'

'He's very different away from the hospital.' Jane had rushed to defend him before realising her mistake.

'Do tell,' Mia said, her eyes gleaming.

Jane took a sip of her beer. 'He's got an old MG car and is very keen on it.'

'And how do you know this?'

Jane, struggling to decide what she should say, opted to focus on Mrs Gupta and hope that would satisfy them. 'Whenever he has a tough day in theatre, he goes to a little Indian place in High St. The proprietor there, Mrs Gupta, cooks him a meal that restores him. I was in theatre one day when we had a lot of problems and he suggested I needed a dose of Mrs Gupta's cooking, so I went. Nothing more to it than that.'

'Yes there is.' Gwen wasn't going to let her off the hook. 'I heard Brookner say it was Townsend who found you at short notice when Ingrid Johansen pulled out.'

'Good for you.' Mia patted Jane's back. 'I'd say there aren't too many women around who can bring Townsend to life.'

Two days after their arrival in Saigon they went to Bien Hoa and moved into their accommodation on the upper floor of a building which housed the office of the United States Agency for International Development on the ground floor. The doctors had separate bedrooms but the nurses were disconcerted to find they needed to share. It was decided Ellie and Mia would room together as would Gwen and Jane. The small kitchen immediately brought a comment from Ellie. 'Pretty cramped to cater for all of us.'

'I believe there are some local restaurants,' Mr Brookner said 'but we would be wise to prepare our own food. There's a range of fresh food — eggs, fish, chicken, fruit and that sort of stuff — to be had at a local market and the Government has organised a pass for us to purchase red meat, flour, salt, sugar and the like from the American food store.'

'We'll need to take it in turns to shop and cook,' Ellie said, scanning the range of pots and pans hanging over the stove. 'I hope you men are up for it.'

Dr Townsend said, 'I can cook the basics. Nothing flash.'

'I was hoping you might treat us to some Indian food,' Mia said and Jane could not prevent the colour coming into her cheeks.

'I regret to say one clear distinction has been made between us,' Brookner said. 'It has been arranged that our clothes will be laundered by local staff while you nurses are expected to do your own washing.'

'I haven't seen a washing machine,' Ellie said.

'I suppose we'll make do in the shower,' Gwen said resignedly.

Next morning, they set off to make their first visit to the hospital. Jane enjoyed the sight of local families sitting outside their small houses eating breakfast. The children who approached them with beaming smiles and greeted them in piping voices were charming. Her delight with the children was not dimmed by the need to hop over the untreated sewage which crossed their path. They turned a corner and saw the hospital ahead of them.

It comprised a series of single-story white stucco buildings with ochre tiled roofs. The buildings stood among trees Jane could not identify and were separated by unpaved walkways. Young children played in the open spaces. They provided an air of exuberance Jane had not seen at a hospital before. 'Where do all these children come from?' she asked.

'I'm told there's an orphanage next-door which has no outdoor space,' Brookner said.

The scenes which met them within the wards were not as benign. Some of the patients lay on stretchers on the floor. Most of the beds had at least two occupants and children were squashed in up to five at a time. The wards were crowded, not only with patients, but also family members and friends. One of the largest buildings was a maternity centre. Jane, who had almost no experience of childbirth, was surprised by this discovery, her theatre involvement inclining her to think only of surgery. She chastised herself for needing to be reminded that children were born in all conditions including war zones. The surgical suite was much smaller and had no more than basic equipment.

Their survey was interrupted by cries and moans from the hospital entrance where they found a stream of badly injured people arriving. They ranged in age from the elderly to young children. A few came by car, more were on wheeled bicycles or in pedicabs and some were carried by distressed relatives or friends. Some had lost limbs, others had severe gashes to their bodies and others grotesque head wounds. Blood was everywhere. Jane stood among the chaos dumbfounded by what she was seeing. Had these people been caught in crossfire or was there a bomb blast? Is this what confronted Danny every day? Is that why he wrote so little and never mentioned his involvement in battle?

'Sister Glover, come with me,' Dr Townsend said. He hurried her to the surgical suite. 'We'll be able to get by running two operations at a time but I'll have my work cut our keeping everything under control. I'll need you to back me up, by keeping a lookout for any adverse signs. Before that you should set up the IV while I sort out the gas.' Almost as an afterthought he said, 'See if you can find any gowns, masks and gloves.'

A succession of difficult and diverse operations was carried out as quickly as possible. Despite needing to maintain her concentration on the condition of the patients, Jane was able to observe how competently Ellie and Mia assisted the surgeons. That was not the end of their duties. At the conclusion of each operation they had to carry the survivors on stretchers to reach Gwen who was in charge of the recovery area. Their path was down slippery steps and across what had become a muddy yard in the afternoon monsoon. Returning on one occasion, Ellie gave a laugh and said, 'Hey Mia, Saturday night back in Casualty at the Alfred will be a breeze after this.'

The work continued into the early evening, by which time Jane had become so enmeshed in her duties that it came as a surprise when no more patients were brought for attention. Mr Brookner surveyed his dishevelled colleagues and said, 'We probably did pretty well to lose only two of them but I'm worried a couple more may not last the distance. Next time I hope we can be better organised before we start. Let's go and see how our patients are doing.'

All Jane could think was, 'Next time? What have I got myself into?'

She became conscious of Dr Townsend standing beside her. 'Pity we can't call on Mrs Gupta,' he said.

'Oh, I'm sorry.'

'What?'

'I shouldn't have told the other nurses about you going to be restored by Mrs Gupta.'

He glanced at her with an expression she couldn't read. 'She told me you'd been in to see her. I'm glad she could help you as well.' Jane hoped he didn't think she had gone looking for him. 'We'd better go and see how they're doing in recovery,' he said.

Recreation

Danny left in a small convoy of trucks carrying those sections granted leave. Their lodgings were in an old three-storey villa on the shoreline of Vung Tau. It was surrounded by a high fence topped with barbed wire but, more encouragingly, carried a large sign across the front of the building proclaiming: 'WELCOME TO THE VUNG TAU R AND R CENTRE'. Apparently, whoever painted the sign preferred recreation to convalescence.

After stowing their rifles and changing into civies, they were keen to begin exploring the town but had to sit through a lecture in which they were called upon to act as ambassadors for Australia and do nothing to bring their country into disrepute. They were instructed to remain within the patrolled areas and approved establishments. The audience came to life when told they would be issued with condoms and warned that the consequences of failing to use protection would almost certainly be long-lasting and painful. After a final edict that the curfew was absolute, they were free to go.

Pug Preston, a corporal from another company who was an old friend of Smacka, came over to him and said in his gruff voice, 'You and Taffy set?' He was a bulky man with the square head and the neck of a rugby forward. Smacka had told them stories about Pug which portrayed him as a fine soldier who could become a wild man when off the leash. Danny, Skeeta and Simmo were glad to be left to find their own way around Vung Tau.

Immediately on leaving the Centre they were set upon by a horde of street children lugging wooden boxes packed with cigarettes, lighters and watches which they pressed the trio to buy. When unsuccessful there, the boys shifted to take on the role of money changers and some of them even offered their sisters who they said were 'very beautiful, very cheap.' Danny thought of the charming children in Binh Ba whose curiosity eventually overcame their shyness. These boys were neither shy nor curious, but their hard eyes and tense faces showed their desperation. Searching for a way to help them, he asked the smallest, 'How much for a thousand piastres?'

'That's not how you barter,' Skeeta said. 'Tell 'em what you're willing to pay and make it very low to start with.'

'You'd be much safer at one of the Cash Offices,' Simmo said.

'I was forgetting you worked for the National,' Skeeta said. 'Over here I reckon the black market is the place to go.'

The boys had been waiting impatiently for Danny to make up his mind. When another group emerged from the Centre, they left Danny and, like a flock of birds descending on the branches of the same tree, ran over to try their luck there. Danny and his mates turned to walk along the road into the centre of Vung Tau. From the ridge of a nearby hill a row of colonial villas looked down upon them. The buildings in the immediate vicinity of the Centre were far less impressive: some concrete block factory buildings and a scattering of small houses. Further along they passed a number of narrow lanes lined with huts and lean-tos which could have been put together with material from a tip. Fetid waste clogged the gutters of the lanes. The road itself contained an unending stream of cars, trucks, horse-drawn carts, motorcycles, pedicabs and bikes.

Closer to the centre of town they passed a few four-storey office buildings, a street market and a number of food stalls, the smell of frying mixing with the fumes from the choked traffic. The footpaths were no less crowded with local Vietnamese and servicemen from America, Australia, New Zealand and South Korea.

'One or two Charlies with a machine gun could make a good dint in the war effort here,' Simmo said. 'Or maybe drop the occasional mortar bomb on the town.'

'Nah,' Skeeta said. 'I've heard the VC like to keep the place ticking along. Even come in here themselves for a bit of R and C when they feel like it.'

The centre of Vung Tau was marked by a concrete and tile monument which bore on its face the flags of those nations supporting South Vietnam. Danny realised this must be what Smacka had meant when he told Pug he would meet him at the Flags. Down a nearby street they saw a plethora of bars offering food, drink and — as they soon found out — other services. Each of the bars had a narrow shopfront and carried a buzzing neon or brightly painted sign with its name. The names were all of a kind: Tex-Mex Bar, Hong Kong Bar, Blue Angel, Washington Bar, Sydney Bar. So was the layout of each: a narrow counter at the back, a line of stools along one wall and several sets of tables and chairs taking up what remained of the space. They bore a resemblance to the small coffee shops which were springing up around Melbourne, although none of those would offer the battered stools, the scarred tabletops or the ill-matching chairs which were typical in Vung Tau.

On entering the World Number One Bar the bartender greeted them with, 'You like a girl? Very nice girl.'

'Three beers, thanks, mate,' Skeeta said. He turned to Danny and Simmo. 'I'm keen to give it a go but I reckon I'll check a bit further first.'

As if responding to him, a young woman with bright lipstick, a low-cut blouse and miniskirt sidled towards them carrying a tray with their three beers.

'You like I sit,' she said and made as if to drop onto Danny's lap.

Skeeta waved here away. 'He's already spoken for. And we'll concentrate on the beer for now.'

They visited two other bars to complete their round of drinks and returned to the main street where Simmo noticed a sign for Bob's Hong Kong Tailor Shop. 'I wouldn't mind a new shirt,' he told them. 'This one is a bit daggy.'

Danny knew Goldie was very clothes conscious and would not have been surprised to find him in Bob's. He had never heard Simmo say anything about his clothes except to complain at how quickly they disintegrated in the jungle; they all suffered that. Perhaps the bar girls were getting to him. They came out of Bob's with a new shirt each and a supply of piastres — as well as providing express made-to-measure shirts, Bob offered the best exchange rate Skeeta had found.

Further along the street they came to a dance hall from which came the sound of a slow waltz. 'Do either of you blokes like to dance?' Danny said. 'I haven't been to a dance for ages.'

'Yeah, I used to have some fun at the B and S balls we had around the district.' Skeeta smiled as if recalling fond memories. 'They could be pretty rough affairs at times, but if you struck it lucky you could end up with a sheila on a hay bale.'

'What's B and S stand for?' Simmo asked.

'Bachelor and spinster, of course.'

Danny could see that, despite no declared girlfriend, Skeeta's sexual experience was greater than his. 'Let's give it a try.'

Inside there was no shortage of scantily clad women willing to dance. Simmo and Skeeta appeared to be enjoying the experience but Danny was disappointed to find that achieving anything more than a shuffle with these girls was impossible. He was also embarrassed by the way they pressed themselves against his body and stroked him. The drinks the girls insisted they must share with them at the end of each dance made the whole exercise very expensive. When a fight broke out between two Americans who wanted to dance with the same girl, the trio decided to leave. Outside it was beginning to darken and Danny felt unsteady on his feet. He had drunk more today than ever before. 'Reckon we should get a feed,' he said.

'What about that place over there?' Skeeta said. 'The Grand Hotel.'

Inside they found Smacka, Taffy and Pug lolling at a table by the bar as if they had been there all day. Only Pug noticed them come in.

'Here are your nasho boys,' he said to Smacka, rousing him with a poke in the side. Come over boys and have a drink. It's your shout.' He waved to one of the bar girls. 'Hey, Chloe, brings us another round. Get one for yourself as well and join us. These guys'll pay.'

After Chloe returned with their beers, she sat sipping her drink and watching Pug expectantly. 'Ya look like cherry boys to me,' he said. 'Can't have that can we, Chloe? Time they learnt.' He frowned at Danny. 'What d'ya say?'

Danny glared at him and it was Skeeta who answered. 'He has a girlfriend in Oz. I'd be interested, though.' He grinned at Chloe who smiled back.

'What's that got to do with it? Chloe'll show him tricks he'll never learn back home. Get him ready for the big night when he's back with the girlfriend. She'll love it and so will he.'

Danny arrived in Vung Tau hoping for a release from the drudgery and danger of the past months. He expected to have fun and to relax without having to deal with any kind of pressure. The disenchantment which began on his encounter with the street boys had continued to grow during the day and become not just disenchantment but disgust, disgust with what the war was doing to Vung Tau and what it was doing to him and his friends. Now he was being told he should abandon his commitment to wait until after he was married and cheat on Jane by having sex with a prostitute. 'Leave her out of it, you bastard,' he spat.

Pug lifted his head and gave an ugly sneer. 'You're not having trouble getting it up, are you?'

Danny clambered to his feet and swung a punch which fell well short of the mark.

Smacka and Skeeta both dived to intercept him and the three ended in a tangle on the table in front of Pug who had got to his feet, emitting a low growl like a roused dog. As they freed themselves Smacka moved between Danny and Pug. 'Get out Dreamer. Go.' When Skeeta and Simmo began to follow, he snapped at them, 'Stay you two.'

They hesitated until Danny said, 'Yeah. I need some time on my own,' and walked unsteadily from the hotel. He had no idea which direction he should take and did not care. Passing the Flags, he was accosted by a herd of cab drivers, but he shook them off and continued away from the centre of town. Surely there must be some parts of Vung Tau he might enjoy. The villas he had seen on the ridge this morning might on closer inspection display the same elegance he had found at Binh Ba. Someone had said the Back Beach had good sand and surf. A swim might cleanse him of the filth he felt sticking to him as firmly as the mud of the jungle.

He was now sufficiently far from the centre of town that there were few lights, but a bright moon lit his path. A narrow track meandered off on the left. This one, unlike the lanes he had seen earlier, was not cluttered with rubbish and led to a number of small but neat houses from which he could see the glimmer of lamps.

The track turned to the right and he found himself on a low cliff above the sea. Framed by overhanging trees, a light breeze caused the moonlight to shimmer on the water. He drank in the beauty of the scene like a parched desert traveller reaching an oasis. He sensed rather than saw a movement near a bush at the edge of the cliff. Stepping towards the bush he trod on a twig which gave a sharp report as it snapped in two. From behind the bush a woman rose to face him.

'Don't be frightened,' he called. 'I will not harm you. You are quite safe.' He did not move towards her, concerned she would not understand the assurance he was trying to give her.

To his amazement she smiled at him and said, 'You are an Australian.'

Her voice was soft with a musical lilt and her pronunciation, unlike the other Vietnamese he had heard, was close to flawless. He could now see she was a young woman, with abundant dark hair, an oval face and high cheek bones. She was clothed in the folds of a white garment consisting of a tightly fitting silk tunic worn over trousers of the same material. Small and delicate, the moonlight transformed her to a porcelain figurine.

Eventually he managed to say, 'Yes I am. I'm sorry to disturb you.'

She took a few steps towards him. 'You are from Nui Dat?'

'Yes I am. I'm in Vung Tau for a couple of days leave.'

Now she came within touching distance. 'Do you know my brother, Tuan Mai? He is at Nui Dat.'

'Are you sure? I haven't seen any Vietnamese on our base.'

Her smile had gone and her voice carried a hint of impatience. 'He is in the ARVN, the army of South Vietnam. He is an interpreter. He goes with you to the villages.'

Danny had to revise his image of her. Certainly, she had the beauty and the tranquillity of a figurine but not the fragility. 'Ah, yes. I've seen the interpreters at work but I haven't met any of them.' Now he began to understand her grip of the language. Was it a family trait or had her brother taught her?

'I worry about him. I write but I do not know if he sees my letters.'

'You speak very good English.'

'I teach English and French in school but my brother is much better than me.' At last her smile returned. 'You Australians, you have a strange accent. That is how I know.'

Danny was happy to continue speaking with her for as long as she would stay. 'I'm sorry to barge in on you. Were you enjoying the view? It's superb.'

She turned to scan the sea as though checking his claim. 'I come to this place to pray.'

'You are a Buddhist?'

Again, the smile and he realised that part of its charm was the hint of sadness which lay below its surface. 'I am a Roman Catholic.'

'So am I.'

'Would you like to pray with me?' Danny was taken aback by her invitation. Since coming to Vietnam, he had got out of the way of regular prayer. It was something that had crept up on him through the scarcity of times when he could enjoy the privacy he needed to pray. His most satisfying prayers were not the ones said with other people at church or at school. Parroting someone else's words gave him no satisfaction and asking God to do him favours was just selfish. What he most valued was the chance to sit quietly and share his thoughts with God. What would this woman expect from him? Perhaps she sensed his reluctance because she said, 'I do not recite the rosary or speak out. I like to commune with God.'

Danny had not heard anyone use that term in years. How strange for him to hear it from a Vietnamese woman. 'I would be honoured to join you,' he said.

They moved to the cliff edge where Danny saw the flattened rock on which she had been sitting had room for both of them. After a time of silence, during which Danny found it hard to think beyond the miracle that had transformed his view of Vung Tau, she stirred and said, 'I must go now.'

She stood up and he rose reluctantly to join her. 'I don't even know your name,' he said. 'I'm Danny McBride.'

She bowed to him and said, 'My name is Linh Mai,' before turning away and walking towards the track that had brought Danny to the cliff. They made their way along the track in silence and Danny sensed that Linh Mai was wrestling with some private thoughts. When they came to a path, which led through a small garden to a box-like house with single windows either side of the front door, she said, 'This is where I live.'

He thought she might have been considering whether she should invite him in and he wondered if she lived alone but did not dare to ask. Instead he said, 'It has been a pleasure to meet you,' and inwardly cursed the stiffness of his words.

'There is one thing,' she said hesitantly. 'A favour. If I brought a letter to you. A letter for my brother. Would you give it to him when you return to Nui Dat?'

'No need to bring it to me. I could come here to pick it up tomorrow night. It would be a pleasure for me to enjoy such a beautiful view again.'

'That is kind.' She bowed again and walked away from him along the path to her door.

Danny was late rising the next morning — one of the benefits he had hoped for. The headache was less welcome but could not dim his pleasure in recalling each detail of his meeting with Linh Mai. He soon found that his headache was mild compared with those being suffered by Skeeta and Simmo, although they had compensating memories as well.

'Pug was right,' Skeeta said in a husky voice. 'That Chloe is really something else.'

'Yeah it wasn't what I was expecting,' Simmo said. The expression on his face suggested to Danny a complex mixture of guilt and pleasure. 'The girls I've been with in Sydney were nothing like that.'

Now Danny was the one to be surprised. First Skeeta and now Simmo showed themselves to be more experienced than him. Again, he thought of Jane's offer that night in her flat. Was he the only one out of step? 'I knew Skeeta was up for it, but you're a bit of a dark horse, Simmo.'

'Talking of dark horses, where did you get to last night?' Skeeta said. 'I assumed, when you left the Grand, you'd come straight back here and was worried about you, but Tich was still up when we got back and told me you came in not all that long before us. He also said you were surprisingly cheerful. I checked on you and there you were sleeping like a baby.'

'I went for a long walk. It cleared my head.' Skeeta gave Danny the look he had seen before: unconvinced by his story but unwilling to pump him — not yet anyway. 'I reckon some time on the beach and a swim would be good for all of us,' Danny said. 'What do you say?'

Before they could reply, Smacka joined them. He frowned at Danny and said, 'Just in case you're wondering, Dreamer, Pug doesn't bear grudges.'

Danny came out of the water, his headache gone, and plumped himself down beside Skeeta who was stretched out on the sand. 'Just what I needed.'

'Yeah not bad. I wondered if you were ever going to come out. And check out Simmo, the little lamb has gone right off.' Skeeta edged over so their heads were almost touching. 'While he's away with his dreams, tell me what you did get up to last night. I haven't seen you so cheerful since we got to Vietnam.' Danny hesitated, weighing his options. 'Come on mate. Just between us.'

'So long as it is. I did go for a long walk last night.' Danny described leaving the lights of central Vung Tau and finding his way to the cliff top. He had intended to give Skeeta a mere outline of his meeting with Linh Mai, but his pleasure at the memory of the moonlit encounter led him to give more detail than he intended.

'An ao dai,' Skeeta said.

'What?'

'An ao dai. That's what she was wearing. Goldie was salivating over them when we were coming down in the truck. He said they cover everything and hide nothing. You were a lucky sod to trip over her.'

Danny picked up a piece of dry seaweed and tossed it down the beach. 'Don't speak about Linh like that. She's not one of your bar girls. She's a devout Catholic and a teacher.'

'And don't take that tone with me.' Simmo stirred and Danny thought he was about to wake up but he settled down again. 'The ao dai is the traditional Vietnamese costume worn by ladies, not bar girls. Obviously, you had a good chat with her. I'm sure Miss Bluebell will enjoy reading about that. Make a nice change from your descriptions of jungle, mud and dead VC.'

'She has a brother in the South Vietnamese army who's an interpreter — one of those working with us at Nui Dat. That's why I need your help.'

'What do you mean?'

'Linh wants me to take a letter from her to him. I'm to pick it up tonight. I need to slip away without anyone getting the idea it would be fun for all of you to come with me or, worse still, follow me and jump out when I meet her.'

Skeeta eyed Danny uncertainly. 'You sure she's dinky-di?'

'Of course. Why wouldn't she be?'

'Charlie isn't above putting spies in Vungas. She might want to get a message to one of their undercover people on the base.'

Danny sneered. 'Devilish clever these VC. Unbeknown to me, they lure me to that isolated cliff-top just when this Vietnamese Marta Hari needs to get a message to her collaborators at Nui Dat.'

'OK. OK. But I reckon Miss Bluebell might have something to fear from Marta. She's in Bien Hoa now, isn't she?'

'I suppose so. I haven't had another letter since the one telling me she was going. I guess she's been pretty busy.'

Skeeta grinned at him. 'Maybe she's found a charming Vietnamese doctor who is taking up her time.'

They stayed on the beach until late afternoon, interspersing periods of sleep with a swim or a visit to the Beachcomber Club for a beer or a snack while they listened to the unceasing music from the juke-box. As evening approached, they walked once more into central Vung Tau, Skeeta and Simmo debating whether they should return to the Grand or seek an alternative venue for their pleasure. 'I reckon you guys need something to eat first,' Danny said. 'Something to build you up. How about that place over there — Faviora?'

'And see the massage parlour underneath,' Simmo said. 'Very convenient.'

After a plate of fish and chips, each of them was ready for action.

'I'll go for a walk,' Danny said. 'Explore another part of the town.'

The wink Skeeta gave him was so exaggerated Danny could not believe Simmo would have missed it. That he did suggested how focussed he was on the massage parlour.

Once on the street, Danny did not hesitate and arrived at the track sooner than he had the previous night. It occurred to him he might have to wait for Linh but she was already sitting on what he thought of as her rock. She rose as she heard him approaching and welcomed him with a small bow. 'Thank you for coming.'

Danny returned the bow, feeling awkward as he did so. 'I'm very pleased to be here.'

She offered him an envelope she had in her hand. 'This is the letter for my brother.' Danny put it in his pocket and was not surprised when she patted the rock and said, 'Would you like that we pray?'

'Yes, I would.'

Once they were seated together, she bowed her head and he stared into the sea, thinking of the many things he would like to learn about her. After about ten minutes she stirred and he said, 'I've been wondering how you and your brother became so fluent in English.'

'That was because of my father.'

'Your father? Was he a teacher of English like you?'

'He was a professor of languages at the University of Hanoi.' Her tone made it clear she saw her father as having held a prestigious position and was very proud of his achievement.

'Did you enjoy living in Hanoi?'

'We were happy at first.'

'At first?'

'Yes, before the French were defeated by the Viet Minh at Dien Bien Phu.'

'How did that change things for you?'

Danny was proceeding as he usually did when involved in a conversation that interested him, listening carefully to what was said and drawing out the speaker by commenting on what he heard or using it as a base for further questions. No one could doubt his interest was genuine, resulting in his informants being both flattered and happy to tell him more than they would have otherwise. This was not a technique he had consciously developed, but one he had employed from early in his life. Tonight, it led Linh Mai to give him a detailed account of each member of her family and to describe what had befallen them since those early days in Hanoi. She concluded by saying, 'So I came to live here and have been happy making the cottage my home.'

'You must be lonely, living here on your own?'

'I am not alone. The Church owns all the cottages along this lane and the nuns and other church workers who live around me have made me very welcome. Besides ...' She paused and the largest smile he had yet seen from her lit her face. 'Every night a handsome Australian comes along to listen to me as I chatter on.'

Danny did not return her smile, still captured by the tale she had told him. 'I feel greatly privileged you should share your story with me.'

'Now it is your turn.'

'What?'

'I want to hear about you and your family.'

'Not a lot to tell, really.' He checked his watch. 'Gee, I had no idea it was that late. I'm probably going to be locked out.'

He began to rise and she put out her arm to restrain him. It was the first time they had touched. 'You cannot go now. That is not fair.'

'I'm sorry, I must.'

'Tomorrow. You must come back tomorrow.'

'I will,' he promised. 'Tomorrow night. It's my last.'

He hurried away without accompanying her as he had done the previous night. He broke into a jog but on reaching the road slowed to a fast walk. He did not want to draw attention to himself. They had been warned the local police, the White Mice they were called by the Australians, had no sympathy for curfew breakers and, when faced with anything suspicious, did not hesitate to shoot. He arrived at the Centre without being challenged but found the gate locked and the fence insurmountable. A path at the side led past the back of the property to the beach where he had spent most of the day. The back gate was also locked so he continued down to the beach where he discovered two drunken figures stretched out on the sand amid a collection of bottles. He was not the only one locked out. Moving out of range of the drunks, he found a hollow in the dunes where he might be able to sleep and stay out of sight. It was like the shallow grave he had dug for the dead VC woman. Sleep did not come as he hoped and, as he lay listening to the surf sweeping onto the beach, he returned to the story of the Mai family and the particular significance so much of it had for him.

Obviously, Linh's father, Quan Mai, was a highly intelligent man.

His appointment at such a young age as Professor of Languages at the prestigious University of Hanoi, an institution founded in the early years of the twentieth century, confirmed that. But what really set him apart in Linh's view was his commitment to the importance of a shared language as a prerequisite for meaningful communication among people of different cultures. He also maintained it was impossible to gain a proper appreciation of a foreign culture without a deep understanding of that foreign language and literature. She said he proclaimed his beliefs with a religious zeal as strong as his own faith in the Roman Catholic Church. Linh's brother, Tuan, had once described their father as a man of twin faiths.

Linh had been very young when they arrived in Hanoi and it was much later that she gained an appreciation of what had occurred. When he first arrived at the University, the French had already been under challenge from the Viet Minh but maintained enough control, especially in the cities, for Quan to concentrate his efforts on teaching French language and literature as well as developing his abilities as a translator. Those abilities came to the notice of the French authorities in Hanoi and they sought him out increasingly when needing precise translation of important documents or sensitive interpretation for crucial negotiations. Linh's mother, Hahn, who had been a language student herself, was firmly convinced of the good Quan could do if given the power and opportunity. After their marriage, she devoted herself entirely to caring for Quan and their children. When Linh told Danny her mother was an elegant woman of great beauty, he pictured an older version of Linh. Although naturally shy, Hahn overcame her shyness to play a significant role in Quan's entry among the elite society of Hanoi. One of Linh's happiest memories of that time was of the handsome couple her parents made when dressed to attend a prestigious ceremony or social event.

Through his connections with the leaders in Hanoi, Quan was able to appreciate the diminishing power of the French and to see the strengthening involvement of the Americans. There had been a time when he hoped French would become a universal language, allowing his dream of direct communication between peoples of all races to be achieved. He even saw the Catholic Church as a vehicle through which French might be taught across the world. When he took his idea to the Catholic Bishops, they were unenthusiastic, focussed as they were on maintaining the power and authority of the Church under the growing threat from the Communists. Linh gave that small smile tinged with sadness Danny had seen before and said at the time she had thought her father noble to have such a grand vision.

She said, 'I can understand that ordinary people like us are better served by having more modest, more achievable goals, but I think the world needs visionaries like my father was then.'

Danny nodded his agreement and thought of how he had belatedly come to feel the need for a goal to which he could commit.

Quan realised that, if there were to be a universal language, it would be English, not French. He was already fluent in English and, unwilling to abandon his vision, shifted the emphasis in his teaching and scholarship to the English language.

During all this activity, he had not neglected the education of his children. He saw that they went to good schools and made time to give them extra lessons in both French and English. Linh had already told Danny her brother was superior to her in his command of English. Quan came to consider his son as his heir, the one who would continue and further his work after him. It occurred to Danny that both Linh and Tuan were fortunate to have inherited their father's aptitude for language. The picture Linh had given of their father suggested Quan would not have suffered them to pursue other directions and the warm family relations she had described could have been destroyed. Perhaps Sean had been let off fairly lightly by their dad.

After Dien Bien Phu, the privileged life enjoyed by the Mai family began to unravel. The Communists tightened their grip, particularly in the north of the country, and it was no longer an advantage to be closely connected with the French. Nor was it safe to be well-known as devout

Catholics. The partition of the country into two states was the last straw. On a night Linh carried vividly in her memory Quan returned to the house and told them they must pack up and go. Special arrangements had been made for them to leave Hanoi and travel to the south where the Government of the Republic of Vietnam, as it was called, were supportive of Catholics and the Premier himself a Catholic. Up until then Linh and her brother had been shielded from their parents' growing worries, so the announcement came as a shock. She was very sad to be leaving her friends, particularly when told there would be no time for farewells, and she was only consoled when she learnt they were to travel south on a French Air Force plane. She had never flown before and, misled by her knowledge of her father's position in Hanoi society, imagined the flight had been put on for their benefit alone.

The seething crowd at the airport soon disabused her. After hours of delay, her father succeeded in arranging for them to leave and she landed at Bien Hoa airport outside Saigon, expecting to be taken to their new house where she would have to make the best of it until their furniture and belongings arrived and she could start school. Instead they were bussed to a tent city which had been hastily thrown up on the outer fringes of Saigon. There they found a chaotic morass of refugees. They had little beyond what they brought with them, conditions were primitive, food was scarce and disease a constant danger. This was their home for the next three years.

Her father fell into deep depression, only saved by the extraordinary efforts of her mother who somehow managed to keep the family together, fed and clothed at a subsistence level and free from other than minor illness. Aid agencies, funded in the main by the United States, brought some relief and their circumstances improved marginally. Hahn prevailed on her husband to stir himself and undertake the education of their children for there was no school in the camp. Only years later did it occur to Linh that her mother was as much concerned to save her husband as she was to educate her children. The school gathered a number of students and brought Quan to the notice of the authorities who began to call upon his interpreting and translating skills when dealing with foreign aid agencies.

It was through these contacts that he learnt of the recent establishment of a university in the central highlands by the Council of Vietnamese Catholic Bishops. Immediately he regained some of his former energy and resolution. Just as he had on that last day in Hanoi, he told his family they must leave immediately and travel to Da Lat where they would live in much greater comfort and safety and he would be able to take up his academic career again. There was no plane this time and they reached Da Lat after an exhausting trip by bus and cart along roads that were never free from the threat of Viet Cong attack.

Immediately on arrival Quan went to the university where the welcome he received was far less effusive than he had expected. Linh well remembered him returning disappointed and angry with the reception he was given. For a start he was told the senior posts had already been filled by staff from South Vietnam and it was made clear to him that refugees from the north had little standing. Later it would become clear to the Mai family that this attitude was not unusual. Many of those who had been in the south for their entire lives saw no reason to share what were already limited resources and resented the newcomers being offered what they considered as their land and their jobs. At least the Da Lat University was more generous than that, offering Quan a junior position at a modest salary. His dignity offended, he was on the brink of refusing the offer until Hahn convinced him to swallow his pride and think of the post as a first stepping stone. They found a cottage which was far smaller than their villa in Hanoi but a palace compared with their tent in Saigon. Hahn set about turning it into a comfortable home while Linh and Tuan returned to school. Quan again took up tutoring them in English and French.

Linh remembered Da Lat as one of the happiest interludes in her life. Her voice took on a new zest as she described 'The City of a Thousand Pine Trees' as it was called by some. Located in the Central Highlands and blessed with a mild climate, early in the century it was designated by the French as the site for a resort centre. In addition to the abundant trees the French endowed the city with boulevards and villas, health facilities, parks, schools and even a golf course. Children from across Vietnam had come to boarding schools in the city where they were taught by French priests, nuns and expatriates. No longer serving the whole of the country, the schools remained and were able to provide a sound education for Linh and Tuan. The Church resumed its place in their lives. Linh liked the French nuns who taught at her school and she made some good friends.

Her father's drive to improve the teaching of languages in his department met with growing hostility from those senior to him who lacked his ability and experience. Seeing himself blocked, he returned with vigour to the notion of grooming Tuan to be his academic heir. It was only when she was older that Linh could see that the long and intense sessions between her father and brother fulfilled a need in her father but were far less congenial for a teenager with a variety of interests. One of these was the military.

Da Lat had been the home of the elite Vietnamese Military Academy and, while it was no longer active, a unit of the South Vietnamese army was stationed in the town. The military tradition left its mark on the boys and men of Da Lat, some of whom aspired to make a career in the army. Among them were a number of Tuan's friends. As Tuan approached the end of school, his father readied him for his entry to the University. It came as a blow to Quan's pride and a frustration to him when the Languages Department refused to grant Tuan advanced standing and insisted he enrol as a first-year student. After fuming for a day or so, Quan decided he must suffer this latest example of the Department seeking to assuage their jealousy of him, so that Tuan could be set on the path to his academic career.

What followed was the most bitter argument between father and son Linh ever heard. Tuan would have none of it, shouting that he already knew everything they taught at undergraduate level. His father sought to persuade him by pointing out he still had a lot to learn but this tactic

176

misfired when Tuan, either genuinely or as a ploy — Linh had never been sure — construed his father's remark as evidence he could never aspire to reach the level of his father. He said he was far better suited to joining the army and made it sound like a religious calling: defending the Catholics of Vietnam against the attacks of the Communists. Danny was delighted to hear this. He and Tuan had a shared commitment. He looked forward to meeting him. Their father was furious with Tuan and only Hahn's intervention prevented Quan from immediately sending his son from the house. Nevertheless, he departed soon afterwards and joined up. Danny found an odd irony in the parallel: Tuan had fallen out with his father because of his commitment to the war against the Communists; Sean because of his opposition.

After Tuan's departure, Hahn became convinced her son would soon be killed and was obsessed with the need to ensure her remaining child would be safe. At the time the Viet Cong were gaining increasing power across much of South Vietnam and she feared they would soon attack Da Lat. In fact, Linh explained, the presence of the detachment of the South Vietnamese army in the city discouraged the Viet Cong from outright attack and, while their control of the villages around Da Lat increased, the city remained undamaged and able to carry on much as it had up until then, a situation which continued to the present. Danny recalled someone — was it Goldie or Butch? — telling him the French had renamed Vung Tau as Cap St Jacques and turned it into a seaside resort for bureaucrats from Saigon and plantation owners from Phuoc Tuy. No one could claim, as Linh did for Da Lat, that much of that colonial charm remained. The damage had not been inflicted by the Communists but by the presence of the foreign forces sent to protect the South.

Hahn learned from one of the nuns who taught Linh that a similar school operated in Vung Tau and, believing Vung Tau to be much safer than Da Lat, she agitated for Linh to complete her schooling there. Her father raised no objection and Linh arrived four years ago. She had been here ever since. Danny realised her language skills must have been immediately apparent because she was asked to help with the teaching of language subjects before she reached the end of her own schooling. Subsequently she became a full-time teacher and had continued in that role for the past two years. Her mother would have liked to join her but her father clung to his menial role at the university and they remained in Da Lat. Travelling between the two cities had become increasingly difficult and dangerous, so she had to make do with an occasional letter from her mother and even more sporadic communication with her brother. Even so, when she heard what was happening in the country, she felt blessed to have been spared.

Danny had been deeply moved by Linh's story and the way she had told it. He felt great sympathy for her parents: the flawed man with such talents and dreams, his ever-faithful wife who had watched over the family through good times and bad. He appreciated his link with Tuan and was inspired by the faith which sustained Linh. He owed it to people like these to do all he could to rid them of the scourge of Communism.

When Danny entered the Centre early next morning, he was immediately spotted by Smacka. 'Where the hell have you been, Dreamer?'

'I've been sleeping on the beach.'

'I can see that. You look pretty much like you did the first day I saw you, after you slept on the train. But that isn't what I meant. How did you miss the curfew?'

Danny certainly did not want to give Smacka any details. 'I lost track of time.'

'Typical!' Smacka scoffed. 'Hey Skeeta, come over here.'

Skeeta came over to join them without saying a word.

'Now Skeeta, don't let this dreamy mate of yours out of your sight for the rest of the day. And remember the truck leaves for Nui Dat sharp at sixteen hundred. Miss that and you'll be on a charge.'

'Sixteen hundred?' Danny said in a shocked voice. 'This afternoon?'

'Made other arrangements, have you?' Smacka said.

'I didn't think we were going back until tomorrow morning.'

'Let Skeeta do the thinking for you today. He's better at it.' Smacka turned away and left them staring at one another.

'Fancy a swim?' Skeeta asked.

After the swim Danny felt refreshed but no happier. Skeeta waited until they were sitting on the sand to begin his questions. 'Did you spend the night with her?'

'No, of course I didn't,' Danny said in a shocked voice. 'I just lost track of the time. Linh told me about her family and how they had to leave Hanoi. Her parents are extraordinary people who have really had a bad time. When ...' Danny could see Skeeta had no interest in Linh's family. 'I'm pretty sure Linh shared more of her story with me than she has with anyone else and it was a great relief for her to do it. That's why I'm so upset we're going back this afternoon. I promised I'd go back tonight. She'll think I welshed on her. She's had more than enough disappointments without me adding to them.

'Very noble of you.' Skeeta stared at Danny who could tell his mate thought he hadn't heard the whole story. However, when Danny didn't react to his taunt, Skeeta said, 'How can we get in touch with her today and explain?'

'She'll be at the school where she teaches. I've got no idea where that is.'

'But you know where she lives.'

Danny thought of the neat cottage. Would he ever see inside it? 'Yeah. She lives in this little cottage. It's got ...'

'Right.' Skeeta climbed to his feet. 'I didn't bring a pen or paper down to Vungas, but we can get that from the office. Write a letter to her explaining the army has called you back early — no need to explain you got the timing wrong — and we'll deliver it so she'll get it when she arrives home from school.'

Danny jumped up, reinvigorated. 'Great idea. No need for you to come. You'll want a farewell performance in town, I guess.'

'You heard what Smacka said. I'm sticking with you.'

It was several weeks since Jane's traumatic introduction to the hospital at Bien Hoa and she was still coming to terms with the commitment she had made. While there had been nothing to match the scale of that first day, which it turned out had been caused by the Viet Cong blowing up a bus with satchel charges, the work remained extraordinarily demanding. Surgeries ranged from dealing with blown off limbs, to treating hernias, removing appendices and repairing damaged thumbs or fingers. The pressures on the surgeons meant they placed much more reliance on the nurses to prepare patients for surgery and Jane welcomed this.

Almost everything was in short supply. Drapes, swabs, gloves and dressings often ran out. There was no morphine, little pethidine, few antibiotics. IV sets and fluids were scarce. At times they ran out of blood and could use only saline. One of the doctors suggested they should seek blood from the relatives of the patients who, once they understood what was required, were happy to volunteer. The process almost came to an untimely end when Mia was seen to be drinking tomato juice from a can they had obtained from the US store and was thought to be swilling blood. Gwen saved the day by persuading one of the Vietnamese to drink from her can and confirm the 'blood' was indeed tomato juice.

A bureaucrat in Australia had arranged for the team to be provided with nylon uniforms and briefing notes on how to dress for Embassy functions. While no one received an invitation to the Embassy, the briefing notes caused no harm. On the other hand, in the tropical climate the nylon uniforms became sweat boxes and were quickly discarded. Indeed, the surgeons were often to be found operating in shorts and thongs.

Water was always a problem — either too much or too little of it. Leaking roofs diverted the daily monsoon rain onto the floors of the hospital so that even the doctors needed to help mop up. The main water supply was unreliable and frequently turned off during the early afternoon and the night. Washing of patients often took place under taps. When the water did run, sinks often blocked.

Amid all this chaos the character of the Vietnamese people shone through. Forced to lie in squalid beds without a change of the clothes, the stoicism of the patients amazed Jane. The limited number of Vietnamese nurses, despite their lack of training, did their best in trying circumstances and responded well when Jane and her colleagues had time for teaching. An essential part of the treatment of the patients was provided by their families and friends who tended them and brought food to supplement what the hospital kitchen could provide.

The difficulties caused by lack of a common language were ameliorated to an extent by the unlikely presence of a Vietnamese lad who had attached himself to the hospital. Perhaps he was a refugee from the next-door orphanage. No one knew. They soon appreciated, though, that his quaintly accented English was far better than any of the Australians' Vietnamese and he was often called in to act as interpreter. The tendency for all the patients and their families to call the nurses 'doctor' was one error Jane and her colleagues made no attempt to correct.

Jane had also formed a very positive view of the local staff who did the cleaning, cooking and laundry. In the kitchen they prepared large quantities of rice and various forms of soup in vats set in concrete and heated by wood fires. Avoiding the stray dogs waiting for any spillages, they transferred the food into bowls for the patients. Perhaps the most amazing of the achievements of the local staff was the performance of the laundry. In large concrete tubs of cold water, they hand washed everything, including all the linen from the theatre and the wards, hung it on a barbed wire fence to dry and produced spotless white sheets. Jane and the other nurses could not fathom how they did it.

'You up for the party next week?' Mia asked Jane

'What party?'

'Hasn't Ellie told you? Some of the doctors at the US base hospital are coming over to join us.'

'How did she manage that?'

'You know we're not the first team from the Alfred to come to Bien Hoa. When some of the girls who had been here were telling us about it, they mentioned how the Yanks like to socialise and gave us some contacts at the air base.'

Jane was amazed. 'So, you knew what it would be like before you arrived and yet you still came.'

Mia gave Jane a disparaging smile. 'You've got a lot to learn. After you've done your time in Casualty like we have, nothing much can faze you. We saw this as a great chance to get out of the routine of the Alfred, see a bit of the world and have a good time. What brought you here?'

Jane hesitated. She wasn't going to say it was a spur-of-the-moment decision triggered by the disappointment on Gordon Townsend's face. 'I thought it would be good experience and ...' Again, she hesitated. 'My boyfriend is a nasho over here with the army.'

'One of those poor buggers, eh.' Mia laughed. 'And I thought you were after Townsend. What's your boyfriend's name?'

'Danny. Danny McBride.'

'Don't reckon you have much chance of catching up with him while you're here.' Mia paused to eye Jane. 'No reason for holding back with these Yanks tonight. If we play our cards right, we'll have a great time and get invited back there. Apparently, if we get them properly interested, they'll help us out with stuff from all those excess stores and equipment they have over there.'

'How far do we have to go to achieve that?' Jane asked in a dubious tone.

'Don't know. But it could be fun finding out.'

Jane had been to quite a few hospital parties but never one like this. It wasn't the location — the living room into which they were squeezed was no smaller than the rooms in which some of the nurses' parties had been held in Melbourne. The collection of bottles on the kitchen table was not unusual, either — until the Americans arrived with their Bourbon. In Melbourne there tended to be a majority of women hoping to attract the attention of one of the men who turned up. This time, with their numbers swelled by the four Yanks, there were twice as many men as women. It was common for one or two doctors to come to those parties but not for every one of the males to be a doctor or surgeon.

Nor did they have the likes of Mr Brookner presiding. Jane had been impressed by the way in which Brookner commanded attention no matter the circumstances. He was not an arrogant man — in fact quite personable — but everyone deferred to him. It was the same tonight. Immediately on arrival the visitors presented themselves to him, giving their names and ranks with that air of cordial formality the Americans managed with such ease. When Brookner responded by introducing the home team, his guests had difficulty taking their eyes from Ellie. The vivid green blouse she wore was moulded to her figure and complemented her shining red hair. 'We should get you a drink,' Brookner said. He ushered the guests into the kitchen and individual conversations started up. The senior American, Major Conway, soon disengaged from Brookner and went in search of Ellie.

The party was already taking the standard form: a group of men around the bar (the kitchen table in this instance) with the women collected in the living room awaiting the attention of the men. Jane, who noticed with mild disappointment that Gordon Townsend was one of those content to drink in the kitchen, was approached by the largest American, Calvin Schultz, a bear of a man who hailed from Beaumont, Texas. He was surprised to find she had never visited the States and told her she would find a warm welcome in Beaumont. Or at least that is what she thought he said. Calvin had the slowest drawl she had ever heard, most words including extra syllables. He also had a way of leering at her which gave her the creeps.

A few weeks earlier, Graham Fisher had unearthed a record player and a pile of records, including recent ones from the Beatles and Neil

Diamond, as well as some big band dance music. He put on a record and asked, 'Now, who's going to dance with me?'

Jane put down her drink and went to join him. 'OK. I like to dance.' She could escape Calvin's attention and, besides, it felt like years since she had enjoyed a dance with Danny.

She was disappointed that Fisher had none of Danny's style but he persisted and others began to join them. Ellie insisted that Chuck, as Major Conway had become, dance with her. Another of the Australian surgeons, George Brown, invited Mia to dance and as one record followed another most of the party joined in. Jane noticed that only four had yet to participate. She was relieved to see Calvin retreat to the kitchen. Less happily she saw Townsend and Brookner locked in conversation and, worst of all, Gwen being ignored. No, wait a minute. Townsend had left Brookner and was leading Gwen onto the floor. Good for Gordon. Surely she could use his first name tonight. The Americans were all doctors and they insisted on using first names.

As the party continued, Jane enjoyed herself much more than she had expected. She was a little miffed Gordon had not asked to dance with her — he had with the other nurses — but she hit it off with two of the other Americans. Jerry and Hal, were good dancers — not as good as Danny — and it was great fun to dance with them. After Hal had insisted on doing the Twist and she had matched him, he introduced her to what he called the Madison and they ended up putting on a solo performance to great applause. It was strange to dance with the Australian doctors, particularly those with whom she had worked closely, but it was fun. After her gaffe over Mrs Gupta, Gordon probably wanted to avoid any further gossip. Or was he more deeply offended by her indiscretion than he had shown?

It was getting late when Calvin rolled out of the kitchen and up to Jane. 'Ya all haven't given me a dance,' he slurred and didn't wait for an answer, grabbing her and pushing her into the centre of the room. Gripping her right hand too tightly and pressing himself along the length of her body, he began a slow gyration out of time with the beat. Jane shuffled along with him as she sought unsuccessfully to loosen his grip of her. She grimaced as he slid his right hand down her spine and began to explore the separation between her buttocks. Mia had said it would be fun to find out how far they needed to go to get the interest of the Americans, but this was no fun. Jane frowned at him and stiffened to show her displeasure. If he persisted, she would stomp on his foot. Her stiletto would make a good weapon. She would probably undo any good Mia and Ellie might have done, but that couldn't be helped. Suddenly she felt his arm release her and their bodies separate.

'Wassa you doin, ya bum?' Calvin said.

'Sorry, it's my turn,' Gordon said in his quiet, firm voice.

Jane turned to find him holding Calvin's wrist and staring at him with that unruffled expression she knew well.

Calvin lifted himself and reared over Gordon. 'Piss off you ...'

'That's enough, Calvin.' This time the voice was not quiet and conveyed even greater firmness. Major Conway was not as heavily built as Calvin but had the height to bore straight into his eyes. Calvin looked as though he was about to confront his senior officer but thought better of it and wandered back into the kitchen.

'I apologise for my colleagues' behaviour,' Conway said to Jane. He turned to Mr Brookner who, like everyone else, had come into the room. 'I think it's time we left. We've greatly enjoyed your hospitality.' He smiled around the gathering. 'And look forward to having you come to us very soon.'

Next day Jane was checking on the condition of the patients who had been in surgery that morning when Gwen approached her with a quizzical expression. 'Someone to see you,' she said.

'Someone to see me? Who is it?'

'Outside the entrance.'

When Jane reached the road outside the hospital, she saw Calvin leaning against the bonnet of a US Air Force van. He straightened himself and in an abashed drawl said, 'I came to say sorry to ya. I reckon you're a might pretty girl and I'd had a bit much.'

Embarrassed by the meeting and sure others would be watching, Jane mumbled her acceptance of his apology and told him not to worry. She went to turn away, but he said, 'Wait. Somethin' to show ya.' He led her to the rear of the van. 'Major Conway reckons we could help ya out with your shortages. So here ...' He threw open the doors to reveal an array of medical equipment together with drugs, antibiotics, IV sets and fluids, surgical gloves and masks.

After the material had been safely stored and Calvin had gone, Ellie whacked Jane on the back. 'Well done, my girl. I put our sob story across to Chuck Conway and let him know how a little help would ensure my continuing good will in his direction but I didn't expect to score anything like this the first time. If you hadn't got that oaf, Schultz, over-excited, we wouldn't have done nearly so well.'

'I didn't do anything. I was about to stomp on him.'

'You didn't have to do anything. A pretty youngster like you only has to stand around to incite the lust of types like Schultz and bring out the protective instincts of men like Conway and our own Dr Townsend.'

'Now you know how far you have to go,' Mia said with a smirk.

'It wasn't fun finding out.'

'Maybe next time.'

Later in the day during a break in activity, Gordon Townsend stood resting against a bench. When he saw Jane approaching him, he looked away as though wishing not to be disturbed, but she was undeterred and said, 'Thank you for coming to my rescue last night.'

'You didn't mind me interfering?'

'Mind?' Jane's voice rose to match her indignation. 'Why should I mind? You don't think I enjoyed being pawed like that?'

'No. No, of course not. I thought you might have preferred to handle him yourself.'

'Handle him? He was the one doing the handling.' Jane saw she needed to laugh to show him she was joking. She thought of how often she told Danny to lighten up. 'Am I such a dragon?'

'What?'

'Apart from Mr Brookner, who didn't dance at all, you were the only other of our doctors who didn't dance with me.'

'I was about to,' he said defensively, 'but those Americans monopolised you and when I saw how well you danced with Hal I didn't like to intrude.'

'I saw you dancing with Gwen and the others. You're no slouch. Next time I'll ask you if you don't ask me.' Again, she laughed and this time he managed a grin.

The Reconnaissance Platoon

Immediately Danny arrived back at Nui Dat he went in search of Tuan Mai. The small detachment of interpreters, the only Vietnamese allowed to stay on the base, was housed in a far corner that Danny had trouble locating. Eventually he found a man who was able to tell him Tuan was involved in a cordon and search operation with 6RAR and was expected back before nightfall. Danny left a message asking Tuan to contact him.

He was in his tent after mess that evening, reading a letter from his mother which had been waiting for him on his return from Vung Tau. She told him that Sean had not been called up for National Service but had been accepted to do his Dip. Ed. next year. It was clear she was pleased about both. Danny guessed Sean would now be free to re-join the protests against the war in Vietnam — something that would not help him return to favour with his father. Danny's attention was drawn away from the letter when he heard the voice of Pug Preston outside the tent. 'What are you doing here? These are Aussie lines.' Through the entrance to the tent, Danny could see Pug standing over a Vietnamese man.

'Hey,' Danny called as he scrambled out of the tent, 'Are you Tuan Mai?' The man nodded and Pug glared at Danny. 'I have a letter for you. A letter from your sister.'

The discomfort on Tuan's face changed to surprise. 'A letter from my sister?'

'Did you invite him over here,' Pug growled.

Danny ignored him. He stepped back into the tent and came out with the letter. 'Here it is.' He held it out for Tuan to take. In a cheery voice which was aimed to reassure the Vietnamese but also — he hoped — to mystify Pug, Danny said, 'It's quite a story. Let me walk back with you and I'll explain how I became a postman.' He steered Tuan away from Pug and dropped his voice so Pug would not be able to hear him. Tuan listened attentively but said nothing as Danny told him of his chance meeting with Linh when escaping the grotesquery of Vung Tau. Danny laughed as he described how Linh had recognised his accent and asked if he knew her brother. He made no mention of their second evening together.

Tuan did not share his amusement. 'What is in the letter?'

'I have no idea,' Danny said.

'Why did she give it to you?'

'She's worried that her letters are not getting through to you and saw a chance to make sure this one did.'

'I get her letters. She has no need to worry.'

Tuan Mai's prickly attitude disappointed and irritated Danny. This was the man he had wanted to meet: the Roman Catholic who shared his commitment to protecting the South from the Communists. 'Maybe it's because she receives few responses from you.'

This brought a change to Tuan's face. 'Do you write home much?'

Danny knew he had a good point. 'You mean it's hard to find much to say which you're happy to tell them?'

Tuan nodded. 'My sister is a good girl. She is very different to many of the girls you meet in Vung Tau.'

Angry at Tuan Mai's insinuation, Danny said, 'I know that. I admire and respect her. She has nothing to fear from me.' Danny thought he sounded like an actor in a period movie and wished he could have put it differently but the Vietnamese seemed satisfied.

'Thank you for delivering the letter.' He turned away.

Danny walked back to his tent where he found Pug and Smacka waiting for him.

'What d'ya mean bringing nogs into our lines?' Pug said.

'You mean the people we're fighting for and with.'

Smacka came between them, reminding Danny of his spat with Pug at the Grand. 'Take it easy both of you.'

'We're fighting here because that's what our government sent us to do,' Pug said. 'That doesn't mean we have to like or spend time with them.'

Danny saw Pug's behaviour at the Grand as symbolic of all that disgusted him about Vung Tau. 'Is that what you said to Chloe?'

Pug took a step towards him, clenching his fists. 'You're a cheeky bastard.'

Again, Smacka came between them. 'Shut it you two. Danny, go in the tent. Pug, come with me up to the boozer.'

A large contingent of Americans was scheduled to land at Vung Tau and make its way up Route 15 to Bien Hoa Province. Maintaining the security of Route 15 during the transit required a major operation. For a start, the VC had to be cleared from Nui Thi Vai, a jungle-clad mountain of 1500 feet which commanded a long stretch of Route 15 and was known to harbour a significant number of enemy soldiers. With straight deep faces to the north, east and west and a long ridge of lesser peaks to the south, the mountain also featured a Buddhist pagoda, a red-tiled building of grey granite, sited just below the summit. Fifth Battalion was given the task of clearing Nui Thi Vai and had five days in which to do it.

For Danny, the ride out to the vicinity of the mountain was unexpectedly pleasant. The dry season was almost upon them and the day was fine and sunny. Their trip along Route 15 took them past small villages of brick houses with cream-plastered walls and red-tiled roofs, some of them encircled by grass huts. As they came through each village, they saw women in conical straw hats with babies strapped to their backs. When children ran out to cavort and wave at the passing soldiers, Danny was reminded again of the contrast between those boys in Vung Tau and the ones he saw in the countryside.

Having been dropped on the road, they had to slog through thick scrub and marshy ground until they reached the foot of the mountain.

Next morning, the company was cautiously making its way up the southern slope of Nui Thi Vai when they heard a burst of gunfire and two loud explosions. They took up defence positions and waited. Eventually Smacka was able to tell them the forward platoon, which had been climbing a narrow track ahead of them, had been fired upon by VC snipers. Seeking to take cover, two of the men had stepped on mines laid beside the track. The VC had escaped while the wounded were being attended and a landing space found for the dust-off helicopter to pick up the casualties. The company was told to retire, since a substantial number of VC had been seen by another company and it was believed there could be an unexpected major force on Nui Thi Vai. Instead of participants, the men of 5RAR became spectators at a spectacular demonstration of military force.

First, the battalion mortars and artillery located on Route 15 began to pound the area. Shortly afterwards helicopter gunships arrived to unleash salvos of rockets. Undeterred by the heavy return fire this brought from the ground, the gunships swooped with door gunners spraying the black-clad figures who scuttled back into their bunkers. After the gunships departed an eerie silence took hold, soon broken by the scream of approaching F100s. The scream became a howl as they swooped and soared over the target area preparing for the bomb run. The planes came one behind the other across the hillside, released their bombs and zoomed into a near-vertical climb to avoid crashing into the slope. Two 500-pound bombs glided down before the deafening shock wave of their explosion. The planes circled, their wings flashing in the late afternoon sun, and returned to deposit a barrage of cluster bombs which made a dull thud as their outer cases exploded and sent a swathe of bomblets across the slope.

After the aircraft departed, the artillery and mortars kept up pressure until, just on dusk, the F100s returned to repeat their earlier performance prior to a grand finale with Napalm. On impact the Napalm canisters exploded in a glowing ball of orange and crimson, sending showers of flaming jelly which sucked the oxygen from the air and left a cloud of suffocating vapour.

Night had fallen, denying the ground troops any chance of following up the air attack, so the VC who had survived were able to retreat, harried by the mortars which continued to fire through the darkness. Early next morning the battalion resumed its sweep through Nui Thi Vai. The VC had gone, taking their dead and injured with them but leaving much behind. Danny's section was part of the force which came upon a major VC installation. Under camouflage nets made by sewing thousands of leaves into massive quilts, they found a complex of buildings and, under the buildings, a maze of tunnels containing workshops, a hospital, a training centre and a huge arsenal. The range of items which had been left behind included tools, clothing, several hundred tubes of penicillin, surgical packs, beds, ten tons of rice and several sacks of documents which included records and registers, training pamphlets and news sheets. The arsenal contained anti-tank mines, anti-tank rockets, grenades and a horde of other ammunition.

'Got to hand it to them,' Smacka said. 'I reckon Charlie could have stayed here for years and a small ground army wouldn't have been able to shift them. It was only when we turned on that fireworks show yesterday that the survivors sneaked away.'

'It'll take us ages to go through all of this stuff, take what we want and destroy the rest,' Taffy said.'

Smacka shook his head. 'No time for that. We've got to get down along the road. The Yank convoy comes through in a day or so.'

Danny was incredulous. 'You mean we're going to leave all of this?'

'We'll be back, I bet,' Smacka said.

Skeeta pulled a face. 'And so will the VC.'

A fortnight later on the night of their return to Nui Dat as they sat in the mess, Danny took the lead in the conversation. This was unusual but his experience on Nui Thi Vai had crystallised a concern which had been growing within him for some time. 'When we first got to Nui Thi Vai we slogged around the jungle for the best part of a week, two guys stepped on mines and we didn't fire a shot. All the real work was done by the boys with the bombs and the big guns. We've been struggling round the jungle for months without achieving anything much and the first time we find a sizable force we sit back and call in the heavies to do it for us. Is that all we're good for?'

Smacka grinned at Danny. 'Come on Dreamer. That force we found on Nui Thi Vai was much bigger than anything we were expecting. The boss reckoned we weren't set up to deal with them on our own and didn't have the time for a planned stoush. I reckon he was right. After we'd seen the Yanks safely along Route 15, we went back and had a good go — successful, too. You heard what the boss had to say. We captured a lot of useful material, blew up the buildings on the surface and laced the tunnels and caves with tear gas crystals so no one can use 'em for months.'

'Yeah, but the bulk of the VC got away, as they always do when we run across more than a few. More often we set up ambushes and patrol with no contact at all.'

Smacka grinned again. 'Yeah? Well, the boss agrees with you.'

'What?'

'He's setting up a new unit: a reconnaissance platoon. The platoon is to scout up to two hours ahead of the main units. It'll gather intelligence and report back to HQ. It will close with the enemy only if unavoidable or the force is small. This is his way of making the whole battalion more effective, like you want. Are you going to volunteer?'

'Me?'

'It's what you wanted, isn't it? You're the fittest guy in the section and you're the best shot.'

Danny shook his head. 'I don't know. I'm pretty happy where I am.'

Smacka widened his eyes. 'Didn't sound like that a few minutes ago. Let me know if you change your mind. They're after a squad of about forty volunteers which will go to Vungas to train and then be cut down to twenty-eight, so no-one's a shoe-in.'

'Training in Vungas?'

'Not in the town of course, Dreamer, but quartered at our base there.'

As Skeeta and Danny were walking back to their tent, Skeeta said, 'I thought the mention of Vungas would get you in.'

Danny squinted up at the sky. 'It might be better to be in a recce platoon than keeping on doing what we're doing.'

'Do you reckon they'd take me as well?' Skeeta asked

'You've got the best eyes in the section if not the company. Ideal for a recce platoon, I'd say.'

When Ellie invited Jane to accompany her on her regular trip to pick up medical supplies from the official Vietnamese Medical Store in Saigon, Jane was surprised. Previously Ellie had taken along one of the Vietnamese staff. As Ellie drove their jeep along the crowded road, she explained. 'I like almost every one of the Vietnamese people I deal with at the hospital. These bureaucrats at the Government Store come from another planet. Each time I go, I have to fill out five forms. I hand them in and they tell me it will be two weeks to fill the order. When I return in two weeks, they say it'll be another two weeks. Next time they say the order has been filled and I already have whatever it was I included on those forms. So, I've come up with a different strategy. When we get there, you'll see it's a bit like a warehouse with umpteen shelves. In front of the shelves is a desk where a lazy bastard spends the day doing nothing but being difficult with whoever comes in. You'd think his job is to make sure no one gets what they need.

'Lately I've taken to arriving with a collection of bags and several packets of cigarettes as well as my forms. I hand over my forms and, while the guard pretends to read them, I edge away leaving my

Vietnamese accomplice to chat with him and ply him with cigarettes. Meanwhile I slip into the shelves, take what I've asked for and fill my bags before returning to hear why I can't have anything. I'm pretty sure the guard isn't so stupid that he doesn't know what I'm up to, but he prefers a chat to stirring himself and he likes the cigarettes even more, so he's been letting me get away with it. I must have been pushing it a bit hard lately because last time he chased me out before I had everything I wanted. Your job today is to feed him the cigarettes and engage him in conversation while I go about my business.'

'But you know I can't speak more than a few of words of Vietnamese.'

'He's got a bit of English. You'll need to speak slowly. Make him know it's important he understands you. Get close to him. Don't worry about the smell.'

'You mean I'm supposed to seduce him?'

'Of course not. Just be yourself. You're seductive enough as you are. Think of him as another boofhead Calvin, but don't stomp on him. I don't muck around, so you won't have to keep it up for long and I reckon he'll be pretty confused when you lob on him and start handing out the ciggies, so he won't give you much trouble at all.'

Despite her misgivings Jane tried to do what Ellie had asked and was surprised by how smoothly it went. She was even promised a guided tour of Saigon if she came to stay for a day or two. Once they were out of the store with bulging bags, Ellie's congratulations again took the form of a hearty whack on the back. 'You're a natural, I reckon.'

On the return journey Ellie was subdued. The light was beginning to fade and, knowing that Viet Cong activity heightened around dusk, Jane thought she must be worried about that. They were not far from Bien Hoa when Ellie relaxed and said, 'I hear you have a boyfriend who is over here with the army.'

'Yes, Danny's a nasho. He's been here since May.'

'Are you serious?'

'I think we'll get married after he comes home.'

'Think? You're not sure?'

'We haven't set a date yet. There's a few things to be sorted out with his family but we'll get there, I'm sure.' Listening to herself, Jane was conscious of the doubt which continued to lurk.

Ellie had to brake sharply as the truck in front of them came to a sudden halt. After edging around the truck, she said, 'So, poor old Gordon Townsend hasn't got a chance.'

'What?' Jane chuckled. 'He's not interested in me. Yes, he took me for a meal at the Indian place once, but ever since he's treated me with that polite reserve he uses with everybody. I had to complain to him before he'd dance with me at our parties.'

Ellie turned her head to regard her. 'You haven't noticed the way he watches you?'

'Come on. He hardly ever looks my way. Not like some I could name.'

'Exactly. He goes to a lot of trouble to make sure you don't catch him out and tries to avoid you in public.'

Jane tried to hide the pleasure Ellie's words had given her and hoped Ellie was not observing her as closely as she had Gordon Townsend. On those odd occasions when she was with him at the house Jane had tried to draw out the man she had discovered that night at Mrs Gupta's, but he had remained hidden. 'Why on earth would he do that?' she asked.

Ellie pulled out to pass a slow-moving cart and was forced to brake suddenly when a motorcyclist coming the other way veered into her path. Once she was settled, she went back to Gordon Townsend. 'A shy man who doesn't like to stand out and does like to stick to the rules. I'd say he's toeing the line Brookner laid down about not getting too friendly with any of the nurses. He's not finding it easy though.'

'You're taking a lot of interest in him.'

'The more I see of him, the better I like him but, no, he's not my type. I reckon he'd suit you though. If things don't work out with your Danny, you could do a lot worse than our Doctor Townsend.'

Jane shook her head, dismissing the suggestion but intrigued by the idea, nevertheless. She had wondered when Gordon first invited her to go with him to Mrs Gupta's, but his behaviour that night and since had dispelled any notion of him being interested in her. Could Ellie possibly be right? It was rather touching and did match Gordon's strict adherence to protocol. She would have to see.

⚡

The recce platoon commander made it clear from the first day they were not on R and C in Vung Tau this time. Formed into six-man teams they undertook exercises in the Ganh Rai hills. They practiced patrolling in enemy territory, maintaining coverage of their total surroundings by devices such as resting back-to back by day and laying up at night in a circle with feet touching. They honed their methods for setting ambushes, including the use of mines and special explosives. They practised how to hit and run after enemy contact, something never done in 5RAR before. Helicopters were brought in for them to practice withdrawal of casualties, swift insertion when going on patrol and hot extraction when under attack. Their mornings began with gut-wrenching runs across sand dunes and in the sea. After dark they would often be sent on night training exercises. There was no respite.

After a fortnight, Danny was exhausted and resentful. 'Doesn't seem like I'll ever get to see Linh Mai.'

'Serves you right,' Skeeta said.

Their spat might have developed further had not they been ordered to go to the platoon commander's tent. They arrived to find a queue lined up for an audience with the lieutenant. Skeeta went in before Danny and came out grinning. Danny was next and had no chance to find out why his pal was so pleased. As soon as he entered, the lieutenant said, 'Just wanted to tell you we've made our selections and you're in. Before you ask, your mate Skeeta is in as well. He's already spun me the line about how you two have been together since you joined up and I shouldn't disturb that. You're both in Pug Preston's section.'

'What?' Danny had seen Pug on the first day of the course and made sure to avoid him since then.

'Pug's a very good soldier who knows how to party when off duty. You'll have a lot of fun with him.'

'Yeah? That's not my experience so far.'

'Well, Private McBride, it's time for you gain that experience. Meanwhile, you're free to do whatever takes your fancy in Vungas tonight as long as you're back here by twenty-three hundred. Fail that and you'll be on a charge.'

Outside the tent Danny found Skeeta standing with Pug. 'Can't say I was pleased to have you dropped on me, Dreamer, but the boss wouldn't budge. I've seen what a fit bugger you are. I'll give you that. And Smacka says you're a bit of a marksman. I'll wait to see whether he's right.' He turned to Skeeta with a less hostile expression. 'Smacka also tells me you're a good forward scout. We'll need one of those. At least you've got a spark in you. Coming with me for another session at the Grand? With what we're getting into, it could be our last.'

Skeeta nodded uncertainly.

Accepting his nod as agreement, Pug turned back to Danny. 'You can suit yourself. That'll be a last time for you, too. Come tomorrow, I'm your boss, not Smacka.'

It was still light when Danny reached the end of the track and he could see Linh was not there. Turning back, he walked down the path to her cottage, hesitated for a moment and then knocked tentatively on her door. He heard footsteps crossing the floor and the door opened to reveal her. 'You kept your promise. I did wrong to doubt you.' She gave the small bow she had used previously and Danny was not sure whether she was greeting him or apologising for doubting his sincerity.

'How are you, Linh Mai?'

'I am preparing a meal. Have you eaten? Would you like to join me?'

'Thank you. But you were not expecting me and will have made only enough for yourself.'

'Pff. Some more rice. A few extras in the pot. Come in.'

Danny entered a room that spanned the width of the cottage. A small wooden table with two matching chairs stood in the right half. Two easy chairs covered in a raffia-like fabric were on the left in front of a narrow book case. On the back wall opposite each of the front windows were two doors. Danny guessed the one which was shut led to a bedroom. Through the open one he could see into a kitchen.

'Please excuse me while I finish what I was doing,' Linh said, indicating he should sit in one of the easy chairs. She appeared totally at her ease whereas Danny could not overcome the feeling he was an interloper and wished they could be sitting together on her rock. Once he was seated, she went into the kitchen and he took the opportunity to examine the room more carefully. Long, green and yellow curtains hung beside each of the windows. There were about forty books in the bookcase. From what he could read on their spines, he guessed they were a mixture of language textbooks and novels. A number of small figures carved from wood and possibly jade occupied the vacant places on the shelves and sat on the top of the bookcase. Above them a bamboo cross hung on the wall. The other walls displayed unframed watercolour paintings of coastal scenes. In one of them he recognised the view from the end of the track and wondered whether Linh was the artist.

'Only a little longer.' Linh returned to draw the curtains and switch on a lamp hanging above the sitting area. Something was bubbling away in the kitchen and an enticing aroma wafted into the room. She returned to the door of the kitchen and turned back to say. 'Thank you for giving my letter to my brother.'

'How did ... He has written to you?'

'Oh yes. Quite quickly. Wanted to warn me about Australians.'

Before Danny could ask her to explain she disappeared into the kitchen again. Shortly afterwards she returned and began setting the table.

'Can I help you?' Danny said.

'Not with the meal, thank you. It will be ready soon.' She hesitated before adding, 'I would like you to tell my brother you have seen me and I am well. I wish I had a letter ready for you to take to him.'

'It would be a pleasure.' Danny doubted Tuan would gain pleasure from another meeting with him. Completely ignorant of Vietnamese table manners and cuisine, Danny was anxious not to offend Linh. Although embarrassed, he thought confession was the best option. 'Linh Mai, I have to tell you I know almost nothing about Vietnamese food or how to eat it.'

She was astonished. 'So how have you eaten?'

'The army does its best to provide us with the kind of food we're used to eating. It's not all that good but we get by.'

'Vietnamese food is so good. You must learn. I eat simply but it will be a start. I will show you. It will be fun.' He wasn't sure whether she was ordering him to relax or predicting they would enjoy themselves. 'Do you use chopsticks?'

'I tried once but couldn't get the hang of it,' he said.

'That is where we will start. Come and sit with me at the table.'

So began a meal in which Linh played the roles of chef, teacher and companion. Under her guidance he achieved a minimal competence with chopsticks. Each time he failed he was encouraged to try again and each time he succeeded he was applauded. He could see the school teacher at work. The pleasure she took in teaching him was infectious so that during the meal they often laughed and Danny was delighted to see her so relaxed and obviously having the fun she predicted — so different from her attitude when telling him of her family history.

When they had finished eating and were sipping the green tea she had provided, she smiled at him and said, 'The last time we met you asked me many questions and I told you about my family and myself. You promised to speak about yourself and your family when next we met and I have been waiting expectantly for that. I hope you will be able to speak as candidly with me as I did with you.'

He wondered if he could. He began by telling her about his parents.

When she said they must be worried about having their son at war in a distant country, he agreed that was true of his mother but said his father was proud he had committed to saving the South Vietnamese, the Catholics in particular, from the Communists.

Linh said, 'Fathers hold great ambitions for their sons and gain great pleasure when they see them achieve those ambitions. Daughters have it easier, I think. Was your father a soldier?'

For a moment Danny wondered whether she had been guided by some sixth sense but then realised she had been thinking of her father and his ambition for Tuan to follow him. 'He owns and runs a newsagency. That is where I work, too.' Was it because of Linh's appeal for him to be as candid with her as she had been with him or did he need to confide in someone like Linh: someone with whom he had great rapport, someone who would never meet his father? He was never sure. 'He did fight in the Second World War and that left a deep scar.' He went on to describe his father's brief stint in the army, his shame at having misled people over his war service and how Danny's commitment brought his father some kind of redemption.

It was the same with his account of Sean. He described the rift between Sean and his father over the war in Vietnam and, trying to be just to Sean, found himself putting Sean's point of view almost as though he shared it. He hesitated over mentioning Sean's homosexuality, partly from fear of shocking and upsetting Linh and partly because he had still properly to resolve his own attitude. When he did go ahead, though, he was surprised by how concernedly Linh listened to him and by the relief he gained from speaking with her. Most of all he was taken aback when she said, 'He is lucky to have you for a brother.'

She rose to her feet. 'More tea?'

He smiled at her and said, 'Yes, thank you,' wondering if she realised he was just as thankful for the break as he was for the tea. When she was in the kitchen, he consulted his watch. He still had some time before he must leave. Thank goodness he had come as early as he had. He still hadn't mentioned Jane.

On her return and after taking a sip of her tea, Linh said, 'Tell me about your girlfriend.' She grinned at him. 'Or should I say girlfriends?'

'Just one. But how did you know?'

'Handsome young Australians. They all have girlfriends.'

Was she just joking with him again, or was she being coquettish? Again, he couldn't be sure. He told her about Jane, her career as a nurse and their mutual enjoyment of dancing together.

'You will marry Jane when you return.' It wasn't a question.

'I guess so.'

She made no reply but this time her face did ask a question.

'We have to sort out a few things. She's not a Catholic.'

'But you love one another, so you will find a way.'

Linh's certainty came as a jolt to Danny, making him realise he was not as confident as she was, something he had been reluctant to admit even to himself. 'Thank you. You have been so kind to me in so many ways tonight. I am most grateful, but I must go. If I do not hurry away, I will miss the curfew and be in deep trouble.'

Both of them stood up, but Linh kept her eyes down. He fought an urge to embrace her. She might well misunderstand and that would shatter the rapport between them, something he could not afford to risk.

'Finally, she spoke. 'I will pray God keeps you and my brother safe and look forward to the next time we meet.'

On their return to Nui Dat, the members of the Reconnaissance Platoon moved from their previous locations to take up quarters together. Their tents were at the south-west corner of the battalion area. A short walk brought them a view of Luscombe air strip where Caribou aircraft on the Wallaby Run landed daily with their cargo of stores and men.

When they were settled, Pug called his section together, made introductions and allocated roles. Mick Williams, a raw-boned regular army man, was given charge of the M60 machinegun. Bunny Warren, a Nasho from Grafton, was the signaller and given the radio. Ritchie

Richardson, a short, quiet regular, became the section medic which meant he carried the rudimentary first aid kit. Skeeta was the forward scout. Danny was given the dual roles of covering the rear and carrying additional belts of ammunition for the M60. In Smacka's section Taffy, the 2IC, had come at the rear but Pug made it clear he didn't consider a 2IC was warranted for a section this small. Danny doubted whether he would want one in any case. Pug told them that, as members of his team, their duty was to support one another in meeting the standards he set for the section and carrying out the orders he gave. Danny recalled, when Smacka emphasised the importance of teamwork, he made it clear the obligation was as much upon him as everyone else.

Later, Danny went in search of Tuan Mai, but he was out on another cordon and search operation with 6RAR. Danny did not leave a message this time. He didn't want to risk Tuan having to run the gauntlet of Pug's hostility again.

Next morning they began what was a long four weeks away from the base. Kitting up to leave was itself a major task. Apart from the standard items — a meagre change of clothes, ration packs for five days, eight bottles of water, Hootchie, rifle, bayonet, ammunition for the rifle and spare belts for the M60 — the members of the section had to share Claymore mines, machetes, shovels, radios, spare batteries, rocket launchers, grenade launchers, medical kits, and smoke canisters. Danny counted himself lucky if he escaped carrying a load in excess of a hundred pounds.

Sometimes they operated as the forward platoon of the battalion, seeking enemy concentrations and radioing back intelligence to headquarters. Sometimes they were deposited by helicopter or armoured personnel carrier in an area safe from observation and moved through the jungle to set up ambushes and hit enemy outposts. The APCs were hot and uncomfortable, the noise and fumes almost unbearable, but they had the advantage of completely hiding the presence of the troops within. Although the Hueys, as they called them, were more visible, they gave an exhilarating ride, dipping and weaving at treetop level and sometimes bringing the fear of ejection through the open doorway.

In Bien Hoa the wocka wocka of an approaching helicopter again broke the peace of the group enjoying a Sunday afternoon break from duty by sunbaking on the roof of the team house.

'Here comes another one,' Graham Fisher said. He turned to Gordon Townsend, who was sitting in a canvas chair beside him. 'I don't know why those Yanks should be so interested in observing you and me in our shorts.'

Gordon glanced across at Mia, Ellie and Jane who were stretched out, sunbaking in swimsuits. 'No. Got me beaten, Graham.'

'If it helps get those supplies from the Yanks we're so dependent on, I'm happy to be ogled,' Ellie said.

'Come on, my love,' Graham said. 'You're happy to be ogled any time.'

Ellie ignored him and turned to Jane. 'You'll get plenty of that when you go swimming on the Back Beach at Vung Tau next weekend.'

'Yeah, it will be good to have a couple of days down there. I'm so glad you managed to arrange for the Yanks to give us a lift to Vung Tau when we have a break. Swimming will be good, but what else is there for me to get some exercise.'

'I wouldn't go dancing in Vung Tau,' Graham said. 'The dance halls are very different from what you'd be used to.'

'I haven't seen any sign the Vietnamese play tennis,' Jane said. 'The Yanks or the Australians haven't put in any tennis courts, have they?'

'Do you play tennis?' Gordon said, sitting up quickly and turning to face her directly.

Nothing else she had said to him recently had received such a lively response. In the past weeks she had continued trying to engage him in off-duty conversation. She had some success but seldom got very far before he retreated into his shell. It was a good description of him, she thought. He did wear a protective shell. Here was another chance. 'I used to be play regularly,' she said, 'but haven't had much opportunity lately. Do you play?'

'I used to be very keen. Not much talent, but that didn't stop me trying to improve.' Jane was pleased to hear Gordon shared her ambition to excel at tennis despite his lack of much natural ability — the direct opposite of Danny. 'Not much lately. A few games with friends. When we get back ...'

'Can we talk about something else? All this focus on activity is exhausting me,' Graham said.

Jane wondered whether Gordon had been about to invite her to play before that wretched Graham Fisher intervened. Having had his advances turned down several times, Graham probably didn't like the possibility of one his colleagues having better success with her.

Gordon chuckled. 'You subscribe to that famous quote: "Whenever I get the urge to exercise, I lie down until it goes away".' He had been slow to show it but did have a sense of humour after all.

On the day after they had been sunbaking, Gordon came to her at the hospital and she wondered whether he would speak of tennis again. Was he about to issue the invitation Graham might have prevented? 'Did you know the Australians at Nui Dat take recreation breaks in Vung Tau?' he said, disappointing and interesting her with the one sentence.

'No, I didn't. Danny hasn't mentioned taking a break at all. In his last letter, he said he had applied to be in a special reconnaissance platoon and would be training in Vung Tau. I think he'll have finished that now but I'll check when I go.' She had wondered how Danny would feel if she did turn up while he was still training in Vung Tau. The few letters he had written in recent months said very little about what he was doing. He was never one to go into a lot of detail as she was prone to do but, prior to telling her about the reconnaissance platoon, he had written as though bored with the whole experience. At least he had been buoyed by the possibility of joining this new platoon.

'I guess it might be difficult if he is in the midst of training,' Gordon said, mirroring some of her thoughts. 'He might be given a break if training is over. In that case he'll not be at the base but at a hostel which is further along the beach road. You could check there.'

Jane wondered how Gordon had come by this information. Perhaps he had been speaking with some of the Australians when he had been in Vung Tau recently. 'Thank you. I really appreciate you telling me.' She saw he was pleased with her thanks. 'And thanks for breaking your protocol to do so.'

'I don't understand. What do you mean?'

She smiled at him. 'I've noticed how you never deviate from the task at hand when in the hospital and don't indulge in the slightest idle chat. I was very surprised when you took me to Mrs Gupta's and I found you much more forthcoming.'

'I don't consider giving you some useful information idle chat.'

He sounded quite huffy but Jane pressed on. 'Surely you know what I mean, though. I think it must have been hard for you to adjust when the dividing line between hospital and home became so blurred over here.'

'There have been some difficulties for me over here.' His tone suggested to Jane his difficulties were other than the ones she had suggested, but he did not elaborate. She was about to respond with something encouraging when he cut her off. 'We'd better get back to work. Revert to protocol.' The small grin he gave her was something.

The short helicopter trip to Vung Tau was great fun. The country-side appeared so much more benign from the air. Jane saw the waves breaking on the beach as the chopper came into land at the US base, but swimming was not her first priority. Despite a nervousness that surprised her, she made her enquiries at the Australian base and was relieved to be told the reconnaissance platoon had left over a week ago. Was she nervous about how Danny would greet her? Would he have been annoyed if she had turned up when he was at the base? From the very first day they met she had always been the one to take the initiative and Danny had been comfortable with that. Perhaps too comfortable. On the other hand, she was not sure how she would feel if Danny arrived to see her at Bien Hoa. Fortunately, there was no chance of that. He had made that clear when responding to her letter telling him she would be there. If Danny did spend breaks in Vung Tau, he could have suggested they meet. She had told him some of the Alfred group had arranged to come to Vung Tau when she first learned of it, but he had not responded.

She followed the instructions she had been given at the base and now stood in front of house which carried the sign WELCOME TO THE VUNG TAU R AND R CENTRE. She had no expectation Danny would be there but had come so she could tell Gordon she had followed his suggestion. It occurred to her they might keep a record of who had been in residence. On enquiring, though, she was told he could have visited any time in recent months and there were so many of them her informant did not have the time to trawl through the records. The man did say he would be happy to stand in for Danny but she was not interested.

After spending the rest of the afternoon in the water or lying on the beach, she set off with Gwen to search for Faviora, a restaurant Mia had recommended. Although she had given them directions, it took some time to find it among the sleazy bars, massage parlours and dance halls. Jane was sure Danny would hate the place. If he had come once, that would have been the only time. At least she had the consolation that Mia was right about the food at Faviora.

She would write to Danny as soon as she got back to Bien Hoa and tell him how she had just missed seeing him in Vung Tau. She could also tell him what she had done while in Vung Tau and how she had seen enough to convince her Danny would not want to go there if he could avoid it. It was irritating he so seldom responded to what she said in her letters. When he did write he gave her very little detail of what he had been doing. Early on he had told her of some of the people he had met but now it was just a dull account of training or patrolling. She had written quite a bit about her experiences at Bien Hoa and told him some of the stories of the people she had treated in the hospital. She had not mentioned the business with Calvin or anything about Gordon.

⅄

It did not take Danny long to appreciate why Smacka and the platoon commander had both described Pug as a fine soldier. The first time Danny saw him at Vung Tau, he thought Pug resembled a rugby forward. He certainly had the build and quickly showed the strength and stamina. In addition, he had remarkable balance and was able to make his way through tangles of jungle undergrowth and thickets of dense bamboo with apparent ease. He was an excellent map reader and always knew where they were, a skill Smacka lacked. As forward scout, Skeeta's feel for country and keen sight often gave them advanced warning of dangers or opportunities ahead. Sometimes, though, they were saved by Pug's experience and his ability to sense rather than see an impending threat. He insisted they should move in absolute silence and had developed a comprehensive set of hand signals to indicate his commands and directions. He was ruthless in berating any who were careless or reckless. Anyone performing well could expect no more acknowledgment than a 'right' or 'OK', but it was clear he never asked anything from them he would be unable or unwilling to do himself.

As they approached the time for the platoon to return to Nui Dat, they were engaged in an exercise to disrupt the defences of a suspected VC camp, which lay on the top of a steep hill. The platoon had been dispersed to encircle the hill and Pug's section was climbing through thick jungle beside a narrow track. They had reached a point where the track took a sharp turn to the left and rose steeply towards the summit. Pug signalled for Skeeta to scout ahead while the rest waited. On his return Skeeta indicated he had located a densely camouflaged machinegun bunker. They could be almost certain this bunker would be accompanied by another one sited to provide crossfire and Pug was sure it would be on the other side of the track somewhere near the corner. The plan they had already used with success was for Pug and

208

Skeeta to go forward and lob grenades into the upper bunker while the remainder spread out and waited to pinpoint the lower one. When it raked the upper slope with fire, they would be able to locate the muzzle flashes and Mick, set up opposite where Pug expected the bunker to be, would let loose on the M60.

The grenade explosions brought the expected stream of fire from the lower bunker, Mick pressed the trigger of the M60 and set off a very short burst before it jammed. Now he was the target for the enemy machinegun. He was hit in the upper arm and gave a strangled cry. Ritchie crawled towards him but was halted by a stream of bullets. From lower down the track Danny had a good view of the crossfire with its tell-tale muzzle flashes. He fired hoping to do some damage or at least draw the machine-gun away from Mick and Ritchie. To his surprise all went silent. He saw Pug, who had used the diversion to cross the track, come up behind the bunker and enter it with his M16 poised. The sound of a short burst signalled he had finished off the machinegun crew.

On his return to the other side of the track he abandoned signals, for once. 'How's Mick?' he asked Ritchie.

'His arm's a mess. I've bound it up and think I've stopped the bleeding for now. We need to get him out.'

'We all need to scram,' Pug said. 'Mick, put your good arm around my shoulder and I'll help you along.' He began to return through the jungle the way they had come, half carrying, half-dragging Mick with him. 'Skeeta take the lead. Get us back to that small clearing we passed through about half an hour ago. Bunny get on the radio and call in a dust-off.' He paused to pull out his map, scanned it for a moment and gave Bunny a reference. Tell them that's where they should be able to get a Huey down. Dreamer, bring the M60 and cover us from behind. If the other guys in the platoon have been doing their job, the nogs won't be rushing after us, but you never know.'

They returned down the hill much more quickly than they had climbed it. Skeeta led them to the clearing which, now Danny saw it again, raised doubts it could accommodate a helicopter. They took up defensive positions and Pug spoke to the platoon commander on the radio. 'The boss says we've done our job and should go home. Seeing Mick is not likely to cark it on us, they won't take him to hospital in Vungas. The Regimental Aid Post can fix him up and we can have a ride home with him. Let's hope the dust-off pilot's happy to take us.' The sound of an approaching chopper brought Danny back to wondering whether it could land far less take any of them off.

It hovered over them, as if the pilot was having second thoughts as well, but then descended to cover them in dust, leaves and the remnants of small branches. Pug lifted Mick on board and waved for the others to follow. Danny handed up the M60 and scrambled in just before the pilot was away, clipping a sizable branch, which caused the Huey to lurch before he regained control.

Skeeta picked up the M60, began to dismantle it and wipe the parts on his sleeve. 'There it is,' he said triumphantly and used the penknife he always carried to prise a sliver of bamboo from the firing mechanism.

'Better put it together pretty quick,' Pug shouted over the noise of the helicopter. 'We'll be landing soon.'

After they had landed and Mick had been taken by the medical orderlies, Pug turned to Danny and said, 'Was it you who fired into that bunker after the M60 jammed?'

'I did,' Danny said. 'Maybe some of the others, too.'

Pug didn't smile but his face had a different shape from the usual uncompromising one. 'Reckon the rest of them were a bit busy taking cover. I'd say the nogs in the bunker were already dead but I made sure of it. So, Smacka was right: you can shoot. Under fire, as well.'

After he had abandoned his tattered uniform, cleaned himself up and tended to his blistered feet. Danny went in search of Tuan Mai. He found him sitting outside his tent. 'G'day Tuan,' he called. 'I saw Linh again and she asked me to tell you she's fine.'

'I know.'

'She wrote to you?'

'You took a long time coming to tell me.'

There was an empty chair beside Tuan but he made no effort to suggest Danny should take it. He sat like a headmaster in his office confronting a naughty student. If creating that impression was his intention, Danny's height took away from the effect by forcing Tuan to look up at him. 'You weren't here when I got back from Vungas and I've been on patrol ever since.' He was irritated by Tuan's manner the first time they had spoken. He wasn't going to let it pass again. 'Why are you so hostile to me?'

'Linh says you were very attentive to her when she told you about our family.'

If Tuan had been an Australian, Danny would have heard sarcasm in his voice. Perhaps the Vietnamese used words and tones differently. Did Tuan believe Danny, the foreigner, was being unduly intrusive? Danny sat on the empty chair. 'We shared. I told her about my family and my girlfriend in Australia.' The first time they spoke Tuan had hinted he thought Danny was viewing Linh as some kind of upmarket bar girl. Mentioning Jane might help allay that concern.

'You think that makes it better?'

'What?'

'She says you have come here to save Catholics like her from the Communists.'

Danny saw a chance to find a link with Tuan. 'Yes, just like you. We have that in common.'

'Like me? I suppose she told you that.'

Danny repeated Linh's description of Tuan's commitment to defending the Catholics of Vietnam from the Communists, a commitment she said Tuan pursued despite disappointing his father.

This time Danny was in no doubt Tuan was sneering at him. 'You Westerners amaze me. You don't believe everything you hear but you do believe anything that fits with the ideas you already hold. I see it when I'm translating at interviews of captured Viet Cong or villagers.'

'Are you calling your sister a liar?'

'No. Sometimes I wish she was. It might make it easier to deal with her. My sister is like a nun. After years with the nuns at school and now teaching there herself, she might as well be one.'

The same thought had occurred to Danny after the first two nights they had spoken, but the way she behaved when they ate together had dispelled that idea.

Tuan continued. 'She chooses to believe the best of people. When you listened to her account of our family, I am sure you formed a picture of my father as a highly gifted man who suffered great hardship and disappointment. Yes, he was a great linguist with great ambitions, but in pursuit of his dreams he became a tyrant. Our mother sacrificed herself in serving his needs. He saw that merely as his due.'

Tuan had slumped in his chair. He pushed himself upright and crossed his legs before continuing. 'I suppose my sister told you I was a great linguist, not as gifted as my father, but well suited to follow him. In fact, if he had the wit to see women as anything other than servants and adornments for males, he would have recognised it was Linh who had his talent and I was a pale shadow. She should have gone to the university. She should have become a professor of languages. Instead she is hidden away in a backwater of Vung Tau, teaching children languages they will never use. He insisted I must be brought to the standard worthy of following him and made me miserable for years as he drove me on. At least it gave me a facility which has enabled me to occupy a relatively safe position in the army, but I joined up, not to save the Catholics from the Communists, but to save myself from him. My religious zeal for the role was to make my mother happier.'

Tuan glared at Danny as though challenging him to disagree. When he said nothing, Tuan gave an exaggerated sigh and said, 'Beware of foreigners who say they have good intentions and know so little of our ways. How true that is. They do great damage to Vietnam.'

'What?'

'You are just the latest but you are a danger to my sister and I cannot allow that.'

'I still don't understand you.'

'No. Foreigners never do. I will have to explain.' Tuan sighed as though compelled yet again to undertake a task which had become boring. 'When we first met, you assured me my sister had nothing to fear from you. Of course, you did not mention she is a haven for you from the stresses of battle, a temporary relief you will remember with fondness after you return and marry your girlfriend in your wealthy and peaceful country. In return you listened carefully to her and assured me of your good intentions.

'Knowing my sister and reading her letters, I can see it is very differ-ent for her. She is a young woman who, like a nun, has never come close to any man. You arrive as if by magic, charm her with your attention and she is able to speak with you in a way she has not achieved with anyone before. Perhaps, if you had more openly sought to seduce her, she would have been more wary. She knows you will be leaving and can expect nothing from you. She will not remember you merely with fondness. She will think of you as the perfect lover she could never have. No other man will be able to compare with the image she will carry of you, so she might as well become a nun.'

Now Danny could understand Tuan's hostility to him, but there was a good deal more to Linh than the picture of the weak, self-deluding girl Tuan had painted. 'You said I was just the latest to come with good intentions. What did you mean?'

'The Americans, of course. They became interested in Vietnam when the French were being ousted. The Geneva Peace Conference called for a temporary separation between north and south until elections were held. The Americans would not agree to this. The Viet Minh, already in control of the north, began their campaign to unify the country under their control and the Americans announced their good intention to save the people of South Vietnam from the Communists. Their real aim, of course, was to block Communist influence spreading through South-East Asia.'

'You don't see that as an important for the region?' Danny said. He shouldn't let this harangue go on without some challenge.

213

'The Americans and you Australians have very little understanding of what actually occurred in South Vietnam prior to it gaining their interest. There was a twenty-year history of Communist-led guerrilla warfare against the French, which had strong support from the majority of the population. The Viet Minh had a long-standing network of cadres through the villages of the south which were reactivated after separation to undermine the government of the south. The Americans sought to counter this threat to their ambitions by providing military assistance and by trying to strengthen the government and administration through the appointment of leaders they saw as sharing their aims. They were happy to see a tyrant depose the President, since the usurper was a Catholic and would not be inclined to compromise with the Communists like they feared so many in the south might. He rigged elections, promoted incompetent Catholics over more deserving Buddhists, dealt ineffectively with the insurgents from the north and became an embarrassment to the Americans, so what did they do? They backed the generals to replace him without any idea of how trustworthy these men might be.'

Tuan, whose voice had become more heated the further he went, wiped the sweat from his face. 'The result was a series of coups and further instability. Saigon politics descended into a farce of internal warfare: Catholics against Buddhists, civilians against the army, young officers versus the old guard. Meanwhile the Communists have a clear strategy. They do not fight for territory but for the minds of the peasants. They are able to blame all the peasants' grievances on the government and promise to provide solutions when they come to power. They instituted a military force, the Viet Cong, from local men led by officers from the north. Local men fighting for their land. They did not embark on all-out assault but took control of the open country and the jungle from which they could harry the government forces. It took twenty years to oust the French. They know how to be patient. Step by step they pushed back the government forces and the cadres returned to each of the villages after they came under VC control.

214

'Faced with this worsening situation the Americans pour in more and more military effort and call upon their obedient supporters like the Australians and South Koreans. Through all this it never occurs to the Americans they may have taken on a fight they can never win. I would say that possibility hasn't occurred to you Australians, either.'

Tuan had become less vehement and now sounded more regretful than angry. 'You are effective soldiers. I will give you that. You have regained control of a number of villages and you have killed some VC. But is this enough to wrest control of Phuoc Tuy from the Communists in the long term? The Government will not endure unless it can establish popular support and that will only be achieved if it can provide ongoing safety for the people and improve their living conditions. Almost the first thing you did on arrival was to destroy villages and shift the residents away from their land. Hardly the way to win the trust of the local people. Your efforts will go for nothing unless your military achievements are matched by the same ongoing success in improving the lives of the people. I see no sign of that occurring.

'The Americans will not save us from the Communists. The killing and the destruction will continue until the Americans tire of it and then you will all go home and leave us with the Communists to put the pieces of our shattered country together.'

When Danny returned to his tent, there were three letters on his bed. One was from his mother and the other two were in scented blue envelopes. It was as if they had come from an entirely different world, a world he once knew but no longer had any reality for him. Now his world teemed with contradictions which challenged the beliefs and attitudes he formed in that old world. His unease had grown through the seven months he had been in Vietnam. Tuan said Australians believed anything that fitted their prior ideas. Danny thought that was wrong but wondered if he was clinging onto ideas his experience in Vietnam was showing to be flawed. Be honest. Meeting Linh Mai had been a magical experience — one he desperately needed at the time, one he still desperately needed. By acting honestly, being kind to Linh and keeping a safe distance from her, he was not being unfaithful to Jane and he might even bring Linh some happiness. What was wrong with that? Tuan said that by failing to understand Linh's true feelings he was doing great harm. There must be a way to enjoy her friendship and avoid hurting her.

Tuan's tirade on the damage done by well-meaning foreigners also shocked him. Before Christmas he'd become frustrated with what he saw as their ineffectiveness in dealing with the Viet Cong. He had seen the Reconnaissance Platoon as a positive development, ensuring search and destroy missions dealt heavier blows to the enemy. Since the platoon was formed, there had been an increase in enemy casualties and the severity of destruction to their camps. But would a continuation of that win the war? And was his growing distaste for killing just another sign of his growing exhaustion. He had no trouble shooting to kill in the heat of a fire-fight and knew he was pre-empting casualties on his side by taking out the enemy in ambushes, but he'd lost the satisfaction from a successful ambush and now considered them as a necessary evil. Tuan was certain all this effort wouldn't achieve the goal that Danny had seen as pre-eminent — the protection of the Catholics. Indeed, Tuan saw all this well-intentioned effort leading to long-term damage to the very people he was aiming to help.

End Game

After only one night in camp the platoon was sent out again. Before they left Pug called his section together to introduce the replacement for Mick, a swarthy man with tightly curled black hair who went by the name of Jake Jacobi. As usual Pug chose to make his welcome a challenge and this time added his views on national servicemen. 'I hope you're up to it, Jake. Don't let me down. I see you're another of those nashos. Can't say I have a lot of time for them. Some of you are alright, I s'pose.' He glanced in Skeeta's direction. 'Trouble is none of you signed up to make the army your career like we permanent guys did. Some nashos — better not be any in my section — think they shouldn't be here. Many think they're only in for a while then it's back to their real job, so they don't need to give it all they have. If that's what you think, you're wrong. There'll never be anything more real than the job you're doing right now.' He eyed Danny before saying, 'And that job is to carry out the orders we're given, whether we like 'em or not. It makes no difference whether or not you believe in the cause, hate the Commies or like the nogs. You do the job you're given. The worst thing a grunt can do is try to weigh the pros and cons.'

Despite his opening tirade, once the section was on patrol, Danny found Pug treated him more like the way he dealt with the permanent guys and Skeeta. Poor Jake was the one always having to prove himself. Perhaps Pug needed at least one. The platoon conducted a series of ambushes, intelligence gathering and some hit-and-run operations with a fair measure of success and no further casualties. When on patrol, each of them was so taken up with ensuring their survival there was little opportunity for musing on other things. On those rare occasions when Danny was free to reflect, he found his thoughts turning to Linh. Should he continue to seek her company? There might be one more chance before he left but certainly no more. No good trying to decide in the middle of an operation. Perhaps he should stop worrying and just let matters run their course.

Scanning the section one day when they were taking a break, Danny was struck by the depressing sight they made. Their clothes were ragged and they gave the impression of being refugees from a concentration camp rather than a crack army section. All of them had suffered from various forms of illness. Diarrhoea was common, skin diseases abounded and everyone's feet were in poor shape through saturation in the wet and chafing in the dry. He wondered whether any of them also carried worries and doubts like he did.

Out of the blue, Skeeta said, 'Only a few months and we'll be home.'

'Yeah,' Danny said. 'Had enough?'

Skeeta stepped towards him so they were almost toe-to-toe. 'You saying I'm losing me bottle?'

'Get out of my space,' Danny said without moving an inch. 'I'm asking if you're getting fed up with this grind.'

'So, you're the one who wants to cut and run.'

Danny drew back his fist. 'Don't you ...'

'Shut up, both of you.' Pug glowered at them and they separated.

They got over it soon after, but it wasn't the first spat over nothing between members of the section.

They were just finishing their dinner when Gwen received a call from the hospital. She returned to the table frowning and shaking her head. 'It's that Chau Tran, again. She'll be a good nurse one day and I enjoy mentoring her, but I wish she'd stand on her own feet more.'

'What's her problem?' Jane said.

'The usual. The trouble is she's such an attractive young woman who treats all her patients with great care and concern. The men, in particular, are forever calling on her when there's nothing seriously wrong and she gets bothered she's missing something. I'm sure, after I arrive there tonight, I'll settle the two patients she's worried about and be back quickly. No need for anyone to come with me.'

'Don't worry, Gwen,' Jane said. 'You know Brookner insists no nurse go alone to the hospital at night. Besides, there's something about the hospital in the evening I enjoy, particularly when there are no problems.' She did not tell Gwen she had come to view the hospital at night as a haven. The lights were low, the noisy bustle of the day silent, the shrill cries of patients awaiting treatment replaced by the soft sounds of the sleepers and sometimes Jane could be free to sit alone. She had always thought of herself as one who enjoyed the company of others but here at Bien Hoa, whether at the hospital, the house or on the street, she was surrounded by other people. Danny was much less gregarious than her, so he probably suffered more. Or was the jungle at night his chance to lie quietly by himself? She would ask him in her next letter. Not long now and she would be writing from home.

When they reached the hospital, Gwen went into the ward where Chau Tran had her problems and Jane lingered outside the entrance, enjoying the tranquillity of the night. The dry season was now firmly established so the sky was clear, lit by a three-quarter moon, a myriad of stars and the glow from the air base just above the northern horizon. A faint breeze rustled the leaves of the trees and Jane felt a rare contentment.

Suddenly there was a flash of orange light and the shock wave from an explosion knocked her to the ground. Many of the hospital windows were shattered and the lights snuffed out. Dazed, she clambered to her feet. Had the hospital been bombed? Was it the Viet Cong? Why would they bomb a hospital? Some of them had been brought here for treatment of their wounds. Was this the prelude to a further attack?

In the short silence which followed, Jane wondered whether she had been deafened until she heard the thud of feet. A group of armed men were running towards the hospital. What would induce anyone to attack patients in a hospital? Were the staff the target? Or was it just the Australians — citizens of a country at war with the Viet Cong? Frozen by fear, like an animal caught in headlights, she cowered in the shadows of the gateway and shook with relief when the men continued past without even glancing in her direction.

Now Jane could see it was not the hospital which was under attack but the jail in the next block. She could see flames and billowing black smoke. The bomb must have been intended to breach the walls of the jail or target the military guard mounted there. The shooting intensified as other attackers — presumably Viet Cong — converged on the jail from different directions. The rattle of a machinegun came from the jail. Despite the bomb blast, the guard must have retained sufficient strength to fight back. The darkness was lit by the flash of guns and intermittent explosions. After a few minutes she heard the racket of approaching helicopters. Two choppers, which must have been summoned from the air base, swooped from the sky, their flood lights sweeping the streets and their guns spraying a stream of red tracer bullets. A group of men, some with rifles, some unarmed, ran back towards her. Escapees from the jail? Those caught in the light were cut down from above. Jane feared the survivors would take shelter in the hospital but they ran further down the street.

A jeep driven at high speed skidded around the corner, sending the escapees scrambling to avoid it, swerved through the gateway and screeched to a halt. Was this the beginning of a renewed attack on the jail from within the hospital? Jane shrunk back in the shadows. The door of the jeep was thrown open and Gordon Townsend leap out.

'Gordon. Gordon over here.' She ran to him and collapsed sobbing in his arms.

'You're safe now Jane,' he said in his matter-of fact voice. When she could not stop from shivering, he tightened his grip of her with one arm, stroked her back with the other and cradled her head against his shoulder. 'The shooting's died down. I'd say the worst is over.'

Jane listened and could hear only the more distant sound of the helicopters, which were still circling but had climbed to a greater height. She began to relax and stopped trembling but had no wish to leave Gordon's embrace. After a few more minutes he loosened his grip and asked, 'Are you OK to go inside now?'

Her fear was replaced by embarrassment. Here she was blubbering away when she had never been in real danger — merely a spectator. Driving as he had when he couldn't have known what lay ahead of him, Gordon had been taking a much greater risk. She brushed the tears from her face and said, 'I'm sorry for being such a sook.'

'You had every reason to be terrified: the bomb blast, the gunfire, the injuries and deaths on the road in front of you. You must have feared the hospital would be drawn into the battle — collateral damage to use that euphemism. We were very worried.'

Gordon's use of the word 'we' suddenly made Jane aware he had arrived alone. 'The others? Are they OK?'

'Oh, yes. We were shocked by the bomb blast but were not concerned the house would be attacked. It was those of you at the hospital we feared for.' He paused before saying, 'Sounds like it's all over. The others should be here soon.'

'Why did you come alone?'

Now she could see Gordon was the one to be embarrassed. 'When the battle was in full flow and we had no idea of the extent to which the hospital site was involved, Brookner ruled, sensibly in my view, that we shouldn't risk lives by racing in but wait until it was safe.'

'But you came?'

'Someone had to see you were OK.' He hadn't mentioned Gwen.

'For the second time you've stepped up to protect me — this time taken a huge risk. I'm deeply grateful.' She kissed him.

She saw he was taken aback but then he smiled at her and said, 'We'd better get inside and see what needs to be done. As I said, the others will be here soon and I'm sure we'll have a busy night dealing with the casualties from the battle.'

The battalion was planning a sweep through the Long Hai Hills where it was known the VC had many bases. The strength of VC concentration had varied in recent times but was thought to be building again. The Reconnaissance Platoon was given the task of locating the precise positions of VC bases and estimating troop strength within them. On the third day the platoon was two hours ahead of an advancing rifle company. Through a small gap Danny caught a glimpse of Skeeta who was up ahead in his role as forward scout. He had stopped dead and was turning his head from side to side like a hunting dog seeking a scent. Danny guessed he had heard a sound or noticed some disturbance in the foliage. Had another patrol been through before them? If so, it could not be one of theirs and must be Charlie. Pug signalled for the section to remain where they were while Skeeta disappeared in the thick jungle. After he returned, Pug signalled for the section to continue forward and make no sound. They soon came to a narrow, overgrown track where Danny could see only a few footprints, suggesting this track seldom carried many troops. Most likely it was a little-used part of a web of tracks leading to one of the underground bunkers the section had been sent to find. They needed to continue along the track and try to confirm the size and precise location of the bunker.

A few minutes later Pug signalled for them to conceal themselves. From his position Danny could see nothing which might have triggered the alarm until a single unarmed man in the black uniform of the VC came around a corner of the track, strolling down it as though taking some exercise. Danny tried to bury himself more deeply in the foliage as the man continued to come towards him. There was a rustle when Jake repositioned the M60 and Danny feared the man may have heard it. His fear grew when the man stopped at a point directly opposite. Just then a bird flew from a tree and the man turned to watch it soar into the

222

sky. He loosened his trousers stepped off the track on the other side and squatted to defecate. That done, he hitched up his trousers, stretched his arms high above his head, yawned, and turned to walk back up the track.

He had gone only a short distance when Pug signalled to Danny: a thumb and forefinger standing above his remaining curled fingers, followed by a single raised finger — one shot. Danny aimed his rifle but then lowered it and shook his head, his thoughts chaotic. Pug repeated his signal and scowled at Danny. Again, he shook his head. Furious now, Pug fired his M16 and felled the man with a short burst. He then signalled for the section to disappear into the jungle.

No one was keen to meet Danny's eye for the rest of the day. When the section was safely harboured that evening, Pug came to him. 'What the bloody, hell came over you?'

Danny had been struggling through the afternoon to understand what had led him to hold his fire. It must have been bound up with the doubts he was having. Or was it just exhaustion preventing him from thinking clearly? How could he explain to Pug what he didn't understand himself? 'I'm sure he hadn't twigged we were there.'

'And I'm just as sure he had. But, you dickhead, that's not the point. The point is you ignored a clear order. No, you began to obey but pulled out and then refused when the order was repeated. That's a serious offence. You'll be on a charge.'

'Yeah, you're right,' Danny said, surprising Pug. 'I've been thinking about it. I was worried about shooting an unarmed man who posed no threat to us.'

'No threat? He was on his way to raise the alarm. They would have been onto us like a ton of bricks.'

'All right, then. I found it hard to shoot an unarmed man.'

'What's happened to my sharpshooter, the guy who put out a machinegun crew with his rifle?'

'They were firing at us.'

'The ambushes. The hit and runs. You staying at home now?'

'Of course not. It's been a hard couple of months.'

Pug scowled at him. 'You think too much, Dreamer. I've told you before. Just focus on the job and forget the rest. I should report you but I won't this time. We're shorthanded as it is.'

On the night before the medical team was to return from Bien Hoa there was a celebratory dinner at which the participants were uncharacteristically subdued. Mr Brookner made the speech expected of him. He thanked each of them for their work, described the achievements the group could be proud of and wished them well in settling back at the Alfred. Despite the reasons Brookner had given Jane for feeling satisfied with her efforts and despite her relief that she would soon be safe in Melbourne, she could not escape the feeling she was abandoning the Vietnamese after making no more than a token effort to assist them. Judging by the general air in the room, she was not alone.

She could see Ellie was trying to lighten the mood when she said, 'After our experience up here, will we have to go back to treating you surgeons and doctors with undue deference?'

'I imagine you'll behave just as you always have, love,' Graham Fisher said. 'Passive insubordination.'

Most of them showed no interest in prolonging the occasion and went to complete their packing. Jane was about to go when she saw Gordon waiting for her. 'Have you got a moment?' he asked before ushering her into the small hallway inside the front door. 'I've been thinking about tennis,' he said.

Was this the long-delayed invitation?

'I wondered whether you might like to join our group for an occasional game. The standard isn't very high, but my friend Peter is quite good and I'm sure you'd be very welcome.'

'Thank you, Gordon. I'd enjoy that.' Jane was surprised to find she had accepted without a moment's thought.

'I don't know when the next game will be. Probably not for a while after we get back' He hesitated as if weighing a tricky decision. 'Perhaps, if you gave me your phone number, I can call you when I do know.'

Mia, who had come from the kitchen, was passing behind Gordon on her way to her room. She raised an eyebrow and winked at Jane who began to wonder whether she was wise to be so forthcoming. If Ellie was right, she was giving false hope to Gordon? Was Ellie right? Was she giving him false hope? With Danny out of reach it was pleasant to have someone she liked paying attention to her and being so shy about it. Should she suggest Danny as a possible player? He wouldn't be back until April or May and, anyway, it was hardly polite for her to start suggesting others when she had only just been invited, herself. Plenty of time for straightening things out later.

Over the next few weeks Danny found he had returned to the bottom of Pug's approval list. At least this brought some relief for Jake. Even greater relief for Danny came when Pug announced that the section had been granted three days R and C in Vung Tau. After they arrived at the Centre and received the usual pep talk, Pug said, 'Right, off you go to take your pleasure. See you all at the Flags, seven tonight.'

Danny and Skeeta opted to spend the afternoon lazing on the beach. As the time for going into Vung Tau approached Skeeta said, 'You coming tonight or are you going to slip away to see your Vietnamese girl?'

'You heard Pug. Since that business over the bloke I didn't shoot, I've been back where I started with Pug. I'll need to turn up tonight.'

Once the section had gathered at the Flags, Pug took them to a nearby bar and signalled this was to be the first in a long list. By the time they were well down Pug's list, the privations of the past months began to fade as did the alertness of most of the party. Danny had managed to stay relatively sober and was biding his time. 'Now for the Grand,' Pug said. 'Get some food and call on Chloe and her pals.' He glared around until he located Danny. 'Love-sick lads are excused. But if you want to watch, I'm sure you'll learn quite a bit.' This time Danny did not respond to Pug's suggestion.

They set off for the Grand in a ragged line rolling along the pavement. Danny allowed himself to fall behind and, without any of them noticing, turned down a lane and headed towards Linh's cottage. When he reached it and found no lights showing, he continued down the track to the headland. There was no moon this time and the shadows of the trees, instead of framing the view, loomed up as if to block him. He saw no sign of Linh until he was almost upon her and she rose to face him. 'Danny, it is you.' In the dark the expression on her face was unclear but her voice held a reserve or maybe even a fear he had not heard before.

'I'm sorry to come so late. I thought you might even have gone to bed.'

'I was about to go home. Would you like to pray with me?' He came to stand beside her and was surprised when she chuckled. 'You have been drinking.'

'I'm afraid so. I couldn't get away from my section until now. I'll try not to get too close.' She sat down and Danny, ignoring his undertaking, sat beside her. In the silence he could hear the sea lapping on the shore below while he tried to frame what he should say to her. After a while she lifted her head and said, 'I must go.' They walked together towards her house in silence until Linh said. 'You will be leaving Vietnam soon. Is this the last time I will see you?'

She must have learned this from Tuan. Danny wondered what else he had told her. 'A couple of months yet, but this will probably be the last time I'm able to visit Vung Tau.' He still could not find the words he wanted as a farewell and chose instead to delay. 'I will be here tomorrow and wondered ...'

'Tomorrow is Sunday. Would you like to come to church with me?'

'I would like that very much.'

'Come here at nine o'clock in the morning and I will take you.' She paused to give him the small smile that so captivated him. 'Afterwards I will make a special lunch for us. A farewell lunch.' She turned to walk down the path to her cottage and said over her shoulder. 'I will see you tomorrow.'

⅃

'Dreamer, where did you get to last night?' Pug was the only one of the section out of bed when Danny went for breakfast.

He never felt comfortable lying but did not hesitate this time. 'I thought you said I needn't go with the rest of you to the Grand.'

'No, that's not what I said. These couple of days are for all of us to have some fun together. I don't want you wandering around on your own. So, tonight, stick with us. That's an order.' Pug rubbed his forehead and Danny thought he might not be as hale as he pretended to be. 'What are you planning to do this morning?'

'I'm going to church.'

Pug made no response and took a mouthful of his egg and bacon, instead.

⅃

When Linh Mai opened her door, Danny was stunned. Today the tunic of the ao dai she wore was of pale cream silk embroidered with swirling golden vines which ran across one shoulder and down her body to her feet where the hem opened to reveal her trousers underneath. In her hair was a cream tropical flower. He had showered and shaved carefully, even chosen his most presentable shirt, but how could he accompany this oriental princess to church? She did not invite him in but closed the door, took a key from the small handbag she was carrying and locked it.

She chatted happily as they walked to the church. They approached the centre of Vung Tau and turned into a wide street which led to an impressive church building. The plastered outside walls of the church were a similar colour to Linh's dress and bore a high-pitched roof of small red tiles. A square tower, also in cream plaster, rose beside the church. It was topped by a white cross above a small pyramid roof. The inside walls of the church carried various icons and crosses. The floor

227

consisted of gleaming black and white square tiles and the pews were of highly polished dark wood. Already there was a substantial gathering of white-garbed nuns, well-dressed school children and adults. The air bore a hint of incense. The whole effect was so foreign to the garish sights and filthy lanes only a short distance away that Danny felt he had entered another world, just as he had done on the first night he met Linh.

As they took their places, Danny noticed many of the congregation were watching them. He hadn't expected the presence of a round eye would cause such interest. There would be other committed Catholic foreigners in Vietnam; probably some based at Vung Tau. Surely he wasn't the first to attend this church. Linh turned her head to smile at him and he saw the amusement in her eyes. Of course, he wasn't the one creating the interest — not him directly. Linh Mai would be well known to many in the congregation: the nuns, the schoolgirls, probably their parents and others as well. She would have a lot of explaining to do. It didn't seem to be bothering her, though.

Danny was thankful the priests stuck to the standard form of the Mass so, despite his very limited knowledge of Vietnamese, he was able to follow most of the service quite well. Afterwards Linh was greeted by a number of people and, quite unfazed, introduced Danny to them. They showed considerable interest in him and asked a variety of questions he was able to answer with the aid of Linh as interpreter.

They took a different route on their return, passing through a market where Linh bought a range of seafood, spices, tropical vegetables and fruit. When they entered her house, she excused herself and disappeared into her bedroom where she changed into a more commonplace ao dai. She made green tea for them but did not ask Danny to sit in the main room while she prepared their lunch. Instead, she invited him to watch, describing the ingredients of each dish and what she was doing to prepare them.

The result was a banquet of lavish dishes that Danny thoroughly enjoyed. He did show some improvement with the chopsticks but still gave Linh opportunities to chuckle at his efforts. Pressed to tell her his favourite dish, he plumped for what she had called Banh Khof: shrimps cooked in coriander and served in small, crispy rice and turmeric cups. When she heard his selection, she laughed and said, 'You know,' in an accusing voice.

'Know what?'

'Really? You have not had Banh Khof before? It is a speciality of Vung Tau.'

'We don't eat food like this in Vung Tau or Nui Dat. I wonder whether I'll be able to find Banh Khof in Australia.'

Mention of Australia reminded Danny he had still to make his farewell speech and time was running out. Uncomfortable about what to say and how to start he blurted out, 'Your brother says I have been wrong to become your friend when I knew that one day I would leave here and return to Australia.'

'My brother fears you will spoil my life. He is mistaken.' She paused, allowing Danny to absorb the directness with which she spoke. 'I will miss you when you go but I will have the memories of the times we have shared and they will bring me happiness. I will not mope over what could never be and with God's help I will live a full life and raise a family like my mother did. You need not worry over me.' She hesitated for a moment before saying, 'I fear, though, I may have brought unhappiness to your life.'

'How could that be?'

'You told me of Jane, the girl you love in Australia, and how you will marry her. You are very polite to me but I see how you look at me and that brings me both happiness and fear. I would hate to have caused any damage to your love for Jane. Whatever you may think of me, there is no need for that. Jesus said we should love one another. He put no bounds on who we might love and how we might love them. All of us need love and we should never regret having love for another. I hope you will remember that and think kindly of me when you are in Australia.

Skeeta was waiting for him when Danny returned to the Centre. 'Glad to see you mate. I was worried you might miss Pug's party tonight.'

'No, much as I might like to. He made it clear this morning he was giving me an order to turn up. I got away with it once but ...'

'He said you were going to church.'

The disbelief on Skeeta's face made Danny laugh. 'Yeah, I did go to church. What I didn't tell Pug is that Linh took me. After that she cooked us a fabulous lunch.'

'A farewell performance?'

'I guess so.'

Skeeta scrutinised Danny. 'Are you OK, mate?'

'At this stage I don't think any of us are really OK, but today with Linh has given me a boost.'

'Really? I can see she's had a big effect on you. You're not the kind of guy to take anything like that lightly. Are you going to have problems settling back in Oz?'

Danny knew what Skeeta was really asking. 'Linh Mai is a remarkable woman. Her brother told me I was doing her great damage by being so friendly and then shooting through. He told her the same thing. He talks about her becoming a nun but he doesn't understand his sister nearly well enough.'

'And you do?'

Danny nodded. 'This afternoon she told me I'd be a happy memory for her and she'd get on with her life. What bowled me over was when she said she'd seen the way I looked at her and feared she might have damaged my love for Jane. She said we all need love and should never regret loving anyone. Walking back here I could see she's right. I love quite a few people. I love all my family for a start. I even love you, you old sod. And each of those loves is different. I love Jane and, yes, I love Linh and those loves are different, too.'

'And now you're all for free love?'

'I wish you would take me seriously.'

'No need, mate. You do enough of that, yourself.'

When the section dutifully gathered at the Flags, Danny discovered the previous night had taken its toll on most of them and few were in shape for a crawl through the bars. Reluctantly and with some colourful language about the weak bastards who could get into the army these days, Pug gave in, providing they went back to his favourite, the Grand. Danny, still feeling remote from the revellers, became aware of a guy sitting alone at the next table. He was a lean, wiry man with long dark hair tied in a ponytail, dressed in a dark green T-shirt and faded denim jeans. He was taking no interest in anyone around him as he sipped his beer and smoked a cigarette.

'G'day,' Danny said to him. 'I'm an Aussie — Danny McBride.'

'Ya don't say,' came the reply in a southern American drawl. 'Jed Powlett.' He didn't offer to shake hands.

'Which unit are you from?' Danny asked.

Jed examined at him as if deciding whether it was safe to share such information. 'None now. Cut out on the army when I was in Saigon a while back.'

He laughed at the surprise on Danny's face but became thoughtful when Danny said, 'That must have been a tough decision for you.'

Once again Danny became the interested listener while Jed explained how he had not wanted to come to Vietnam in the first place but didn't have a better option at the time. He struck a chord with Danny when he described how the constant patrolling had got him down and, when he heard there was a bunch of deserters living at the back of the Ganh Hai Hills, went to join them. He had no idea how long he would stay but the longer he was there the easier it became to put off thinking about the future. He described his life enjoying the beach, fishing and coming into Vungas for a night out every now and again. He gave no explanation of how he supported himself. Jed said there were many Yanks opting out now. Some like him formed small communities in the hills or on the outskirts of towns like Vungas. Others never returned from R and R in Hong Kong or Taipei. Danny wondered at the risk he faced of being picked up by the local or military police when he came into town. Jed, in a tone that did not invite further questioning, said he had that sorted.

After sharing a few beers Jed said, 'You know there's not a bugger in the country who knows why he's here. I'm surprised there aren't more of us who skip.'

When Danny said he knew of no Australians who had deserted, he could see Jed did not believe him. He left soon afterwards, leaving Danny to toy with the idea of what it would be like to be the first Australian deserter. Jed had said the longer he was here the less he worried about the future. Danny had to admit there was great attraction in the idea of not having to worry about what to do next. What would Linh say if he arrived on her doorstep to tell her he had gone to live in the Ganh Hai Hills? Of course, he would eventually be arrested and returned to Australia in disgrace, but indulging in such impossible dreams was a way of keeping reality at bay.

Despite having denied significant areas of the province to the Viet Cong, the VC were still able to move across southern Phuoc Tuy from the jungles and coast in the east to the populated food-producing centres in the west. To deny this route to the VC, the Task Force planned to construct a fence which would run from the South China Sea past Dat Do, a town of several thousand, located several miles to the south of Nui Dat. The fence would consist of two parallel belts of barbed wire, six feet high and six feet wide, separated by one hundred yards in which a minefield of 20,000 mines would be laid. Several gaps were to be left in the fence so that the local farmers could work their land outside the fence by day. These gaps were to be manned by Vietnamese police during the day and closed at night. Patrols of South Vietnamese troops would prevent the VC breaching the fence after it was completed.

5RAR was given the task of constructing the fence. During

construction, the role of the Reconnaissance Platoon was to patrol during the day and lay ambushes at night to intercept any VC attempting to lift mines and lay them where they would be a hazard for the Australian patrols.

Late one afternoon, in a break from patrolling, Danny and Skeeta sat watching farmers from Dat Do leading their water buffalo home through a gate in the partly constructed fence. This had to be done before the 6 pm curfew was signalled by the firing of a flare. Anyone found outside the fence after curfew risked being shot.

'Those guys will need to get a move on if they're going to beat the curfew,' Danny said.

'I can understand why they're pissed off,' Skeeta said.

'Better than being shot.'

Skeeta continued to watch the men and their buffalos. 'Don't forget I'm a farmer. We farmers don't like being told when our day must end and those people, who say we're stupid and lazy just because we move slowly, give us the shits. I remember when the local council wanted to take a bad bend out of the road past our place and thought they'd do it by running the new stretch through one of our paddocks. All hell broke loose over that. I can't imagine what would have happened if they'd wanted to erect a barbed wire fence and lay mines, cutting our place in two.'

Danny was reminded of Tuan's condemnation of the Americans and Australians for alienating the villagers when he saw gaining their goodwill as essential to long-term success. Surely Tuan would see this as another example. Danny's thoughts were interrupted by the order to move out to where they were to set up an ambush that night.

The location for the ambush was in a disused paddy field not far from the Suoi Ba Tung creek where two tracks surrounded by scrubby bush met in the shape of a V. The platoon, well-armed with a variety of automatic weapons and grenade launchers, settled into the familiar triangular formation they used in such circumstances. It was just on dusk, giving time for their eyes to adapt to the changing light. Danny was in support of Jake who had his M60 covering the track.

They had been in place for a few hours when four VC came jogging along the track with their weapons held at waist height. Suddenly red tracer bullets streamed down the track from another section's machinegun. The enemy dived to the ground before Danny heard the distinctive sound of an AK-47 returning fire. A volley of the green tracer bullets used by the VC homed in on the muzzle flashes of the M60 which had done the initial damage and Blue, the gunner, writhed from the pain of bullets smashing into his leg. Instead of the usual silence which followed an ambush, a hail of enemy fire thrashed the trees above their position. Charlie had regrouped quickly and was systematically attacking the Australians. Unlike some of the VC Danny had encountered on other ambushes, these men knew what they were doing. The muzzle flashes from small arms and bursts of red and green tracer bullets from automatic weapons flickered in the low trees. The ambush had become a full-scale fire-fight.

After an ambush, the Reconnaissance Platoon would usually melt away in the manner they had been taught during training, but this time they had a badly injured man and could not break from the enemy. In the midst of the battle Danny heard the chilling scream of another soldier who had been hit. He couldn't tell whether it was one of the enemy or one of their own. After the howl had died away, he could hear the voices of VC officers organising a counter-attack. Clearly the Reconnaissance Platoon had run into a group much larger than a single platoon and was heavily outnumbered. The M79 grenade launchers were used on the enemy position and brought a fierce response. Now bursts of fire were coming from their flanks as the VC spread out around them. Danny was no stranger to the fear of battle but that was usually before and after engagement, not during it. This time his fear was more than personal. He faced the prospect the whole platoon could be overrun.

The platoon commander radioed in for supporting fire from artillery at Nui Dat. Danny would later learn that the enormous whoosh and crump of shells descending on the enemy came from American 155's and 175's at Nui Dat and a US destroyer in the South China Sea. Pieces of shrapnel from the explosions flew over his head as the commander called directions into his handset. A mistake here and they'd be killed by ill-named 'friendly fire'.

'Time to go,' the commander called and in the silence after the onslaught the members of the platoon slipped away from the ambush site, four of them carrying the injured gunner. Suddenly the barrage of shells resumed. As if in brave but fruitless response to the might of the artillery, orange flashes from VC mortar bombs covered the position they had just abandoned. 'Nice timing,' Pug muttered.

Now all attention was focussed on bringing the dust-off safely in for the injured Blue. They prepared to provide cover if there was any sign of Charlie. The chopper descended and, when the pilot put on the spotlight, Danny feared the onslaught of enemy fire but Blue was loaded and the helicopter lifted off safely. The platoon sergeant led the men across the paddy while the commander called for another round of artillery to cover their withdrawal.

When they finally reached safety there was an air of unreality. Did the danger, the fear, the destruction of the past hours really occur of was it a nightmare from which Danny had just awoken.

'I reckon we're right now,' Skeeta said.

'Yeah, of course we are,' Danny said, concerned Skeeta might not be free from the nightmare.

'I don't mean just now. I mean for the rest of our time here.'

'How do you make that out?'

'Well, we only have six weeks to go and I don't see us running into any strife as big as that in the rest of our time.'

'Six weeks is it?' Danny was surprised to find Skeeta was counting.

For the next two weeks, while they continued to patrol and lay ambushes, Skeeta was correct. They met no major problems and it was clear the large force they had encountered had withdrawn from attempting a direct assault on the fence. Instead there were some incursions by one or two-man parties who avoided detection and relayed some of the mines where they posed a danger to the Australians. The Reconnaissance Platoon patrolled closer to the fence during the day and at night mounted multiple ambushes along approach tracks. At the end of each day Danny watched the farmers returning before the curfew and wondered again about the wisdom and effectiveness of the army's strategy.

And it wasn't just the fence. He would soon be returning to Australia having not achieved the mission he had embraced when coming here and now doubting its achievability or worth. What could he commit to when he returned to Australia? The newsagency wasn't the answer. And he had to tell Jane about Linh.

One morning he was surprised to see a young woman lead a line of children through the gate from Dat Do and set off along the track towards the Suoi Ba Tung creek. Were they on a picnic or was this a nature excursion? He thought of the havoc created by the artillery barrage a fortnight ago and wondered what the children would think of the destruction when they saw it. He also wondered what Linh would now be doing with her class.

When the farmers were slowly wending their way through the gate that evening, he looked for the children and was disappointed to find no sign of the them. It then occurred to him their teacher would have brought them home well before the curfew and they would have returned when he was on patrol out of sight of the gate.

The fence was now close to completion and Pug set the ambush that night along a narrow track close to the southern end. Dusk had not yet darkened to full night and they were hardly in place when a single figure came towards them along the track. He was not dressed like a soldier and strolled towards them apparently unconcerned by any danger. Skeeta who was closest to him called out, 'Hurry up mate. Curfew.'

The man stopped, peered into the clump of bamboo from which Skeeta's voice had come, suddenly leapt to the side of the track and fired a shot from a weapon he had concealed. Skeeta gave a stifled cry and Jake let fly with the M60. Ritchie and Danny, conscious this might be the start of a counter-ambush crawled as quickly as they could towards Skeeta while the others provided cover. Danny found Skeeta lying on his back with his head turned to one side, as though enjoying a good sleep. When Ritchie arrived, he checked Skeeta's shallow breathing and searched his body for the wound. It was only when he turned Skeeta's head that they could see a single bullet had entered his left temple which was bleeding profusely. There was no sign of exit. Ritchie staunched the bleeding with a pad and bound Skeeta's head in a tight bandage. 'Bloody bad luck to cop this from a single shot,' he said. 'Still he's breathing.

'We need to get a dust-off,' Danny said.

'Already called one.' Danny became aware that Pug was beside them. 'I've given them a location down the track near the fence. I'll take him. Dreamer, you and Jake cover our rear.' He lifted Skeeta gently before walking down the track cradling him as though carrying a sleeping child.

For the next few days Pug made sure to tell Danny whenever he had any news of Skeeta. He had arrived in Vung Tau in a critical condition but the doctors were able to stabilise him and next day undertook an operation to remove the bullet which had passed through his brain and lodged in his skull. The operation was successful but the damage to the brain was severe.

'I don't like it,' Pug said to Danny and gave a deep sigh, one that Danny had never heard from Pug before. 'They reckon he's still got a chance to pull through, but I can't see how he'll ever be properly right.'

'Yeah,' Danny said. 'It would be tough for him to be invalided out and he'd hate to be a burden to his family. If his mind's affected ...'

'You'll have to pray for him. What has me beat is why he called to the bugger who shot him.'

'Skeeta must have thought he was a farmer. He had a soft spot for the farmers round here, having to cope with the fence and the curfew. He just thought it was one of them taking too long to get home.'

Pug shook his head. 'It just goes to show when you're in a war it doesn't pay to be kind.'

Danny assumed Pug was having a go at him again. 'He didn't look like VC. Who do you think he was?'

'A farmer, Charlie, one of the ARVN skiving off, some crook from Dat Do? Who knows? The weapon he had couldn't have been more than a pistol. Not VC gear. Meanwhile, we need to get out on patrol. Something to keep us occupied while we wait. Without my forward scout you need to do the job for me, Dreamer.'

Danny was pleased to see the teacher — he thought it was the same woman — leading her class out for another excursion. He took their presence as a good omen for Skeeta.

The patrol was uneventful but when they returned Pug approached him with a long face. 'He didn't make it.' It was as if Pug had whacked him in the guts. 'Like we said the other day, maybe it's for the best.' He gazed intently at Danny before adding, 'Don't let it distract you out there.'

'It won't distract me,' Danny said. He didn't say that Skeeta's death altered everything. He didn't care what was right or wrong any more. He wanted to go home and meanwhile would kill anyone who threatened him or his mates. He didn't care who they were — peasants, ARVN, Viet Cong, North Vietnamese Army — it was all the same to him.

He was thankful the section did not return to where Skeeta was shot. Instead they set up an ambush along the path which led to the gate in the fence about half way to the Suoi Ba Tung creek. They were hardly settled in position when Danny could see two figures approaching through the gloom — one of average height for a Vietnamese, the other shorter. Was this a repeat of the other night? Was the taller one the man who had shot Skeeta? Was this his chance to avenge Skeeta?

He raised his rifle, took careful aim and, although he should have held his fire until the couple had come closer, could not wait. A single shot felled the taller one. Danny readied to fire at the other when the unmistakable howl of a crying child came to him. He stood up and ran down the track. A young child cowered away from him while the schoolteacher lay lifeless on the track.

⟍⟋

The enquiry held at Nui Dat cleared Danny of grave misconduct but sanctioned him for not following the rules of engagement and wait-ing until the enemy suspect had come closer before opening fire. The explanation for the presence of the two on the track after curfew was that the child had wandered away and become lost towards the end of the day and the teacher had brought the rest of the class back to the Dat Do gate before returning to search for the child. A formal apology was made to the people of Dat Do, reparation made to the family of the schoolteacher and further warnings made about the dangers of going outside the fence after curfew. The platoon was relocated to Nui Dat where it undertook guard duty on the base.

None of this was any consolation to Danny who remained distraught at the two deaths. His suggestion he go to the funeral of the school-teacher was immediately rejected. Pug had a better idea. 'I've had a word up the line and got you leave to go to Vungas and pay your respects to Skeeta before he's sent home.'

'I don't know, Pug. I like to think of Skeeta as I knew him. Seeing him dead in a box isn't my idea of a good way to farewell him.'

'Suit yourself, Dreamer, but go anyway. I've got you one day and one night in Vungas. Go and see that girl of yours. You need a shoulder to cry on and I reckon hers will be a lot better than any of ours.'

'How do you know ...'

'Skeeta had a word to me. Wanted me to know you were OK when you skived off on your own in Vungas.'

⟍⟋

Danny waited until he could be confident Linh would be home from

239

school before he went to her house. He hesitated before knocking and almost walked away when she did not immediately come to the door. When she did open it and saw him, her face clouded. 'Danny! Danny, what is wrong?'

'Skeeta is dead and I killed a schoolteacher from Do Dat. She was just like you,' he sobbed.

'Come in. Come in.' She drew him in, closed the door and wrapped him in her arms. 'Tell me everything.'

On awakening Danny was unsure where he was until he smelt Linh's musky perfume on the pillow. Opening his eyes, he found her sitting at the end of the bed watching him. Her face showed concern and her eyes were soft. 'Do you feel a little happier? Are you rested?'

Linh was fully dressed but he was naked under the covers. 'Linh, I'm so sorry.'

'We have nothing to be sorry about.' He noticed the emphasis she put on the word 'we'. 'You needed to speak of your sadness and remorse. You had to rid yourself of so many dark thoughts. And then we needed to fill you with loving thoughts and memories.' She gazed at him as if fixing his image in her mind. 'Now, get dressed and I will serve you a Vietnamese breakfast.'

Her latter words brought him fully awake and he checked his watch. 'Ten o'clock. Is that really the time?'

'I think that might have been the best sleep you have had in months. You needed the rest.'

'But I was s'posed to be on the truck at nine. I only had leave for a day.'

'In that case you have time for breakfast before you report in and see about alternative transport.'

Linh left him and went into the kitchen. When he came to join her, he had a new concern. 'Shouldn't you be at school?'

'I sent a message with one of my neighbours that I wouldn't be in today.' She smiled at him. 'I didn't say why.'

Danny received a frosty welcome when he arrived at the transport depot and was told to report to his platoon commander immediately on return to Nui Dat.

He spent the trip switching between memories of his time with Linh and contemplating the consequences. It was a revelation to him that lovemaking could relieve grief but what did he know about love? Linh said that expressions of love were all-powerful, enhancing joy and bringing balm to pain. It had been pure and lovely. For a time it had brought him peace, but now he knew the results were catastrophic. Surely there would be neighbours, people he had met at the church, who would have seen when he came and when he left. The consequences for Linh, her reputation, her standing in the Catholic community of which she was such an integral part, maybe even for her job, all of them irreparably damaged. His first reckoning would be with the army. He wondered what his punishment would be. Pug had tried to help him out and would be furious. And this was the least of his problems. Only a few weeks and he would be on his way home. He had planned to tell Jane about Linh but what could he say to her now? His mother would be wretched. It had been hard to take his father treating him like some kind of hero before he left. It would be unbearable when Danny returned. He knew he couldn't go back to the newsagency. But what could he do instead? Was there any part of his life that wasn't a total mess?

Pug was waiting for him when he arrived. 'Where the bloody hell did you get to?'

'I slept in.'

Pug sneered at him. 'If it was up to me, I'd put you in the slammer for the rest of your time over here but we have to see the skip. Remember to salute when we get there. You're on formal report.'

The lieutenant came straight to the point. 'Private McBride, being AWOL is a serious offence warranting a significant penalty. Corporal Preston has assured me that prior to this you have performed well.'

Danny shot a glance at Pug who was staring straight ahead. What about their various run-ins and the business of not shooting the unarmed VC?

'All of us are aware of the events of recent days,' the lieutenant said.

Was he to be given a reprieve?

'However, in your current state, I have no confidence you could go on active duty without being a risk to the operation and to your fellows. I was considering a change of role for you but higher command has now taken the matter out of my hands.'

Was the boss telling him he would have let him off lightly but the brass wanted more? Was he to be made an example, a scapegoat? How would they know what it'd been like? He had not expected to feel resentment at whatever punishment was in store for him, but there it was.

'Do you recall the date you entered the army?'

The question had Danny flummoxed. Why did he want to know that? From the depths of his memory an image appeared of Sean reading out the letter telling him he had been called up. 'It was April. I think it might have been the twelfth.'

The commander checked a sheet of paper he had in front of him. 'Yeah, that's what it says here. The army adheres strictly to the two-year period you signed on for. Today is the tenth of April. You're to be sent home forthwith. You fly out tomorrow.'

Danny was having trouble grasping what he had been told. 'But doesn't the battalion have another few weeks here?'

'We do. You don't.'

Home Again

After their return from Bien Hoa, Jane had been in theatre with Gordon several times. He had reverted to his usual hospital manner, softened only by a warmer smile of greeting than had been his habit. After a month, just as she was regretfully accepting he must have had second thoughts on the tennis, he called her. 'I'm ringing about the tennis. Sorry about the short notice but we're having a game next Sunday afternoon. Perhaps you already have a commitment. Would you like to play?'

Jane thought he was making it easy for her to say no. She was supposed to be having lunch with her parents but she knew her mother would be delighted to hear she had been invited to tennis by a doctor, no less. 'Thank you. I'd like to come.'

He picked her up in his gleaming MG and told her they were going to Brighton. 'The court is at the home of the parents of my best friend, Peter Trethowan. We went to school together.'

'Where was that?' Not for the first time, Jane was struck by how little she knew of Gordon's personal history or circumstances.

'We went to Scotch.'

She thought of Richard St John and his friends. Gordon was nothing like them. Surely his friend wouldn't be, either.

They came to an imposing house on a large block overlooking the Bay. 'This is where I played my first game of tennis,' he said.

They were greeted by Peter, a large man with a genial smile, who immediately put Jane at her ease. His open, straightforward manner contrasted with Gordon's multifaceted personality and she guessed their longstanding friendship stemmed from the way they complemented one another. Waiting by the court was Peter's girlfriend, Claudia, a willowy blonde who, Jane would learn, could play well when of a mind to do so, although she preferred not to exert herself unduly. Shortly afterwards they were joined by Heather, one of Peter's colleagues from the stockbroking business owned and run by his father. The remaining player was Nick, a successful entrepreneur, who was one of Peter's clients. It was apparent Peter was a man who liked to mix business with pleasure. He was also deft at mixing the pairings so that Jane played with each of the men in a series of enjoyable games.

While they sat watching the others, Gordon surprised her by suddenly telling her that he had grown up in Glen Iris where his father owned a pharmacy. He added that he had two sisters, one of whom had followed her father into the pharmacy while the other was a journalist. This was more information on his family than he had revealed in the months at Bien Hoa. Perhaps he was concerned she might be overawed by the grandeur of the house and its surrounds.

When it was her turn to sit out with Peter, he chatted away about the house, his parents and his hopes to take over from his father as the head of the stockbroking business. He then turned his attention to her and asked about her family and her life as a nurse, speaking admiringly of her courage serving in Vietnam. 'I was pretty scared at times,' she admitted but did not mention how she suffered from the occasional flashback to that night of the break-in at the jail. 'Gordon was the one with the courage.'

Peter immediately told her what a fine man Gordon was and how lucky he was to have him as a friend. This gave her the opportunity to mention the different personalities Gordon exhibited in and out of the hospital. Peter laughed before saying, 'Yeah, when the task at hand is important to him, he gives all his attention to it and ignores everything else. Doesn't matter whether it's an open-heart operation or trying to improve his backhand. At other times, as I'm sure you've found, he becomes a lively and interesting companion.'

Jane nodded her agreement and was surprised when he frowned at her and said, 'He's a very private person who keeps his deepest thoughts and feelings well hidden. You need to know that.' She was disappointed when they were called back onto the court and the chance to learn more was lost. For the rest of that first day, though, Jane was conscious of Peter taking every opportunity to spend time chatting with her and encouraging her to tell him about herself. Accustomed to being flattered by such attention, this time she was bothered that Peter might be more like Richard St John than she had first thought. She felt sorry for Claudia and would have been concerned for Gordon had he shown the slightest sign of minding that Peter was taking such an interest in her. Had she read too much into Gordon's invitation to join him at tennis?

When she sat with Peter on a second afternoon of tennis, his questions became even more personal. 'Gordon tells me you have a boyfriend who's serving in Vietnam. I s'pose you miss him.'

'Yes, I do. I'll be very glad when he's back home.' She wasn't going to tell Peter she was increasingly worried about Danny. The gaps between his letters had been growing and those that did arrive were brief and stilted. Something was amiss with Danny and she didn't know whether it was to do with Vietnam or with her.

'You're not engaged, though?'

Jane's first impulse was to tell him to mind his own business, but she thought of a better response. 'I didn't think such things would be of interest to you. Have you popped the question to Claudia, yet?' She smiled at him archly. 'Do tell.'

The impact of her response surprised her. He stiffened and his face reddened as though she had slapped him. 'I'm sorry. I shouldn't, but ... Oh, never mind.' He stood up, but the game on court was far from over and he had nowhere to go. 'Can I pour you another drink?'

Jane had not meant her words to be as harsh as Peter had taken them but was not sorry. Perhaps it was the only way she could stop him pestering her. For the rest of the day he did not try to speak with her except in the most cursory fashion, but she noticed he kept glancing in her direction. Could it be he was actually smitten with her?

When Gordon rang the third time, Jane was planning to tell him she couldn't come, but he surprised her by saying, 'I guess you're excited. Won't your Danny be home any day now?'

It was the first time he had mentioned Danny since they had been in Bien Hoa. 'Yes, it must be very soon, but we haven't heard an actual day yet. The army isn't good about notifying the family.' She didn't say that neither she nor Mary had received a letter from Danny for weeks.

'I'm sure you won't have much time for tennis when he's back, so I thought you might like to squeeze in a game next Sunday.'

He made it sound like a farewell performance and Jane liked that idea. It was a kinder way of breaking off with Gordon than saying no to his invitation. 'I guess you're right. I've enjoyed our games and it would be nice to have one more.'

Jane watched as Gordon gathered himself for his second serve to her. His first had been fast but well wide of the sideline. He took several slow breaths, bowed his head and bounced the ball three times before serving again. By now Jane had seen enough of Gordon's game to know how he strove on every point to recall and emulate his coach's instructions. She could almost hear him reciting: 'Relax the tension in hands, arms and shoulders, throw the ball straight up, coil and release through the shot.' His intensity was often his undoing, tightening his grip and stiffening his body. If only he had some of Danny's ease and balance, he would do far better. This time the serve was in court but short and she had no difficulty sending the ball speeding into the gap between Gordon and Claudia. Claudia did well to reach it and parry a weak forehand down the sideline, but Peter had anticipated the shot and was able to volley the ball away for a winner.

'Too good,' Gordon said with a laugh. 'Claudia, we'll have to lift our game if we're ever going to beat these two.'

As Jane and Peter left the court and the others began their game, she wondered what he might say to her. He was not at all like a man who had just won a set of tennis with her as his partner. In silence he ushered her to a court-side chair and poured a drink for her before seating himself beside her and taking a mouthful from his glass.

Eventually in a voice hardly louder than a whisper, he said, 'Jane, I have a favour to ask of you. I need to speak with you privately. Could you have a drink with me after work one day next week?'

So, she hadn't got rid of him last time after all. What a pest! 'What does Claudia think of this idea?'

'She suggested it.'

'What?'

'I made such a mess of speaking with you last time I was reluctant to try again, but Claudia encouraged me to persist. It's for Gordon's sake.'

'I don't understand.'

'Yes, I know. But can we meet? At the Chevron, perhaps. It's just along from the Alfred. I don't want to put you out.'

'I'm in surgery next week and can't be sure I can be clear before about six ...'

'That's fine. Let's say tomorrow, 6.30 at the Chevron.'

Jane had not been to the Chevron before and was struck by the fading opulence of its dark wood and claret velvet furnishings. Men in suits and women in cocktail dresses mingled in the bar and made Jane wish she had taken more trouble over her dressing. She could not see Peter until he rose from a small table in the far corner of the room and walked towards her.

'Thank you for coming,' he said in a relieved voice. 'What would you like to drink?'

'A Pimms, please.'

He returned with a tray holding her Pimms, a dish of nuts and olives and what she thought was a glass of whisky 'Cheers,' he said his face unsmiling. 'I hope your day has been rewarding.'

'Best for us both, Peter, if you tell me what you want to speak about.'

He sipped his whisky as if uncertain how to begin. Eventually, he said, 'I don't know if you remember … The first day we met I told you Gordon is a private person who keeps his deepest thoughts and feelings well hidden.'

'Yes, I remember. And you told me I needed to know that. You didn't say why, though.'

'We both know Gordon can become intense, even obsessive, about things that matter to him.' The crowd in the room had swelled and Peter was speaking softly, so Jane had to lean forward to catch his words. 'Sometimes those obsessions are obvious to even a casual observer. His car for example. But when it comes to his deepest feelings, matters of the heart for example …' Peter paused to take another sip of his drink. 'Sometimes he confides in me and I always try to help him out. My ham-fisted attempt to speak with you at tennis a few weeks ago was the result. This time I want to start by telling you about Gordon.' He leant back and sighed. 'If he knew I was doing this, he'd probably kill me, but I think it's in his best interests … and I guess yours as well.'

A bray of laughter came from a man in the group next to them and Peter glanced around quickly before turning back to Jane. 'About five or six years ago, not long after he finished at uni, Gordon started taking out a girl we all liked. Her name was Christine. Everything went along fine and, just when we were expecting to be told of an engagement, Chris dropped him and went off with another guy. Gordon took it hard. He immersed himself in his work, which became the sole purpose of his life. Gradually he recovered. He started to enjoy being with his friends again and regained some of his enthusiasm for his car, tennis and the like. And then you came along.'

'I came along? What do you mean?'

'He started telling me about this nurse he'd met in surgery and how she had impressed him.'

Jane threw back her head and widened her eyes. 'Wow! I know what a glamorous figure I cut in my surgical gown, cap and mask.'

'No, it was your manner.' Peter was unmoved by her attempt to lighten the conversation. 'At least that's what he said. He was impressed by the conscientious and efficient way you went about your work. I thought there might be more to it than that and was delighted he was taking an interest in another woman.' Jane remembered Mrs Gupta saying something similar. Perhaps Gordon had taken Christine for meals there. 'I encouraged him to take you out but he said it was too soon. What he meant of course was that he was frightened of being disappointed again. He hung back, enjoying every time you worked together, until he got the chance to suggest you go with him to that Indian place. He was very pleased with himself for being able to make it like his invitation was just a follow-on from a hard day in theatre.'

'But that night at Mrs Gupta's I told him about my boyfriend, Danny.'

'Yeah, that was a disappointment for him. But the rest of the night went so well he was unwilling to walk away. What's more, you sighed before saying you were going to a family party for your boyfriend who was going to Vietnam.'

'I don't remember that.'

'Gordon does. It made him wonder just how closely attached you were to this boyfriend. I told him he should ask you out and see what you said.' Jane was distracted by a tall, elegant woman in a chic red dress who walked past them. She joined a much older man who had been drinking alone and kissed him on the lips. '... and he engineered your inclusion.' Was Peter speaking about Bien Hoa? 'He was even more pleased with himself than he had been when he took you to the Indian's.'

'But he made such little effort to get to know me better. Out of the hospital he tried to avoid me. It wasn't until I asked him if he thought I was a dragon that he had anything to do with me on social occasions.'

Peter opened his hands in appeal. 'Don't you see? Every time you took the trouble to engage with him, he saw that as a sign of growing affection for him. He wrote me a number of letters from Vietnam and they were filled with his pleasure at your kindness to him. I found it embarrassing to read his account of the night you hugged and kissed him.'

'But that was after I thought I was going to die and he came to rescue me.'

'Exactly. How many movies have a scene like that?'

Jane could see Peter had now overcome his diffidence about speaking with her and could even chuckle at his friend's passion. This time she was the one slow to smile. 'I think Gordon is a lovely man. I admired him the first time I worked with him and felt I was rewarded for my efforts to have him open up to me during our time at Bien Hoa. But that doesn't alter the fact I love Danny and expect to marry him in the not-to-distant future.' She should have said 'hope' rather than 'expect' but didn't want to show any doubt to Peter.

'Forgive me, but you are sure?'

'I just said so.'

'It's just that Gordon clings to the hope he might still have a chance with you. Coming to tennis as you have ...'

Jane took an olive from the dish. She needed something to settle her thoughts. What a cheek this man had, suggesting Gordon's problems were all her doing. If he hadn't been so diffident about declaring himself, she wouldn't have tried to draw him out. How dare Peter suggest that coming for a game of tennis meant she was thinking of ditching Danny in favour of Gordon. Tennis was a way to get some exercise, enjoy herself and not be stuck at home, worrying about what was going on with Danny. The olive had been marinated in a fiery sauce. She coughed and took a mouthful of her Pimms. 'Just last week Gordon suggested, with Danny soon to return, Sunday's game might well be my last and I agreed with him.'

'He was fishing, of course. You must have known that.'

Now Peter expected her to read Gordon's mind. Gordon was a sweet man and she had enjoyed the attention he'd been paying her — she needed something to make up for Danny's indifference over the past months — but it had to stop.

'I'll miss the exercise and the enjoyment of playing with all of you but, let me assure you, last Sunday was my last game.'

Danny stood at Sydney's Central Station oblivious to the crowd of people scurrying past him. When a woman carrying a red suitcase cannoned into his leg and glared at him before hurrying on, he began to look around. A mother was urging her children on as she dragged them towards the station exit, a man bustled through the crush towards a platform where departure bells were sounding, a group of schoolboys laughed and jostled one another as they entered the doors of the station cafeteria. Everyone was intent on going somewhere. Everyone except him. It had been like this on the flight from Vietnam. He kept aloof from the other nashos who spent their time swapping experiences and talking about what they would do after they arrived home. Did they know his story? Is that why they were happy to ignore him? Certainly, the bloke at the airport who issued his travel warrant to Melbourne was keen to be rid of him.

Danny ambled over to join the line at the booking office. The man there took his time scrutinising his warrant before giving him a ticket for the evening train. Danny didn't mind — he had hours to fill before it left. He walked outside the station to the small triangle of parkland where he saw four or five winos slumped under a tree. One of them waved a bottle in what Danny took to be an invitation to join them. He had no interest in accepting but liked the idea of a drink and sought out a nearby pub where he sat for the next couple of hours slowly putting away schooners of Tooheys. Several other patrons attempted to start conversations with him but he brushed them off. As the time for his train's departure approached, he left the pub unsteadily, found the designated platform and took a seat in a second-class carriage no different from the one he had occupied on his trip up to Sydney.

As soon as they were under way he leant back and shut his eyes in the vain hope sleep would allow him to escape his thoughts. Some of the time he dozed, but mostly he wrestled with the problems which continued to torture him. What should he have done? What would have made a difference? He had to work out what he was going to do when he got home. What was he going to say to them? He saw the shocked faces of Jane and his family and opened his eyes. Through the window of the carriage everything was black. Not a glimmer of light. No hope.

Eventually exhaustion brought a troubled sleep until he was woken by a garbled announcement that the train was about to reach Junee. He remembered that was somewhere near Skeeta's property. 'At Mundarlo,' Skeeta had said, 'between Junee and Gundagai.' Danny shook himself, stood up and grabbed his pack. He would go and pay his respects to Skeeta's family. Anything was better than reaching home.

The handful of other passengers who left the train hurried away and Danny stood alone outside the station. An icy wind blew directly down the street and Danny, acclimatised to the humid heat of Vietnam, began to shiver in his greatcoat. The station was now locked, so he lay on the floor of the entry hall to wait for the town to stir. At least he was out of the worst of the wind.

When the dark began to give way to a frosty morning light, Danny roused himself and went in search of some food. He was cold, stiff and had a bad headache but found a pub which was willing to serve him a hot breakfast. The bacon and eggs were greasy and the toast dry, but he left feeling less depressed. He had thawed out, been given directions for reaching Mundarlo and had a purpose: he would visit Skeeta's family, tell them what a great mate he had been to Danny and offer his condolences.

He found the road to Gundagai without difficulty but was unsuccessful in thumbing a lift until a truckie delivering a load of hay picked him up. 'Not goin' into Mundarlo,' the man said, 'but I'll drop yer at the turnoff. Not much goes down there but a young bloke like you can walk it.'

After the truckie dropped him, Danny set off along the dirt road through lush sheep country and found, contrary to the man's forecast, there were some cars heading for Mundarlo. None stopped to give him a lift until a battered ute pulled up and an elderly man with a ruddy, wrinkled face gestured for him to climb aboard. The man wore a well-pressed suit he must have owned for many years. He also wore a collar and tie — unusual for a farmer. It wasn't Sunday.

'Dunno you'll find much casual work round Mundarlo,' the man said.

'I'm not here for work. I want to visit the Phillips family. Do you know them?'

'You goin to the funeral?' the man asked in a surprised tone.

'What funeral is that?'

'You dunno?' The man was even more incredulous. 'For Skeeta, one of the sons.'

'I've just got back from Vietnam. Skeeta was my mate. I was there when he was shot.'

The man nodded sympathetically. 'What a bugger. I know how hard that is. Saw a few of me mates get it at Tobruk.' He turned his head to scrutinise Danny carefully. 'Sorry for thinkin' y'were after work, but y'don't look like a bloke going to a funeral. I'm in me weddin' and funeral suit. Don't get to many weddin's these days but plenty a funerals. For young Skeeta, though? That's a real bugger.' He gazed at Danny. 'Thought the army'd treat ya better.'

'Had to kip on the station at Junee last night.'

'Won't be much time when we get there. Don't even know if there's somewhere y'can give yerself a lick and a promise. Best stick with me and we sit up the back. I reckon there'll be a crowd.' They travelled in silence for a while before the man said, 'Forgot to say. I'm Vin Prentice.' He held across a gnarled hand and Danny was surprised by the strength of his grip.

'Danny McBride.'

Mundarlo had a general store, a garage, a timber merchant, a small school, a muddy sports field beside a creek and a few houses. On a small hill above Mundarlo Danny saw a bluestone church beside an old cemetery. A hearse was drawn up on the road outside the church with cars and utes parked along the verge. After joining them, Vin climbed from the ute and said, 'Follow me, Danny.' He marched him past some curious onlookers gathered on the grass in front of the church and mounted the steps. For a moment Danny hesitated. He had seen the sign Mundarlo Methodist Church and Catholics were not supposed to attend Protestant services without permission of the bishop.

They entered the church and Vin piloted him to a pew where there were two vacant places. Danny was eyed off again as those already in the pew shuffled down to let them in. The bare walls and absence of stained-glass windows struck Danny as cold and stark compared with the churches he knew. A woman at a small organ was playing a sombre tune. A darkly polished casket stood at the front. The casket was draped with an Australian flag and bore Skeeta's slouch hat beside a wreath of white roses. Danny couldn't remember when he had last seen Skeeta in his slouch hat. In Vietnam they always wore floppy canvas ones.

Apart from an empty pew at the front, the rest filled quickly and several lines of men stood in the space at the rear of the church. The organist lifted her volume and a gap formed, allowing the minister to walk down the aisle. He was followed by three men of strong build, each apparently as uncomfortable as Vin in their suits and ties, although theirs were of a more recent fashion. Behind them came an older man who appeared as fit and strong as those that preceded him. He stood erect, staring straight ahead and reminded Danny of a sergeant-major. He held the arm of a small, dark-haired woman in a black dress who was bent over by grief or by some physical ailment; Danny could not tell which. Skeeta had inherited his mother's build and colouring while his brothers were younger versions of their father.

As soon as the minister began the service, Danny took a dislike to him. He was a weak-chinned man whose lack of gravitas robbed the service of the dignity Danny wanted to honour Skeeta. 'Friends,' he said, smiling at the congregation, we begin with a hymn I'm sure is well-known to all. Danny knew neither the words nor the tune and, to judge by the efforts of the congregation, neither did most of the mourners. The bible reading, undertaken haltingly by one of Skeeta's brothers, was from a modern translation which lacked the grandeur Danny expected.

The priest shuffled some papers and began his eulogy. 'We're here today to mark the passing of one our town's sons, a young man dear to us all.' Skeeta had made it clear he and the rest of his family were not churchgoers but this priest was pretending to know him well. 'John Richard Phillips, the man we are here to honour, achieved much in his short life. John, who was known by some as Skeeta, was the fourth son in the Phillips family and ...'

Danny's shut his eyes. Skeeta was his name, not John. They were here to honour Skeeta.

'John was born in Mundarlo ...' The priest checked his notes. '... just over twenty-two years ago.' Danny listened with mounting anger as the priest, working from what he must have gleaned from the family, described the life of the man he continued to call 'John'.

'Call him Skeeta,' Danny wanted to shout. The priest continued to survey Skeeta's life but failed to convey the essence of his personality to a church filled with people, Danny guessed, who would have known him well. The last straw was when the minister said, 'And finally John gave his life in the service of his nation.'

Danny jumped to his feet and called out. 'No, you're wrong. Skeeta went to Vietnam to serve his nation but he died thinking he was saving a farmer. Skeeta was a farmer through and through, and that's how he died. The army won't have told you this, so I owe it to him to tell you how my best mate, Skeeta, met his death.' For a moment Danny paused. What was he doing? Where had his words come from? Could he go on? He was aware that many of those sitting in front of him had turned to see who had interrupted the service.

The silence in the church encouraged him to continue. He told them how he and Skeeta had met on their first day as nashos and remained together throughout their time in Vietnam. He reminded his listeners of Skeeta's skill as a repairman and explained how in the army he demonstrated how to get on with people and 'wangle things'. He described Skeeta's stoicism and cheerfulness, his unmatched ability to read country and see what others missed, resulting in him becoming the forward scout in the Reconnaissance Platoon. He told them about the creation of the fence, the need for the farmers to pass through the gate before the curfew and how Skeeta's sympathies had been entirely with the farmers. Finally, he described how Skeeta died because he thought a farmer had stayed out too late and might be killed. Danny's voice shook when he said, 'I wanted you to know that's how he lived and died.'

When Danny awoke, he was slow to recognise the bed in which he lay. This time he did not have Linh's scent but the musty smell of a seldom used room. He pushed back the blankets and swung his feet onto the timber floor, but before he could get up a voice from the doorway said, 'Thought I heard a bit o' movement.' Vin Prentice stood there with his craggy smile. 'I've just brewed some tea. Stay there and I'll bring yer a cup.'

Danny sank back onto the bed, recalling with remorse what he had done yesterday. Where would he be without Vin? After his extraordinary outburst, which must have embarrassed everyone, Vin stood and put an arm around him while the minister announced another hymn. When the whole congregation was on its feet, the old man said, 'Come on, mate. Better we go,' and began to guide Danny out of the pew. Danny was slow to move and felt Vin's bony fingers tighten their grip. Vin took him through the crowd at the back and down the steps to the ute. They drove in silence until well out of the town when Danny said, 'I'm sorry. I don't know what got into me. I'm usually pretty quiet. I must have offended all those people — particularly Skeeta's family — carrying on like I did.'

'Dunno 'bout that,' Vin said. 'After the way that minister was carryin' on I reckon Skeeta's mates ud be queuin' up to buy ya a beer. I didn't reckon y'were in a good state to deal with anyone right then. That's why I got us out o'there. What I reckon y'need most is a shower, a shave, somethin' to eat and a good night's sleep. Don't reckon you've had any of them for a while.'

Vin saw Danny through each item on his list and apologised that his wife, who died three years ago, would have provided much more appetising food. After a dinner of grilled lamb chops, tomato and chips, he poured Danny a stiff whisky from an old bottle and packed him off to bed in the room he said hadn't been used for a while but didn't explain why.

Danny came out of his reverie when Vin returned with a mug of tea and the smell of oats. 'Put on the porridge. Best way to get y'started these cold mornin's.'

Danny had not eaten porridge since sleepovers with his grandma and grandpa when he was little. In those days he knew he must eat the stodgy stuff without complaint and hoped he hadn't lost the knack. As it turned out Vin's porridge was far easier to get down than his grandma's. When he had emptied his bowl, he turned to thank Vin and became conscious of how steadily Vin was regarding him. 'Had a call from Meg, Skeeta's mum.'

'When was that?'

'Last night. Y'were asleep.'

'Any chance I could see the family today? I want to apologise.'

'She doesn't think that's a good idea,' Vin said.

Danny dropped his head. 'So I did upset them. Bugger.'

'You didn't upset her. Matter of fact, she was worried about you. That's why she rang. No one knew who y'were, o'course, but Skeeta had told her a good bit about ya in his letters, so she thought it must be you. She'd like to see ya but reckons now's not the right time. We had a long talk about it.'

Vin used his thumb and forefinger to scratch his bristled chin. 'The problem is Jim, Skeeta's dad. He's a difficult bugger. The family's been here for generations and Jim wants everyone to remember that — treat him with the respect he reckons is due to him. For him Skeeta's funeral had to be done right. I guess he'd call it givin' him a decent burial. When you jumped up, he thought some loony derelict had got into the church.' Vin gave Danny his crooked grin. 'Can't say I blame him. When, first up, y'said Skeeta hadn't died serving his country, Jim was furious. If his son was goin' t'die, he had to be some kind o'hero. Everythin' y'said after that he heard as y'tryin' to cut him down t'size.'

'But he was a hero to me,' Danny said. 'That's what I was trying to say. That minister mouthed his clichés and didn't say anything about Skeeta's real character. I couldn't stand it. He had all those qualities that distinguish people from the bush and we needed to pay tribute to that. Skeeta's death was a tragedy — the greatest tragedy I've ever had to deal with and ...' Danny choked back a sob.

Vin reached out a hand to him. 'Steady down mate. Meg understands that. From Skeeta's letters she knew how close y'were.'

'Since Skeeta was shot, everything's gone wrong. Now I've mucked up his funeral when all I wanted to do was see he was properly honoured.'

'Everythin's gone wrong? What do you mean?'

'I don't want to talk about it. It's too complicated.'

'Fair enough.' Vin scratched an ear before saying, 'You haven't said anythin' about your family. Don't even know where y'come from.'

Vin's change of tack took Danny by surprise. 'My family? We live in Melbourne. I used to work in my dad's newsagency. I've got a younger brother who doesn't live at home these days. He goes to the uni.'

'And your mum. Get on well with her?' Vin said.

'Why do you want to know about my family?' Danny was becoming annoyed with Vin's probing.

'Meg and me, we're both concerned about ya. We wondered why y'came here straight off before goin' home.'

'I told you when you picked me up. I wanted to call on Skeeta's family and pay my respects. Fine mess I made of that.'

Vin did not reply immediately but continued to regard Danny with a concerned face. Eventually he said, 'It's just, Meg and me, we've seen it before. She was a nurse y'know. War weighs heavy on some blokes. Y'need to tell someone what's buggin' ya.'

'And you need to stop bugging me,' Danny said. 'OK. If you must know I have to tell my mum and dad the truth about me. Not just them but my girlfriend as well. It's going to be hard for me and a lot worse for them. But don't worry, I'll be telling them. So, will you just shut up and leave me alone.'

'I'll drive ya into Junee. The Daylight'll come through in a few hours.'

Danny continued to glower at Vin but his anger had now turned on himself. The old man had gone out of his way to be kind to him and all he could do was be rude to him.

Danny rang the doorbell softly. He could hear the television in the front room, but no one came to the door, so he tried again, more loudly. From upstairs he caught his mother's voice calling down, 'Bernie, someone at the door.' Now he could hear his father's footsteps in the hall and the door opened.

'Sorry. I seem to have lost my keys.'

'Son, it's great to see you.' Bernard took Danny's right hand and pulled him into a hug with his free arm. Danny could not remember his father greeting him so effusively before. 'I can't wait to hear all about Vietnam.'

Over his father's shoulder Danny saw his mother flying down the stairs. Bernard let him go and Mary wrapped him in her arms. 'Danny. Danny. Are you alright? I've been so worried.'

The army must have notified his family of his travel schedule. 'Took a bit longer to come home than I thought,' he said defensively.

Mary gazed into his eyes as though searching for the truth. It was the same look she gave his dad when he stayed late at the pub. Had she smelt the beer on his breath? He'd had a few this afternoon but surely not that many. 'It was just, when you hadn't written for ages to us or to Jane, we began to fear something bad had happened to you.'

For a moment Danny thought of telling her it had. It would be the truth. Best to wait. 'Can I come in?'

'Oh, I'm sorry, dear. I'm so pleased to see you. Have you eaten? Can I get you something?'

'No thanks, Mum. I am pretty weary though, so, if you don't mind, I might go off to bed.'

'A bit early, isn't it?' Bernard said.

'Your room's ready for you,' Mary said, 'and we can catch up with all your news in the morning. You are looking a bit peaky.'

'A good night's sleep's all I need.'

'And you're very thin,' Mary said. 'I'll need to fatten you up. I know: we'll have a welcome home dinner for you tomorrow night. I'll see if Sean can come.'

'As long as he behaves himself,' Bernard said. Turning to Danny, he said, 'When he missed out in the ballot he went back to protesting against the war in Vietnam. Seems to have gone a bit cold on it lately, though.' Bernard paused and Danny wondered what was coming next. 'We could ask that girl of yours, Jane. You know she went to Vietnam, too? Haven't seen anything of her since she got back.'

'We've been in touch,' Mary said. 'I think she had her share of adventures. It'll be good for you to compare notes.'

'No. Not Jane.' Mary and Bernard stared at him. 'I'll see her later.'

'Of course. Of course,' Bernard said. 'Been quite a while since you two have been together. Don't want your aged parents getting in the way.'

Danny was late for breakfast the next morning. He had been awake for hours but waited until he heard his father leave before coming down.

'Ah, Danny,' Mary said. 'How is it to be back in your own bed? Did you sleep well or was it strange?' She didn't wait for an answer before going on. 'Now breakfast. The usual or have you different favourites, now?' Danny was irritated by her constant questions. Why couldn't she just leave him be? He had tried to give nothing away but perhaps she had twigged something wasn't right. She didn't miss much and was hard to fool.

'Just the usual, thanks, Mum.'

'Dad is keen for you to start back at the shop, but I've told him you need to have a break, get into the swing of things before you do. He also wanted you to join him for a drink at the pub after he finishes tonight, but I vetoed that, as well. I want all of us together. Sean is coming and I've told him not to be late.' Again, she gave him her 'tell-me-the-truth' stare. 'Is something troubling you, dear?'

'Something troubling me. 'That's one way you could put it.' He wasn't going give her the whole story now. Maybe when all of them were together tonight. She'd keep at him, though, unless he said something. 'A week before I left Vietnam, Skeeta, the best friend I ever had, was killed.'

'Oh, dear, how terrible.' Mary went to embrace him but he pushed her away. 'There are other things troubling me but I don't want to talk about them, yet. Maybe tonight. Just leave me alone, please.'

After he finished his breakfast Danny returned to his room. In mid-morning he was lying on his bed when Mary appeared in the doorway. 'I wondered whether you'd like me to wash anything for you.'

He decided the quickest way to get rid of her was to give her some washing and rummaged in his pack for it. 'Thanks, Mum,' he said, dismissing her.

He was still on his bed in the middle of the day when she returned. 'Danny, I've made some tomato soup. Please come and have it with me.' He wasn't at all hungry but what could he say? 'OK. I'll just go to the toilet before I come down.' He didn't like the unkempt bristly face he saw in the mirror but didn't have the energy to do anything about it.

They sat in silence having their soup until Mary said. 'I've been so sad since you told me about your friend. How did it happen?'

'It was a terrible mistake.' Danny stood up, his soup unfinished. 'I think I'll go for a walk.'

He thought his mother was going to object but, after a moment's hesitation, she said, 'Good idea, dear. It's not a bad day and some fresh air will do you good.'

'Yeah, maybe.'

When Danny returned, Mary let him in and said, 'I should have given you a key.' She led him into the living room where he found Bernard and Sean waiting.

'Great to see you, mate,' Sean said as he shook hands and gripped his arm with his free hand.

'Just about to get us a beer, son,' Bernard said. 'Care to join us?'

'Yeah, why not, thanks Dad.'

'Don't sit down again,' Mary said. 'The meal is ready to serve.'

After they were seated at the table with plates of roast lamb, potatoes, parsnips, tomatoes and peas before them, Sean said, 'Your favourite meal, again, mate. I guess you've been looking forward to this?'

'Yes, son,' Bernard said, raising his glass of beer, 'A toast to you. Welcome home.'

'I have a different toast,' Danny said. 'I want to drink to my mate, my best friend, Skeeta. God rest his soul.'

They raised their glasses and muttered Skeeta's name before drinking.

'Don't let your food get cold,' Mary said. 'After we've eaten, Danny, you might like to tell us what's on your mind.'

Danny felt a stab of resentment. 'You want to know what's on my mind, do you?' He saw the pain on Mary's face and was ashamed. He had to get it over with. 'I'll tell you all that's troubling me after we've eaten.' Not all. He had to face Jane. He picked up his knife and fork and began to eat.

There was an awkward silence, broken only by the click of cutlery and the muted sound of food being chewed and swallowed. Eventually Sean said. 'I feel like I've crashed a Trappist supper.'

'OK let me get it out of the way.' Danny put down his knife and fork and drank the remainder of his beer.

'But you haven't eaten half of it,' Mary said.

'Not hungry, Mum. We didn't eat much in Vietnam.'

'Well, go ahead, son. Say what you want to say,' Bernard said.

Danny sighed and wiped his hand across his face. He had worked on his speech in the pub last night and rehearsed it while having a drink this afternoon. Now he could not find the words. He saw how intently the three of them were watching him. 'Sorry. I'm sorry. I've let all of you, everyone, down.'

'How can that be, son?'

'Skeeta's death was such a waste. He didn't die serving his country. I told his family but that only made his dad angry. He could have killed the man — the army would say should have — but Skeeta thought he was a farmer and Skeeta was a farmer, himself, on the farmer's side. I've done terrible things — killed a young woman, a teacher, and ruined the life of another — all because I was hell bent on avenging him.'

'Terrible things happen in war,' Bernard said. 'You have to put those things behind you, son. You can't dwell on them.'

'No, Dad, I have to confront them.'

Bernard maintained his encouraging tone. 'Take your time. Settle back into your old life. A few weeks in the shop and you'll see things differently.'

Danny frowned at his father. 'Dad, you know that's not true. You've been trying to hide your shame for years and years but you haven't succeeded, have you?

What are you talking about?' Sean asked.

Danny ignored him. 'You deluded yourself into thinking my service in Vietnam would somehow make it right for you. It was never going to do that and, even if it could have, I failed you. In the end my commander told me I couldn't go on active duty without being a risk to my section. I was sent home in disgrace. I don't know how I'm going to do it but I have to atone for my sins.'

'I thought Jesus had already done that for you,' Sean said, drawing angry frowns from both his parents.

Danny ignored him again. 'What I do know is I can't step back into my old life: work in the shop and live here at home. I have to find a new life, one where I can do something worthwhile. I have to do this on my own. I can't stay here. I don't know where I'll go but I have to leave. Now I've told you, I'll go. You can be free of me.' He rose quickly from the table, overturning his chair. 'Sorry,' he said and righted it before hurrying from the room.

Reaching the stairs, he heard his mother say, 'Bernie, leave the boy be. Let him calm down.' In a much louder voice, his father said, 'You heard what he said about me. I've got to have it out with him.' The sound of their voices trailed him up the stairs. Their tones were enough to tell him that, just as she had done so often before, Mary was trying to calm an angry Bernard.

Danny was stuffing his things into his kit bag when Sean came in. 'Mate, I have a suggestion.'

'I don't want your advice.'

'Of course not. But where will you go? Not easy to find somewhere at this time of night.'

Danny stood with one of his shirts in his hand. 'I saw some cheap hotels when I arrived at Spencer Street.'

Sean shook his head. 'You wouldn't want to stay in one of those flea-infested doss houses. There's a spare room out the back of Guy's place. I'm sure he'd be glad to let you stay there for a few days while you decide what you'll do. You could hang out there without having anything to do with us if that's what you want.'

'You sure he wouldn't mind?'

'Wouldn't have suggested it if I wasn't sure.'

Danny hesitated. It would be good to have a day or so to get himself set. 'Well thanks.'

Sean grinned at him. 'Great.' The grin disappeared and he said, 'There's something else I could do for you, if you like. Would you like me to explain to Jane what's happened?'

Danny fell back into his previous gloom. 'No, I must speak with her myself. It's different but all part of the mess I've created. I've betrayed her. She must forget me and get on with her life.'

'Betrayed her? You had it off with another woman? Is that what you're telling me?'

'It wasn't as crude as you make it sound, but yeah.'

Sean gave a broad smile. 'Danny, it's the swinging sixties, not the Victorian era. While you've been in the jungle, the sexual revolution's arrived in Australia. Confess to her. Tell her you're sorry — a result of all you've had to cope with. Ask for her forgiveness. I'm sure she'll give it.'

'I can't do it. It might be alright for you, but I can't.'

Sean's drew in his breath. 'You mean we poofters have looser morals?'

'That's not what I meant.'

'The world's changing for queers, too, you know. In England their laws against homosexuals are being done away with. Guy and I are hopeful the day will come here when we won't have to hide our love. We ...'

Bernard burst into the room glaring at Sean 'What's that you're saying?'

'Ah, Dad, masterful timing. I've wanted to tell you this for ages. Tonight seems to be the night for confessions. Yeah, I'm queer. A kinder term is 'gay' but you probably haven't heard that one.'

'And that Guy is another one. You ... You ...'

'Yes, Dad, Guy and I are lovers.'

'How could you do this to me, both of you?'

'What?'

'With my gammy leg killing me, I keep the newsagency going for two years so Danny can serve his country and take over when he gets back. He makes a total mess of his war service and wants to run away from his obligations to the family. Now you tell me you're a homo and show not the slightest bit of guilt. In fact, you sound bloody pleased with yourself. Why do you want to do this to me, both of you? What have I done to hurt you?'

'Dad, I'm sorry,' Danny said. 'I know how important it is for you to keep the business going. I know the cost to you of keeping the good name of the family. I can't hide the truth like you were forced to do. That's what I was trying to say before, but it came out all wrong.'

'What *was* that all about?' Sean said.

'Dad was no war hero. His father put that about after he came back injured before his unit was involved at Kokoda. Dad's had to live with that for the rest of his life.'

'And I'd do it again. Can't you two see how you're betraying the family? Destroying the good name we've had for generations. Why are you doing this to me?'

'Dad,' Sean said. 'We're not doing anything to you. You're doing it to yourself.'

Bernard gave a growl and his face convulsed. 'If that's what you think, go into that den of iniquity together, then. There's no place for you here.'

Aftermath

When they arrived outside Guy's house in North Melbourne, Danny was struck by its similarity to their home in East Melbourne. It was smaller but a terrace house of about the same age and style. Inside the similarity ended. Straight from the street they entered a spacious living room which led through a wide archway to a space for dining and beyond that a modern kitchen. Indian rugs covered most of the polished floorboards; discrete lighting gave a glow to the room and highlighted the array of contemporary paintings on the walls. In the centre a low glass-and-chrome table was surrounded by ergonomically designed black leather easy-chairs and it was from one of these that a tall man rose to greet them.

'Guy, this is my brother, Danny.'

'Danny, it's good to meet you,' Guy Norton said in a sonorous voice as he took Danny's hand in a firm grasp and smiled directly at him. He was a handsome man with neatly arranged dark curly hair and blue eyes. What impressed Danny most was his air of calm assurance. Occasionally Danny's mother would describe someone she had met as 'having presence' and it was clear to him that Guy Norton had abundant presence. Danny could understand how Sean would be charmed by him and was relieved — he had feared he would be unimpressed, even repulsed, by his lover.

'Danny doesn't have anywhere to stay right now and I said he'd be welcome to use the back room for a day or so while he gets himself sorted,' Sean said.

Danny had expected Sean would have cleared this with Guy before they turned up but it must have been a spur-of the moment offer. If Guy was puzzled that Danny should not be staying with his parents, he showed no sign of it. 'Good idea. Why don't you take him down there and show him what's what, then come back for a nightcap?' He gestured at a bottle of red wine standing on the table. 'I've just been trying out a Cab Sav from a new winery in the Yarra Valley.'

Sean shook his head. 'We're pretty phased out. It's been a ...'

'Thanks. I'd like a drink,' Danny said.

The back room, as Sean and Guy called it, consisted of a comfortably furnished bed-sitting room with its own bathroom and toilet. On closer inspection Danny saw Sean's quilt on the bed, a few of his posters on the wall and a number of his text-books on the shelf over the desk. 'But this is your room.'

Sean laughed. 'Glad you think so. Guy holds quite a few meetings here in the house and we need to be careful. When people we don't know well or can't trust arrive, I retire down here. The rest of the time I spend with Guy in the front of the house and upstairs. Unpack your gear and, if you're sure you want that drink, come up when you're ready.'

It took very little time for Danny to unpack but he suspected Sean had gone to explain why Danny needed a bed and did not hurry back, even though a drink was waiting for him. When he did approach the living room, he heard Sean say, 'The good news is I've told my dad about us.'

'Was that wise?' Guy asked.

Danny came to a halt just outside the room. Should he interrupt? Should he return to the back of the house?

Sean said, 'I hate having to deny you and I want my family to know who I really am.'

'How did your father take it?'

'He seemed to think I chose to be gay to embarrass him.'

'Will he make a fuss?' Guy sounded sufficiently anxious that Danny decided he should not hesitate any longer.

He walked into the room saying, 'The last thing Dad will do is to make a public fuss. I'd say he's more frightened of Sean's sexuality coming out than you are.'

For a moment Danny feared he had offended Guy by his candour but, without losing his frown, Guy said, 'I hate that we have to slink around being so careful. It's just that the lead I've taken in opposing the war in Vietnam has given me a public profile and my enemies would not hesitate to use our relationship to tear me down.'

'Guy's making his way in the Labor Party,' Sean said proudly. 'Expect to see him in parliament soon.'

'I'd be interested in your opinion, Danny,' Guy said. 'Are you OK about Sean and me?'

Danny was taken aback to be asked so directly but he had chosen to enter the conversation and felt he owed Guy an honest reply. 'I'd be happier if Sean was otherwise, but we've always been close and I hope we remain so.'

'Thank you for your honesty and your compassion,' Guy answered before smiling at him. 'That's the best we should hope for from our families.'

Danny realised he'd considered Guy in isolation and given no thought to the man's family or friends.

'Enough of that, though,' Guy said. 'Danny come, sit here and try this wine.' He poured a glass and held it out to Danny. 'The Barossa in South Australia and the Hunter in New South Wales have been given all the publicity, but I've been exploring the wines of the Yarra Valley and the King Valley here in Victoria. I think both have a great future. Go ahead. Tell me what you think.'

'I don't know much about wine.'

Norton waved his denial away. 'Doesn't matter. The experts with all their knowledge can be stuck in their ways. If the wine industry in Australia is to flourish like I think it should, we have to appeal to people like you, not the experts.'

Danny sipped his wine. 'Yeah, I like it.' He felt embarrassed by the flimsiness of his response.

Guy did not pursue him but said, 'You know I've been involved in the protest movement for a few years now, but I've never met anyone who has actually fought in Vietnam. The Government tells us everything is going well but the Americans are drawing us further and further into the mess. Tell me, what's the real situation on the ground? Are we winning the war or are we wasting young lives in a fruitless campaign?'

Danny was surprised by how his spirits lifted. Here was a chance to talk to an intelligent and interested listener about his concerns over the war in Vietnam — a relief from continually revisiting his own failures. 'Militarily the Australian Task Force has achieved a good deal and can be proud of its achievements,' he said and paused to gather his thoughts.

'But?' Guy said.

'Let me tell you about a Vietnamese interpreter I met. His name is Tuan Mai and he's attached to the Task Force. He's a Catholic whose family had been driven from Hanoi by the rise of the Communists in the north. He took me to task one day.'

Danny paused as he realised that, during all his recent soul-searching, he had not given a thought to Tuan Mai. Once Tuan had said it was a pity Danny hadn't more openly tried to seduce Linh, so she would have been more wary. What would Tuan think of him now? Danny became aware of both Sean and Guy waiting for him to go on. 'He said to be suspicious of foreigners who say they have good intentions and know so little of Vietnamese ways. He made it sound like a local proverb but maybe he made it up. I don't know. His main target was the Americans.' Danny took Guy and Sean through Tuan's account of the American's failure to understand properly what had occurred before their arrival and the mistakes they made as a consequence.

'A pity your Tuan Mai can't talk to our Government,' Sean said impatiently. 'We've been telling them this for ages but they won't listen.'

'Hush, Sean,' Guy said. 'Let Danny tell us more. What about the Communists? Why are they proving so hard to dislodge?'

'Tuan had a clear explanation. They didn't battle for territory but for the minds of the peasants. Tuan saw it as highly significant their military force, the Viet Cong, consisted of local men led by officers from the north — local men fighting for their own land. He was sure the Government would not endure unless it could establish popular support and would do this only if it could provide ongoing safety for the people and improve their living conditions.'

'Sounds delightfully simple,' Guy said. 'Aren't we doing anything along the lines he suggests?'

'Their Government does have some programs but it's not in the brief of the Task Force. Tuan thinks that's where we've got it badly wrong. He pointed out the first thing we did on arrival was destroy villages and shift the residents away from their land — hardly the way to win their trust. Not long before I left Vietnam, we began building a large fence, laced with mines, to prevent easy movement of the VC. This fence was a huge disruption and inconvenience to the farmers in the area. My pal Skeeta was a farmer and all his sympathy was with the farmers. That's what led to his death.' Danny realised he was veering back to his own problems.

'But that's another story. The fence is a massive example of the approach Tuan Mai had criticised. He was intensely gloomy about the future, saying we wouldn't save the South from the Communists. He expected the killing and destruction to go on until the Americans tire of it and then they and we would go home leaving his people and the Communists to try to put the pieces of their shattered country together. The longer my time in Vietnam, the more I came to believe Tuan Mai was right.'

Danny drained the remainder of his glass and saw Guy nodding thoughtfully. 'Your Tuan Mai strikes me as a very perceptive man.'

Sean stood up. 'You blokes can keep chatting for as long as you like but I'm on a teaching placement in Frankston tomorrow. I'm going to bed.'

'And I'm in court.' Guy rose to join Sean. 'I hope you sleep well, Danny. I look forward to another chat soon.'

Danny did not immediately get up from his chair, reflecting on how the combination of Tuan's critique and his own experience had taken such a powerful hold of him.

⅄

Jane entered her flat and turned from closing the door to find Danny standing in the doorway of the living room. 'Danny!'

'Sorry to startle you,' he said. 'Carol let me in. She's gone out now. She said I could stay.'

He remained standing in the doorway as if waiting for her to make the next move. When Mary called Jane to say Danny was back, she said he was a bit thin and peaky but she hadn't mentioned how wooden he'd become. 'Are you going to kiss me?' Jane said.

'Yes. Yes, of course.' He took her in his arms and kissed her on the lips, but this was not the embrace she had been yearning for. It was as if he had been sedated. 'Danny, what's wrong?'

'Come and sit,' he said and led her to the couch. He neither touched nor looked at her.

'I know about Skeeta,' Jane said. 'That must have been terrible for you. I could tell from your letters how close you were.'

'It started when Skeeta was killed,' he said. 'No that's not right. I was going to tell you. But when Skeeta died, everything went to pieces. There was this schoolteacher.'

Had Danny fallen for a Vietnamese? Is that what he was trying to tell her? 'I liked many of the Vietnamese I met at the hospital in Bien Hoa. Some of those nurses were lovely.'

'After Skeeta … Maybe revenge. I don't know.' His voice was hoarse and he stared at the wall as though watching a film. 'The schoolteacher … All she'd done was go back searching for one of her kids who was lost. I thought she … the man who shot Skeeta. One shot and she was dead.'

'You … You fired at her?'

Danny nodded.

How appalling. No wonder he was traumatised. What could she say to ease his pain? She took his hands in hers. 'You shouldn't blame yourself. Awful things happen to innocent people in war. Many of the people we treated in Bien Hoa were civilians, bombed by the Viet Cong or caught in the cross-fire.'

'It got worse. The woman I met in Vung Tau taught me you could love more than one person.'

He had taken his pleasure in Vung Tau. The good Catholic wouldn't make love to her when she gave him the chance but went with some prostitute in her sordid bed. 'I imagine the girls of Vung Tau all say that.'

Suddenly Danny became animated. 'She wasn't one of them,' he said. 'I told you she was a schoolteacher.'

'The one you killed?'

'No not her,' he snapped.

'Danny, no need to get stroppy with me. You're all over the place. I'm confused.'

Danny irritated Jane further by taking the tone of an adult explaining something quite simple to a child. 'Linh Mai is a girl I met in Vung Tau. A Catholic. She's a schoolteacher; not one of those bar girls. We became friendly. You'd like her, too. I was going to tell you about her and her family — the terrible time they've had. But after I killed the schoolteacher, I went to see Linh and she ...' Danny dropped his head. 'She comforted me.'

Jane tried to contain the surge of jealousy but couldn't prevent her sneer. 'That was kind of her.'

Danny shook his head sorrowfully. 'I never meant for this to happen. I betrayed your love for me and I'll regret that for the rest of my life. I came to confess to you and tell you to forget me. Find someone worthy of your love.'

They sat silently staring at the carpet.

Jane could not accept her love for Danny must be put aside, cast off. Why didn't he ask for her forgiveness, beg her to let him make amends? After all, she'd hugged and kissed Gordon when she had been no more than a witness to a battle. Danny had been enmeshed in war for a year and seen his best friend killed. No wonder he'd sought the comfort of the Vietnamese woman. But would her forgiveness be enough? He was so determined to break off from her. If she took the initiative and offered her forgiveness, he might still leave her. How abject would that be?

The unfairness of it all took hold of her and she burst into tears. 'You've always held back from me, haven't you? The reluctant lover. The earth didn't tremble for you the first time we met. I wasn't a Catholic and, when I offered to become one, you wouldn't have that. Making love was something that had to wait. This Vietnamese school teacher gives you another excuse. You don't ask me to forgive you. Oh, no, that would mean we'd marry.' Jane stood up, separating herself from him. Yes, she'd get on with her life without him and be glad about it. She should have broken free from him ages ago.

⎯⅄

Danny took the tram back to the city and sought a pub where he might have something to eat and drink. After a steak and chips with a few glasses of beer, he felt no better. Once more he had made a mess of explaining himself. He wanted so much to comfort her. His ability to do that in the past had been one of the bonds between them. Sean had urged him to ask for her forgiveness and she sounded as though that might have been what she was expecting. It could have given him the chance to salvage a bit of his previous life. But he couldn't do it. He loved Jane, yet there was a part of him that cherished his time with Linh. He couldn't make his peace with Jane, marry her and turn his back on Linh, denying her existence. He must do penance for his sins against both of them.

Another couple of drinks and he began to feel better. He still had the link with Sean, which was now more important than ever to him. Not only that, he'd formed an unexpected bond with Guy, a man he liked and admired. Tomorrow, though, he must set about finding his own place and getting a job. He had a fair reserve of cash from the money earned and not spent while in the army, but that wouldn't last forever.

He needn't rush but he must be on the lookout for the opportunity he craved to make amends — a job, even a career maybe, to which he could commit himself in the knowledge he was doing something worthwhile.

He needn't rush but he must be on the lookout for the opportunity he

Sean opened the door. 'Well, how did you go, mate? Did you do what I told you?'

'Probably worse than our scene with Dad, but at least it's over.' Danny was surprised by the depth of disappointment on Sean's face.

'Bugger. When it got late, I started to hope you'd stayed with her for the night.'

'I made a mess of it like I always do these days and she was pretty upset.'

'I'll give her a call.'

'No need for that, Sean.'

Sean frowned at him and shook his head. 'I'm not doing it for you. You're my brother, but Jane is the only girl who's ever been a good friend of mine. You two have been great for one another but, if it's not to be, I'll support you and I'll comfort her as much as I can.'

'Come on you two,' Guy called to them. 'Don't spend the rest of the night on the doorstep. I've got a Shiraz from a small place near Avoca I want you to try, Danny.'

After they had sampled the wine and discussed it for a few minutes Guy said, 'Danny, I was greatly impressed by what you said to me about Vietnam last night. I know a TV journalist who's always keen to explore behind the direct news of the war in Vietnam. How would you feel about doing an interview with him — telling him about Tuan Mai and his views? I'm sure he'd be interested in what you'd have to say to him.'

Sean sat forward and glared at Guy. 'Cut that out. I know you mean Rick Greer. Danny's a man who set out to serve his country in a war you and I believe is wrong but he saw as an opportunity to protect the Catholics of Vietnam from the Communists. Now he has doubts, but I'll bet he remains loyal to the cause and to his mates. Rick will lead him on and destroy him in the glare of the TV studio just to give you some new material for the campaign.'

Guy smiled at Sean reassuringly. 'You need have no fear for Danny. He's a man of integrity who doesn't flinch from giving his opinion. Remember how he replied when I asked him what he thought of you and me being together. His story of the Vietnamese interpreter warrants a wider audience.'

'Stop bullshitting me, Guy. Danny's a supporter of the war and its objectives who believes the current approach won't succeed. Rick will twist his words and make him out as wanting the war to end right now. He'll be seen as a traitor to the army and to his mates. I won't let that happen to him.'

'Sean. Sean. You always have to overdramatise the situation.' For the first time Danny saw Guy lose some of his unruffled air. 'Besides, it's not for you to decide what your brother will do. That's up to him.'

'I'm going to bed,' Danny said, hoping to calm the storm he saw breaking out. He walked to his room and sat on his bed, regretting he had spoken as he had the night before. Meanwhile the ruckus in the front room was unabated. He could not hear all that was said but snippets kept reaching him:

'... using him for your own ends ...'

'... we have a responsibility ...'

'... whatever suits your cause. You use people, regardless of the harm to them.'

'... the public must be told the truth. They must be roused.'

At each exchange Sean's voice became louder so that Danny eventually caught every word. 'It's the same with those guys you encourage to burn their call-up papers. Makes for great television but just lands them in further strife. Most of the people you defend in court have no genuine objection to the war. They just don't want to go. You seldom win but your name and your face become better known. As soon as you get elected to parliament, you'll drop this cause, I bet.'

The only reply Danny heard from Guy was his footsteps on the stairs and the slam of a door. He wondered whether Sean would be down to cadge a place in his bed. It wouldn't be the first time they had slept head-to-toe in the same bed. When he heard nothing for the next ten minutes he undressed and tried to sleep, eventually dozing off in the early morning.

He made no attempt to get up when he heard them moving in the kitchen. His relief that the shouting had not started up was tempered by concern over the lack of any conversation, at all. He feigned sleep when he heard Sean approaching and was pleased his brother did not attempt to rouse him. After he was sure both had left the house, he showered and dressed, ate some cornflakes and drank some tea before packing his kitbag and leaving two notes. One, addressed to Guy, thanked him for his hospi-tality and said he needed to move on. The second, a rather longer one to Sean, said that he deeply regretted causing the argument with Guy the night before, but everywhere he went he caused disagreements to break out. It was best he struck out on his own. He wished his brother well.

Walking from the house, he reflected that his connections with the only people who really mattered to him had all been severed: his mother, father, Sean, Jane, Skeeta and Linh.

When Jane awoke from a night of troubled sleep, she could not decide whether she was most angry with Danny or with herself. Was he incapable of making the commitment to marry or was he frightened? Whatever it was, there was no changing him and she should have realised that much earlier. To be rejected in this way was also a blow to her pride, but she refused to dwell on that. She needed to decide what she was going to do now and, most urgently, have an explanation for Carol who was sure to be wondering.

Sean rang in the evening. It was clear from his concerned voice that Danny had told him. 'I'm OK thanks, Sean. Relieved, actually.'

'What do you mean?'

'Remember you once told me if you love someone, you know it for sure, and if you're not sure, you don't. In the past year I've come to know a man who is sure he's in love with me and has made me realise Danny and I are not meant for each other. I didn't want to say anything to Danny or anyone else until he was back from Vietnam and I could tell him face to face. I was worried when your mother told me how down Danny was but, as it turned out, he'd come to the same conclusion, so I'm relieved.'

Within a couple of days of leaving Guy's place, Danny had found an inexpensive boarding house in Fitzroy. His room was dingy but clean and would do for now. Finding a job proved to be much more difficult. He had no need to worry yet, because he had sufficient money to get by for some time, but would like to settle into a regular job as soon as he could. A work history of two years in the newsagency followed by two years in the army was nothing out of the ordinary and his inability to produce any references counted against him. He gained some amusement from imagining what his father would say if he had asked him for a testimonial.

Bernard looked even more tired and disconsolate than usual when he returned from the shop but Mary did not hold back. 'Danny's gone missing,' she said.

Bernard sank on one of the kitchen chairs. 'What do you mean, "Gone Missing"?'

'I rang Sean to see how ...'

'You shouldn't have done that,' Bernard said.

Mary could not contain her exasperation. 'Bernie, when are you going to see sense? I'd be much happier if Sean was not as he is. I wish Danny had returned well and happy, ready to take up his role in the shop. But these are realities we have to accept. Those boys are our sons. We should be doing all we can to help them whatever their situation.' Bernard started to object but Mary would not let him speak. 'Bernie, listen to me. I know you're deeply upset by Sean's situation and I know you feel Danny has let you down and insulted you, so I can appreciate why you told them to go the other night. It may take you a while to get over the hurt but for their sakes and for ours you must. They need you and we need them.'

'That's all very well but ...'

'But nothing.' Mary shook her head. 'While you come to terms with your disappointment, I'll do what I can to stay in touch. Carry on all you like, but I'll continue to call Sean and see how he is. While you're so hostile, I won't invite him to come here, even though it's his house, but I will stay in touch. I'd do the same with Danny but Sean tells me Danny left him a note saying he was causing disagreements wherever he went, so it was best he struck out on his own. He didn't say where he was going and he hasn't been in touch since.

'He'll turn up,' Bernard said with an unconvincing smile.

Danny was alone in a hostile jungle. Trees bent their branches to block his way. Vines reached out to entangle him. As he tried to crawl to safety, the monsoon rain beat upon him and shrouded his view. He saw ahead of him the crouching figure of a VC soldier lining him up with his AK45. Danny fired and the man slumped forward onto the floor of the jungle. In that instant Danny saw it was not a VC but Skeeta he had felled. He scrambled forward to where his friend lay face-down in the mud. Turning his body over he found Linh Mai, her face frozen in agony as blood spurted from her forehead down onto the tattered jacket of her ao dai. 'No!' He woke sweating in the cold May night.

These dreams had been troubling him since his return. He didn't have them every night — getting any sleep at all was a more persistent problem — but, whenever they came, they brought images of him killing someone dear to him. When he came down late and bleary-eyed

279

in the mornings, his landlady, Mrs Garrety, would shake her head and mutter about the evils of drink. It was true he liked to finish his day with a drink or two at the Duke. No harm in that.

Seeking respite from the disappointments of job-seeking, he'd stumbled on the Duke of Cornwall, an old pub in a side street near his boarding house. It was clear the Duke's best years were long past, but the dingy atmosphere of the place did not deter Danny. It suited him that the regulars, of whom there were relatively few, kept to themselves. Even Tom, the burly barman, was reluctant to interrupt his viewing of the small television set he had placed behind the bar and showed little enthusiasm for chatting with the drinkers.

When Danny approached the bar for a beer, Tom was watching the TV news.

'Hey, Tom, turn up the sound,' Danny called to him.

On the screen, ranks of slouch-hatted soldiers marched along a city street while the newsreader announced, 'Members of the Fifth Battalion, returning from their tour of duty in Vietnam, marched through Sydney today, watched by an appreciative crowd.' Danny thought he caught sight of Simmo and a little later might have seen Pug but wasn't sure.

'Why you interested in them?' Tom asked.

'I was with those blokes in Vietnam,' Danny said and immediately regretted having spoken. Tom was sure to ask why he wasn't with them now and he would have to lie or admit he had been sent home and no longer belonged.

'Another beer, digger?'

Danny stiffened. To be a digger was an honour. He'd blown any chance to earn that name.

During the operation Jane whispered to Gordon, 'Could we have a word after surgery?' He nodded and she saw the surprise on his face.

He was waiting for her when she came out of the change-room. 'I want to bring you up-to-date with some developments in my life,' she said, smiling at him as if she were joking.

'Sure,' he said but Jane could see he was puzzled. They hadn't spoken for weeks but she thought he might have heard about her breakup with Danny. She had told Carol and a few others and thought the word might have got around.

'The last time we played tennis you said you thought I wouldn't have much time for tennis after Danny returned. He has returned and I've been able to tell him my feelings have changed. I no longer want to marry him. I didn't want to say anything to Danny or anyone else until he was back and I could tell him face to face. But now I've done it and I'm greatly relieved.'

'How did Danny take it?' he asked.

'He was very understanding.'

'So, you're free to play tennis with us again.'

'Yes, I'd enjoy that.'

When Jane and Gordon arrived for tennis, Peter and Claudia were there to greet them. Jane saw Peter's restrained smile as a sign of his bemusement at her change of heart. Claudia was less subtle. 'Good to see you,' she said. 'I'd thought we'd lost you for good.' The arrival of a young couple, Bob and Sophia Jorgenson, who had recently become Peter's clients, was a welcome intervention.

The Jorgensons were better players than those Peter had invited previously. Jane did not play well, put off her game by the way he kept glancing over at her. It was similar to his behaviour in the early days when she mistakenly thought he was keen on her. This time, she knew he was mindful of their conversation at the Chevron.

When it was their turn to sit out, Jane put on her jacket but did not zip it up. Although a cool southerly blew across the court, she felt quite warm. Was this a result of her exertions or because of her anxiety over how she would handle Peter? He poured drinks for them and sat staring fixedly at the court where Gordon was straining hard not to let Sophia down while Claudia was having the same problem with Bob. Eventually Peter said softly, 'I hear your marriage is not going ahead.'

'I guess you're wondering why.'

'I was surprised.' He hesitated and turned to face her. 'And sorry, too.'

Jane did her best to smile at him. 'No need to be sorry.'

Peter did not smile back. 'Why do you say that?'

'Did you know Danny and I became friends when we were still at school? There were a few ups and downs but we remained friends and I came to take it for granted we'd marry one day. Danny has been a good friend and I hope we can become friends again sometime. Friendship is great but ... You could say I'd become more in love with the idea of marriage than I was with Danny.'

'But at the Chevron ...'

Peter had annoyed her at the Chevron and was doing it again. 'Did you expect me to tell you how I was feeling before I'd spoken with Danny?'

Peter was distracted by Claudia's shouted of appreciation for a winner hit by Bob Jorgenson. He turned back to Jane and said, 'It's really none of my business ...'

'You're dead right there.'

Peter's face flushed but he did not avoid her eye. 'Your relationship with your boy... your ex-boyfriend is none of my business but I've told you, Gordon's welfare is my business. That's why I'm anxious about you taking up with him again.'

Jane sniffed derisively. 'Taking up? You make it sound so cheap.'

Peter sighed. 'Yes, I'm sorry. I don't know how to put it.' A ball from a mishit bounced towards them and Peter got up to retrieve it before re-joining her. 'I'm sure of Gordon's feelings towards you but I don't know what your feelings are towards him.'

'Does Gordon use you as his spokesman in all his relationships?'

'What?'

'You say you're sure Gordon is strongly attracted to me and yet he's never said or done anything to make that plain to me. Even you can't bring yourself to be frank with me. Having ditched my boyfriend, am I coming after Gordon on the rebound? That's really what you're asking me?'

'Now you're putting it crudely.'

'When we were at the Chevron, I told you I admired Gordon and thought he was a lovely man but made it clear I did not love him. After the soul searching I've been through recently, I'm damn sure I'll take it very carefully before I fall in love with anyone. When I told Gordon, I'd broken up with Danny, he was the one who suggested I come back to tennis and I was pleased to do so. I enjoy playing, the exercise is good for me and, most of the time, I enjoy the company of the other players. However, if you're not happy with me coming, just say so and I'll not come again.

⎯⎯ℓ

Sean phoned Jane several months later. He was diffident — not like Sean at all. 'I know it's a long shot. But have you seen anything of Danny?'

He might be apologetic, but she prickled. 'No, I haven't. Nor would I expect to.'

'Yeah, it's just he's disappeared, gone missing.'

'What?'

'He went off the day after he last saw you and we haven't heard from him since.'

'Why would he do that?'

Sean described the dinner at which Danny had told them of his remorse at what he had done, letting down his family, his unit and his mates. She could add herself to that list. For the first time Jane began to understand some of the garbled story Danny had tried to tell her in the lead up to his confession of having slept with the Vietnamese woman. When Sean ended by telling her Danny had said he needed to find a way to atone for his sins, she said, 'Why didn't you tell me about all this when you last rang?'

'I got the impression you weren't interested in hearing anything about him,' Sean said. 'If I wasn't at my wits end trying to find what's happened to him, I wouldn't have called you now.'

'Please let me know if you hear anything.'

When she rang off, Jane sat reflecting on how she had failed Danny. She'd been so upset by what she saw as his lack of concern for her that she'd failed to understand the depth of the trauma he'd suffered. If only she had remained calm, listened sympathetically and given him time to settle. That's what he always did when she was upset. She couldn't escape the conclusion her reaction to his confession had been the last straw for him. Where was he now? She shuddered at the thought he might have harmed himself. Surely the family would have heard if he'd done that.

After months of occasional temporary jobs, Danny's money started to run out. In February he enquired at a local factory just after a storeman had been sacked. 'He was a lazy bastard and I got fed up with him,' the boss said. 'Save me a bit of trouble to put you on. If I do, you'd better not let me down.'

When Danny assured him he wouldn't, the boss remained dubious but told him to report for work the next day. It was nothing grand but a first step in his recovery. After the turmoil and frustration of the previous year, he was delighted by the prospect of settling into a steady job and planning his next steps. Tonight, though, he would celebrate with a few drinks at the Duke. He'd also phone Sean from the pub. He had been reluctant to call him until he could report something positive which Sean could pass on to their parents. That had taken much longer than he expected.

Danny had already enjoyed more than his usual quota of beer when three men he had not seen before entered the pub. They were a rowdy bunch, wearing cheap suits and loud ties. His father would have called them 'two-bob lairs'.

'Lively joint this is,' one of them said.

'No worries,' the largest of the three, an overweight man with a florid face, told his mates. 'Get a few down here and we'll move on.' He turned to the bar. 'We'll have double whiskies and beer chasers.' When Tom was slow to leave the television, the man said, 'Get a move on. We're as dry as a pommy's bath towel.'

Tom glared at him but provided the men with their drinks and returned to watch the quiz show he had been enjoying. The big man who had placed the order called for a toast to their success in clinching a deal with someone he described as 'that mug, so stupid we should have fleeced him for double.'

'Yeah, you're spot on there, Bull,' one of his mates said.

They were on their third round when Tom called to Danny, 'Hey, digger, over here.' The quiz had given way to the news, where the Tet Offensive, the coordinated attacks by North Vietnamese and Viet Cong on the towns and cities of South Vietnam, was receiving prime coverage. When the focus moved from a survey of the breadth and extent of the attacks to views of the damage inflicted on Ba Ria, the capital of Phuoc Tuy Province, Danny was staggered. During his time in Vietnam Ba Ria and Vung Tau had been the two totally secure towns in Phuoc Tuy. The war must be going really badly.

'Did he call you Digger?' Bull asked.

'I did a tour in Vietnam,' Danny said brusquely and tried to get back to his seat but was blocked by Bull.

'Tour? That'd be right.' He laughed and wiped his lips. 'You'd be one of those nashos, playing soldiers for a while before escaping back here as soon as you could. A bunch of pretenders.'

Anger began to simmer within Danny but outwardly he remained calm. 'Know a lot about what's going on in Vietnam, do you?'

'Too right I do. Me brother is a proper digger. Signed up a few years ago, did a stint in Vietnam and now he's at Pucka. He reckons the nashos were close to useless — couldn't wait to get in from patrol and run off to Vung Tau after the women. Mind you, all the girls in

Vung Tau are up for it and know quite a few tricks me brother hadn't seen before.'

Danny's face flushed. 'Your brother didn't get past the bars and prostitutes of Vung Tau and meet some of the fine people who live there.'

'One nog is pretty much like any other, I'd say.' Bull shrugged as if this was of no consequence. 'Getting back to the point, they've just been showing the bloody mess you buggers left behind when you scuttled back here. Tell me, how can you have the cheek to call yourself a digger? What did you nashos do in Vietnam except save your skins?'

'My best mate was killed just a few days before he was due to come home. Doesn't matter about me. Does matter you show him proper respect.'

'How did he die?'

'He was shot.'

'Who shot him?'

Danny struggled to give a clear explanation, just as he had with his parents and with Jane. Or was it he'd had a bit too much to drink? 'We don't know. It was ... We thought it was a farmer.'

Bull gave a laugh that came from deep in his chest. 'He gets himself shot by maybe a farmer, but you don't know. What did I say about a bunch of pretenders?'

Fury took hold of Danny, just as it had when he sought revenge for Skeeta and shot the teacher. He stepped towards Bull, hit him on the jaw and felt a surge of pain in his knuckles.

For a moment Bull was silent, shaking his head. Then he lunged forward and roared. 'I'll fix you, you bastard.'

Grief, anger and beer combined to slow Danny's reaction, but even so, he had no trouble avoiding the hay-maker aimed at him. Danny had done a bit of boxing at school and disappointed the priest who coached him by not taking it further. The agility and balance, which made him such a good dancer and footballer, also made him a difficult target and Bull had no speed at all. Now that he had settled, Danny was able to skip around Bull, hurting him with jabs to the body and taking no blows himself. The other regulars and Bull's two mates came to stand in a ring as the fight continued. Danny had never owned a knockout punch and could only wear his opponent down. The fitness he still retained from the army gave him a clear advantage over Bull who was gasping for breath.

When Danny ducked out of range yet again, he felt arms encircle him as one of Bull's pals pinned him in a bear hug. Bull ambled towards him with an evil grin and drove his fist into Danny's stomach, taking all his wind and making his knees buckle so that he was not just pinned but held up by his captor. Danny saw the fist coming towards his face and tried to turn away but was taken to the side of his left eye by a blow that made his head spin. No longer held, he fell to the floor and was about to be kicked by Bull when Tom intervened. He pushed Bull from the side so that he, too, fell to the floor and as he lay there puffing Tom, said. 'That's enough.' Danny had never seen Tom come from behind the bar or provide such a formidable presence before.

The door of the pub swung open and two policemen entered. 'Well, Tom, we decide to drop in on you while doing our rounds and find two of your patrons on the floor. What's been going on here?' The question came from the older of the two in the bored voice of a man who had arrived at many similar scenes during his career.

'That guy attacked my mate,' the one who had pinned Danny said as he pointed at him.

'He deserved it,' one of the regulars said.

'And you held him while the big guy took to him,' another said. 'If Tom hadn't stepped in, he would have murdered him.'

'That's a lie,' the third of the newcomers said, 'If he hadn't ...'

'Shut up, the lot of yer,' the policeman ordered them. 'Tom, tell us what happened.'

Danny, still lying on the floor, was surprised by the comprehensive account Tom gave while the second policeman, a fresh-faced young man, made notes. He had never heard Tom speak for so long before.

'Thanks Tom,' the senior officer said. 'Anyone want to disagree or add anything to what Tom has said?'

'He attacked me,' Bull said, sitting on the floor with his back to the bar. 'You should charge him with assault.'

The policeman went over to examine Bull more closely. 'A bit of blood on your chin but you're not badly hurt.'

'I've got bruises all over me,' Bull whined.

'And you've got a foul breath,' the cop said. 'I'd say you'd had more than a skinful before the fight began.'

The man who had earlier said murder was about to occur bought in again. 'If anyone's goin' to be done for assault, it ought to be the big bloke and the gutless one who held the young guy while he tore into him.' The policeman walked across to Danny. 'You've been very quiet so far. Anything you want to say for yourself?'

Danny gazed up at him blearily, shivered for a moment and then spewed vomit over the policeman's boots.'

'Right, that's it. I'm charging the three of you — drunk and disorderly. A night in the cells will sober you up and you can tell your stories to the JP in the morning.'

The sergeant in charge at the Fitzroy Watch-House gave Danny the once-over before saying, 'You'll have a nice shiner there but no need to bother the hospital. I reckon you can clean yourself up before we put you in a cell.'

Danny found it difficult to sleep on the narrow bench, only partly because of his splitting headache and the pains in his legs, chest and stomach. More painful to him was the conviction he had let down those he cared for again. Those two-bob lairs had demeaned Linh and others like her in Vung Tau, they had insulted his mates and, worst of all, dishonoured Skeeta. He had good reason to have a go at them, even insist on an apology, but hitting Bull only made everything worse.

At nine-thirty the next morning the three of them were arraigned before the JP at the Fitzroy Court. Like the policeman the previous night, the scornful glare the JP gave them as the charges were read made it clear he had seen many similar cases and had no sympathy for any of them. After Bull and his mate had pleaded not guilty and protested their affronted innocence, the JP sighed and said, 'You really want to take up the court's time?' He turned his eyes to Danny. What about you?'

His quiet reply of 'Guilty' drew a less hostile glance from the JP.

The young policeman was the one who was called to provide the evidence. Perhaps the older one was giving his junior some experience on an unimportant case. He read from his notes to give the JP an account that sounded very much like Tom's original version, except that he added evidence of the degree of their drunkenness.

The JP immediately found the charges sustained and asked if the offenders wished to say anything. Bull did not get very far before the JP cut him off, telling him he was not rehearing the case and was only interested in what might influence the sentence he would impose, noting that both Bull and his pal had been found guilty of similar charges several times before. When it was his turn, Danny repeated the thoughts which had been uppermost in his mind the previous night. This triggered some questions from the JP who then said, 'I note your early plea of guilty and accept your remorse is sincere. I also note this is your first offence and will release you without recording a conviction. I'll not be so lenient if you reoffend and I urge you to limit your drinking. You are free to go.'

The remaining two scowled at Danny as he walked from the court and the JP began to address them in a much harsher voice.

It was now midmorning and Danny hurried to the factory where he had expected to begin work earlier that day.

'Where the hell have you been?' the boss said. 'You look terrible.'

Danny told him what had happened but, unlike the JP, the boss had no interest in hearing any explanation for what had triggered his unacceptable behaviour.

'Bugger me. I take a chance on you because I'm desperate and what do you do? Get into a drunken brawl the night before you're due to start with me. Get out and don't let me see you round here again.'

He sounded like Danny's father.

Redemption

A short distance into the narrow, cobbled lane, which ran off Young Street north of the Rainbow Hotel in Fitzroy, stood the rear of an unused factory building. The brick wall of the single-storey building had an inset to provide an unloading platform in front of a rusted roller-door. The cobbles had subsided over the years to provide a depression under the platform rather like a shallow, open grave. In the years since Danny had been forced to live on the street he had become more and more reclusive, so this hideaway suited him well. He had chanced upon it when searching for a place to sleep and had used it ever since. The lane was unlit so that, when stretched out in the depression, he became invisible to the very few who might stray into the lane. He was even safe from the police who made periodic sweeps through the area to arrest vagrants. As he entered his lane it was beginning to rain but this did not bother him. The platform provided a roof for his bed and the slope of the cobbles meant he could remain dry through the night.

Over the time he had been on the street he had found a few pubs and cafes which were prepared to offer leftover scraps to the hungry. He moved around them to avoid becoming a nuisance. Tonight he had eaten through the generosity of The Green Parrot, a recent addition to his list. As he entered his lane it was beginning to rain but this did not bother him. The platform provided a roof for his bed and the slope of the cobbles meant he could remain dry through the night.

He had drifted into a fitful sleep, rather like the way they slept on patrol, when he was woken by the sound of ragged laughter. He sensed that three or four drunks had wandered into the lane and from the sound of their voices he guessed they were under-age drinkers — it wasn't hard for kids to get a drink in this area if they had the cash. He flattened himself and waited for them to discover the lane was a dead end. Footsteps suggested to him they had come to stand beside the loading platform and shortly afterwards streams of beer-laden piss rained down on him. He gave a cry of protest and tried to struggle up but was prevented by one of the lads pushing him back with his foot. 'What we got 'ere?'

'Bloody, dead-beat, I'd say.'

'Can't you swim?' another cackled as the streams of urine continued.

'Get away, you stupid kids,' Danny shouted and struggled again to get to his feet. This time he was forced back by a kick to the chest.

'We'll give ya kids,' one of them said and the kicks spread across his chest, stomach and legs. He tried to roll over to protect himself and a foot planted on his head drove his face into the cobbles. It was a common sport for gangs of youths in this area to bully and beat up people who were homeless. He had been able to escape several attacks by outrunning them. No chance of that tonight.

'Let's get on. The others'll be waiting.' Danny had been thrown a lifeline by one of the gang, less rabid or more impatient than his pals. He lay, not daring to move until he heard them walk back to the street. When he was sure they had gone, he gingerly climbed into the lane. Much of his body ached and blood ran from his face but what worried him most was the sharp pain which speared through his chest with every breath. He needed to get to St Vincent's.

After a slow and painful walk, thankful the rain was keeping many off the street and washing some of the filth from his coat, he reached the Casualty Department at the hospital. It was warm inside, the air filled with the fug of waiting bodies. Painfully he took off his coat before being attended by a sharp-face nurse whose first question was, 'You been drinking?'

'No,' he replied. 'The smell's from a gang of hooligans who pissed on me and laid into me with their boots. I think they've broken some of my ribs.'

'You are a bit of a mess,' the nurse said with a more accommodating expression. 'You're not going to die, though, so you'll have to wait until the doctor can examine you. That could be a while. It's always busy on a Friday night, but tonight's worse than usual.'

Danny slumped on a chair in a line of injured or ill-looking men and women. Perhaps it was the stuffiness of the room or the toll of what he had been through but, despite his aching body and head, he nodded off until woken by a voice saying, 'Dreamer? Dreamer, it is you, isn't it?'

Was he back in Vietnam? Was this one of his dreams? He hadn't heard that name in years. He hadn't liked it when Smacka first called him Dreamer, but now it had a comforting ring to it. He knew that voice. Blearily he opened his eyes. 'Simmo! What are you doing here?'

Danny winced as he went to get to his feet and Simmo stretched out a restraining hand before taking the chair beside him. 'I thought it was you but I wasn't sure. It's great to see you.'

He beamed at Danny who reflected on what a sight he must make with the grime of street life and his damaged face. But that didn't seem to bother Simmo and his words were the friendliest Danny had heard for ages. 'Not surprised you had trouble recognising me,' Danny said. Simmo showed no sign of injury or illness. He looked a lot better than when Danny had last seen him in Vietnam.

'I just brought in a guy who has pneumonia. They've admitted him and I was about to go home when I saw you sitting here. It's great to see you,' he repeated.

'Daniel McBride,' a nurse called from a doorway and he stood to go to her.

He held out his hand to his friend and said, 'It's been good to catch up with you.'

Simmo did not take his hand. 'I'll wait here for you. We can go to my place for a drink. I live pretty close in Carlton.'

Danny had to strip for the doctor to examine him. 'The abrasions on your face don't need stiches and will clear up quickly so long as you keep them clean,' he said in a stern voice. Danny did the best he could to wash regularly but understood why the doctor used that tone with him. When he examined the bruises over Danny's body and legs, he was more sympathetic. 'They certainly gave you a pasting.' Danny winced as the doctor felt around his rib-cage. 'Yeah, we'd better have an X-ray of your chest. Get yourself dressed again. The nurse will treat your face and show you where to wait.'

During the wait for the X-ray, Danny reflected on the way Simmo had treated him as an old friend rather than a homeless person. Danny had become used to the variety of attitudes people displayed towards those living on the streets. The harshest saw him as a repulsive creature who had no right to intrude in their world. Others treated him as a bludger, whose failure to make his way was no responsibility of theirs and therefore warranted no assistance from them. Occasionally he encountered people who were sympathetic — sorry that he should have descended into what they saw as such an abject state. Sometimes these latter ones were the hardest of all to take. Simmo was the first person in years to speak to him as though they were equals. He hadn't shown any curiosity in Danny's circumstances, yet he must have noticed. His delight at meeting Danny could not have blinded him to that extent. And he wanted Danny to go back to his place for a drink!

The X-rays showed no breaks but three of his ribs were cracked. He was probably lucky his assailants were neither strong nor sober. His chest was tightly bound, he was given painkillers and told to rest. He was also warned of the danger of pneumonia developing unless he continued to breathe fully and avoided becoming cold and wet. Finally the doctor frowned and said, 'You need to keep off the street for the next few weeks.' He didn't say how Danny could achieve that.

When he emerged from the treatment area, Simmo was waiting with an anxious frown. 'What did they say?'

Danny told him without mentioning anything about keeping off the street. The only way he could think to do that was to be arrested as a vagrant and he would rather face pneumonia than Pentridge. Danny could not understand the mentality of some of the homeless people who viewed a month in jail on a vagrancy conviction as a form of R and C. They enjoyed having regular meals and a bed which was softer than the pavement. A couple of years ago, when he was still new to the life, he had been caught. In Pentridge he felt like a caged bird. The daily session in the exercise yard allowed him to see the sky but reinforced his sense of entrapment. He swore never to go back there, no matter how desperate he might be.

'Let's go,' Simmo said. 'My car's up the street a bit.'

His house was one of a row of old brick cottages wedged together in a side street in North Carlton. The front door opened onto a narrow passage which had a small sitting room off on the left. The room had a gas fire set in what had once been an open fireplace. To one side of it was a bulbous three-seater couch which faced a TV set. A couple of beanbags lay against the far wall. As he lit the fire, Simmo said, 'Make yourself comfortable on the couch and I'll get us a beer.'

Returning with two stubbies, he handed one to Danny and dragged one of the beanbags in front of the fire where he sat looking up thoughtfully at him. 'Cheers,' he said before tilting his head. 'You know, I missed you when you went into the Reconnaissance Platoon. I reckon I wouldn't have made it through Vietnam if it hadn't been for the start you gave me.'

'Really? What did I do?'

Simmo considered him thoughtfully. 'Remember that gut-busting confidence course at Canungra. You could have got through that far more easily if you hadn't hung back to help me make it. That was the first time. Once we got to Vietnam you were always there to back me up and help me out.'

'You were the one who ripped your hand unsnagging my webbing from the barbed-wire,' Danny said, enjoying the memory.

'Yeah, we did help one another. After we finished that course, I said nothing in Vietnam would be as bad. Fat lot I knew. Still, even in the bad times, we managed to get some laughs, didn't we? Remember when we were on that cordon and search of Binh Ba and were told to tie a rope between ourselves and the bloke in front of us so we would stay together in the pitch dark? What a circus that turned out to be.'

Danny was surprised by Simmo's good-humoured take on their time in Vietnam, but mention of Binh Ba triggered several happy memories of his own. 'Binh Ba! Do you remember that priest riding so slowly through the town we were amazed he stayed upright and, speaking of amazement, remember how Goldie had those kids mesmerised with his conjuring tricks?'

'Yeah,' Simmo said. 'I lost track of him after we got back. Do you see any of the blokes?'

'The last time I saw any of you was when I caught TV coverage of the battalion marching through Sydney after its return from Vietnam. I picked you out but didn't recognise most of them. After the way we dressed over there, the slouch hats and smartly turned out jungle greens made you hard to recognise.'

'Yeah that was a good day.' Simmo's voice became gloomy. 'I was sorry you weren't there — you and Skeeta.'

Danny had been waiting for Simmo to raise the subject and thought how tactfully he had worked up to it. 'You know what happened?'

'The news spread through the battalion like a kind of poison gas, devastating all of us. It must have been terrible for you. I don't know how I would have coped.'

Was this Simmo being kind or was that how he really felt? This was not what Danny had expected.

Simmo got up from his beanbag. 'I reckon that's enough for tonight. You look buggered. No wonder after what you've been through.' Only got one bed here, I'm afraid, but why don't you kip on the couch? Sad to say, I'm carrying more weight than you, but we're about the same height, so you'll fit into a pair of my pyjamas and have a bit of room to spare.' He didn't wait for Danny to respond. 'Could have a shower now or you might prefer to do that in the morning. Good job it's Saturday tomorrow. We can both have a lie-in.'

The thought of a shower was so enticing that, despite his exhaustion, Danny lingered under it for much longer than he should have. Fortunately the pyjama trousers had a draw string which allowed him to pull the waist tight around him. Within moments lying on the couch he was asleep.

Shafts of pain kept breaking into his sleep. Before it became light, he heard the carolling of a couple of magpies. From time to time he had awoken in East Melbourne to similar calls and he wondered how they were getting on there. It was over three years since he had been in touch with them. He started to think about Simmo and the unlikely coincidence which had brought them together, but sleep reclaimed him.

He next woke to sounds of activity from the kitchen and wandered into the small room where Simmo, in jeans and black T-shirt under a thick green jumper, was scooping scrambled egg onto a plate. 'Great timing mate. I don't have much time on weekday mornings, so like to indulge myself at weekends. There's toast and I think I remember you like eggs. Tea or coffee? I can do either.' Danny eased himself onto a stool at the bench which served as a kitchen table. 'How are the aches and pains this morning?'

'Eggs will be great and I'd like a cup of tea, please.'

'Have you got enough painkillers?'

'I'm OK,' Danny said curtly. Simmo's concern was beginning to bug him. What was the point? Soon he would have to get back on the street and fend for himself.

After they had finished the eggs, Simmo poured another mug of tea for both of them and said, 'Let's go into the front room. You must be cold in just those pyjamas.'

Danny shook his head, denying the suggestion. He did feel cold — something he was not unused to — but was reluctant to swap the clean pyjamas for his old clothes. He settled on the couch and pulled one of the rugs Simmo had given him over his legs. Every time he twisted or stretched pain shot through him. After lighting the fire Simmo sank onto the bean bag he had used last night and gazed questioningly at Danny. 'Dreamer, I have a favour to ask of you.'

'Sure,' Danny said. What else could he say after Simmo had made him so welcome?

'It might be hard for you, but I'd like you to tell me exactly what happened to Skeeta. There were various stories floating around and you'll know the truth. It's stupid, I guess, but I feel I need to know so I can properly accept his death.'

'That's not stupid.' Danny said. 'It's just the way I felt when I made a fool of myself trying to set people straight at Skeeta's funeral.'

'You were at his funeral?'

'I didn't know it was on but went to pay my respects to his family and lobbed there the very day.' Danny started to tell the story of his visit to Mundarlo and, encouraged by Simmo's close attention, went into detail about his dissatisfaction with the service, his interjection and its unhappy aftermath.

'Good on you,' Simmo said. 'You shouldn't regret what you did. Everyone should have thanked you for telling them how Skeeta died and what that said about the kind of bloke he was. That's exactly why I wanted you to tell me what happened. If it's not asking too much, I'd like you to take me through it in as much detail as you can.'

Danny didn't mind at all. He was heartened at last to find someone he knew would properly understand how Skeeta's death had come about. Now he was free of the difficulties which had inhibited him and caused him to mess up his previous attempts. As he described the details and saw Simmo's response, he felt as though a load he had been carrying was being lifted from him. Finally he described how Pug had come to him with the news of Skeeta's eventual death and fell silent.

Simmo nodded slowly several times as if absorbing the totality of the story. 'Thank you. I know it got even worse for you. Again, I've only heard the rumours. Could you bear to tell me what happened to you after Skeeta died?'

Danny said nothing, dropped his head and brought his clasped hands up under his chin. He remained deeply ashamed of what he had done and thought of his recent life, not as the atonement he had set out to achieve, but as a form of punishment. If he spoke, he would have to tell the full story, just as he had when describing how Skeeta died. He mustn't deny any of his failures to Simmo. Better to stay silent? Yet there had been relief in speaking of Skeeta. Could there be relief in confessing to Simmo? He'd taken confession to the priest very seriously when he was a kid but had grown out of that as his awe for the clergy had faded. Perhaps the Church was right after all: there was value in confession. But that depended on you respecting and trusting the receiver of your confession. Simmo certainly met those requirements.

Danny took a deep breath and said, 'I hope you'll still think of me as a mate when I get to the end of this. It could take a while.'

'Better get started.'

Danny reached the end of what he had come to see as his confession by saying, 'I left Vietnam having let down the battalion, disgraced the woman who was kind to me, betrayed Jane, the girl I was planning to marry, and determined not to continue in the family newsagency where my father was waiting to hand over to me. I had to tell them what a mess I'd made of things and get out of their lives.'

Simmo, who had listened attentively without saying a word, stood up. 'I could do with another cuppa. One for you?' When he returned with their refilled mugs, he said, 'What of the past few years? How's that gone?'

Danny was irked by what he felt was Simmo's undue tact. He must know it had gone badly. Yet his concern seemed entirely sincere. 'I set out to get a job which would support me while I searched for something which might give me the chance make up for some of the harm and hurt I'd caused. I made a mess of that, too.' He would have left it there but Simmo wouldn't let him.

'You're on the street?'

Danny nodded, ashamed to admit it.

'Let me tell you what I think,' his friend said. 'I think you're wrong to be so hard on yourself.' Danny went to disagree but Simmo continued, 'We can talk about that some other time. What you should do, as soon as I can organise it, is meet Jakub Kowalski.'

Danny imagined he was a social worker or psychologist and had no interest in taking that route. 'Who's he?'

'He keeps a low profile, so I'm not surprised you haven't heard of him: a wealthy man who owns and runs White Eagle Transport. The reason I'm in Melbourne these days is the bank sent me down from Sydney to join the team set up to serve the banking needs of high wealth individuals in Melbourne. That's how I met Jakub. Let me tell you about him and why I think you should meet him.'

Simmo began by saying Jakub had just been called up to the Polish army when the Germans invaded. His unit was decimated and he became a fugitive from the advancing forces. He saw the best chance of surviving was to escape Poland and find a safe haven. He set off at the start of winter and walked through a ring of Eastern European countries aiming to reach neutral Switzerland. Along the way he was constantly in danger of capture or death from police, soldiers, border guards, roaming bandits, hunger, snow and bitter winds. When he reached Zurich, he thought his travails were over but had not appreciated the difficulty of finding work and lodgings in wartime Switzerland. Homeless and without work, he managed to survive, and at the end of the war entered a displaced persons camp in Italy from which he was brought to Australia and sent to the camp at Bonegilla, near Albury.

At Bonegilla he was given the job of mucking out railway vans used to transport sheep and cattle. He had endured far worse experiences in Europe, but this latest indignity hit him hard. Was this all he could expect after travelling across the world? He could feel the determination to survive, which had sustained him until now, crumbling away. Fortunately for him, Alesky and Brygita Mazur, an older Polish couple in the camp, encouraged and took care of him so that he became like a son to them. Alesky had operated a furniture removals business in Warsaw prior to the war and was determined to start again in Melbourne. He had sufficient funds to buy one old van but no longer had the strength needed to do the heavy lifting required and persuaded Jakub to come with him as his assistant. Jakub not only demonstrated the necessary strength but also delighted Alesky with his speed in learning the business. Slowly they began to prosper and were able to buy a larger van and expand their coverage.

After some years Alesky decided he could retire from active involvement, confident Jakub now had the knowledge, experience and business acumen to run the enterprise. Shortly afterwards Jakub saw a pick-up van parked in the street where he lived with Alesky and Brygita and noticed it was for sale. He found the owner was a man who had operated a small courier service. He was a good and reliable driver but had no talent for running a business and was forced to sell up. After speaking with him, Jakub bought the van, offered him a job as driver and went to tell Alesky they now owned a courier service. This was the first occasion on which Jakub demonstrated the entrepreneurial flair that saw the White Eagle Transport Company, as it became known, grow to its current prominence and make both men wealthy.

Two years ago Alesky died and was soon followed by Brygita. Jakub was determined to provide an ongoing memorial to the couple. Despite his wealth and position, Jakub retained a modest lifestyle and had ample funds he could use for charitable purposes. He thought of the years he had endured in Europe, the impasse he had reached at Bonegilla and his rescue by Alesky and Brygita. He believed the lessons learned through his early, harsh experiences and the mentoring of Alesky had combined to make him the successful man he became. Perhaps he could use his money and his experience to rescue those trapped by poverty in Melbourne. Where better to start than with people who were homeless?

Simmo paused and at last Danny could see why he had embarked on his account of Jakub Kowalski. 'I know you mean well, Simmo, and, believe me, being with you has been great. But I've already received the help some charities offer. All they can do is give temporary relief. How could this Kowalski man do any better?'

Simmo smiled at him. 'That's why I'm so keen for you to meet him. He came to the bank for advice in setting up what he's called the Mazur Foundation and I was the one given the job of helping him. He can be a hard man to deal with, but I'm convinced he's onto something. The Foundation's been running for just short of a year and has already had some success. Jakub insists on vetting everyone who joins the program. He likes to look for candidates himself, but that's time-consuming and he's a very busy man, running White Eagle and the Foundation. I volunteered to help out by going round the streets on a Friday night, talking to any homeless people I came across and seeing whether I think there's a fit with the Foundation's approach. If I think there is, I arrange for them to go into temporary accommodation prior to Jakub making his assessment. I knew the poor wretch I found shivering in a doorway last night couldn't benefit from what Jakub offers, so I took him to St V's instead. On the other hand, I reckon you are a good fit. That's why I want you to meet him.'

Simmo went into his bedroom and closed the door, but Danny could hear enough to know he was on the phone and speaking about him. When Simmo returned he was grinning broadly. 'We're on with Jakub after lunch.'

Simmo drove them to West Brunswick and parked outside a two-storey red-brick house, which was protected by a tall fence built of similar bricks. In the middle of the fence was a sturdy wooden gate and, beside it, an intercom. There was a delay before a deep voice said a curt, 'Yes,' and after Simmo announced himself the snap of a relay which unlocked the gate and allowed it to swing open. They walked down a gravel path which bisected a green lawn surrounded by dense bushes. As they approached the front door, it opened to reveal a thickset man of average height dressed in a red woollen roll-neck jumper and faded jeans. Coming closer, Danny could see the man had a squarish face topped by steel-grey hair cut very short. His ice-blue eyes showed no welcome but studied him carefully.

'Thank you for seeing us this afternoon,' Simmo began in a voice Danny thought was unduly deferential. Perhaps this was required when junior bankers addressed wealthy clients. 'This is Dream... This is Danny Mc Bride.'

Kowalski took Danny's offered hand but did not smile and continued to scrutinise him. 'Do I call you Danny or Dreamer?'

'Dreamer is reserved for old army mates,' Danny said firmly, causing one of Kowalski's eyebrows to lift.

'You'd better come in.' He led them into a large room which retained an open stone fireplace where the fire was set but not lit. Facing the fireplace was a burgundy Chesterfield couch with matching armchairs to either side of it. Under the window, which gave a view of the front garden, was a mahogany sideboard and on the far wall a painting of a large bird poised on a craggy outcrop as if about to swoop down on them. 'The white eagle,' Kowalski said. 'The national bird of Poland.' He gestured at the couch. 'Sit there.' Danny took his place on the couch while the others sat on the chairs either side of him. 'Tell me about yourself,' Kowalski said and sat back.

Danny had no intention of repeating the comprehensive account he had given Simmo that morning. Instead, he briefly described himself as the son of a newsagent who had been called up for national service, sent to Vietnam and returned a different man. He could no longer work in the newsagency or stay with his parents. He set out to make his own way but found the going tough and had spent the last two years on the street.

'Do you drink?' Kowalski asked.

'I did to excess for a while but no longer.'

Kowalski nodded, apparently satisfied with Danny's response. 'You are a displaced person.'

'No one's called me that before.'

'The term is often used to mean a refugee but it's more than that. As far as I'm concerned, a displaced person may be a foreigner or living in their native country. What distinguishes them is they have no money, no home, no job and no friends they can fully trust. I was one for years before I came to this country and you're one now. I was able to survive and prosper because of the generosity of Alesky and Brygita Mazur. I have named my foundation after them. Their generosity and my determination are what saved me. It can save you, too. The Mazur Foundation can provide you with a home and a job which will allow you to earn money. You already have a friend you can trust in David Simmonds. What we can't give you is the determination to make good. That's up to you.' He paused as if giving time for his words to sink in. 'Some displaced persons don't have that determination. Some have had it knocked out of them. Some never had it in the first place. Whatever the reason, I can't waste my time and money on them. David assures me you've got what it takes and I'm inclined to give you a chance, but show any sign of letting me down and you'll be back where we found you.'

'I've let enough people down for one lifetime,' Danny said.

Kowalski smiled for the first time, although it was more of a sneer than a grin. 'You telling me you make a habit of it?'

'No, I'm saying I've finished doing that.'

'Good.' He turned to Simmo. 'David, take Danny to the flats and hand him over to Max. Tell him I'm happy for Danny to start on the program. Max can allocate him a flat and kit him out. He'll start work on Monday with the Removals Group.'

Simmo pursed his lips. 'I forgot to tell you Dreamer was beaten up last night. He's got three cracked ribs and is carrying a lot of bruising. Might I ...'

'You didn't tell me he gets into fights.'

Danny answered for Simmo. 'I don't. I've only ever been in one fight and that was three years ago. Last night I was asleep when three or four young tearaways set on me.'

Kowalski surprised Danny by asking, 'You got a driving licence?'

'Yes, I have.'

Kowalski turned back to Simmo. 'We'll start him on courier work.'

⟋⟍

The flats, Danny discovered, were not far away in East Brunswick. They appeared to have been recently built — about a dozen in the block. Max was a small man with sharp brown eyes who acted as live-in caretaker and occupied the ground floor. He gave Danny a key to number seven. 'Did the boss tell you? You pay no rent for the first three months and if you're still here after six, we throw you out. Come in here.' He led Danny to a room fitted out like a charity clothes shop. He looked Danny up and down before handing him a change of clothes, a coat and a pair of shoes together with toilet gear and a shaving kit. Danny was reminded of his first day at Puckapunyal when he collected a much more comprehensive wardrobe. The clothes were not new but they were spotless.

'I've done me best but if anything doesn't fit too well, let me know and I'll see what I can do.' They walked back to the office where Max asked, 'Where you workin'?'

'Kowalski said I was to start on courier work.'

'You're on courier?' Max stared at him as if looking for an explanation. 'He usually starts blokes like you on removals.'

Danny did not enlighten him.

'Jerry Torrens in number four is a courier. He can take you to the base in the mornin' where you should see the boss, Tony Delgardo. Jerry aint home right now, but I'll tell him when he comes in.'

Thinking they were done, Danny turned away, keen to see his flat.

'Hold on.' Max went to a safe which he unlocked and withdrew an envelope he handed to Danny. 'That's your first week's pay. You'll need most of it for food and some more clothes, so don't splurge it.'

⟋⟍

Jerry Torrens had red hair, freckles and the build of a jockey. On their walk to the courier base he showed no interest in asking about Danny or

304

speaking about himself. He took Danny to a small office where he introduced him to Tony Delgardo, a dark-haired man with a barrel chest and
a challenging manner, similar to Jakub Kowalski. 'Been told you were
coming,' he said. 'You need to learn the ropes and when you're up to speed
I'll check out your driving and see whether I can trust you to run your
own van.' He turned to Jerry and said, 'He can go with you to start with.'

Danny could see Jerry did not like being burdened with a learner
but it would take a lot worse than that to dim his pleasure at the turn
in his fortunes. After a few frosty days his willingness to do the leg
work of picking up and delivering the items they couriered saw a thaw
in Jerry's attitude. Danny welcomed the opportunity for a brief chat
with whoever was sending or receiving the couriered package. It was
so good to be treated as just another human being.

Soon Jerry was happily telling Danny about himself, encouraged by
the interest Danny showed and the questions he asked. It was a long
time since Danny had engaged in such a conversation but he hadn't
lost his touch. 'Grew up on a dairy farm near Leongatha with me two
brothers and a sister.' Danny thought of Skeeta. Would he ever get back
to Mundarlo to see Skeeta's mum? Jerry gave a small grin. 'I'm the runt
of the litter. Not built for farm work. Not interested, either. Came to
Melbourne to make me fortune.'

'I know how tough that is,' Danny said.

'Yeah. Didn't help hittin' the bottle, but.'

When Danny was given his own van, he missed Jerry but they continued
to chat after work at the flats and found others there who came to join
them. The residents were a shifting population. Some of them moved on
to other accommodation and some to other jobs. A few didn't meet the
obligations Jakub had placed on them and were shifted out. New ones
took their places, tentatively at first, but more confidently as they realised
it was safe to engage with those already there. For Danny it had some of
the elements of being in the army. There wasn't the danger, but men who

started as strangers were brought together by their common past experience and their shared struggle to overcome the difficulties they faced.

On Friday nights Danny began to go with Simmo seeking others the Foundation might be able to help. He had suggested he accompany Simmo as a way of staying in touch without imposing on him, but it soon became apparent Danny knew far better where to go and how to engage with people who might benefit from the help of the Foundation. He said it was because his own experience enabled him to connect with them, but Simmo told him there was more to it than that.

Danny had been at the flats for almost three months when, one Friday night, he and Simmo had found no one they could recommend to Jakub and were sharing a beer before going their separate ways. Simmo wiped his lips and asked, 'You been in touch with your family yet?'

'Not yet. Wanted to make sure I was settled before I did.'

'How settled do you need to be? You shouldn't put it off any longer. I bet they're anxious to hear from you?'

'OK I'll ring my brother. That's if he's still reachable on the number I have. I'll do it tomorrow.'

'Do you know the number?'

Danny grinned at Simmo. He'd written it on a slip of paper and, after he went on the street, ended up with only two things in his wallet: his driving licence and Sean's phone number. 'Yeah, I've got it here.' He began to pull the wallet from his pocket.

'Hold on. Come to my place. You can phone from there. It's not all that late. Besides, your brother won't care how late it is.'

Danny had expected the phone to be answered by Guy and wondered whether Sean was still with him. He was both surprised and delighted when he heard Sean's voice.

'Sean, it's me, Danny.'

There was a long silence before Sean said, 'My God, it is really you. You're not dead. Where are you?'

'In Carlton. A long story.'

'I bet it is. Come over here and we can talk.'

'I don't want to intrude on you and Guy.'

'No problem. He went to Sydney earlier this evening. You're lucky to get me. I'm teaching in Frankston these days and have a bed-sit down there. I only come here at the weekend.'

⚓

Danny stood in front of the terrace house in North Melbourne, the only sound coming from Simmo's departing car. He remembered the day he left. He had taken the closing of the door behind him as symbolic of shutting out his old life and taking up a completely new one — a melodramatic notion for what had so far turned out to be a failure to find any commitment to a worthwhile cause or occupation. What should he make of the door opening again? He wasn't going back to his old life.

The door was thrown open and Sean stood silhouetted by the light from the room behind him. 'There you are. Come in where I can see you properly.' He stood aside and Danny entered. Sean turned to examine him from head to foot. 'A bit dowdy but you were always that way inclined. Everything in working order?'

'I'm fine.' Danny had been making his own appraisal. He had the feeling Sean was not so fidgety and more settled than he had been in the past. Or was this merely the awkwardness of their meeting? 'Can I sit down?'

'Yeah. Yeah, of course. Sorry. Can I get you something to drink? A beer? You started to show an interest in wine when you were here.'

'Nothing thanks. Tell me, how are you? You're teaching, you said.'

'Yeah. Had a stint in Hamilton and have moved to Frankston. It's as good as I hoped. But you can't fob me off with your old tricks. Tell me about yourself. Where have you been? What have you been doing for these years? What are you doing now? Where do you live? Why take so long to get in touch?'

Danny shook his head and opened his palms. 'OK. OK. But first, tell me about Mum and Dad.'

Sean pursed his lips and drew in a breath. 'Physically they're OK. A bit older. But I don't think either of them is happy. Dad struggled on with the shop for a few years. I think he was kidding himself that you'd see the light and return but eventually gave up and sold the business. Don't think he's happy in retirement, although they live comfortably enough. I should tell you I get all my news from Mum. Dad still views me as having been captured by the devil. He won't speak with me or let me anywhere near the house. I think he tried to get Mum to toe his line but she refused. She rings me fairly often and every now and again we meet for coffee. She isn't hostile to Guy but won't come here to visit. I think she's walking some kind of tight-rope with Dad.' Sean had slumped down in his armchair and now sat up straight. 'No more from me until you answer those questions you were so keen to avoid.'

'I'm a courier driver for White Eagle and live in a small flat in East Brunswick. Neither the job nor the flat are anything special but, after a rough time I prefer to forget, I'm making progress. That's why I thought it was time I got back in touch. You'll tell Mum?'

'Come on mate. That's not good enough. Tell me the whole story.'

Danny glanced around at the paintings. He didn't remember the one which in which an army of pencils marched across the canvas. It must be new. 'Things went badly until I met one of my old army mates who rescued me, introduced me to Jakub Kowalski, the boss of White Eagle, who likes to give blokes like me another chance. Tell Mum I'm fine, say what I'm doing now but leave out most of what I've told you about the earlier times.'

'That won't be hard. You've told me nothing. You know Mum will be busting to see you.'

'What about Dad?'

Sean sat back and scratched his chin. 'That could be tricky. Mum doesn't say much, so I don't know whether he still feels the same way he did the night he kicked both of us out. He certainly hasn't changed his opinion of me but maybe he's mellowed towards you. You haven't committed any mortal sins ...' Sean paused to consider. 'Not any I know about.'

'And you and Guy are still together?'

Sean grinned at Danny. 'Remarkable as that might seem. I don't know whether Dad prevailed on God to interfere, but the fates have been making things difficult for us. I was shipped off to Hamilton and later Frankston. Meanwhile Guy has become prominent in the Labor Party. He's forever going to a conference or a planning meeting or a demonstration. And the higher his public profile the more important it is to keep our relationship secret. Yet, somehow it survives. Perhaps we do really love one another.'

'You still involved in the marches? They're getting a lot of interest.'

'I did at first.' Sean gave a humourless laugh. 'I've had a chequered career as a protestor. Remember me telling you how I lost enthusiasm for protesting against National Service when I saw too many of the protestors acting out of self-interest rather than genuinely campaigning for peace. After I missed being called up for National Service, I went back to campaigning against the war but my enthusiasm dwindled away again. That was your fault.'

'What?'

'It's been very tough for veterans like you. I saw how Vietnam affected you and knew you'd lost your best mate there. Then I met a few other nashos back from Vietnam. They hadn't suffered what you had to deal with but they were mightily pissed off. With all the protests and the marches, they feel they're now being seen as the bad guys. They reckon they had to put their lives on hold for two years to go and serve our country while those who missed out on the ballot steamed ahead in their careers. Now they're home again they get blamed and abused for doing it.' He paused and shook his head. 'The more I thought about it the more I couldn't hack it and pulled out of the protest movement. It triggered another one of those arguments between Guy and me that sent you on your way, but we got over it as we always do.'

'You were right,' Danny said.

'Right about the war in Vietnam?' Sean's forehead creased in a frown of frustration. 'No one was right except perhaps that interpreter guy

309

you told us about. I remember he said the killing and destruction would go on until the Yanks got tired of it and then they, along with the Aussies, would go home leaving his people and the Communists to put the broken pieces of their country together again. Nixon's trying to invent a way out and, now McMahon's deposed Gorton as Prime Minister, he's saying all our troops will be home by Christmas. That'll leave your interpreter's people and the Commos to get on with the Humpty Dumpty exercise he forecast. Don't like his chances with the Commos. It could get very nasty in the south.'

Immediately Danny thought of Linh. Would she be safe? How had she got on? It was over four years since he had seen her. He wasn't going to share these worries with Sean, though. 'What else have I missed?'

Sean leaned forward and brought his hands together, interlacing his fingers. 'I'm not sure how you'll take this. Jane married a doctor at the Alfred a couple of years ago. They live somewhere down Beaumaris way.'

Danny hesitated before saying, 'Good for her.'

'Do you really mean that?'

'When you told me, my first thought was to regret I mucked up with Jane, but I'm pleased she's got on with her life and married. Could be a long time before I do that.'

Nest morning, when Danny answered the knock on the door of his flat, it was Max. 'Jakub wants to see you.'

'Is he coming this morning?' Jakub liked to drop by the flats from time to time and speak with whoever he found there.

'No. He wants you at his place right now.'

As far as Danny knew, there had been only three occasions during his time at the flats when one of them had been summoned to Jakub's house. Twice the men called to see him were fired from their jobs at White Eagle. The only survivor was severely chastised but given another chance.

As Danny hastened through the streets, the overcast sky and chill wind were not good omens. What had he done to fall foul of Jakub? His boss at the courier service was hard to please but hadn't berated him like he did some. He was coming up to the time when he would be required to pay rent but he knew he could stay another three months before being 'thrown out' as Max had put it. He hadn't kept his flat very tidy but Max had not complained and, after all, it was his flat. If he wasn't to be fired, perhaps he was going to be moved on. Perhaps that was it: he was going into removals or heavy transport.

Just like his first visit, the front door opened as he walked up the path and Jakub stood waiting for him. Again, there was no smile of welcome but, unlike the first time, Jakub did not study him directly and appeared rather less sure of himself.

'Come in. I've lit the fire,' he said and led Danny to the couch. When they were seated, Jakub said, 'Your injuries, they are completely healed?'

He was to be moved on. 'I'm fine.'

'And the courier job? How are you finding that?'

If he was going to be moved on, he might as well say what he really thought. He had already seen that Jakub preferred direct answers. 'I've enjoyed the job. It's given me the opportunity to speak with a lot of people in a way I haven't been able to do for quite a while. I suppose that's a bit like my old job at the newsagency. I'm starting to look around, though. What I really want is a job where I can be of some direct benefit to people. I don't know what that might be, yet. I'll never be a nurse or a teacher or anything like that but maybe I can find something.'

'Yes.' Jakub leaned forward excitedly. 'I was right.'

This was a side of Jakub Danny had never seen. 'Sorry?'

Jakub took a deep breath through his nose. 'Better I explain. I have several problems pressing on me. Good problems, most of them. First, my business. White Eagle has been doing very well and is now poised ...' He glanced over at the painting as if he had been speaking of the bird rather than his business. Perhaps he saw it as a talisman. 'There are new opportunities I'm ready to grasp, but this will need hard work and close attention. Less time for the Foundation. Yet it, too, is ready to expand. The plans are drawn up for a new block of flats in Fitzroy and building will start in a few weeks. I need to increase the number of volunteers finding suitable participants in the program and they must be trained.

'Then, most concerning, I have a problem which is not a good one. Remember I said that displaced persons have no money, no home, no job and no friends they can trust. I said the Foundation can provide these to anyone who has the determination to take them up. I was kidding myself. Yes, we can provide the money, the job, the home but friends they can trust are not so easy. You were fortunate to have David Simmonds, but many of the men who come to the Foundation have no one. I thought, because of my experience as a displaced person, I could play that role.'

Jakub broke off and began again in a humble voice, something Danny would have thought impossible. 'But I am an abrupt man. I do not make friends easily. I can be intimidating. The determination which has enabled me to overcome difficulties and thrive has its cost. I have come to realise my successes in the Foundation are due more to the determination of the men, themselves, than to my influence. On the other hand, every one of my failures, can be traced to those men not being able to find a find friend they trusted who could support them through the inevitable hard times.

'On my recent visits I see the change in the atmosphere at the flats, the building of friendships between men who were struggling to survive pretty much on their own. Max tells me you've provided the seed for this change. I am grateful and I am envious of you. I wonder how you would have got on if you hadn't had the support of your friend Simmonds.' He gave a modest smile, not the sneer he had used last time. 'Probably you had the determination that would have allowed you to succeed, despite having only my help. And, speaking of Simmonds, he has told me about your success when you go with him. Put all of this together and the solution to my problems with the Foundation is obvious. Use the successful participants in the program as recruiters and mentors. Not all will have the interest or, like me, the aptitude.

But some can be trained. I see one who I think is ready-made to take the lead and when I ask him to come and talk with me about my idea, he tells me he wants a job in which he can help people. My instinct is correct.' Now he was beaming at Danny.

'You know I was only recently in an abject state. You hardly know me. How can you risk giving me the responsibilities you're suggesting?'

'My instinct needs no time and has seldom let me down. Neither will you.'

———⟍

As soon as Bernard entered the front door Mary came to him. 'Bernie, oh Bernie, he's OK.'

He had not heard her sound so excited for a long time and there could be only one explanation for that. 'Has Sean seen him?' He knew Mary hurried home from Mass each Sunday and phoned Sean while he lingered at the church. It was best for both of them that he wasn't around when she spoke with Sean.

'Yes, he called Sean last night and then dropped in for a chat. Sean says he seems healthy, has a flat in Brunswick and works for White Eagle Transport. Danny wouldn't tell him where he's been and what he's been doing, but Sean thinks he's had a pretty hard time. Still he's OK now and it's so good to have him back.'

Bernard took off his coat, hung it in the hall and walked past her into the living room where he sat in his usual armchair. 'He's not really back, though, is he? Besides, with the business gone, it's too late for him to make amends.'

He saw some of Mary's joy leak away as she took her place next to him. 'Don't you think we should invite him here so we can assure ourselves he's OK? I'm not suggesting he move back here to live — just a visit.'

Bernard gave a sigh of frustration. 'We've been over this before. Can't you understand? When Danny came back from Vietnam, I was willing to give him whatever time he needed to get over his troubles before taking over from me, but that was never his plan.'

'He went to work with you straight after leaving school when he could have gone to university instead.'

'University! Huh!' Bernard spat out the words. 'You know what university did to Sean. Corrupted him into committing unspeakable acts and have no shame. All the shame falls on us.'

'I'm saying Danny was committed to the shop and it was the damage he suffered in Vietnam ...'

'He was not,' Bernard shouted at her. 'I've told you. Before he left Danny said to me he'd been searching for something he could really commit to and thought serving in the army was it. He wasn't interested in the shop. He didn't want to go to uni and saw working in the newsagency as a soft option until he found something that suited him better. If he'd only been straight with us from the start, we could have made other arrangements. We could have put Sean into the shop, avoided losing the business my family built over the years and saved Sean from the degradation he's suffered.'

Mary began to respond but Bernard would not allow her. 'If that wasn't bad enough, Danny had the gall to tell me he can't hide the truth when that's exactly what he's been doing. No, my dear, talk with them if you wish, go and spend time with them if you must, but don't ask me to have anything to do with them or suggest they come to this house.'

Reunion

Danny glanced around the hall where he stood chatting with some of his father's old customers and saw Jane next to a white-clothed table which carried party pies, sandwiches and cakes. She held a plate with two sandwiches on it and was standing alone scanning the crowded hall. When her head turned in his direction, he was too slow to look away. He nodded a greeting and after excusing himself walked slowly towards her.

He remembered her as a very pretty girl and was not surprised to find she had become a beautiful woman. What was different, though, was her air of calm composure, putting him in mind of those experienced nurses he sometimes met in casualty. They instilled confidence they could deal with the direst of situations by conveying an attitude which said, 'Don't worry, I've coped with far worse than this.' Was that how she felt about speaking with him?

He began to worry about how he should greet her. To make no gesture would be rude, shaking hands too formal and distant, a peck on the cheek risky and one of their old hugs unthinkable. She avoided the problem for him by turning away to place the plate she had been holding on the table and saying as she returned to face him, 'I'm sorry about your father, Danny.'

He noticed that she struck just the right tone: appropriate regret without indulging in false grief. 'Thanks Jane. I ...' He began again. 'You know I was a big disappointment to him.'

She said nothing but he read *Not just to him* in her eyes.

'We didn't agree on a number of things,' Danny said, 'but he had his principles and held to them throughout his life. I respected him for that.'

'Yes, I thought the priest put it well.'

'Dad had a hard time as a young man, worked to build a successful business and had every right to be proud of his achievements.'

'How is your mother coping?'

'Coping fairly well, I'd say.' Danny paused to wonder if that were true. His mother was so good at hiding disappointment and sadness. 'We were all shocked by the suddenness of it.'

'Hello there. What have we got here?' The greeting came from Sean who was dressed in a pin-striped navy suit and colourful tie. He gestured at them with a half-full wine glass. 'Together again after — what must it be? — going on for ten years. Wow! And to think the old man had to die to achieve it.'

'Hello Sean,' Jane said.

'You haven't got a drink.' He made it sound like an accusation. 'What can I get you?'

'A cup of tea would be nice, thank you.'

'Tea?' This is a Catholic wake, not one of your prissy Proddy affairs. You needn't have any of the hard stuff but surely wine. Red or white? They've forgotten the champagne.'

'No, a cup of tea will suit me fine.' The calm assurance with which Jane saw off Sean's challenge again reminded Danny of the casualty nurses. In the gallery of images which haunted him was one of a tearful, uncomprehending Jane. He still regretted the hurt he'd caused her. What a difference the fall of a marble had made to their lives. Now, coming to appreciate the woman she'd become, he might be able to remove one disturbing image from his gallery — one less to deal with. On the other hand, he used to take pleasure in knowing Jane turned to him for support and assurance whenever she was troubled. She had no need for that now and he was surprised by the prickle of regret this caused him.

'What about you, elder brother? A beer?'

Danny nodded and Sean departed.

'He's still the same irreverent Sean,' she said.

'At least that's what he'd like us to believe,' Danny said and changed the subject. 'Your Mum and Dad? How are they?'

'It took a while but they've settled down very well now.'

'Sorry?'

'Oh, I thought you might have heard,' Jane said. 'They down-sized and moved to Point Lonsdale. They missed being in East Melbourne at first but now there's no way they would come back to the city.

'They sold the house?'

Jane shook her head in mock disapproval. 'You are behind the times! Gordon and I bought the house from Mum and Dad. We'd been searching for a place closer to the Royal Melbourne and the University.'

'You'll be neighbours again.' Sean had returned with the drinks and an arch expression.

'How come?' Jane asked.

'I'm moving back with Mum,' Danny said. 'She claims she'll be fine on her own, but we think one of us should be with her at least for a while.' He thought Sean might have told him Jane and her husband had moved in next-door. Ever since he had re-established his link with his mother, she had never mentioned Jane and neither did he, but Sean was usually keen to pass on any gossip. Perhaps it had occurred to him the day would come when one of them might have to move back and he wanted to make sure it was Danny. Did Sean think he would be put off by having Jane and her family next-door? The idea of them once again living beside one another clearly amused him.

'Where have you been living?' Jane asked.

'I've been renting a small place in Fitzroy.'

'You'll have to get Danny to tell you what he's been up to since he saw you last,' Sean said. 'When he does, let me know what he says. I've been quizzing him for the past five years but still haven't been able to get him to tell me much.'

'Yes, I'd like to do that,' Jane said. 'But not now. I'm already late for picking up the children from the child-minder.' As she turned away, she said, 'See you again soon.'

✗

'James, stop that splashing.' Jane glared at her son who merely grinned cheekily from his end of the bath and whacked the water again, sending a spray of soapy water into the face of his sister who let out a shriek.

'It hurts. My eyes hurt. Mummy, stop him.'

Jane leant into the bath to grab his arms and, when he tried to wriggle free, was doused with water herself. 'Anne, get that cloth, wipe your eyes and then give it to me.'

Gradually Jane restored order and dressed them in their pyjamas. It was always the same when they came home from the child-minder. Mrs Dennison was a nice lady who took good care of them, but they had come to expect at least one of their parents would be with them at all times. There were tears when she left them and bad behaviour after they returned home. James disrupted their tea by poking faces at Anne while she refused to eat the custard Jane had prepared for them. When she thought she had them ready for their bed-time stories, Anne started up again. 'Want Daddy to read.'

James agreed with her. 'Yes, want Daddy.'

'Daddy can't read tonight. He's at the university. If you want a story, then I have to read it. If that won't do, you'll have to go to sleep without one. What do you want?' She didn't know whether it was the glare she gave them or her ultimatum, but they settled down and she was able to enjoy the pleasure of their kisses after she tucked them in for the night.

Still, as she mixed herself a stiff gin and tonic, their last grizzle continued to rankle. It was Gordon who had been loath to leave them with others during the early days, and Gordon who had established himself as the favourite story-reader. When Anne was on the way, Jane had been surprised how Gordon read everything he could find on parenting. She was used to the vigour with which he pursued his passions — It was one of the things that attracted her in the first place — but she hadn't considered parenting as being in a similar category to tennis, MG cars or even anaesthesiology. He was obsessively attentive to Jane during the pregnancy and to both of them once Anne was born, spending every moment he could spare, and some he couldn't, with them. When James arrived, Gordon had been less intense but remained closely involved in caring for the children.

His appointment to the chair at the university on top of his leadership role at the hospital had eaten into his time at home as they had known it would, so Jane had been pleased their move to East Melbourne had brought him closer to his work. Increasingly, though, his time was taken up by the administration of his department and by his new obsession: to build it into a world leader in the teaching, research and application of anaesthesiology. That's what had kept him at the university tonight, hosting some important overseas visitor. He had given her the details but she couldn't remember them now.

As she ate her solitary meal of pesto pasta, she thought back to the funeral this afternoon. She had prepared herself for her inevitable meeting with Danny and was annoyed to be shaken when she first caught sight of him. Just like the old days, it was his companions who were doing most of the talking while he paid close attention to them. Focused as he was on the other three, Jane had time to compose herself and appraise him more closely than had been possible in the church. He had lost a little of his athletic bearing but did not appear as damaged as she feared he would be. His hair remained as thick and unruly as ever, the knot of his black tie had loosened and his suit could have done with a press. Not much had changed, even though it was getting on for a decade since she last saw him. She had looked away but was quickly drawn back to him and found him staring at her. What had he thought of her?

He was more like the Danny she once thought she knew so well: not the troubled and confused man she last saw in her flat. Had he recovered from the guilt and trauma which assailed him? She had known that meeting him again would be awkward, no matter where and when it occurred. There were so many things she would have liked to ask and tell him, none of them appropriate this afternoon.

She had been warmed by the affection she still felt for him. Her anger had burnt itself out and the hurt had ebbed away. That had begun when Sean called to tell her Danny had gone missing. What had he been doing during those years and what had brought him back? Had he found the atonement he sought? Was it through his work for this charity she knew so little about? She would dearly like to restore her friendship with Danny. She couldn't go back to where they had been. That was impossible.

She remembered the visit she made to see Mary after her engagement to Gordon had been announced. She had been reluctant to go, having had little to do with Mary since breaking up with Danny, but Mary had sent a message through her mother, asking her to call.

Mary was so kind, throwing her arms around her and then leading her up to the quilting room. On the floor lay a double quilt. The off-white backing sheet was covered in interlocking rings made from fabric segments in a variety of rich, harmonising colours. 'You may have read about the Double Wedding Ring Quilt in one of the books I loaned you,' Mary said. 'It has been a favourite wedding gift for quilters since the nineteen twenties. 'We do hope you like it.'

Jane scanned the quilt, struggling for words. Eventually she said, 'This is exquisite but I can't accept it.'

'Why not dear?'

'You know why not. You haven't just run this up. It must have taken many hours. This was for Danny.'

'No, dear,' Mary said in a firm voice. 'When I started it, I thought that one day I might give it to both of you. He has no use for it. I want you to have it.'

Jane sniffed before saying, 'You are very kind. I thought you might mind me marrying Gordon.'

Mary took Jane by the shoulders and looked into her eyes. 'You know there was a time when I hoped you and Danny would marry. That time has passed.' She let go of Jane's shoulders but continued to gaze at her. 'I think life is a bit like a patchwork quilt. You can have all the hopes and plans you like but, in the end, you have to make the best quilt you can with the fabrics you have — not the ones you might have wished for but the ones you have.'

Jane had seen the wisdom in Mary's words, though living her life that way was more difficult than she'd imagined.

'I'm feeling rather tired,' Mary said. 'If you boys don't mind, I'll go up to bed. You sure you don't want to stay overnight, Sean?'

'No, Mum, I'll have a chat with Danny and then be off.'

Danny and Sean stood to kiss her and watch as she slowly left the room. Danny sank back into his armchair but Sean remained standing. 'Like a beer?'

'No, better not. I had a few at the wake and that will do me for the day.'

'What's got into you guys?' Sean said. 'First, Jane sticking to tea this afternoon and now you.'

'You know I used to hit the bottle pretty hard. These days I watch myself.'

Sean sat opposite him and leaned forward. 'Isn't it time you told me more about those days. You disappear on me for close to four years until, out of the blue, you ring up to say you're back. Like I told Jane, I've never been able to get you to tell me where you were back from.'

'Oh, the brink. That's all you need to know.' Danny cleared his throat. 'I saw Guy on the TV the other night.'

'Guy's pretty disappointed. After Whitlam's dismissal last year, he managed to hold on to his Senate seat but is frustrated his ambitions to be a minister have to be put on hold. He's gone back to his human rights agenda and is pushing for Fraser to do more about the refugees coming out of Vietnam.'

'Yeah, that's been a terrible mess,' Danny said. 'A lot of us tried to do

321

our best but in the end achieved nothing. We probably made things worse.'

Sean shook his head and sat up, straightening himself. 'I don't know about that. The Communists are making life very tough for those who opposed them.'

'I try not to let it bother me anymore but that's hard,' Danny said. 'I was the first veteran to be helped by the Foundation but we have a number of them coming through these days.' He put his hand to his cheek before giving a small smile. 'Nothing to be proud of, but I do get a sense of relief from knowing I wasn't the only one to come back with a heap of baggage.' Embarrassed by his confession he went back to speaking of Sean and Guy. 'Must be difficult for the two of you with him being away so much.'

'Our relationship has always been like that. Often apart or having to pretend we are. It does have the benefit of making the time we spend together more precious.'

'Given all the difficulties you two have to confront, it amazes me you can have the arguments you have and yet stay together.'

'We agree on the basics and often fall out over the details and the methods of achieving our aims. We always have. It's part of the chemistry between us. To have a big argument with someone you love doesn't mean it's all over. If only you and Jane had understood that, you'd be the one living next-door with a couple of kids.'

Danny was not rising to that. 'Now the funeral's over, how do you think Mum'll get on?'

'She really loved Dad, but he must have been very hard to live with.'

'Yeah,' Danny said. 'He could be such an affable bloke when things were going well but the way he took on over us was so fierce and implacable.'

Sean surprised him by laughing. 'Did I tell you about my visit to the psychologist?'

'What?'

'In the early days after you went off, Mum persuaded me to see a psychologist. Dad had it in his head — actually I think it was old Father Maloney who put it there — that homosexuality was a kind of fixation which could be treated. You can imagine what I thought of the idea, but Mum begged me to go. She hoped it might placate Dad. When I said I'd go, Guy was furious — accused me of betraying the cause. We had one of those rows you're so frightened of, but I went anyway. The psychologist was one of those tweedy-suited gents with a pipe and a kind expression. After I told him my story and explained why I had come to see him, he eyed me over his glasses and said, "You seem pretty well-adjusted to me. I think your father is the one with the problem. Would you like to have him come to see me?" I didn't pass on his suggestion to Mum or Dad.'

Mary lay under the quilt, staring up at the ceiling. After all these years, longing to have Danny and Sean in the house, it was paradoxical she should hasten away and leave them on their own, but she wanted some time by herself now the funeral was over. Properly reacquainting herself with Danny and Sean could wait a little longer.

The funeral and the gathering in the hall afterwards had been a strange experience. She felt that she went through the motions of the grieving widow while her real self watched on as a disembodied specta-tor. So much of what was said about Bernie had fallen short of the full story that she had an urge to cry out but, of course, she didn't do that. Much of the day was a blur but she carried a number of vivid images.

Not unexpectedly the priest spoke at length about Bernie being a committed member of the Church and scrupulously following its teach-ings throughout his life. She would have liked to ask him why Bernie had been dogged for so long by his inability to follow the Lord's Prayer. He found it so hard to forgive those who transgressed and impossible to forgive himself. She never understood why he didn't debunk the story of his war heroism at the outset but came to appreciate the store he put on protecting his father's good name. Some of his deep shame over that surely lay behind his inability to forgive his boys for being as they were.

Up until the time Bernie banished the boys, he was known as a man devoted to his family. That was downplayed today. Only she had been able to see how he missed them and hoped he might relent, but right up until his death he remained adamant. If it hadn't come so swiftly, there might have been a chance for reconciliation but there had been no time. She had to work hard to persuade him she should stay in touch with Sean and then with Danny after he returned. Yet, despite his pretended lack of interest, he always listened carefully when she told him about her conversations with them.

At one stage today she had spied Danny, Sean and Jane in close conversation. What a bittersweet scene that had been for her. She still regretted that Jane and Danny had not married but hoped, now they were neighbours again, there would be the chance for some kind of reconciliation. Not that she wanted anything to undermine Gordon.

Jane cast a concerned eye over the living room. The irises she had bought were lovely, but she wondered about the savouries she had prepared. Bits and pieces on cracker biscuits looked good but could be tricky to eat without creating a mess. Gordon had not arrived home as early as he promised but had made it in time to read to the children, so they should get off to sleep without any problems. It was Gordon who had suggested they host this dinner. He said he felt guilty he hadn't been able to come to the funeral and saw this as a kind of recognition and apology. Jane wondered if his real reason was curiosity to meet Danny. She felt uneasy at the prospect of having them together and suggested that, if Gordon thought it neighbourly to invite Danny and his mother for dinner, they should include Sean, as well. Of course, she had to do all the work but that was true of all their dinner parties. Tonight at least she would be spared the need to pretend to be fascinated by esoteric medical research, hospital politics or the efforts to gain recognition for anaesthetists in the College of Surgeons, topics which so often dominated discussions at the dinners she attended with Gordon or they hosted here.

At the sound of the bell, she took off her apron and went to the door. Mary came in first, giving her a kiss on the cheek. Sean, carrying a bottle of wine, followed his mother's example and embarrassed Jane with his attention. Danny came last holding out a bunch of red carnations. She was relieved to find the carnations served to keep some space between them, just like the plate she put on the table when Danny approached her after the funeral. 'Thank you. They're beautiful,' she said. 'Gordon will be with us in a moment. He's just finishing the bedtime stories. Dad's the favourite for reading stories.' She was pleased to have the opportunity to boast of his skill with the children.

'Sorry. Just getting the kids off to sleep.' Gordon came into the hall and kissed Mary. 'You must be Sean,' he said shaking his hand and taking the bottle Sean offered him. After a quick inspection of the label he said, 'A very good wine. Thank you.' Jane was surprised when Gordon held out his hand to Danny and said, 'Good to see you again.' That was right: he had mentioned bumping into Danny in the street with Mary.

As Gordon ushered them into the living room, Mary said, 'That's a lovely dress you're wearing, dear.'

Jane smiled her thanks. 'I wasn't sure whether the colours suited me. She had told Mary there was no need to dress up but decided at the last minute to wear her new dress. Her guests had also ignored her advice. Both Danny and Sean were wearing ties and jackets with Danny rather more spruce than he had been at the funeral. She was reminded of the time he took her to the school dance. Probably Mary was responsible for the improvement on both occasions. Gordon had not had time to do more than remove his suit-coat which was probably just as well given the way their guests had dressed.

'Now, what would you like to drink?' he asked.

Having taken their orders, he left the room and there was an awkward pause before Sean broke the silence. 'I have some news. Next year I'm going to Richmond High as Head of the English Department.'

'Congratulations,' Jane said.

Mary smiled at him and said, 'It might suit you to stay here during the week, like you do at Frankston now.'

'Pity you didn't know earlier,' Danny said in what Jane thought was a rather crabby voice.

'How are the children?' Mary asked. Was there something going on between the brothers Mary wanted to nip in the bud?

'Very healthy and getting more of a handful every day.'

'If I can help out any time, let me know,' Mary said.

Jane stood to hand around the savouries. 'Do have some nibbles.'

After Gordon returned with the drinks and offered, 'Cheers', Sean affected a serious expression and said, 'It's wise we get things straight from the beginning. What footy team do you barrack for?'

Gordon took a moment before answering. 'Hawthorn's my team.'

'What?' Sean feigned outrage. 'Bad enough your wife goes for the Demons. You're in Tiger country now you know.'

As far as Jane could recall Gordon had never shown the slightest interest in football and she wondered whether he had cast around for a reply like she had done when Sean asked her the same question the first time they met.

'The kids at Scotch who were really good at footy went to play for Hawthorn, so I decided to follow them,' he said.

Sean shook his head slowly. 'Danny could have played for Richmond.'

Over dinner Jane was able to relax a little. The meal had turned out well. She had wondered about serving Danny's favourite roast lamb but thought better of it. The chicken, prune and bacon casserole — one of her mother's old favourites — was a success and, having dragged the children to the bakery in Smith Street, she was pleased by the reception her guests gave the apricot pie. On that trip she had been surprised to find Cafe Georgette still existed. It seemed such a long time since she had been there with Danny.

She was also relieved the conversation had begun to flow. Sean started them off with stories of the kids in his classes. Over desert, Danny asked Gordon to tell them about his work. Gordon's ability to speak simply and enthusiastically about his research seldom failed to excite the interest of his listeners. He made her proud to be his wife.

Just like in the old days, Danny said very little but he did appear more relaxed than she feared he would be. As Gordon paused to raise his glass to his lips, she saw her chance to draw him out. 'Danny, now it's your turn to tell us about your work with the Mazur Foundation. I'd like to hear about that.'

'Good idea,' Sean said.

'OK,' Danny said, 'but to understand the work of the Mazur Foundation and my place in it, I need to start by telling you about Jakub Kowalski. He's a complex man. If you met him, I'm pretty sure you'd see him as a hard-nosed businessman, well fitted to run a substantial transport company which, of course, he does. But there's a lot more to Jakub than that.'

As Danny proceeded, Jane could see he was trying to be brief, but Gordon would not allow him, frequently breaking in to gain further details. Familiar with Gordon's drive to know all there was to know about any topic that caught his interest, she was concerned for Danny. Some people were intimidated by Gordon's persistent questioning and others became offended when he raised points they were either ill-informed about or, worse still, had never considered. Danny's approach of gently leading the speaker down a path they found congenial was much more comfortable and often more revealing. Surprisingly, for someone who used to have little to say, except when speaking with her, Danny was not put off by Gordon.

When he reached the creation of the Foundation, Gordon was quick to ask, 'So how does the approach of the Mazur Foundation differ from other charities?'

'Many of those well-meaning people who try to help the homeless are limited in what they can do — like putting a band-aid on a wound requiring stitches. Jakub says displaced people have no home, no job, no money and no friends they can trust. Unless all of these needs can be met, they'll be unable to get back on their feet. His aim is for the Foundation to provide each of those necessities.'

'And how do you do this?' Gordon asked.

Danny described the initial jobs provided in White Eagle Transport and the accommodation in the flats where there were now blocks in Brunswick, Fitzroy and Kensington. Again, Gordon wanted more information and led Danny into explaining the rental arrangements and the pressure to move on to free the space for others.

Jane said, 'You haven't mentioned how you provide the friends they can trust.'

'No I haven't yet,' Danny said. Was she kidding herself or had he been particularly pleased she asked that question? 'This was the issue which allowed me to gain a better understanding of Jakub and led me to the role I've played in the Foundation for some years. I'd been there for about three months when Jakub called me to see him and asked me how I was enjoying the job. I decided to be frank with him and told him what I really wanted was a job where I could be of some direct benefit to people.' Danny paused to grin at Jane. 'You'll probably be amused to hear I told him I'd never be a nurse or a teacher or anything like that but maybe I could find something.'

Jane reacted with mock amazement. 'Danny! You're not telling us you wanted to achieve something in your life that mattered to you? Who could have convinced you of that?'

'Sorry, Jane, I've always been a slow learner.'

'Do you two mind enlightening me on what you're talking about?' Sean said.

'Golly,' Jane said. 'I think it was after the first game of tennis we had when we were still at school.'

Danny smiled at her. 'Pretty much our first conversation.'

'I was explaining why I wanted to be a nurse and Danny had other ideas about ...' Jane suddenly realised she was leading him into some deep water. '... about what he should do.'

'Getting back to your conversation with Jakub,' Mary said. 'How did he react?' Jane wondered whether Mary was bothered she and Danny were enjoying their trip down memory lane too much.

'He treated me as though I'd just provided him with the solution to some pressing problem. I've never seen him as happily excited before or since. Then he bowled me over by telling me he wanted to use the successful participants in the program as recruiters and mentors and he wanted me to be the leader.' Danny looked around the table. 'There you are. That's my story and that's what I've been doing for the past five years.'

'That's not all your story,' Sean said. After you went off you became a displaced person, as you like to call them. Tell us about that.'

Danny sighed. 'You never give up, do you, little brother?'

'Sean's right.' Jane leant forward to urge Danny on. 'Tell us what happened before you came into the Foundation. We'd all like to know.'

'OK. When I cleared out on all of you, I was determined to start a new life. I found it much harder to get a job than I'd imagined. I made some mistakes and I had some bad luck and, yes, I ended up on the street. I was fortunate to bump into one of my old army mates, Simmo, who introduced me to the Foundation and, furthermore, was a friend I could trust.'

'We have a lot to thank him for. I'd like to meet him,' Mary said.

'The bank sent him back to Sydney a couple of years ago, but he does come down occasionally and we catch up. He's still very interested in the Foundation. I'll invite him home for dinner next time he's in Melbourne. You're right, though. Goodness knows where I'd be now if he hadn't chanced upon me. But that's behind me now. If I hadn't gone through that bad patch, I wouldn't be doing what I am now.'

Jane remembered Danny had once told her God had a plan for each of us and we had to be ready to take up that plan when the chance came. She wondered whether Danny saw all that had occurred to him as God's plan and the unlikely appearance of Simmo as the chance he had to grab. Surely he couldn't. She wasn't going to ask him. Not now.

Jane closed the door, positioned the wash selector and pressed the start button. 'I'm so glad we bought the dishwasher. The worst part of any dinner-party is cleaning up afterwards and it does take some of the tedium out of it.'

'It was a good party,' Gordon said. 'I'm glad we invited them in and I enjoyed getting to know our neighbours better.'

Jane nodded her agreement. 'When you suggested it, I had my doubts but you're right. It was interesting and it was fun. Better company than those earnest members of the medical profession you like to bring home.' She turned to give him a wry grin. 'As usual, though, the men did all the talking. Mary and I hardly got a word in.'

'Whose fault was that? You were the one egging each of us on.'

'And each of you were good value,' Jane said, relenting. 'We poor housewives couldn't compete.'

'Would you like to keep baiting me or should we go to bed instead.'

'They're both attractive propositions, but I'll settle for the latter.'

As Jane was cleaning her teeth, she recalled with pleasure how impressive Gordon had been. If any of them had doubted it, they would now be sure she had married a man of stature — she had made a good choice.

In a different way, Danny had been impressive, as well. After sinking so low, he had found a role which clearly brought him great satisfaction. Perhaps she could feel less guilty over her failure to recognise the depth of his suffering. Making love with Gordon would be a great way to end the night. Too often lately she'd been worn down by the unrewarding drudgery of her day.

When she returned to the bedroom, Gordon was already in bed but sitting up with that expression on his face she knew well. It came when a particular topic had captured his interest and he would not be satisfied until he had explored it in depth. She had seen it when he questioned Danny tonight. Is that what he wanted to continue discussing now? She had other priorities.

As she slipped in beside him, he said, 'You were right about Sean and Danny being good value. I was impressed by both of them. Very different personalities. Hard to see them as brothers. Sean is such an outgoing entertainer but I was most impressed by Danny and the story he had to tell.'

OK, if he wanted to talk about Danny, she would tell him what she thought. Not all of her thoughts, of course. 'It was strange for me listening to him. He's changed quite a lot from when I knew him, but bits of the old Danny kept showing through.'

'I hadn't realised that you and he went back so far.'

'What?'

'When you ribbed him about searching for a role where he could achieve something that mattered, you said you'd talked about it when you were still at school.'

'That's right. The McBrides moved in when Danny and I were still at school. You must have known that.'

'I did, but I didn't realise the two of you were an item then.'

'An item?' Jane chortled as she turned to face Gordon. 'Far from it. I thought he was a droob and he had no interest in me. Apart from my other failings, I wasn't a Catholic — not even worth considering. We only played tennis because I was annoyed at the way he spoke to me and I wanted to challenge him.' She paused, recalling their conversation that day. 'The thing was that after that first hit of tennis we talked about serious things — whether you should always strive to be the best you could at something, what we planned to do when we left school, a bit on his religious views and he even told me he thought everyone should get married and have a family.'

'That's quite an agenda. And you still remember it.'

'I'd never had a conversation like that with a boy before. That's why it was so memorable.'

'But your feelings for one another must have changed.'

Jane didn't like the direction their conversation was taking. 'If you want to carry out a full analysis of my love life prior to meeting you, I'd better tell you about Richard St John.'

'Who was he?'

'He was a boy from Scotch. After him, I swore never to have anything to do with any boy from Scotch again. But there you are. Your charm overpowered me.' She ran her hand down his thigh and lifted her face for a kiss. 'Come and overpower me again.'

'Thank you, Mary.' Jane beamed at her hostess. 'The meal was great and you could see what an adventure it was for the kids as well. They're so fond of you and to sleep in your house instead of their own was a thrill for both of them.'

'You don't need to thank me, dear. It was a pleasure to have you and I'm always delighted to see the progress the children are making. With Gordon away at that conference of his, I thought you might enjoy a night out, even if it was only a meal with the neighbours.

'You're so kind,' Jane said, 'but now I must take them back to their own beds and hope I don't disturb them too much.'

Danny stood up. 'I'll give you a hand.'

'Thanks, Danny. If you could take Anne. She's becoming quite heavy for me to lift.'

The air outside the house was cold and Danny enjoyed the way Anne snuggled into his shoulder without waking. James grizzled for a while before Jane was able to settle him in his bed. Danny had never tended to children before and, standing beside Jane as she smoothed the covers and murmured her endearments, he felt a rare contentment. He'd always believed people should marry and have children but, until tonight, he hadn't realised how special the experience of parenthood could be. A shame this was probably as close as he would get.

He was preparing to bid Jane good night and leave when she looked appealingly at him and said, 'Would you mind waiting a minute? There's something I want to say to you. Come into the lounge.'

Danny sat on one of the off-white couches and recalled that first occasion when he came to take Jane to her school dance. The furniture was less formal and more stylish than it had been then, but he felt the same unease. What could it be she wanted to say to him?

'Danny, I wanted to say I'm sorry.'

'Sorry? What do you have to be sorry about?'

'When you arrived back from Vietnam and came to see me, I didn't understand all you'd been through and I showed you no sympathy, just focussed on myself.'

'Understandably so,' Danny replied guardedly. He was surprised she should apologise after all this time and wondered what she expected from him.

'The next day you went off on your own and we didn't hear from you for years while you were having a terrible time. I've always thought you wouldn't have done that if I'd been more understanding.'

Danny was moved by her words and more particularly by the intensity of her troubled expression. His first impulse was to take her in his arms and comfort her like he once did. Instead he looked into her eyes and spoke softly. 'You're wrong there. I was deeply sorry for betraying you and thought you were completely justified in what you said. I didn't go away because of your reaction. I was ashamed of what I'd done in Vietnam and how I'd let everyone down. Now I reckon I was running away, but I told myself I wanted to make a fresh start and atone for what I'd done. Those years were hard but they taught me important lessons. One of them was that, whatever your situation, you need to concentrate on the future and not be mired in the past. Easy to say but never easy to do.' Danny paused and, in the silence, it occurred to him that perhaps Jane was apologising for more than she had said. 'But surely you know that. I really like Gordon — an impressive man who's devoted to you — and your two kids are great. It makes me happy to see them.'

'The old patchwork quilt.'

'Sorry?'

Jane grinned at him shyly. 'Your mother once told me she thought that making the most of your life was like sewing a patchwork quilt — you had to make the best quilt you could from the pieces you had and not spend time worrying about the fabrics you would have liked but did not have.'

Danny knew his mother had various sayings but had not heard this one before, although he could see how she had applied it to her own life.

'From what you said the night you had dinner here,' Jane said, 'I'd say you've taken the same approach. Best of all, at long last, you've found a role you think is important and are doing well at it. We've changed positions.'

'I don't understand ...'

'No, you wouldn't. I used to be the one who had a satisfying career being the best nurse I could possibly be while you meandered along in the newsagency. Now you're the leader in a successful charitable foundation while I'm at home with the kids.'

'Just being with them, tonight I could see what I was missing.' He'd spoken quickly, wanting to encourage Jane to focus on the joys of being a mother but now he wondered whether she heard him as complaining at being denied the privilege.

Jane smoothed the folds of her dress over her knees. 'Oh, it was great at first. I really enjoyed being a wife and mother. Gordon didn't spare himself in making all of us happy. But the more successful he becomes in following his dream to raise anaesthetics to new levels of achievement, the less time he has for us. We all miss him. Not just me but the Anne and James as well. When they're not happy that just increases the load on me. It's worse at times like this when he's away. That's why tonight has been such a godsend for me. I have such limited opportunity for adult conversation and none of the challenge I once had as a nurse. I didn't think I would ever envy you, but ...'

'Have you thought about a part-time job?'

She gave a wan smile. 'That would be good. The trouble is I have to be on hand caring for or taking and fetching the children through the day so there's not much chance for a regular job — even a part-time one.' She stopped and gave a humourless laugh. 'We're back to old times: me pouring out my troubles while you sit listening so attentively and encouragingly. Perhaps we should go dancing. I haven't had a decent dance for years. Gordon has little interest and no great talent in that direction, I'm afraid.' Danny thought of the joy he had when he and Jane would sweep around the floor together. 'Don't worry,' she said, 'I'm just kidding. You still take me too seriously.'

'There has to be a way to help. I'll talk with Mum. Perhaps you should, too. She must have been through the same thing.' Danny paused to reflect on the crucial difference for her. 'I'd never thought of living over the shop as an advantage but it would have given her more contact with people.'

'She'll be wondering where you've got to.' Jane stood up, bringing Danny to his feet. 'Thank you for listening and being concerned for me. I can't talk with Gordon like I can with you. He'd feel I was blaming him and wanting him to be less involved in his work.'

She came to stand in front of Danny, gripped him by the elbows and softly brushed his cheek with her lips.

When Danny re-entered the house, his mother was waiting for him. 'You took your time,' she said. 'Is anything wrong?'

Danny wasn't sure how to respond. 'No crisis, if that's what you mean. Jane wanted to talk and I thought it best not to hurry her. She's feeling a bit tied down at home with the children and apparently Gordon doesn't have as much time to spend with them as he used to.'

'It's a problem many young mother's face,' Mary said in a voice he thought sounded rather dismissive. 'I'm sure it would help if she could spend time with other young mothers. And it would be good if she and Gordon could leave the children and have some time out just by themselves. I'm very happy to babysit. Otherwise there's not a lot we can do.' She paused to fix her eyes on Danny. 'Nor should we.'

A couple of nights later Danny called over his shoulder to his mother as he went out the door, 'Just going to check on Jane and the kids.' If she didn't like that, too bad. He had no ulterior motive and Jane had made it clear she valued being able to talk with him. A misty rain was falling so that he had to hurry from one porch to its neighbour. When Gordon opened the door, Danny was surprised. 'Oh, hello, Gordon.'

'Danny! Good to see you. Do come in.'

He had thought Gordon wouldn't be home until tomorrow. There was no chance to escape — Gordon had already turned to lead him inside and call to Jane, 'Darling, Danny's here.'

As he ushered Danny to the same couch he had occupied a few nights ago, Gordon said, 'Can I get you a drink? Coffee or something stronger?'

'No, I'm fine thanks.'

'Hey, I hear you're quite a reader. I'm told on the best of authority that the man next-door has all sorts of voices when he reads the stories and is very funny.'

Danny smiled, remembering the pleasure he's had. 'When they were in with us the other night, I was as surprised as they were. Dad used to love acting out the different characters when he read to us as little kids and was very good at it. Without thinking about it, I found myself doing the same thing and it did go over well. They're a great pair, your two.'

'Seriously, though, I'm most grateful to you and your mother. The way you looked out for the three of them while I've been away has been great.' He laughed and said, 'I get the feeling they can't wait for me to go again.' There was something in his tone which made Danny wonder whether Gordon was as pleased about Danny's success with the children as he made out.

When Jane came into the room, Gordon turned to her and said, 'I've just been telling Danny how I've been superseded by the man next-door as the reader-of-choice.'

'Yes, he was a hit. We'll have to get him married off so you don't have to face the competition.'

Was Jane suggesting competition for more than the affection of the children? 'I came in with a request for Jane. No, not a request. More a suggestion she might be interested in but is probably not.' He saw the puzzled expressions on both of his listener's faces and knew his embarrassment had caused him to revert to the garbled speech he had suffered from in the old days. 'What I'm trying to say is that Jane showed interest in the work of the Mazur Foundation. Mum was telling her how she was making quilts for the beds in the flats where our recruits stay and Jane said how good it was she could help.'

He broke off and turned to face Jane directly. 'It occurred to me we have a need which you would be able to meet. When we find anyone on the streets seriously ill or injured, we take them to hospital but many of our recruits arrive with relatively minor complaints and we do nothing for them. I don't know whether you'd be interested. It wouldn't take a lot of time: a few hours a week at most. It would have to be at night or at least after work when the men are available. I s'pose that could be awkward for you. But would you be interested in checking out the health of our people and tending to them? It mightn't appeal to you and I could understand you wanting to spend all the time you can with Gordon but ...'

'It sounds interesting, but I'm not sure I'm well qualified ...'

'Yeah, probably more of a job for a doctor,' Gordon said.

Jane pulled a scornful face. 'Typical doctor's response. They think nurses are only good for holding the patient's hand and mopping the doctor's brow. What do we do in pre-op if it's not checking the patient's condition, treating it if we can and referring it on if it's more serious?' Gordon began to reply but Jane was having none of it. 'Of course, I'd want to go and see what's involved before I'd be willing to commit, but the prior question is for Gordon, not for me. Are you willing to hold the fort here on your own for a few hours? It would have to be on a night when you were at home, of course.'

'If you're keen to do it, sure.'

'Is there a night next week when I could take you to visit the Fitzroy flats?' Danny said. 'You could get a better feel for what might be involved. Each of the blocks is pretty similar and Fitzroy is the closest.'

Over morning tea with Jane, Mary said, 'Danny mentioned you were feeling down having to cope at home with Gordon so taken up by his work.'

Jane took a sip of her tea and tried to swallow her irritation as well. During their conversation the other night Danny had said he would seek his mother's advice, so she shouldn't object to Mary raising the topic. She did though. 'Poor Danny. It's a long time since I unburdened myself to him. I do feel a bit under the weather. It's worst when Gordon is away and I don't like to mention it to him. I know he worries his work leaves him much less time for us than it used to. The last thing I want is to have him feel guilty or try to limit his involvement at the hospital or the university.' She did think he might have noticed without her having to raise it. She'd been dropping hints for some time.

'It would be good if you and he could go out on your own more. I'd be happy to babysit.'

'Thank you, Mary, that's very kind. You know how reluctant he is to leave the children without one of us being nearby. I'll have to cure him of that first.' She hated being in competition with the kids for Gordon's attention but that was what it had become.

'What about tennis?' Mary said. 'I remember your mother telling me both of you liked playing together but I've seen no sign of that since you've been living here.'

Had Mary been taking more interest in Gordon's and her comings and goings than Jane realised? This sounded more like something her mother would have got up to than the Mary she thought she knew. 'We stopped when I became pregnant with Anne and have never got back to it.' Jane shook her head. 'The problem is finding the time.'

Mary nodded sympathetically. 'It's a shame there aren't more young families living nearby. I had some good friends who were also mothers when I was in your situation. You have a bond from facing the same problems and issues and they understand how you're feeling much better than any man can.'

Jane leant forward to pour herself some more tea. Was Mary telling her not to bother telling her problems to Danny? Is that what this was all about?

'When Anne starts school next year, I'm sure you'll make new friends,' Mary said brightly. 'That's not far away now.'

Jane had heard enough. 'Mary, it's so kind of you to bother about me. I would like to take up tennis again. I need the exercise as well as the enjoyment of the game. And I will try to have Gordon take me out to other than work functions. That would be good. When you come over to babysit you must bring Danny. He's so good at reading to the children. They think he's great.' That would give Mary something to think about. Jane had enjoyed re-establishing her friendship with Danny and Mary had no reason, nor any right to be concerned. Besides a bit of competition might do wonders in stirring Gordon's interest.

⁓⁂

Steady rain fell and the only sound in the car was the regular thump of the windscreen wipers and the occasional swish of spray thrown up by the tyres. Jane had given Danny a tight smile when he collected her and had said nothing since. He hadn't expected her to be nervous. It was, after all, just a visit to see the set-up at Fitzroy and meet a few of those who occupied the flats.

The traffic was light, so it took very little time to arrive outside the flats and scurry into the shelter of the foyer where Charlie awaited them. Charlie, now the caretaker at the flats, had been a self-employed house-painter, bankrupted by his inability to manage rapid growth in his business. Danny had identified him as a man who was capable of caretaking the building and had the kind of personality which would fit him to become a supporter and confidante of the residents.

Danny was grateful for the relaxed way Charlie explained to Jane the layout of the flats and the services he was responsible for providing. 'But you'll be wanting to meet some of the guys,' he said to her before turning to Danny. 'We've got about four or five in the lounge.'

The lounge had been one of Danny's innovations: a ground-floor room containing easy chairs, a pool table, a TV set, tea and coffee making facilities and a collection of newspapers, magazines and books. Danny was disappointed Charlie had been unable to get more of the residents to attend but, when they entered the lounge, he was pleased to find the men who broke from their conversation comprised a mix of new and longer-term participants in the Foundation's program.

He introduced Jane who had taken off her coat and wore a simple, navy skirt and blouse, as though dressed for work. She greeted each of the men in a friendly yet businesslike manner. At the end of the introductions Danny made an awkward start on explaining the purpose of Jane's visit and she rescued him by breaking in to say, 'Danny, before we go any further, let's all sit down. We can make a circle.'

Having taken over from him, she continued after all were seated. 'In case you are wondering, let me tell you why I'm here tonight. I'm an old friend of Danny and was a nurse before I married and had children. He suggested there might be a role for me in maintaining or improving your health. I'd like to hear what you think?' Danny was sitting back enjoying the way Jane had taken charge but was jolted when she said. 'I don't know about you, but whenever I take part in this kind of conversation — and we used to have them from time to time at the Alfred — I always find they go better if the boss isn't present.' It was the first time she had smiled and Danny could see the responding smiles. 'Danny, I know you're not the boss of these men but you do run the Foundation, so would you mind.'

Danny occupied his time examining paperwork in Charlie's office and listening to the sounds coming from the lounge. What he could hear suggested Jane had no difficulty getting the men to talk and the frequent sounds of laughter confirmed they were enjoying themselves. When the door eventually opened, Jane emerged, saying over her shoulder, 'Thank you again for being so frank. I'll see what I can do.' Danny poked his head into the room to say goodnight and found the men regarding him with amusement.

Jane said nothing to Danny until they were in the car. 'Drive away but, when you find somewhere convenient to park, pull in there. We need to talk.' Danny waited until they were off the main streets and stopped opposite the tennis courts. The rain had intensified and was beating a tattoo on the roof. He switched off the engine and turned to face Jane who said, 'I'm wondering why you really asked me to come tonight.'

'I told you. I thought ...'

'I know what you said.' Danny was surprised when Jane gave him a quizzical grin. 'Was that the real reason or were you caught out when you came to see me the other night and found Gordon home, so had to invent some reason for calling in?'

He decided to take his cue from her and chuckled before replying. 'Yeah, I'm afraid that was what happened. Sorry.'

Jane nodded her agreement and Danny had the impression she was satisfied to have that issue out of the way but had more to come. 'I learned a lot tonight,' she said. 'Once they'd torpedoed your plan, we had a lively chat about a number of things.'

'I could tell they appreciated talking with you.'

She smiled, obviously enjoying the memory of her reception by the men. 'For a start I was a woman. Despite my best efforts to present myself as a sexless professional, several of them tried to flirt with me.'

'I'm sorry.'

'Don't be. After my years in the hospital I had no trouble handling it. None of your guys were obnoxious. Quite flattering, really. Allowed me to believe I hadn't lost all my sex-appeal. I could tell they were delighted to have female company and given how they live and where they work it's in short supply. That's one of the things coming out of tonight you might like to think about.'

'The others?'

'Collectively I'd call it *Ambition*. I know the Foundation is focussed on bringing men off the street and giving them the security of a job and accommodation. But, once that's achieved, what then? Take Charlie for instance. Like most of them, he's very grateful for what the Foundation has done for him but he wants to do more than be a caretaker for the rest of his life. He'd love to go back to painting and the freedom of working for himself but is scared he won't be able to cope with the business side. What he needs is some training and mentoring in running a small business.'

'He's never said anything to me about that.' After what he had done for him, Danny felt miffed that Charlie had not spoken with him about his ambitions and preferred to confide in Jane the very first time they met.

A sudden burst of wind rocked the car. 'Of course he hasn't. He reckons he owes you a lot and, seeing you've given him the job at the flats, reckons you'd think he was being disloyal by wanting to get out. I remember you telling us how your Jakub realised he was not the man to be the confidante of the men he was dedicated to helping and you were. I reckon it's time for you to come to a similar realisation — given your personality and having once been homeless yourself makes you an ideal person to support the men in the early stages of re-establishing themselves, but the next stage, the flowering if you like, needs planning and access to a wider range of expertise.

'And it's not just about jobs. When I asked the guys tonight how they thought the Foundation could make things better for them, they spoke not only about their job ambitions but also their desire for improving their education, re-establishing links with their families and forming friendships outside the Foundation.'

Danny was impressed. He was now hearing from the woman whose maturity he had sensed when first seeing her at his dad's funeral. 'I can see what you're saying. It's amazing you got so much out of a relatively short time with them.'

'I'm so glad I turfed you out of the room. They appreciate what you and the Foundation have done for them and would hate to have you think them ungrateful by making criticisms or suggesting anything extra should be done for them.' Jane stretched back against the seat and said, 'I don't suppose you play tennis these days. Would you like a game?'

Danny peered across at the rain-drenched courts before replying. 'I think it's a bit wet and dark for a game right now.'

Jane gave a hoot of laughter. 'Don't tell me you've developed a sense of humour.'

Danny was pleased to find Jane had discovered changes in him. Probably he was a different person from the one she knew and maybe even an improved one. It certainly was enjoyable to sit in the cocoon of the car speaking with her. A bit like the old days.

'I haven't had a game in years,' she said. 'It'd be fun to start again and I thought a good way to do that would be to have a hit with you like we used to.'

'Doesn't Gordon play?' Danny immediately regretted his question. He didn't want Gordon intruding on their conversation, although he had to admit he had been lurking at the back of his mind throughout the evening.

'He used to be dead keen, but once the children were on the way, we stopped playing.' Jane turned to face him directly. 'Danny, can I be frank with you? I could do with some exercise and have always enjoyed tennis but what I miss more than tennis is the kind of conversations we started having after our early games and which continued until you went into the army. A quick game with you on a Saturday afternoon while Gordon minds the kids would give me exercise and conversation. Would you be willing?'

'Willing, of course. Not very able I would say.'

Gordon came into the hall as soon as she opened the front door. 'How did it go?

'Hold on while I get rid of this dripping coat. It's bucketing down out there.'

When Jane walked into the living room, Gordon repeated his question. Jane wondered whether he was worried about her taking a job for which he thought her insufficiently qualified or was he starting to wonder about Danny? She sat down and dealt with the first concern. 'Turns out the job Danny had in mind isn't really necessary. I enjoyed speaking with some of the men who live in the flats and they gave me a number of suggestions I was able to pass on to Danny.'

'Wasn't he there?'

Jane chuckled. 'Not for my discussion with the men. I insisted on meeting with them on my own and they were much more forthcoming without him there. Not that they wanted to complain about him. He's doing a great job and is very popular. They hadn't spoken with him directly for fear of appearing ungrateful or disloyal: another case where men hide their feelings much more than women do.'

Gordon glanced at her and she wondered whether he thought she was having a go at him. That wasn't her intention, but *if the cap fits*. 'Where to now?' he said. Was he asking about getting a job or did he mean with Danny?

'Where to?' She smiled at him. 'Not to the Mazur Foundation but to the tennis court.'

'What?'

'If the weather allows, Danny and I have decided to have a hit at the local courts next Saturday afternoon.'

'If you want to get back to tennis, you should have said. Peter and Claudia still host games at what is their place now. I'm sure they'd be happy to have us back. I know they were sorry when we stopped.'

'Ah, yes, Peter. He's always been your best friend, hasn't he?'

'Since we were at school. But ...'

'What about other friends? Would any others be in the "best friend" category?'

'Jane, what are you on about?'

She leant forward and appealed to him. 'Bear with me, my love. You've always had Peter as your confidante. A man you can rely on to have your interests at heart, who supports you, listens to you and gives you good unvarnished advice. You probably have seen a little less of him since we married, but otherwise nothing has changed.'

'I have you. I talk with you.'

'Yes, you do.' Not as much as she would like these days, but she wasn't going down that path — not now. 'But you have Peter as well.'

'Yes?'

'So, who is my best friend?'

'Me, I suppose,' he said lamely.

'See the difference. I've had two best friends through my life. Sally Courville was my best friend at school, but she went to France and I lost contact with her. The second was Danny and you know what happened there.'

'Are you saying you want to have Danny as best friend again?'

Jane eyed him directly. 'If Danny were a woman would you be bothered?'

'But he isn't.'

Jane laughed scornfully. 'Sean has always been a good friend, as well. Perhaps you wouldn't mind if he became my best friend. He is gay, after all.' Gordon did not respond but sat carefully studying her, as though wondering what she would say next. 'Come to think of it, it was Sean who first told me I wasn't in love with Danny.'

'Unusual thing to discuss with your boyfriend's brother.'

'I told you he was a good friend. After Danny went into the army, Sean had just decided he was in love with Guy, the man he's still with, and asked me if I was in love with Danny. When I said I thought so but wasn't sure, he told me unless I was sure I couldn't be. Turns out he was right, although I didn't think so at the time. There's a difference between a best friend and a lover. You showed me that.'

'What does Danny say?'

'We haven't had the kind of conversation you and I are having and there's no reason we should. Danny is happy to have a game of tennis and a chat from time to time and that's all I want.' When Gordon still said nothing, she said, 'There is another thing,' and was pleased to see Gordon frown. 'I was talking with Mary the other day and she suggested we have more nights out on our own. She offered to babysit. I think we should take up her suggestions — both of them.'

Fete

Since they had started eating out more, Jane and Gordon had gone to a number of restaurants but Bombay House remained their favourite. Entering the restaurant, Jane reflected that Mrs Gupta had developed a stoop and the lines on her face had deepened but her welcome was as enthusiastic as it had always been.

'So good to see you again. The children, how are they? How lucky to have such parents. You must tell me what they have been doing since I last saw you. It's been ages. Must be almost a month. First, though, some of my magic.'

As she bustled away, it occurred to Jane that she had less need of Mrs Gupta's magic these days.

'I haven't had a chance to ask,' Gordon said. 'How was tennis this afternoon?'

Jane laughed. 'I've improved over the past months but I doubt I'll ever get back to the form I had when we played with Peter and Claudia.'

'Still, you have the conversation.'

Jane was sure Gordon was now more relaxed about her friendship with Danny — how could he not be given the lift in her spirits and the enjoyment they both got from what was like a second courtship — but she could see he continued to be intrigued by the value Jane placed on her conversations with Danny.

'Danny was telling me about his latest plans for opening a new block of flats in Abbotsford.' Since the night he had taken her to meet the men in Fitzroy, he had continued to tell her about his efforts to improve the impact of the Foundation. 'I think he values being able to discuss his plans with someone not directly involved who encourages him, yet doesn't hold back on critiquing his ideas.' She smiled at Gordon. 'That gave me an idea. We seldom talk about your work and I think we might both be missing out. There's no way I can discuss your research except in the broadest terms, although I am interested. But what about the other sides of your work? What about running the department and politicking to get a better deal for anaesthesia. I might be able to help you like I think I help Danny.'

'It's an idea,' Gordon said, rather grudgingly, Jane thought. 'There is something I was going to tell you about.' He leaned towards her over the table. 'I've been invited to give a key-note address at a world congress on anaesthesiology hosted by Harvard University. It's a great compliment to me,' he said, unable to keep the smile from his face, 'and it'll be a great chance to present the work we're doing before such an audience.' His smile faded and he dropped his head but continued to gaze at Jane. 'How do you feel about coping on your own? I'll be away for about three weeks.'

Jane had been expecting this. Gordon had dropped a few hints, probably preparing the ground. She lifted her head and pursed her lips as though making a detailed assessment of her feelings. 'Now Anne has settled at school and James spends time at kinder, it's easier for me.' She paused and allowed herself a broad smile. 'Besides, Mary and Danny are always there when I need them.'

Gordon had been gone for a week when Jane arrived at their door one night.

'Hi there,' Danny said. 'If you're here to cancel tennis on Saturday, I'm sure Mum wouldn't mind having the kids.'

'Actually,' Jane said uncertainly, 'I have a bigger favour to ask. One from you.'

'You make it sound quite onerous. You'd better come in and explain,' Danny said light-heartedly.

'No. I've left the children alone while I pop in here. It's just the annual fete at Anne's school is on Saturday and she's mad keen to go. I walk both of them to and from school each day without much trouble but you know how James can be a problem at times. With the crowd I expect to be there, I wondered whether you'd mind coming with us. That's if you're free of course.'

Mary, who had been drawn into the hall by the sound of Jane's voice, said, 'Why don't you leave James here with me? I can mind him and you can go with Anne. No need for Danny.'

Jane shook her head. 'That would have been good, but he's just as keen to go as she is. He's been talking about little else than the fairy floss he's going to have.'

'It'll be fun,' Danny said. 'What time should I pick you up?'

It was one of those autumn afternoons when the cloudless sky had allowed the sun to thaw the frost well before midday. Danny and Jane set out with Anne and James, farewelled by Mary, whose troubled expression was at odds with their gaiety. Anne was wearing a new check smock over a white blouse patterned with small yellow flowers and had her hair tied back in a single plait. She was even more pleased with herself after Danny told her how pretty she was. James in blue jeans and red T-shirt bounced around impatiently, reminding Danny of the way Sean behaved as a child. Jane had chosen a navy denim pants suit and a white ruffled blouse. Danny was struck by how happy she looked. Clearly, the family was expecting a good day out.

As they approached the Punt Road traffic lights, James started to run ahead of them until Danny caught him and held his hand. 'Now you can see why I'm so grateful you agreed to come with us,' Jane said.

After they crossed Punt Road and began to walk down Victoria

Street, Danny said, 'I haven't been back to our shop since I left for Vietnam. I guess it will have changed quite a bit.'

'I'm sure it will have,' Jane said with a grin. 'I know the newsagency was in Victoria Street but I never visited it, fearful of the reception I might get from your dad, I s'pose. Where was it exactly?'

'Further on. Not far past the railway bridge.' Danny stopped and scratched his head. 'Golly the street is so different.'

'The Vietnamese are starting to make their presence felt,' Jane said. Quite a few of the shops have signs in Vietnamese, so I'm not sure what they offer, but I've identified several restaurants and there is a greengrocer who has a wonderful array of bean shoots, kohlrabi, bitter lemon, Ceylon spinach and a host of other vegetables I don't recognise.'

'I'm impressed by the number you do know.'

'I didn't spend all my time in the hospital at Bien Hoa,' Jane said, 'and, unlike you soldiers, we had to feed ourselves.'

Danny thought of the meal Lien had prepared for him. He remembered his favourite dish, Bahn Khof, and how he had wondered whether he could find a restaurant in Melbourne that served it. He hadn't given it a thought since his return. Maybe he'd find such a place along Victoria Street.

'It's, not little Saigon yet,' Jane said, 'but I wouldn't be surprised if that's what it becomes one day.'

'I knew about the boat arrivals and how the government is bringing refugees from the camps in Asia but I didn't appreciate some of them were settling in Richmond.'

'There are two girls and one boy in my class,' Anne said. 'They're not very friendly and don't talk much.'

'That's because their language is different from ours,' Jane said. 'How do you think you'd go if we sent you to school in Vietnam? It must be very hard for them.'

A picture of the boys in Vung Tau, touting their wares in front of the hostel, came into Danny's mind. 'They learn quickly when they need to.' He wondered how those boys — now men — were getting on.

'Here we are, just along here.' He stopped, bemused by what lay before him. Even though he had already seen many changes in the streetscape, he could not easily rid himself of the image he held of the newsagency with its wire-encased newspaper posters lining the bottom quarter of the wide front windows. The posters had gone and above the windows was a painted banner with a line of Vietnamese characters, presumably the name of the restaurant. He could see Formica-topped tables and metal-framed chairs occupied by a few families of Vietnamese. 'Dad must be spinning,' he mused more to himself than to Jane.

'I've been thinking,' Jane said. 'Your Jakub should be very keen to help the Vietnamese who are arriving now. After all, they're facing the same problems he did. Perhaps the Foundation needs to take on a role beyond rescuing homeless men.'

Danny had been surprised and pleased by the interest Jane had taken in the Foundation since her visit to the Fitzroy flats. She was right: it would be a new direction for the Foundation but one that should appeal to Jakub. It would be great if he could do something for Vietnamese refugees — a form of recompense, perhaps. 'We'd need to change our approach a lot,' he said, already starting to plan. 'Treat the whole family. We're not really set up to do that at present. There might be a role there for you.'

They turned down the street to the school where they found the playground already crowded with parents and children clustered around a variety of stalls. 'Wow,' Danny said, 'A gathering of nations here.'

Jane laughed. 'Mum's aghast we didn't send Anne straight to Merton Hall and cannot understand why we would risk her granddaughter among the riff-raff of Richmond, but Gordon and I want her to start nearer to home and think the experience will give her a more balanced view when she does join the ladies of Merton Hall.'

The smoky smell of barbecued sausages wafted towards them as Anne called for them to head for a stall labelled Trash and Treasure where she had seen one of her classmates. James was not interested in trash or treasure. 'Fairy floss. Where's the fairy floss?'

'After we've been over to see Anne's friend,' his mother said.

Approaching the trash and treasure stall, a gust of breeze carried a cloying smell to them and Danny turned to see a woman spinning the pink floss at a stall across the playground. 'There 'tis,' James cried and took off through the crowd.

'I'll get him,' Danny said and gave chase. He did not immediately reach his prey, having to dodge through the crowd, a number of whom watched on with amusement. When he did catch up with James just short of the fairy floss stall, he swept him up and held him against his shoulder. Struggling to keep hold of the squirming boy, Danny became aware that one of those watching him was a woman wearing the white trousers and tunic of an ao dai. Could it be Linh Mai?

James wrenched himself free and Danny, turning to give chase once more, found him heading for Jane who was bringing Anne to join them. 'Mummy, please. Fairy floss.'

Turning back Danny was disappointed to find the woman in the ao dai had vanished. Had it really been Linh Mai or had the shock of seeing a woman in that fondly remembered costume played tricks on him?

'Are you OK?' Jane asked concernedly. That Asian woman. You were looking at her as though you'd seen a ghost.'

Danny laughed. 'Exactly right. For a moment I thought she was someone I knew in Vietnam.'

'Not ...' Jane started again. 'Seeing we're here why don't I buy the kids some fairy floss and you have a scout around, just in case she wasn't a ghost.'

'Thanks,' Danny said and hurried away. His search took him to stalls offering lucky dips, cakes and pies cooked by the mothers of the school, sweets, drinks, second-hand clothing and a comprehensive display of paintings and ornaments created by a local artist. At each stall he scrutinized the crowd for a woman in an ao dai and twice he found one. Neither of them was Linh. He must have fooled himself into thinking one of them was her. The excitement he felt when he thought he had seen her was both surprising and disturbing. Long ago he had accepted he would never see her again.

He was close to the furthest extent of the playground when he became aware the aroma of barbecue and fairy floss had been replaced by a spicier smell. Before him was a stall where a man was cooking Asian dishes which another man was encouraging the predominantly white crowd to try. A banner above the stall proclaimed GANH HOA RESTAURANT and added in smaller letters VICTORIA STREET RICHMOND. What shook Danny was not the unlikely sight of a Vietnamese restaurant offering food at a school fete in Richmond but the appearance of the man trying to cajole custom. He looked exactly like Linh's brother, Tuan Mai. Was Danny undergoing a series of hallucinations brought on by his exposure to Vietnamese people?

The man went to offer a satay to Danny but gave a start before hastily turning away. Danny realised this was no hallucination and Tuan Mai had recognised him. 'Tuan Mai, what a surprise,' Danny called to him.

'Can't you see I'm busy, trying to introduce you Australians to proper food? Go away. I want nothing to do with you.' He walked over to engage with another family which had arrived at the stall.

Danny hesitated before turning to find Jane and the children watching him. 'We were beginning to think we'd lost you. What was that man saying to you? He seemed very surly.'

'He was an interpreter attached to the Task Force at Nui Dat. We had our differences.' Danny paused to collect himself. He shouldn't mention Linh. 'He was cynical about the allied involvement in Vietnam, thought our efforts were misdirected and that we would eventually walk away and leave the Communists in power across the whole country. He was right. He's a very capable linguist and should have a much better job than being a chef's sidekick.'

'There you are,' Jane said. 'A role for the Foundation.'

'He made it clear he doesn't want anything to do with me.'

'You should persist,' Jane said and pointed to the sign above the stall. 'You know where he works.'

James pushed between them. 'Mummy? More fairy floss? Please?'

'How about an ice cream or maybe a cake?' Danny said. 'And I'd like a drink, as well. Come on, there's a lot more for us to see before we've finished here.

To judge from Jane's expression, his suggestions were no better than more fairy floss. He still had a bit to learn about what it meant to be a parent.

When Danny returned from the fete, he had little to say in response to Mary's enquiries. 'Yeah, I think the kids enjoyed themselves.'

'And what about Jane?'

There was that question within a question again. He wanted to tell her she had nothing to worry about but, if he did that, she'd probably take his words as confirming something was going on between him and Jane. 'Have you been past the shop lately.'

'You mean the Vietnamese Restaurant? I rather like the colour and energy the Vietnamese have brought to — let's face it — a pretty dull street.'

In the late afternoon he said to his mother, 'Don't worry about a meal for me tonight. I have to go out a bit later.'

'OK, dear. Where are you going?'

Was she worried he was going in to spend time with Jane? The way she stared at him suggested it. 'Yesterday I bumped into a Vietnamese man who was at Nui Dat with me.'

He thought his mother would be relieved but she didn't look it. 'Did he bring back bad memories? I hoped you'd been able to put all that behind you.'

'Some things will always stay with me. But don't worry about me, Mum. I'm sure Tuan Lai has had a rough time and I'd like to help him. The trouble is he's not too keen to speak with me and I've been puzzling over the best way to approach him.'

Returning along Victoria Street, Danny continued to worry whether he was being foolish. He could understand why Tuan wanted nothing more to do with him, but he kept thinking of the woman he had glimpsed at the fete. Perhaps it was Linh, after all. She might have come with Tuan. It would be so good to know she was safe and well and he might even be able to make his apologies for the way he'd behaved. She'd treated him so tenderly, but what would she think of him now? It would be great if he could establish some kind of ongoing relationship with her. He and Jane had managed that. Danny scowled at himself in the window of a shop he was passing. He was getting way ahead of himself.

Danny passed the turn-off to the school and continued along Victoria Street before he came to the Ganh Hoa Restaurant. It was also housed in a converted shop but was fitted out more handsomely than the one in their old newsagency. The tables were of solid, polished wood with matching chairs and the white walls held large colour photographs of scenes from Vietnam — Danny thought he recognised several spots on the outskirts of Vung Tau. A red banner which ran along the back wall carried golden Vietnamese characters and underneath the words GANH HOA WELCOMES EVERYONE TO ENJOY OUR FOOD. About a third of the tables were occupied by Vietnamese families with their children. Danny was the only white person present and was aware of the interest being taken in him. Almost all the diners watched him enter the restaurant and a young lad about the same age as James pointed at him and spoke excitedly to his parents who tried to hush him. Danny took a seat at a table near the window where he could see whoever came from the kitchen.

After a short time, a young woman emerged carrying several dishes which she placed in front of the diners at a nearby table. He felt sure she had seen him but, instead of coming to him, she hurried back into the kitchen. Shortly afterwards Tuan came through the door wearing a navy and white striped apron over his T-shirt and jeans. He glared at Danny with the same expression as yesterday. Danny braced himself for more hostility, but when Tuan arrived at his table, he bowed and said with mock servility, 'Good evening sir. Welcome to Ganh Hoa. May I provide you with an English menu? I translated it myself.'

He went to the small counter on the other side of the restaurant where he picked up a menu and returned to hand it to Danny who was puzzled by Tuan's feigned politeness but decided to play along. 'Thank you for the menu. What would you recommend?'

Tuan did not hesitate. 'If you are setting out to explore Vietnamese food, no better place to start than with Pho: a traditional dish consisting of flat rice noodles in a warming broth with chicken or beef — I suggest beef would be best tonight — and a variety of spices chosen by our chef.'

Danny glanced down at the menu and saw the description repeated, almost precisely as Tuan had recited it. 'Thank you. And to follow?'

'I'm sure you will not want to dawdle over your meal, so the Goi Cuon should suit you well: fresh spring rolls packed with crispy salad, prawns and pork, served with a spicy dip. You can be out of here very quickly.'

'You're wrong there. I'm determined to make a night of it, so there's no need for me to hurry. Why don't you get me the Pho while I read the helpful descriptions you've provided in your menu?'

Tuan did not return for some time, during which the young woman served the other tables. When he did come back, he was accompanied by a small Vietnamese man with a round face and watchful brown eyes, dressed as a chef. They came straight over to Danny and when they reached him, the man bowed in the customary fashion and Danny stood to return his greeting.

'Mr Nguyen is the proprietor here and wants to thank you for honour-ing him with your presence in his restaurant,' Tuan said, his fawning servility undiminished.

'Welcome. Welcome,' the man said before addressing Danny at some length in Vietnamese. Danny caught a few words he remembered from his time trying to learn the language but had no idea what was being said to him. When Mr Nguyen had finished, he gave another small bow and turned to Tuan for him to translate.

'Mr Nguyen is most grateful to the Australian people for receiving him into your country and believes there is no better way to offer his thanks than by introducing Australians to the delights of Vietnamese food. He set up a stall at the school yesterday, so the local people might sample his food and be encouraged to visit his restaurant.' Tuan paused for a moment and some of his humility slipped away. 'Actually, it was my suggestion we set up there yesterday and, if I hadn't, you and I would have been spared this.' He glanced across at his boss before resuming as interpreter. 'Mr Nguyen is delighted you are the first to come to the restaurant after visiting our stall and hopes many more will follow you. He also hopes the enjoyment you have here tonight will lead you to tell others about the restaurant.' Tuan stopped speaking and turned to Nguyen who nodded to Danny as if underlining what had been said.

'Thank you both,' Danny said. 'Please tell Mr Nguyen I'm delighted to have found this restaurant and its warm hospitality. If he doesn't know already, please tell him you and I first met at Nui Dat and ...'

'Nui Dat?' Nguyen pronounced the words with the Vietnamese inflection Danny was never able to master.

Tuan spoke to him briefly and then turned back to Danny. 'I told him you fought in Vietnam.'

'Say to him it will be a pleasure for me to return here to enjoy the food and get to know both of you better. I'd like to hear about your time after I left Nui Dat and how you came to Australia.' During the day Danny had thought over Jane's suggestion the Foundation should play a role helping the Vietnamese in Richmond and decided now was the time to mention it. 'I work for an organisation which aims to assist those who are having difficulty in establishing themselves in our community. I would like to speak with you about how that would best be done for the Vietnamese who have arrived here.' Danny gestured for Tuan to translate and was surprised he took such little time to interpret his words. 'I hope you gave Mr Nguyen a full account of my remarks.'

'As you know I am a professional interpreter. I told him all that was needed.'

'What time do you close?' Danny asked, surprising Tuan.

'We close at nine o'clock.'

'I look forward to continuing our conversation then and meanwhile will not have the spring rolls after the Pho. Instead I have chosen Banh Xeo.' Danny had been attracted by the description of the dish as pork and shrimp crepe flavoured with turmeric and packed with bean sprouts. He thought he recalled that being one of the dishes Linh had served. There was no sign of Bahn Khof on the menu.

Tuan nodded his acceptance of Danny's order and the two men retired to the kitchen.

Danny slowly worked his way through the food, which was excellent. There was no chance he could keep eating until nine o'clock and all the other tables had completed their meals by eight. Just when he was wondering what he should do, Tuan came from the kitchen having removed his apron. He stomped over to Danny's table where he sank with a sigh onto the chair opposite him. 'Nguyen is determined to make you a regular customer and has sent me out to build on our friendship in the army. You know how strong that was. But I need to humour him, so we'll have to chat for a while before I can be rid of you.'

Danny smiled at him, hoping to dissipate some of Tuan's hostility. 'That's what I was hoping for. But why is he so keen for me to become a regular customer?'

'One thing I'll say about Nguyen is he's a good chef. If you haven't discovered that for yourself there's something wrong with your taste. He had a top-class restaurant in Vung Tau with the same name as this one and he saw the chance to start again by setting up here in Richmond. The trouble is there are too many with the same idea. There aren't enough Vietnamese here yet and those that are can't afford to eat out much. Nguyen believes the way out of his problem is to entice some of you Australians into his restaurant, at least until more of us arrive. That's why he's making such a fuss of you. You're the first of what he hopes will be his salvation.'

Danny could see this was an explanation for Nguyen's behaviour but what of Tuan? Why would he work as a chef's assistant and, more puzzling, why was he so concerned to humour Nguyen? 'How did you come to be working here?'

'He gave me the opportunity to escape from Vietnam. It was his boat we arrived on.'

Danny seized on Tuan's use of the word 'we'. 'Did Linh come with you?'

His question caused Tuan to ignite, not in the flash of an explosion, but in a slow burn. 'What a hypocrite you are,' he hissed. 'I make it clear I want nothing to do with you, but you pursue me, not because you have any interest in me, but in the hope you can prey upon my sister again. What a brute you are. Many lost their friends in Vietnam but only you took revenge on an innocent girl from Dat Do. Oh, yes, the story was all round Nui Dat, even though the army tried to keep it quiet. Most of you foreigners sought relief in the bars and brothels of Vung Tau but that would not satisfy you. I didn't trust you from the day we met. You told me you admired and respected my sister and said she had nothing to fear from you. I could see she was a diversion for you until you could return home to marry your girlfriend — something I see you have successfully achieved.'

Danny, who had been staring down at the table in front of him as each of Tuan's accusations fell upon him like blows, looked up to see Tuan sneering. He had seen him with Jane and the children at the fete. Danny resisted the impulse to put him right. Best to wait until Tuan had finished his tirade.

'I remember saying it would have been better for her if you had more obviously tried to seduce her, so she would be more wary. But you were more subtle than I imagined. I can never forgive myself for not doing more to protect her from you. This time, though, she is out of your reach and you can do her no more harm. If you want to indulge yourself in some slant-eyed sex outside your marriage bed, Mr Nguyen will be happy to oblige you. He knows about such things and has the right connections.'

Danny's face flushed and he had to choke back the rejoinder which Tuan's accusations had triggered. He took a deep breath. Linh hadn't come with Tuan. But where was she and, more importantly, how was she, now. If he could keep him talking, let him blow off steam and relax a little, he might reveal more.

'Oh, yes, he's a resourceful man, Mr Nguyen,' Tuan said. 'He knows how to sniff the wind and doesn't mind what he has to do to prosper. When the Americans arrived in Vung Tau, he could see they wouldn't be interested in coming to his restaurant, so he set up a chain of bars and brothels. You might have been too busy stalking Linh, but I'm sure your mates would have been customers of his. He chose his girls carefully and made a lot of money. He also saw the Communists were bound to seize power in the end and would come down hard on those who sold grog and sex to the foreign troops.'

Danny had heard enough of Mr Nguyen. 'I remember you telling me how the war would end and you were spot on there. Did you stay on at Nui Dat?'

Tuan gave an exaggerated sigh. 'Right to the bitter end. It is hard to bear the pain of predicting a disaster and then having to sit watching it occur when you know there is nothing you can do about it.'

Danny thought of the Vietnam veterans the Foundation had tried to help. 'I've heard from a few of the Australians who were there after me that it got really tough.'

Tuan sniffed derisively. 'You might think that wretched fence which divided the farmers of Do Dat from their lands led to your downfall, but at least you were left in one piece, not dead or maimed like so many of your countrymen.'

'What do you mean?'

'You don't know? No, I suppose they kept it as quiet as they could in Australia. For a while after it was built, the fence served its purpose of making it difficult for the VC to move across that region. Like so many things in the war, it was the failure to follow-up that brought on disaster. Patrolling the fence was shared between you Australians on the outside and local forces on the inside. Just as it was throughout the country, the local forces were poorly led, corruption was rife and morale low, so their patrolling of the fence was neglected. The troops that followed you did a poor job, as well, and by the end of the year the VC had removed thousands of mines and re-laid them where they brought injury and death to many Australians. I saw a steady deterioration in the morale of your men. There were multiple causes for this, but the damage inflicted by the mines was a major one.

'As soon as President Nixon declared his policy on what he called 'Vietnamisation' of the war I knew the retreat had begun. So did many of your troops. They could see they were largely wasting their time and needlessly risking their lives. Morale plummeted at the same rate as drunkenness on the base increased. Even so, it came as a surprise when your Mr Whitlam became Prime Minister and ordered the immediate abandonment of your country's commitment to South Vietnam. In the midst of the rushed withdrawal from Nui Dat the Australian army showed no interest in my future — a foretaste of what was to come.'

'What happened to you?'

Tuan gave a humourless laugh. 'I went to Saigon where the ARVN showed as much interest in my future as the Australians had. Eventually I was shuffled into a position as a clerk, fulfilling an unnecessary role which I endured for close on two years.'

'I'm sorry,' Danny said. He felt genuine sympathy for Tuan but saw little prospect his sincerity would be believed.

'Very kind of you,' Tuan said drily. 'You haven't heard the final kindness meted out to me by you Australians.'

'What?'

'Some six months before the fall of Saigon I could see a full Communist takeover was imminent and those who had fought for South Vietnam or supported the foreign troops in any way could expect a very hard time. I decided to see the Australian Ambassador and tell him your country owed me asylum. Of course, I wasn't allowed anywhere near him, but a junior officer in the Embassy politely explained it was not your government's policy to offer asylum to anyone from Vietnam, even those who had fought beside your troops. He tried to give me hope by saying that were South Vietnam to fall — he was careful to avoid saying it would — it was possible the policy might change. This must have been the end of the recitation he had been briefed to present to anyone like me, because he hesitated before giving me an apologetic smile and adding, "Although, given the messages coming to us from Canberra, I wouldn't bank on this if I were you." I had to admire his candour.'

'So, what did you do?'

'I knew I wouldn't be missed if I left Saigon and needed to find a place and a job where I could hide all trace of my army career, so thought I'd try my luck in Vung Tau.'

Danny tried to hide the quickening in his interest. Perhaps Tuan had gone to be with Linh. Perhaps he thought she or even the Catholic Church in Vung Tau would help him.

'I soon found I wasn't the only former member of the army who was aiming to hole up in Vung Tau and jobs were hard to come by. However, I was in a bar one night when Mr Nguyen approached me.'

'What was his interest in you?'

'I told you he feared the Communist take-over — probably more than I did. He had more to lose. He had bought several boats and sought to portray himself as nothing more than the owner of a fishing business while he found men who might be useful to him in getting away from Vietnam. He had figured out that to escape safely he would need some men who could be relied on to protect him and, wherever he went, it would be an advantage to have with him someone who spoke good English. That's where I came in. He is a man who likes to plan ahead and not be rushed. We recruits were put to work as fishermen on his boats.'

'When did you leave for Australia?'

While Tuan's tone had remained sardonic, Danny had been pleased to see his earlier anger subsiding. Now he erupted again. 'We never left for Australia. After the way I was treated at Nui Dat and later, why would I want to come here?'

Danny felt his colour rise, more with frustration than with embarrassment at Tuan's outburst. At this rate Tuan would never be calm enough for him to find out anything about Linh. He took pains to speak softly when he asked, 'Where were you heading?'

'Nguyen wanted to get to the United States. I did not care as long as it was not Australia.'

'But you ended up here. What happened?'

Tuan's cynicism continued. 'You really want to know?' Perhaps it was the close attention Danny had been paying him or perhaps he needed to tell his story to someone, but he did not wait for a reply. 'Getting away from Vung Tau was the easiest part of our journey. Nguyen had bided his time until the Communists began to close in on him and by then his boats were well-known among the fishing fleet of Vung Tau. The one he chose for our escape was a twenty-metre wooden boat with a small timber wheelhouse. Our captain was an experienced fisherman who couldn't bear Communists, and the crew consisted of me and three other men who had been in the army and kept their weapons. We arrived at the quay before dawn and set out with the rest of the fishing fleet as was our custom. Unlike many of those who tried to escape by boat, we triggered no interest from the patrols the Communist had set up off the coast. Once we reached the open sea, Nguyen emerged from hiding in the wheelhouse. He was opposed to having any women on board and had abandoned his wife and at least one mistress in Vung Tau.'

Danny had already noted how Tuan enjoyed speaking ill of his benefactor — further reason to wonder why he stayed with him.

'We headed towards the shipping lanes where Nguyen hoped to be picked up by a passing ship. Several ignored us without slowing and one nearly ran us down. We could see storm clouds building and in the afternoon the edge of a typhoon burst upon us with drumming rain and tumultuous seas. The captain, who was the only one not violently ill, turned the boat to run before the storm towards the Malaysian coast. A particularly vicious wave broke over the boat sending one of the men into the sea. In a moment he disappeared below the waves and was lost to us. I could not see how the boat would stay afloat for much longer but it wallowed on with its sick and exhausted passengers until, after endless hours, the storm abated. It was then we discovered that some of the food we had brought with us had been ruined and several cans of water had been lost overboard. Each of us was now suffering from thirst but could take little relief as we were forced to conserve our depleted store of water. We didn't know how long it would be until we reached some shelter. Over the next few days of burning sun we survived on an occasional sip of water and a little rice while we edged towards Malaysia.

'Next came a bunch of Thai pirates who preyed upon small ships and boats in this area of the sea. Our journey would almost certainly have ended there were it not for Nguyen's foresight in recruiting men with AK45s to protect us. Eventually we reached land on the southern tip of Malaysia where the authorities offered to replenish our supply of fuel, water and food, providing we left immediately. We made slow progress down the coast to Singapore where we were turned away again. So began a gruelling voyage past the islands of Indonesia. Our engine failed and we drifted for several days before we were able to beach the boat. We were there for a few weeks making repairs. Later we were met by the Indonesian Navy. Having convinced them we were harmless, we were able to make our now customary bargain: renewal of our supplies for a promise of continuing on. This time we were escorted out to sea to make sure we complied. Every day provided some difficulty or other but at least we were free of sea-sickness and, while there were storms, none of them were as terrifying as the first one.

'By now Nguyen had decided our best hope was to make for Australia. I tried to argue him out of it, but he did have a strong point, saying that the Australians could not send us on our way like the other countries had done. After Australia there was nowhere to go. We were not really sure where Australia was but sailed on past a series of islands, always watching for hidden reefs and shallows. When we reached Timor, we were told Australia lay across the open sea to the south-east and there we headed, eventually coming ashore at a deserted beach. We had reached Australia but it was like no one actually lived here. There was an argument over whether we should head east or west along the coast and, thank God, Nguyen chose east, so that after another few days we came to Darwin. Other boats had arrived before us but we were still a novelty.'

'Why did you choose to come to Melbourne?' Danny asked.

'Choice is a luxury not given to refugees. After a few days the authorities flew us over endless desert to Melbourne where they wanted us to enter a government hostel which housed other Vietnamese. Nguyen trusted no government institution and had no wish to be confined in a hostel. Instead he came to Richmond where he knew a small community of Vietnamese were living. He had managed to secrete a nest egg of gold and US dollars throughout our voyage. He used some of it to buy this place and set it up as a restaurant. And there you have it.' Tuan sat back.

Danny, however, was not satisfied. He still knew almost nothing about Linh and, although he could see Tuan owed his escape from Vietnam to Nguyen, he couldn't understand why he remained in such a menial job. He had no safe way of reintroducing Linh into the conversation, so opted for the latter. 'I can understand the debt you owe Nguyen, but acting as a chef's assistant and interpreter is surely a poor use of your abilities.'

'Here we go again.' Tuan scoffed. 'You are so slow to understand. The jobs your country has for us Vietnamese are in factories, sweeping floors, collecting garbage, cleaning toilets. Working here is not much of a job but it's better than that and at least I eat well. Now you know how I came here and what I do, you can go back to your wife and children and have no need to bother me ever again.'

The hostility with which Tuan had burned earlier was gone, replaced by the disdain he had shown to Danny in Vietnam. Here was his chance to let Tuan know he was mistaken about him and justify his desire to know what had become of Linh. 'Yes, my understanding is limited, but so too is yours. I was not at the fete yesterday with my wife and children — I have no wife or child. The woman and children you saw are friends who live next-door to me. You hardly knew me when we were in Vietnam and you know nothing about me since I returned. You fly off the handle when I ask about Linh, but all I want is to know she is safe and well. I have long regretted what occurred between us and, when I thought I saw her at the fete yesterday, I hoped I might have been given the chance to tell her how sorry I am.'

'You thought you saw her yesterday?' Tuan seemed genuinely surprised.

'Just for a moment and then she was gone. I was searching for her when I stumbled on you.'

'A woman in an ao dai?' Now Tuan was amused.

'Yes.' Danny felt a surge of hope.

Tuan sneered at him. 'I used to hear you Australians at Nui Dat saying all Asians look the same. Unlike me, Linh saw no need to flee the retribution of the Communists. She will never be the linguist her talents warranted but, despite your efforts, she has found contentment as a mother caring for her family.'

Danny took a moment to swallow the disappointment that his earlier fear was confirmed — he would never be able to make his peace with Linh. He would like to learn exactly where in Vietnam she lived, some details of her husband and children, but to ask now would risk another tirade. He could still do something for Tuan, though. 'Remember I said I work for an organisation dedicated to helping displaced people get on their feet. I would dearly like us to help the Vietnamese who are now arriving in Australia. You could advise me on the best way to do that and I'm sure we could help you.'

'Huh! Still spouting good intentions for people you know so little about. Won't you ever learn?'

'I have learnt. That's why I want your advice before I try to do anything. You've made your feelings for me very plain. You disdain Nguyen yet have benefitted from him. Why not do the same with me?'

Tuan got to his feet. 'Our time is up. I have spent long enough with you to satisfy Nguyen. Just go and never come back here.'

Hello, dear,' Mary said after she opened the door to find Jane facing her. 'Anne and James, as well! I hear you all had a good time at the fete last Saturday. Have you children come to tell me about it?'

James began to speak about his enjoyment of the fairy floss, but Jane cut across him. 'I suppose it's too early, but is Danny home yet?'

'Oh, no. I'm not sure when he'll be back tonight, but it won't be for ages.' Mary sounded quite pleased about it. 'Anything I can do for you?'

'I hope he won't be too late,' Jane said as much to herself as to Mary. 'When he does get in will you ask him to come into our place? I have an important message for him.'

'I'll tell him when he gets home and have him call in after he's had his meal.' Mary sounded like she was dealing with an unwelcome caller. This was not the Mary Jane knew.

'Oh, please have him come in straight away.'

'When he comes to you will be up to him, of course.'

It was dark when Danny arrived at Jane's door. 'You have a message? What's this all about?'

Jane stepped back, drawing Danny with her, but remained standing in the hallway. 'I understand you spoke with Tuan Mai last Sunday night. I'm glad you did that.'

'How did you know?' Adding to Danny's puzzlement was the thought he'd never mentioned Tuan's name to her.

'I bumped into him at the school.' Danny wondered why Tuan would go to the school. They would have cleaned up their stall last Saturday or Sunday at the latest. 'He'd seen us together at the fete.' Jane's serious expression softened and she laughed. 'He thought I was Mrs McBride.'

'I straightened him out on that. What's the message and why send it through you?'

She had her earnest face on again. 'He said he had no way to contact you directly. I gather your conversation did not go all that well. He's changed his mind and would like to meet with you again. He'll be at the Ganh Hoa tonight. You're later than I imagined you'd be, but I'm sure he'll still be there. You'd better hurry, though.' Jane gestured at the door which had been left open. Danny wondered what Tuan could have said to engender such urgency in Jane.

As Danny made his way down Victoria Street, he continued to wonder what had brought about the change in Tuan's attitude. Towards the end of their conversation, when he had been encouraging Tuan to become involved with the Foundation, he had thought there was a chance, but that evaporated very quickly. Had Nguyen put pressure on him to pursue Danny? Had Tuan decided the opportunity for him and his countrymen was too good to be missed?

When he entered the restaurant, Danny found even fewer diners than last time and no sign of Tuan. The young waitress, who had been there last Sunday, came through the door from the kitchen but turned back when she saw Danny. Almost immediately Tuan appeared. He looked uneasy and made no attempt to greet Danny before sitting opposite him. Danny saw that Tuan was having trouble opening their conversation. 'My friend, Jane, said you wanted to see me.' He smiled encouragingly at Tuan. 'I was surprised by your invitation and its method of delivery.'

Tuan eyed him stolidly. 'Jane has spoken with me.' She had put it the other way around to Danny. What was going on here? 'She is a good friend to you.'

'She was amused you thought we were married. Had you forgotten what I told you last Sunday?'

'I remembered what you said. But I had also seen the way you were with her and the children at the fete. You would have done well to marry her.'

Surprise made Danny more forthcoming than he would otherwise have been. 'At one time in my life I thought so, too. Vietnam changed that.'

Tuan nodded. 'So I have heard.' He paused and looked steadily into Danny's eyes. 'When we last spoke you said I hardly knew you. Jane has persuaded me I should learn more about what has befallen you since you left Vietnam.' Jane had persuaded Tuan? How could this be? 'Last Sunday you encouraged me to speak fully about my experiences. Tonight it is your turn.'

Danny could hear the echo of that early conversation with Linh when, after telling him about herself and her family, she had called upon him to speak of himself. It was clear Tuan had no intention of explaining how Jane had brought about this change in his attitude. And why should he care? This was the chance he had been denied last Sunday. He should get on with it. 'I left Vietnam devastated I'd killed that innocent schoolteacher, let down my platoon and betrayed Jane.' He hesitated for a moment, wondering if he risked having Tuan explode again. 'And there was Linh. I arrived at her house distraught at what I'd done and she gave me comfort. I knew it was wrong at the time and have never forgiven myself for the harm I must have done her.' He paused to eye Tuan enquiringly. 'I suppose it became known I'd been in her house overnight, a sin in the eyes of the Church and bringing shame to her at the school and in her community?'

'It was a very hard time for her. She survived, though, and I have come to appreciate what a courageous and determined woman she is.'

Danny had the opening he wanted. 'It was a great comfort to me when you told me she was happily caring for her family in Vietnam. When I have finished, I would like you to tell me a little about her life now, her family ...'

'Later.' Tuan frowned at him. 'You have still to tell me what happened after you returned to Australia?'

Danny told him of his break-up with Jane and the family. He explained how he believed he had to get away from everyone he knew and build a new life in which he might atone for his past but had failed in this as well, ending on the street where he was rescued by Simmo. Tuan, who sat impassively through most of the story, his eyes never leaving Danny, occasionally interjected to ask for further details. Danny concluded by saying, 'You told me Jane had persuaded you to learn more of me but you didn't say how she did this. Last Sunday you made it clear you never wanted to see or hear from me again.'

'Jane said the view I had of you was wrong. She told me much of what you have given me tonight and urged me to hear it from you directly. Now I have.'

'So, are you now more inclined to work with the Foundation? I'm sure we can assist you and your people here in Richmond.'

Tuan's smile was diffident. 'That can wait. You wanted me to tell you more about Linh. I am not sure what I should do for the best.' He paused and looked away.

'Go on,' Danny said.

Still he did not speak and Danny wondered what it could be that made him so uncertain. Eventually he said, 'Linh and her family came with me to Australia.'

Danny was speechless with surprise and joy. Tuan sat watching until Danny recovered sufficiently to say, 'But you said ...'

'I know what I said and what I was careful not to say. The most convincing liars use truth in their telling. That is what I did when you asked me about Linh. I said she saw no need to flee Vietnam for fear of the Communists and she was happy as a mother with her family — all true. I said Nguyen opposed having any women on board which was also true. I didn't tell you I persuaded him to change his mind.'

'Was it her I saw at the school fete?'

Tuan nodded. 'Like me, when she saw you with Jane and her children, she thought they were your family. She hastened away because she did not want to intrude. That was never her intention. As I told you, we expected to go to North America. My reason for keeping her presence from you was different: I wanted to protect her from having you intrude into her life. However, after speaking with Jane, Linh has changed her mind and would like to meet with you.'

'I thought it was you who spoke with Jane.'

Tuan shook his head as though irritated at being interrupted over a triviality. 'We both have. While Linh would like to see you, I remain unconvinced it would be wise. Both of you have your own lives and I see no good coming from your meeting. She begged me to meet with you, hear your story and see whether that changed my view of you. To some extent it has. I feel sympathy for what you have had to endure and even some admiration that you have rebuilt your life. Yet I remain worried about the effect on her and her family if you should meet. If you really want what is best for her, tell me what you think that is.'

Danny frowned and shook his head. 'Can't you see that's impossible? Knowing so little of her situation and without hearing from her, I can only tell you what would be best for me. I'd like to meet with Linh to say I'm very conscious of what she sacrificed to comfort me and am deeply sorry for the sadness I brought her. I want to tell her I'm delighted she's found contentment in this country with her family and that I, too, have been restored to a life I enjoy. That done, I'll not seek to have anything more to do with her. I do hope you'll reconsider the suggestion I made last Sunday and we can work together for the benefit of your people here in Richmond. But that needn't lead to any further contact with Linh.'

Tuan got to his feet and put out a restraining hand as Danny sought to join him. 'Wait.' He turned, walked to the rear of the restaurant and out through the door to the kitchen.

Danny checked his watch again. A long ten minutes had passed and he was beginning to fear Tuan had abandoned him. Suddenly Linh emerged through the door. She was thinner than when he last saw her and her hair lacked some of its former gloss but, in an ao dai made from inexpensive fabric, she was even more beautiful than he remembered. He struggled to his feet and ran a hand through his unruly hair. She gave him the shy smile which had first captivated him and bowed. He returned the bow before saying, 'Come, sit. I cannot tell you how happy it makes me to see you once more.'

'Thank you for coming tonight,' she said softly 'I wasn't sure it was the right thing to do but, after speaking with Jane, I came to believe I should, and she persuaded Tuan to meet with you again.'

'Jane didn't tell me she had met you.'

'Oh, yes. She sought me out at school the day after the fete.'

'I thought Tuan contacted her.'

'No, he had to say that. It was part of her plan.'

'Her plan?'

Linh hid her smile with her hand before saying, 'I'm sorry. I should tell you what happened. Jane approached me when we were waiting for our children to come out of school. She asked me if I was a friend of Danny McBride. I was torn as to how I should reply. The last thing I wanted was to intrude into what I believed was your family and yet I couldn't bear to deny knowing you. Jane said we should continue our conversation and we agreed to meet the following morning when we were free from our children. We have talked a lot over recent days. I am so sorry you have suffered, but it makes me very happy to know you now have a much better life.'

Linh's words brought home to Danny that he had been so engrossed listening to her he had forgotten all about what he planned to say to her. 'Yes, that is true and I am content. I'm even more delighted you have found happiness in this country with your family. The damage I did to you when consumed by my own distress has haunted me. You wanted to avoid intruding on me and my supposed family. I intend the same for you and your real family. After tonight I will not trouble you further.'

'Would you like to meet my family?' Danny hesitated, unsure what he should say. 'Tuan thinks it is not the right thing to do,' Linh said. 'He has been so good to me, I am reluctant to go against his wishes but I have thought long and hard and believe it would be for the best.'

'If that is what you believe, then yes, of course.' Danny was not at all sure he wanted to meet Linh's husband. It had turned out OK with Gordon but, somehow, Linh's husband was different.

'I will be a minute.' Linh rose and went back into the kitchen. Danny was sorry to have the magic of being alone with her broken so soon. There would be no chance for a repeat.

Linh returned holding the hand of a small Vietnamese girl also dressed in an ao dai. Danny saw the girl as a copy of her mother: a miniature of the figurine he had first seen on the cliff at Vung Tau.

'Danny this is Nhi.'

Unbidden the girl gave a demure bow to which Danny responded awkwardly. 'Does she speak English?' he asked Linh.

'Yes, I do,' the girl replied quickly.

'Of course she does,' Linh said with some irritation. 'I have taught her and am teaching all of the children who come to me. Adults, as well when I can. You know that is my vocation.'

'I am very pleased to meet you, Nhi,' Danny said, smiling down at her. He turned to Linh. 'Your husband? Is he not here?'

Softly Linh said, 'I have no husband.'

Danny was appalled to have blundered into this new sadness. Tuan should have said something. Had Linh's husband been killed in the late stages of the war or died on that gruelling voyage Tuan had described? 'I'm sorry,' he murmured. What else could he say?

To his amazement he saw that Linh was smiling at him. It wasn't a broad smile but one that Linh might well give when chastising one of her students for being slow to learn. 'Oh Danny, you make it hard for me. Jane knew as soon as she met Nhi. Use your arithmetic. Nhi turned nine last January.'

'Nhi is my ... Nhi is our daughter?'

Jane had been awaiting Danny's return for what felt more like days than hours. As soon as she heard his step on the tiles of the porch she raced to the door and flung it open. 'How did it go?'

'Pretty much as you planned,' Danny said laconically. He certainly seemed happy, but that didn't mean Tuan had done more than be civil and allow him to have his say.

'Come in and tell me about it.'

She hurried him into the living room and gestured for him to take seat on the couch. 'Go on.'

'You've been extraordinarily good to me.'

'Come on Dany. Who did you see?' She had promised to tell him nothing of what she knew. If Tuan had not been persuaded by his conversation with Danny, she would have to carry that secret with her for ever.

'I talked at length with Tuan who is a great fan of yours — thinks I should have married you. Whatever I said was enough for him not to stand in the way of my meeting with Linh, although he made it clear he still had doubts it was the right thing to do. She introduced me to our daughter, Nhi. Wasn't that your plan?'

'Yeah, I suppose it was.' She should be congratulating him. Telling him how pleased she was.

'What's the matter?'

'I've been sitting here wondering whether I've done the right thing.'

'The right thing? What are you worried about?'

'You of course ... and Linh ... and Nhi.'

Danny beamed at her. 'I'm so lucky.' She would have agreed with him when she sent him off but now ... At least her frown brought him a bit closer to earth. 'Why are you worried about us?'

'It's not just me,' Jane said. Didn't Tuan tell you how he felt?'

'He did that alright. He told me we both had our own lives and he couldn't see any good coming from Linh and me meeting.' Danny grinned. 'Now I come to think of it, that's pretty much what he said to me at Nui Dat.'

She had to get Danny to focus on Tuan's concerns which had increasingly become hers. 'Linh didn't tell you what Tuan has done for her and Nhi?'

'You mean getting them on the boat?'

Jane shook her head. 'Far more than that. He was the one to save Nhi from the orphanage.

'What orphanage?'

At last he had lost his dreamy expression and was staring at her intently. 'The nuns were insistent that, after her birth, Nhi should go into the orphanage at Vung Tau where there were many children fathered by foreign troops. Linh was adamant this must not occur but is sure she wouldn't have been able to keep Nhi, were it not for Tuan undertaking to support them both and coming to argue with the nuns on her behalf.'

'He told me he'd gone to Vung Tau,' Danny said, 'but didn't say anything about supporting Linh.'

'He did more. When Nguyen first offered Tuan a place on his boat, Linh, urged him to go and not risk being sent off to one of the Communist re-education camps. She assured him she and Nhi would be fine, but Tuan saw a bleak future for the daughter of a foreign soldier and her mother under the Communists. He made it a condition of serving Nguyen that he allow Linh and Nhi to come with them and he protected them throughout the voyage.'

A strand of Jane's hair had come loose and she pushed it back into place. 'Were it not for Tuan, you would not have met Linh again and never known of your daughter. He's enchanted by Nhi and I have no doubt the most important thing in the world for him is that Linh and Nhi should be safe and happy.'

'In that case, why would he have any concerns over Linh and I coming together?'

'Do you really have no idea?' Jane could hear the irritation in her voice. She needed to stay calm. 'He's worried about the problems he foresees in a marriage between a Vietnamese woman new to this country and an Australian man. How will they fit into what he sees as this racist country that fears and demeans Asians? Will you want to take her away from the community where she is safe and accepted? If not, how will you manage in her community? It's going to be tough for both of you. You can't let the thrill of finding Linh and Nhi blind you to these realities.'

Her annoyance increased as Danny grinned at her. 'When I was walking towards you in the hall after Dad's funeral, I was struck by how you put me in mind of those nurses I meet in casualty. They give you confidence they can deal with the direst of situations and convey an attitude which says, "Don't worry, I've coped with far worse than this." Don't you think Linh and I can say that?'

'Have you discussed any of this with Linh?'

'Give us a break. I reckon we deserved one night of joy at our reunion without worrying too much about the future. And we'll have you and Tuan to help us.'

'I'm not so sure I'll be welcome.'

'Why would you say that?'

He couldn't be that naïve, could he? 'Come on Danny. Linh was very happy for me to help bring you two together but — the old girlfriend he was once going to marry and is still good friends with — Linh mightn't want me around too much in the future and I don't blame her. She'll have enough problems settling down with you as it is.'

He gave her that wry grin of his but there was something else in his eyes. 'Surely you and I can remain good friends. I would hate to give that up.'

Did he think she was jealous of Linh? After all she'd done in the past week … At least she'd been able to salve some of the guilt she carried for the way she'd treated him after he returned from Vietnam. 'Funny you should say that. When I haven't been sitting here worrying about what was going on between you and Tuan or whether he was right to keep you apart, I thought back over our torturous history: the droob who came to live next door and irritated me into challenging him to play tennis, the serious conversations I'd never experienced with a boy before. Romance didn't come into it.'

'That's a bit harsh, isn't it?'

'You imagined you'd meet your soul mate one day and immediately recognise her while I looked forward to being wooed by my lover. If you hadn't been called up, would we have married? Would we have been happy if we had? Instead …'

'Who knows. That water went under the bridge a long time ago.'

She wanted to hit him. How could he dismiss their long and complex history so casually? This man who said he loved her but was always daunted by the difficulties he saw in marrying a Protestant. This same man who was so enchanted by Linh he could blithely ignore the far more profound problems in marrying a refugee from a foreign country and culture.

Danny was studying her carefully. Had he guessed what she was thinking. 'I'm so overjoyed with what I've found tonight I wish you could be more optimistic.'

Perhaps he was right. She had found a man who continued to be enchanted by her in a way Danny had never achieved. She had made her reparation to Danny and their friendship was stronger than she had feared it ever could be again. She shrugged. 'Maybe I'm just overtired. It's been a hectic few days talking with Linh and Tuan as well as dealing with Anne and James. I s'pose I want to make sure you aren't deluded into thinking you will now live happily ever after.'

'I can understand you being tired. It's been full on for you even before the last few days. Gordon's home soon, isn't he?'

'Next Wednesday.'

'You must be looking forward to that. You'll have a lot to tell him.'

'He'll be thrilled to pieces.'

'Really? He's always been very friendly to me, but "thrilled to pieces"?'

'Oh, sorry. I wasn't thinking of you. He'll be pleased for you, of course. No, it's my news. I'm pregnant.'

Acknowledgements

In writing this novel I have called upon a wide range of people for advice and assistance and am very grateful they were so willing to help me.

Kevin and Wendy Prendergast and Rod and Marie-Claire Morgan spoke about their memories of being young Roman Catholics in the nineteen sixties. Richard Farrell shared his experience of school dances at Parade.

Carlene Gosbell taught me about the art of quilting, loaned me her books and showed me some of her beautiful quilts.

Elizabeth King and Ros Brown told me of their experiences as nurse trainees in the same era as Jane.

Ross King spoke of his time as a national serviceman at Puckapunyal and recalled being the son of a newsagent.

Paul Delianis shared with me his memories of being a policeman in Fitzroy at the time Danny was on the street.

Rev. Ric Holland talked with me about homelessness in Melbourne and, whilst he is not the model for Jakub Kowlaski, some of Jakub's views stemmed from what Ric told me.

I read numerous accounts of the war in Vietnam and the protests against it in Australia. However, in describing Danny's experiences in the Fifth Battalion Royal Australian Regiment, I drew heavily on two books: *Vietnam Task* by Robert O'Neill and *Crossfire: An Australian Reconnaissance Unit in Vietnam* by Robert Kearney and Peter Haran.

Both books contain personal accounts of the first tour of 5RAR in Vietnam.

All of my informants read and commented on drafts of the sections in the novel relevant to them and this was most helpful. In particular Bob O'Neill and Bob Kearney carefully read everything about Danny's time with 5RAR. Thanks to their work in checking my account I was able to correct a number of errors and inaccuracies.

I was not able to speak with anyone who had been in the Alfred Hospital teams which served at Bien Hoa but I did have the benefit of viewing the DVD *Nineteen Nurses: The Story of Alfred Hospital Nurses in Wartime Vietnam* and was able to incorporate some of what I learned in the story of Jane's time at Bien Hoa.

I was fortunate to have Tania Chandler read and critique my novel. Her corrections, comments and suggestions greatly improved the telling of my story.

As ever, I am indebted to my wife, Jo, who read and commented on every draft and was unfailing in encouraging me at all times.

About the author

Brian Smith was born and grew up in Melbourne, where he now lives with his wife, Josephine. They have two daughters and three granddaughters.

Brian began his professional career as an engineer and finished it as vice-chancellor of the University of Western Sydney, having previously been the head of RMIT.

In retirement he has served on a number of committees, including chairing the board of UniSuper, the company that provides superannuation for the staff of all Australian universities.

Among a range of current activities, the two that most consume him are playing golf and writing stories. He has published two sets of short stories. *A Patchwork Quilt* is his ninth novel.

www.ingramcontent.com/pod-product-compliance
Lightning Source LLC
Chambersburg PA
CBHW020653110726
47901CB00001B/179